"The ultimatum delivered at 0105 hours this morning has not been acted upon. You have had six hours in which to bring Mahmoud Assad to this airport. *You* have failed to comply or your Prime Minister has failed to comply. It is now imperative that you convey to the Prime Minister the following instructions:

"Mahmoud Assad must be brought, unharmed and alone, to this aircraft and permitted to walk unaccompanied to this aircraft. If this is done, no one here will come to harm. If Assad is not here in three hours' time, the entire population of this great city will be put at the gravest risk.

"There is aboard this aircraft an atomic device. I repeat. An *atomic* device. It will be detonated in three and a half hours' time, at 1030 hours, if you fail to produce Mahmoud Assad. Message ends. Out."

DEAD RUNNER

Frank Ross

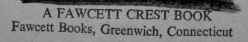

A FAWCETT CREST BOOK
Fawcett Books, Greenwich, Connecticut

DEAD RUNNER

Published by Fawcett Crest Books, CBS Publications, CBS
Consumer Publishing, a division of CBS, Inc., by arrangement
with Atheneum.

ISBN: 0-449-23454-1

Printed in the United States of America

10 9 8 7 6 5 4 3 2 1

FOR **K**—WHO RAN

Acknowledgment

The author wishes to acknowledge his debt to the writings of Dr. Theodore Taylor, a brilliant inspirational nuclear physicist and designer of America's biggest atomic bomb.

For years, Dr. Taylor has contended that anyone of modest technical ability could design, develop and build an atomic device. He expanded that thesis graphically in his technical biography, *The Curve of Binding Energy*, by John McPhee (Farrar, Straus and Giroux, New York, 1974). His reflections in that book, his outline of the elementary bomb-making process, form the basis for the model employed in these pages.

Dr. Taylor has said: "If we don't get this problem under international control within the next five or six years, there is a good chance it will be permanently out of control."

This book anticipates that danger.

PART ONE

GENESIS

The long black Mercedes was on time to the second.

It curled around the corner of Whitehall into Downing Street, its armored glass momentarily alive with rippling rainbows where lances of thin winter sunshine fell.

Instantly, the banners rose, fluttering in the light breeze, and with them the jubilant cries of the crowd jammed along the pavement opposite the door of No. 10.

The faces were predominantly young; bright, shining with anticipation and pride. Their voices fell into a rhythmic chant—"Ash-er, Ash-er, Ash-er"—and rose to a triumphant choral litany.

"ASH-ER! ASH-ER!"

A dozen or so police constables locked arms and lay back against the straining wall of bodies. Two sergeants pushed good-naturedly at a defector from the crowd who ran into the path of the car, arms raised in joyous salute.

An inspector waved the driver into position, but before he could reach the car, the rear door swung wide and a huge young man with cropped, sun-bleached hair stepped into the street and blocked the interior with his body.

A second man, dark glasses sinister, obliterated the crowd's view from the other side. A third slid from the front passenger seat and walked around to the driver's door.

For thirty seconds, the trio eyed the crowd. The inspector approached and shouted into the back of the car but his words were lost in the tumult.

The fair-haired man seemed satisfied. He opened the rear door, reached in and offered a supporting hand.

Asher Landis brushed him aside.

His square peasant's face flinched in the sunshine as he levered his dead leg onto the pavement. He was a burly man, his chest and shoulders deep and powerful; but the face had the color and texture of kangaroo hide and the scars of war had rooted deep behind the eyes.

He reached a hand to his slate-gray jacket and pulled it straight. The three guards settled around him, their bodies crushing in on his. The door of No. 10 opened a few experimental inches ahead of them.

Above the heads of the crowd a flag rose and floated free, the Star of David at its center. The crowd roared with a new orchestrated ecstasy.

"Mit-la! Mit-la! Mit-la!"

Asher Landis hesitated for a moment and looked back. Then he shoved his guards to one side and limped across the street to the crowd. The police line gave under the pressure and suddenly they were all around him, touching him, reaching for his hand.

The fair-haired guard forced a passage to Asher Landis' side. He grabbed a corner of the curling flag with his left hand and, in his right, a Smith & Wesson appeared as if by magic.

Landis raised a fatherly hand to the bodyguard's shoulder, restraining him. There was an odd twisted expression on his face.

"Mit-la! Mit-la!" rejoiced the crowd.

History. Legend, reaching out from a hot summer day twenty years ago.

Mitla Pass. A crushing barrage from Egyptian field artillery had staunched the flow of Israeli armor, pinned down a whole army group, bloodied the sand with the flower of Canaan's manhood. And in the heat of it, Asher Landis, major general, impatient and distraught, had snatched a Star of David pennant from a burning tank and stood with it in the back of his jeep and roared into the pass.

And they had followed him.

He thrust aside the guard and reached out and touched a corner of the flag and the crowd screamed its joy.

Landis' eyes found the standard bearer. He was very young, very handsome; hair blacker than the roots of hell, skin washed with gold. When he saw Asher's pleasure, he lowered the flag in salute and pointed it at the general's chest. The hero smiled and extended a beckoning hand.

The flagpole spat flame.

Asher Landis died with the smile still creasing his face, his blood and exploding flesh splashing the silk suit of his bodyguard.

The Sony Digimatic Litetime screeched like a dying pullet. Julia reached out a half-awake hand and released the alarm. The radio clicked on automatically.

"That was Christopher Morris on the hot line from Madrid."

The breeziness of the host on the "Today" program implied that, while death and destruction stalked the earth, it was still good to be alive if you didn't think too deeply. To prove it, Brian Redhead was addressing himself to a farmer who had doubled egg production by playing Burt Bacharach to his White Leghorns.

Driscoll stirred and opened his eyes reluctantly. His mind groped for the last waking thought before sleep. Lunch at 1230 with Gamal Anis of the United Arab Emirates and Tom Shilton of Defense Sales. Badgoorney, the Iranian military attaché, was to be there too.

There would be the usual flak from Shilton, all designed to clear his and the national conscience before he agreed to play. The sale of offensive weapons in the Gulf was a sensitive issue, but Shilton knew that America, France and Russia were all dangling carrots in the area and, in the end, it was safer to keep them buying British.

Anyway, Badgoorney was there to embody the Shah's interest and the Shah made a habit of winning diplomatic endgames of this nature.

Winning was important.

Driscoll yawned widely and turned his face into the pillow.

Tanks and guns and rockets and planes; the raw material of winning; the base metals of success, power, wealth. In five years they had paved his personal road to—what? Security? Self-sufficiency? Independence? The line of logic, as always, led him into areas he didn't want to explore.

Facts were good enough. His arm stirred under his cheek. It was supple, smooth. Young. He was forty-two; he still had a waistline, his teeth and his hair. If the mood took him—God forbid!—he could still make a showing in the decathlon.

In the last days of Korea, ahtletics had been the key that

unlocked the big time. A bright boy. All muscle and co-ordination. Too good to waste on the muck-and-bullets brain-washing of the infantry. Intelligence, they decided. He was then just eighteen years old and a patsy for death and glory. Six years later they bedded him into the Beirut station as a fully trained field operative. It didn't take long before they started talking about David Driscoll.

There was a lot of talk. Years of it. All good. So good they plucked him home to London in '61 and sent him to the Big House near Maidenhead, then drafted him into Herrick's and gave him a gun to play with.

The radio was giving out the staccato splutter of a sports-caster. It was too much for Julia. With a groan she rolled herself upright and stumbled naked from the room trailing a lace peignoir.

The spirit of Driscoll proved willing. Twenty-seven con-trolled assassinations in twelve years. He became a legend in the time it takes to squeeze a trigger. The names were gone now but he could remember the places: Paris, Beirut, Tripoli, Cairo, Jerusalem, Prague. A lot of places. No faces.

Around about No. 22 he saw the light. How to win.

That first time was sheer accident. A target, a Swiss, had hopped, skipped and jumped from Lausanne to Frankfurt to Athens to Addis Ababa. Driscoll nailed him in Nairobi, in the shower of his suite at the Stanley Hotel. Naturally, Dris-coll went through his briefcase. It was all there: bills of lading, certificates of clearance, export licenses. The Swiss was in the middle of an arms deal with the Eritrean guerrillas of northern Ethiopia. It needed just one final move. Con-tact. Why let it lie? Driscoll flew to Asmara and handed over the documentation. They paid him in deutschmarks. By the hundred thousand.

Within a year he was moonlighting as an arms agent. Within two he had sewn up the volatile end of the Middle East market, forged a supply and delivery contract with the Czechs and forced a half-dozen itinerant dealers into re-luctant retirement.

IMPACT was a natural extension. His own idea. Inter-national Military Protection and Control Teams. Ex-army men—high on warfare, low on opportunity—grouped to-gether in specialized paramilitary protection units. Insurance for despots and dictators who couldn't trust their own troops. It paid well in beautifully stable Swiss francs.

Toward the end he had known the ax would fall. All that

13

interested him was that it didn't fall on his neck. The moment Herrick's pieced together the telltale evidence of free-lance activity in their undergrowth, they hit him like a ton of scrap iron.

Too late. His commercial involvement with the oil sheiks made sure his skin stayed intact. It was nice timing. The Oil Producing and Exporting Countries were suddenly, terrifyingly omnipotent. A month earlier, they had sent the price of oil rocketing and laid the industrial West on its ear. They were Lords of the Earth and Driscoll was their pet bunny. Herrick's swore and fumed and gnashed their teeth but in the end they had to be content with kicking him out. No charges. No pack drill.

And to date he'd had three years of smooth, freewheeling achievement. Winning. His own brand. One hundred and one percent David Driscoll Unlimited. He had learned to close his eyes to the rest; as long as the fine focus was on the things that counted. Anything countable counted.

David Driscoll, self-made entrepreneur, yawned again.

There was a new voice issuing excitedly from the radio.

" 'Plain Bloody Murder!' is the *Daily Mirror*'s headline and in a front-page editorial the paper demands immediate government action. Says the *Mirror*: 'The cold-blooded murder of General Asher Landis proves yet again the real intention of Arab politics. They alone have nurtured, comforted and encouraged the lunatics who believe that the bullet solves all equations. They alone bear the responsibility for bringing these bloody assassins to heel, once and for all.' "

There was a lot more in the same vein.

Julia reappeared with a tray laden with eggshell-thin coffeeware and a George III silver coffeepot. She placed it at the foot of the bed and leaned across and kissed him. She poured him a cup, than padded off again into the sitting room.

Driscoll stirred with interest. Julia had that deep orange tan seen only in advertisements for Italian bronzing gel. Not an inch of her had been spared. Her bottom was taut and smooth, with none of the disfiguring dimples of cellulite. No liquid retention in Julia's cells. She had been dieting with religious dedication since she was sixteen.

He watched her as she returned with a stack of morning newspapers. Her glistening black hair swung like a silk curtain around breasts that moved with sadistic rhythm.

It had been the breasts that hooked him. Cliff Warrender's

14

house in Chester Square. Too many diplomats (because that was Cliff's business) and too much queer talk (because that was Cliff's bag) on a sultry, humid evening when fat men's faces grew marbles of sweat and every shaken hand left a perfumed deposit.

Driscoll had pushed through the crowd gathered around the open French windows to catch the breeze whispering in the shade trees. He nudged her elbow and her drink slopped over the skintight pants of a dyed blond with a dyed blond bum-fluff beard. She'd turned in anger but stayed to stare at him with unselfconscious interest. Cliff had spotted the prelude and came over to wrap an arm around Driscoll's waist and a hand under the fall of Julia's hair, binding them together, channeling their mutual heat.

He had got her out of there fast and they'd walked back along Chester Row in silence. Only their bodies had spoken and the message was compulsive, suffocating.

At the door of his house, as he fumbled with the key, her hands had crept like hysterical spiders under his shirt. When he closed the door, she had pinned his back to it, her face drained of emotion, her eyes glazed, her body vibrating against his. They had lain in the hall for hours. The experience had given Julia ideas. It had given him neuralgia.

Driscoll came out of the reverie with a start. Julia's hand was in his loins. Her face reached down to place fleeting lips on his naked stomach.

"Plain Bloody Murder!" screamed the *Mirror* front page in her hand.

TUESDAY   0845

Rear Admiral Sir Charles Wharton-Stone, DSO, CMG, RN, wobbled his bicycle around the tail of traffic bunching in Grosvenor Square and pedaled majestically into Brook Street. It was a bright, chill morning, pregnant with snow, but the sun reached down and drew pale shadows beside him. He sat astride the light frame, puffed out with warm mufti like a winter robin: bowler hat foursquare on his head and a half size too big, so that it bent down the top of his ears; black greatcoat swathed at the neck with a five-foot black woolen scarf; pinstripe trousers cycle-clipped above black laced ankle boots. He wore no gloves because that was an old man's admission of weakness; anyway, he liked to feel a direct physical control of his bicycle.

The machine had been Ellie's idea, although he had to admit the children had cemented it. Bruce had said: "I bet you daren't," and Alice had fretted because it was so dangerous cycling in London these days, "at your age." So he had bought the Raleigh. All is vanity and vexation of spirit. That's what came of having children late in life.

He beat an irregular passage along Brook Street, curb-crawling to avoid the challenges of buses and cabs and vans, playing the old man's game of foot-on-the-pavement when the dangers were greatest.

The entrance to the house lay between a French patisserie and a pharmacy. Ex-Marine Sergeant Rother was on the steps, as always, a ramrod in blue serge, brown shoes and tartan tie. For three years, Rother had been unable to resist the vertical beginnings of a salute as Flag pulled into the curb each morning, but he had now trained himself to taper it off around the vicinity of his nose. The same involuntary reflex led Flag to reach politely for the brim of his bowler and resettle it on his head.

"Could snow, sir?"

Rother's observations were always couched as questions; a tribute to his professional humility.

"Colder than yesterday," confirmed the admiral.

He squinted up at the circle of blue plaster mounted on the wall between the polished double doors and the first ground-floor window.

Its white lettering read: "In a house on this site lived Robert Herrick, poet, 1591–1674."

Another fragment of the daily ritual. The Greater London Council had raised a commemorative plaque to the English poet years before the Department had moved in, and as a result had blessed the Secret Intelligence Service with one of its lesser-known sobriquets. The house, the operations it pursued and the men it controlled had become, in the lingua franca of intelligence, "Herrick's."

He mounted the stairs slowly, pausing on each landing to catch his breath. There were six stories to Herrick's and no lift.

Mrs. Lamb's radar was tuned to his feet on the stair; she was waiting for him, as usual, on the fourth-floor landing. Ritual.

"Morning, Flag. Colder today."

In Mrs. Lamb's Isle of Dogs accent, the *nom de guerre* rang absurdly. Flag. It *was* absurd. It was also convention. Heads of division had always embraced some kind of childish code name throughout the history of the service. The Secret Intelligence Service itself favored "C"; Naval had traditionally taken the initial letter of the incumbent director's name. Times, of course, had changed and too many security agencies were now masterminded by career civil servants. But old habits die hard.

"Flag" had been Mrs. Lamb's brainchild, an appropriate recognition of his naval flag rank. But nicknames travel fast. He had not been in Herrick's a week before he overheard a whispered reference to himself: "Old Flagstone."

It was eight-fifty. Flag prided himself on being at his desk a full half hour before lay-abed clerks and secretaries.

Besides, he no longer slept as soundly as he once did. Valium was Ellie's answer to that, but he alone knew how much deeper the truth lay. As a serving naval officer, his body had adjusted perfectly to the principle of broken sleep. Now it was his mind and his imagination that had to adjust. And his conscience.

His office overlooked Brook Street and a continuous tide of traffic. It was a quiet room, surprisingly tasteful. Ministry decorators were green-paint-and-cord-carpet men but even their sense of propriety had been overawed by the grace of this house. Mahogany paneling rose from the floor to head height. Above it, primrose walls reached to a primrose ceiling where molded roses and fleurs-de-lys were etched in white. Eight of Flag's own collection of Laurence Bagley marine-scapes hung around the room.

"The eight-o'clock bag's in from the FO, sir," announced Mrs. Lamb, shuffling papers on his desk. "Room 12 have it."

Room 12 was Codes and Ciphers.

"Lot of flak through the night at the Yard. Special Branch are taking a walloping, according to Mr. Rodgers."

Rodgers was Herrick's tame Special Branch pigeon; their friendly neighborhood spy-in-the-ranks. Rodgers had been recruited after the Vassall tribunal, when it became obvious to Herrick's that far more happened under heaven and earth that they should know about than Special Branch were ever likely to tell them. Rodgers was an inspector just five years short of retirement. His reward for covert service to Herrick's would be a doubled pension. He had proved himself worth his weight in disloyalty.

Flag selected a pipe from the rack of five on the desk in front of him. He pressed long, black, stringy shag into the bowl from a battered leather pouch and struck a match.

No one could blame Herrick's, of course. Safe enough there. Diplomatic baby-sitting was not their business. Special Branch had been responsible for Asher Landis and Special Branch had boobed—wasn't that the expression? But the ball would drop at Herrick's feet, no shadow of doubt about it. Herrick's was Middle East CAPE—Covert Action and Political Evaluation.

The whole stinking barrel of fish would be rolling down Brook Street before the morning was out.

At least, it should be. It was important to him that it should. Flag allowed the match to burn almost to his finger ends, then blew out the flame and observed the black carbon stick minutely.

The trouble was, of course, that the whole security machine was becoming far too fragmented, far too complex. And complexity bred jealousy. He could visualize the activity in a half dozen points across London.

Special Branch would be in torment at their headquarters on the top floor of New Scotland Yard's skyscraper block in Victoria Street. They had around a thousand undercover agents on their strength to observe the activities of political groups inside Britain. They were spread thin. A vast amount of their work was concerned with illegal immigration and kept their agents pinned down in ports and airports. It was bad luck for them to have inherited the Landis job. The Israelis had insisted on mounting their own bodyguard. Still, Special Branch would be aching to get back into the game to erase this slur on their reputation.

Presumably, there would be some unpleasant postmortems in session in Barnard's Road, Battersea, the obscure little HQ of the Yard's C11 division. They were responsible there for long-term observation of suspects and a spiteful inquiring mind might well have put the finger on them. Assad may have been in the country for months, at least weeks. C11 were interested in criminal activity, not political, but someone was bound to think they should have been aware. In a crisis, everyone's a target.

Across at Leconfield House in Curzon Street, M15's central filing system would be under intensive scrutiny. The House was one vast filing cabinet, computer-run, with at least two million names in its memory banks. Anything they could establish would be fed out to all points via the communications center on the sixteenth floor of the Euston Center Tower in Euston Road. All telephone taps were handled from the Tower and Assad's name and mission would be checked against information recorded from several thousand calls bugged with the Home Secretary's permission.

It took very little to imagine what was happening now at 100 Westminster Bridge Road, SE 1. C would already be at his desk, high over the South Bank of the Thames in Century House, the central powerhouse where all information gained from SIS agents is assessed and distributed. Available in the same building are the Permanent Undersecretaries of the Foreign and Commonwealth Office, through whom information is passed. They are links in a perfectly interlocking chain but the undersecretaries have great authority and in many cases could make decisions barred to C himself.

That was a virtue in this case. If C could exclude Flag from this or any other operation of importance, it would be to his eternal delight. He might even now, though, be speeding across the river to the Ministry of Defense building in Whitehall, where the manpower and executive machinery of the SIS lived in a state of permanent wakefulness.

Luckily, Century House also quartered one of the chairmen of the Joint Intelligence Committee, so C's theater of operations was likely to be even more restricted in this case. Still, C would have seen to it that he had all the advantages available to him. He would have been at his desk all night if necessary, if only to keep in touch with the Oakley Communications Center at Cheltenham. They described Oakley, in the trade, as the Grain Store. It was the central point for the gathering of all information intended for SIS consumption. Half of the whole complex is given over to a giant ICT computer used for decoding and monitoring.

Flag sucked deep on his pipe. No—he couldn't afford to be excluded from this.

"My respects to Colonel Basey when he comes in. I want him to convene a meeting of the Executive for ten o'clock."

Mrs. Lamb ingested the words like a tape recorder. No one made notes at Herrick's unless specifically instructed.

"That gives you time to telephone Weatherby, Grant, Wernher and Davidson now. I'll accept no excuses for absence from anyone."

Mrs. Lamb scurried into her outer office and shut the door. Flag waited until he heard her making the first call. Then he picked up the red telephone from the battery of instruments on his desk. It had no dial. A voice came on at once.

Flag said: "Good morning. The Prime Minister, please."

TUESDAY   1100

The Prime Minister looked like a man who had flown three and a half thousand miles with a hot coal in his mouth. The caricaturistic Gladstone bags under his eyes were cobalt blue, and jet lag had etched a bloodshot line around the lids. He was a notoriously bad traveler; he found it difficult to sleep in strange beds and impossible to slip into the trance-like state that set Henry Kissinger apart from his fellow men.

He walked to the head of the Cabinet table and eased himself into his chair. The Foreign Secretary, who had been conducting the meeting, tidied three stacks of papers in front of him. The PM waved the fidgeting hands away.

"We'll not waste time," he said irritably. "I've seen the Special Branch report and I've talked with the commissioner. We'll save the recriminations for later. What are we doing about it?"

"Your personal telegram to the Israeli President reached him at two-thirty yesterday afternoon."

The Secretary of State read from penciled notes in a black leather book like a housewife checking a shopping list.

"As you know, Sir Derrick has called a special meeting of the Security Council for this morning and he'll read the text of the statement we prepared. Vanderkar here"—he inclined his head toward a white-haired man on his right— "called Egypt, Syria, Lebanon, Libya, Iraq and Iran to the Foreign Office last night and informed them officially."

The Prime Minister broke in quickly. "And?"

"They expressed concern at our security arrangements for visiting statesmen."

Vanderkar's face was devoid of expression.

"Are they concealing anything?"

Vanderkar looked down diplomatically at his hands. "If there were anything to conceal, sir, they would be the last to know."

20

"So?"

The Secretary of State went back to his shopping list.

"We now have the pathologist's report. General Landis died from major cardiac infarction caused by . . ."

"A dumdum bullet. I've read the papers."

The Secretary of State kept his eyes on his notebook.

"The President called shortly after you left Washington last night. He suggested we might care to consult the State Department's Political Intelligence Unit. They've been studying . . ."

The PM flared. "We'll go our own way on this. Is that understood?" He looked challengingly around the faces at the table. Nobody spoke.

"Intelligence can speak for themselves." The Secretary of State ticked his list.

"Can they indeed?"

The director of the Secret Intelligence Service had rolled a sheet of typescript into a cone. He held it by the narrow end and placed it on the table in front of him. He was very careful to address his remarks to the room at large.

"The assailant is a man called Assad. He's not known. None of the groups working under the PLO umbrella are claiming responsibility, which is curious enough in itself."

"How much of that is guesswork?"

"None of it, with respect, sir. We've had all channels open to our men in the field through the night. There are twenty-three groups operating under the Palestinian flag, some of 'em only educational—political training, that sort of thing. We have—er—associations with all of them. Assad isn't an official card carrier. There is absolutely no question of that."

The Prime Minister stared along the table, daring the SIS chief to meet his eye. He was disappointed. He finally clamped a pipe in his mouth and said through it: "I wish I could share your confidence. What've Middle East CAPE got to say?"

The Intelligence man placed the palm of his hand hard on the cone and flattened it in one savage sweeping movement.

"It's a little early to bring covert action people into the game, sir. This is a central intelligence exercise."

"Precisely."

The Prime Minister's exhaustion shattered like an inferior veneer. He brought his cupped hands together with an ear-splitting clopping sound and his knuckles showed white as he twisted his fingers in anger.

21

"Or to be perfectly accurate, it's a central intelligence *catastrophe*."

He put a match to the pipe bowl with shaking hands. The others watched him uncertainly.

The Secretary of State cleared his throat. He had been a political brother-in-arms of the PM since they were at Oxford. The slightest hiccup of party history and perhaps their roles might have been reversed. The town clerk's son and the miner's bastard; an unlikely fusion of political birthrights, but it had worked. The powder-keg personality who naturally became president of the Oxford Union, Britain's youngest minister, leader of his party at forty—and the slow-burning fuse who time and again had diverted the ultimate disastrous explosion.

"I think we have to accept, *sir*," he emphasized the courtesy, "that all security agencies must be brought into this as quickly as possible. However, I think it would be illogical to approach the matter on a pure intelligence level. There are more urgent elements to consider. I propose that Vanderkar here coordinate a joint diplomatic and intelligence effort. I've already suggested to him that he send his liaison people to see Flag at Middle East CAPE this morning. If you agree, of course."

"I don't want to appear uncharitable . . ." began the SIS chief coolly.

"Then keep your personal animosities to yourself," snapped the PM.

The state of permanent warfare that electrified the relationship of C and the pudgy little rear admiral who ran Middle East CAPE was an institution. It had its roots in a long-forgotten naval action off the Norwegian coast in 1942. Both men had commanded cruisers engaged in convoy protection. The facts were blurred. The memories of the two combatants were not.

"I'm sure," said the Secretary of State soothingly, "that C will have enough on his plate in the next few days to keep him busy. We must know if this man Assad is a lone wolf. Whether he has a backup operation in the wings. And it goes without saying that if Assad is not alone . . ."

"We can expect more shooting," finished the Prime Minister.

"Or worse," Vanderkar added quietly.

"How much worse?"

Vanderkar composed himself. He was a long, gaunt, unhappy-looking man with bloodhound eyes and jowls and a thin mustache the color of his white-gold hair.

"I hesitate to say so, Prime Minister, but I think this is possibly only an opening salvo. I believe Assad *does* have a task force behind him and we must accept that they will now press for his release."

"That, with respect, is guesswork," intoned C.

"Not entirely." Vanderkar smiled thinly. "Nevertheless, it does open up the prospect of retaliatory measures. And fairly quickly—unless we take exceptional steps to counteract it."

"I don't see how . . ." began the Secretary of State.

"What do you mean?" the PM interrupted.

Vanderkar sighed. His eyes fell on the flattened cone under C's bunched banana fingers.

"We've already had a somewhat heated meeting with the Israeli ambassador this morning, sir. He was treated for shock last night. The general was married, if you remember, to the ambassador's sister. Israel has formally demanded—not requested, *demanded*—the handing over of Assad for trial. I don't have to tell you that, emotionally, General Landis . . ."

"Go on. Go on."

"Our refusal to hand over Assad might well lead to a less formal approach from the Israelis. If they believe their cause is best served by putting on a show trial for the benefit of the Arabs, they might feel justified in resorting to terrorist tactics themselves."

"By kidnapping Assad?" The Prime Minister was incredulous.

"I think we'd be naïve to rule it out," said Vanderkar evenly.

TUESDAY   1400

Despite the blistering heat in the street above, the basement was cool and airy.

High in one corner, lashed to a water pipe with string, an electric fan turned slowly, its blades emitting a faint whistle where they brushed the battered mesh guard.

A unit of steel shelves ran the length of one wall, stacked haphazardly with a confusion of cans, flasks, vials, bottles, Kilner jars, retorts and test-tube stands.

An oxygen canister was propped against a steel filing cabinet and beside it lay the goggles and torch that completed the oxyacetylene kit.

In the center of the room was a workbench of Dexion slotted-and-bolted metal. It supported a small furnace. From it, a lead snaked across the concrete floor to a battery of plugs.

An old-fashioned bookcase, its glass doors removed, was jammed with books which overflowed onto the floor around it.

Ten volumes, heavily thumbed and stained, were grouped on a rickety table. Among them:

The Los Alamos Primer (Atomic Energy Commission, $2.60, declassified 1964).

Manhattan District History: Project Y, the Los Alamos Project (Office of Technical Services, U.S. Department of Commerce, $4.00, declassified 1961).

The Plutonium Handbook (Gordon and Beach, New York, 1967, two volumes, $81.50).

The Reactor Handbook (Wiley, New York, 1960–64, four volumes, $123).

The Effects of Nuclear Weapons (Atomic Energy Authority, U.S. Government Printing Office, 1962, $3.00).

Source Book on Atomic Energy, by Samuel Glasstone (Van Nostrand Reinhold Company, New York, 1967, $13.95).

Some of the books carried place markers of torn newspaper; others had whole sections creased over for easy reference.

The young man was the only occupant of the room. He wore white overalls, a black plastic apron, rubber gloves and a rubber head shroud and mask such as fire fighters wear.

He was twenty-six years old and his name was Raschid Sharshir. He was a graduate of the Department of Applied Physics at the University of Cairo.

In a small box on the bench in front of him lay a brown powder not unlike instant coffee.

He took a spatula and carefully measured four and a half kilograms onto finely calibrated scales. After much adding and subtracting he was satisfied. He shook the mixture onto a tray and placed the tray in the furnace. When switched on, the tray would vibrate, shaking the powder at random.

From the furnace, he led a length of rubber tubing to a flask clamped over a small gas ring. The flask contained hydrofluoric acid.

The brown powder on the vibrating tray was uranium oxide.

It had been part of a far greater haul hijacked in America from an open truck at an overnight transit yard. The consignment was en route from the uranium-conversion center at Erwin, Tennessee, to a fuel-fabrication plant at Crescent, Oklahoma.

It had reached the agents of the PFLP through a Mafia intermediary at a cost of twenty thousand dollars per kilogram. At Erwin, the material was logged as MUF—Material Unaccounted For. Since 1950, tons had been lost.

Sharshir pressed a switch and studied the temperature gauge on the furnace. As it rose, a gas began to form in the heated flask.

The gas was hydrogen fluoride. Mixed with the uranium oxide at a temperature of 500 degrees Centigrade, it would form uranium tetrafluoride.

In the coolness of the basement the young man wiped a trickle of sweat from his cheek as he reached across the workbench for a graphite crucible. When the temperature reached 500 degrees, he switched off the furnace, removed the contents and placed them in the crucible. Then, in a ratio of six to one, he added powdered magnesium.

Carrying the mixture gingerly, he crossed the room to a steel cylinder lodged in a wall recess.

He attached two wires to the crucible, added potassium chlorate to the contents, then slid the vessel into the cylinder and locked it.

Electricity, fed through the wires and boosted by the chemical heat of the potassium chlorate, would raise the temperature to 600 degrees.

He stood back and waited.

As soon as the required temperature registered, he switched off the current and attached a rubber hose from the cylinder to a water tap.

He turned the tap and watched the temperature fall.

At exactly 100 degrees, he opened the container and sprayed water inside until it was cool enough to handle.

He removed the crucible.

There was no evidence of excitement or achievement in Raschid Sharshir's eyes. He had followed the procedure many, many times before. It was as routine as any of the techniques he had mastered with such facility at the university.

He took a pair of fine steel calipers and gently lifted from the crucible a tiny nugget of grayish material.

Raschid Sharshir had created four kilograms of uranium 235, known in the patois of nuclear physicists as a Derby.

Meticulously, he removed the hood and the protective apron, washed his hands and, with a final glance round the room, closed the door and double-locked it. There was just time for a brief lunch. Abu Shemali would be arriving in three quarters of an hour.

He was not the kind of man you kept waiting.

TUESDAY   2000

For a week Beirut had burned and stifled in a dry, consuming heat that shredded the nerves and set neighbor on edge with neighbor. There had been forty-six killings within forty-eight hours. In a city where the knife and the gun are ready answers to political arguments, this was remarkable only in that eight of the killings were domestic: husband stabbing wife, youth strangling girl. It was a bad sign when murder needed such a motive.

To add to it all there was a water shortage. A pumping station on the outskirts of the city had trembled to a halt through lack of spare parts. Beirut Radio hinted darkly at sabotage. The spark was enough to put demonstrators on the streets calling for reprisals, retaliation; if there was no water, blood would do. Even now, as an uneasy dusk began to fall, small mobs of teenagers roamed the streets, robbing and beating in the sacred name of righteous indignation.

From a sixth-floor apartment overlooking the rue du Sénégal, Abu Shemali sipped a glass of iced Perrier water and watched a mob stop a car to jostle and ridicule its occupants, the long-haired youths rocking it back and forth on its axles. He shook his head slowly and turned to face the occupants of the room.

"It is a sadness, brothers, that the young use the energies we give them to vulgarize our aims."

The six figures around the table neither nodded nor dissented. They sat with the tenseness of men unused to talking, hands awkwardly splayed across the table, or clenched around the arms of their chairs.

For six years Abu Shemali had nurtured men like these, shaped their hate and cast it in a mold. But for him they were no more than the thugs on the streets below. It did them no harm to suffer his philosophical indulgences.

He drew a chair to the head of the table and sat down, toying with a bowl of olives. The faint hum of the air conditioning filled the room with a steady tone.

Then he relented.

With infinite precision he placed one of the olives on the table before him and, from under hooded lids, raked the gathering with a single look.

"Brothers, we have our weapon. It is ours."

The effect, as he knew it would be, was electric.

They rose as a man, punching, slapping, embracing, voices raised in exultation. Abu Shemali watched it all benignly, waiting for the euphoria to fade, and, when it did, his voice took on a different tone, a tone to dispel all illusions.

"It is good, yes. But now there must be no mistakes. No word, no gesture, no look that can betray our cause. Tonight, all of you will go from here to places I have named. You will carry no identification and will not know your brother, nor your father, nor your mother, nor your woman. Tomorrow, when you reach your destinations, you will hear from me and know what is expected of you."

The figures around the table nodded. There was no doubt they would do as he ordered. Their only collateral was their lives, but the goal was martyrdom.

"If you have any questions, ask them now. There will be no other time," went on Shemali. "We have bought the device and we are satisfied it will work. Now, all that is left is to assemble it and that is being done. I do not need to remind you who financed this historic moment, or the price he has paid. Our Libyan brother expects much of you. Remember: your lives are expendable; our cause is not. May that thought guide you in all you do. There is none so worthy."

He embraced them as they filed out, taking with them the

folded cards that named the houses where they would stay.

Abu Shemali removed his reflecting sunglasses and stretched himself luxuriously. For years he had dreamed of this moment; now, alone, he could at last savor it. And it was Assad, Assad whom he had nurtured like a son, who was to give him his opportunity. Assad, who had, with his tuition, struck the greatest blow for the Palestinian cause, would now be the instrument for striking an even greater one.

Here, in Beirut, the material that had cost over half a million dollars had been fashioned into the very metal of destruction. In Amsterdam, word had come yesterday, work was complete on the casing that would contain it. Three international liberation organizations had conjoined to ensure that the project would succeed. Assad would return a hero and no one would ever again dare ignore their cause.

Abu Shemali walked to the window and stared across the heat-stained city, feeling its pulse beat with his own. Below, unnoticed, a young man lay crumpled beside his car, cradled in the arms of a wailing woman.

Beirut had claimed its forty-seventh victim of the week. There would be others.

WEDNESDAY   0350

Driscoll retreated from sleep for the tenth time in three hours. Damn Shilton and every poncing bureaucrat in Defense Sales.

An hour before the meeting with the Gulf Emirates, Shilton had turned up at Prince's Gate with his morals tacked to his sleeve. The Landis assassination had already got the Arabs walking on eggshells, but Shilton's soulful diatribe on the invidious position of the British government at a moment of high diplomatic crisis had well and truly strangled the project at birth. Driscoll had walked in on a wake. Sorry, Mr. Driscoll—you can appreciate the position.

No, he couldn't, but they weren't buying that tactic. In a few weeks, perhaps, a couple of months?

Hypocritical bastards.

It had set the seal on the day. The shipment of Sturmgewehrs in the warehouse at Lausanne had not been picked up as scheduled, and Schattner, the forwarding agent, had got himself lost "for a few days." Driscoll had spent hours vainly trying to locate him and established only that there was a technical holdup over the completion of the export license. That was bad. His contact in the licensing department collected ten thousand francs a year to make sure there were no holdups. Ever.

And to cap it all, he had arrived home to run head on into one of Julia's insecurity moods.

Well, they were sleeping in the same bed but emotionally they were on separate planets. Driscoll exhaled his frustration through his clenched teeth. She was angling for something and that something didn't figure in his compendium of treasured womanly virtues. She had very nearly come out with it: Where do we go from here? Tomorrow, maybe, she'd pluck up the courage to say it. Tomorrow he'd be busy.

The sound scythed through his thoughts. A click. Definite. Fracturing. Without mobilizing a muscle or changing the pace of his breathing, Driscoll was instantly alert. Again, from the hall downstairs, another click.

Julia turned, groaning in her sleep, and buried her head beneath the sheet. Driscoll waited a full minute. Then a chair squeaked unmistakably as a body lowered into it.

His eyes fought the darkness until the shapes in the room took on visible outlines, then he slid the Beretta from the bedside table, eased himself off the bed and slipped into a robe.

He walked out to the landing. At night an undisturbed house breathes quietly but distinctly. A presence and it stops. The breathing had stopped. He took the first half dozen stairs and saw a faint slat of light edging the bottom of his study door.

Driscoll moved like a stalking panther down the remaining stairs into the hall, tightened his grip on the automatic and reached for the door handle. He swung it wide and fast, the Beretta stomach high and hungry.

Larry Guilfoyle smiled up at him from the Charles Eames chair. He kept his voice low.

"Ah. There you are."

Driscoll shut the door quickly and silently, waited for ten seconds to catch the slightest hint of an awakening Julia, then spun on his heel to face the night visitor.

"What the hell are you playing at?"

Guilfoyle had the weight and build of a ballet dancer. Well under six feet, tiny hands and feet, the face of a starved idealist, restless eyes with too little color and too much confidence. The mouth was petulant and comfortless. The smile it wore was a lousy imitation of the real thing.

He made no attempt to reply but waved the glass of brandy he was nursing as though inviting Driscoll to join him. Driscoll advanced across the room and stood over the chair threateningly. Guilfoyle merely raised his legs and laid them to rest elegantly on the leather footstool.

"Why don't you sit down?" he said. "This might take a little time."

Driscoll's fingers whitened on the stock of the Beretta.

"I'll give you five seconds," he hissed angrily. "Then I'll break your fingers off at the shoulder."

Guilfoyle raised the brandy balloon to his lips and sipped delicately.

"Sit down, please," he said. He had given up trying to smile.

Driscoll made a move downward with one furious clutching hand. A bulge mushroomed in Guilfoyle's coat pocket.

"I wouldn't want to ruin a perfectly good coat, friend, so why don't you just do as you're told and forget the histrionics. We wouldn't want to wake the lady, would we?"

Driscoll glowered but retreated and dropped into a chair.

He said: "All right. Let's hear it. Then get out."

Guilfoyle nodded comfortably. "That's better. Well . . ." He looked interestedly around the room. "This is very nice. Very nice. A bit rare for my taste, but then I don't have your standards, do I?"

Their eyes met, feeling for strangleholds. Driscoll held the stare but the old cold recognition was beginning to tie knots in his stomach. He had stared into his face perhaps three times since he had left Herrick's, but the first was enough to reflect a mirror image of himself. And he had loathed on sight what he had seen that first time in Flag's anteroom. They hadn't been meant to meet, of course. Driscoll, the outgoing hatchet man, and Laurence Dean Guilfoyle, his replacement. They shared nothing in common except the glacial state of their mentalities and the hair-trigger lightning of their reflexes. Driscoll had turned from the frightening face of Guilfoyle as he had turned throughout his life from any close examination of his own motives.

"Get it over with," Driscoll said. The words came with difficulty He was suddenly icily cold.

"Yes. No point in sparring around."

Guilfoyle fell into deep contemplation of the brandy swirling in his glass. He looked up quickly.

"I want you to do a little job for me," he said.

Driscoll began: "You can go . . ."

Guilfoyle interrupted. "We won't get anywhere if you're going to be stubborn, friend. I'd better make it clear, here and now. You make it difficult for me and I'll get very nasty indeed. Very nasty. You're an independent now, remember. No Big Brother to fight your battles. No Herrick's to"—he paused carefully—"to protect your health and home. Think about it."

Driscoll twisted his mouth contemptuously.

"You preposterous little shit! If you think . . ."

"I try not to think, friend. Bad for the digestion. I like to keep things simple. No thinking necessary."

He pushed himself onto the edge of the chair and leaned forward intently.

"Now listen. I'd like this to be nice and friendly. Businesslike. That ought to appeal to you. They tell me you're a good businessman. So we keep it straight. All right?"

He rolled the brandy around the balloon and drained it expertly.

"I'm going to be honest with you, so I expect cooperation. Fair enough?"

Driscoll said nothing.

"The Arab who shot General Landis. We want him."

For the first time, Driscoll forgot his apprehensions.

"Mahmoud Assad? I thought he was in Wormwood Scrubs."

"He is. Your information's good, as usual."

"So what are you bleating about? You can interrogate him anytime you like."

Guilfoyle sighed and closed his eyes in exaggerated torment.

"Try not to be coy, friend. It's wasting time. I'm not talking about Herrick's."

Driscoll stared at him in disbelief. Then the penny dropped and he began to laugh softly.

He said, almost good-naturedly: "You mindless little pimp! Are you telling me you're touting for the Arabs?"

Guilfoyle clicked his tongue wearily.

"I said let's keep it businesslike. So cut out the comedy, shall we? I'll be losing my temper and that would be wrong."

He said it like a small boy, pouring revelation into the confessional.

"No—to answer your question—not the Arabs. There are other interests, but you don't have to worry about causes. Now do you? This is the proposition. Assad is in Wormwood Scrubs. He's there until the SIS or the Foreign Office or Downing Street decide what they're to do with him. There'll be a lot of pressure from all over, so let's say that decision will be made in a week, at most. For the moment he's safe, but not too safe, if you get my meaning. If he's to be sprung, it'll be a lot easier from the Scrubs. There are plenty of precedents."

Driscoll cut in: "That's why there's plenty of security nowadays. Forget it."

Guilfoyle said seriously. "No, we can't do that. Once he's out of the Scrubs and in Intelligence hands, we'd be wasting our time trying to organize an escape. No, it's got to be the Scrubs. Now—that's where you come in. You can see how we're placed. No legitimate security service could afford to get mixed up in springing this kind of prisoner from a British jail. Not in this situation. It has to be an independent job. We have to contract out. Now, our problem is simply sociological. We don't have criminals on our payroll and hiring a free-lance team would be rather stupid, wouldn't it? So we've decided to give you the contract. All clean and businesslike. Fifty thousand for you and fifty thousand for the operation." He rubbed his hands together agitatedly. "A very substantial opportunity for you, I would say."

Driscoll eyed him pensively.

He said: "And when you and your Israeli friends . . ."

Guilfoyle stopped rubbing.

"I said nothing about any friends."

"Didn't you? Now where did I get that idea?"

Guilfoyle tried the smile again. It was still a bad imitation.

"For a hundred thousand, I think we can agree to forget the whos and whys and wherefores, don't you think?"

Driscoll lay back in his chair.

"No, I don't, *friend*. But never mind that. What did you and your buddy-boys decide to do when I told you to go stuff your proposition?"

"Oh, we had that worked out, naturally. It's fairly obvious, I think you'll agree. You're a gunrunner. Well, you'd probably prefer the term arms dealer. Not one of the shabby set, by any means, but when you get right down to it, just another death peddler. Well, we can deal with that. Switzerland is your springboard and it would cost you a fortune to rebase, if it was possible anyway. You rely heavily on three bankers: Zurich, Geneva and Lausanne. They are rather better friends of ours than they are yours. You could say they're in the family, so to speak. Two: You had some bad news yesterday. Little delay over an export license, I believe." His eyes glinted as Driscoll came upright in the chair. "Yes, very bad. You could almost say that license was contingent on your accepting our offer. It was very astute of you, tying up that chief clerk in export licensing. But you have to take care with the petite bourgeoise. Great care. Threaten them, even obliquely, and they run. Even professionals like Herr Schattner run. Oh, don't worry. One word from you and they'll be as free as air."

Driscoll said: "Suppose I tell you to go ahead and prove it."

Guilfoyle held out his hands agreeably.

"We'd do just that, friend. Quick as you like. Overnight. But you haven't let me finish. We realize you're a man of ingenuity. You have . . . resources. Maybe you wouldn't mind losing a fortune. Unlikely, but it could happen. We thought we ought to come closer to home. First, there's a little lady upstairs. I personally think that you wouldn't lose any sleep if she got quite badly hurt, but my colleagues are naïve sentimentalists. They think you might be impressed by that kind of threat. However, I have an idea your ex-wife and your son mean rather more to you than you might admit."

He waved a hand airily.

"We shall have them under continuous observation, anyway."

Driscoll allowed the air to fill his lungs and lay back again in the chair. Guilfoyle was studying the brandy glass again, deep in thought.

"Suppose I put in a call to Flag and told him his pet cobra was doubling for the Israelis?"

"Ah. Now I thought you might think of that. No good, I'm afraid. Flag hasn't seen you in too good a light since you left. It was all very embarrassing for him, you know. He put you on the Restricted Persons List himself. Right at the top. He's not a man to lose his temper easily, but the slightest mention of your name and . . . well, understandable, isn't it? But, you could always try, I suppose. Or Hugh Davidson. Old friend of yours. I'm sure *he'd* listen. But, then, that would do your wife and son no good at all, would it? Or the young lady upstairs. Or Herr Schattner. Or the chief clerk. Or your credibility at the banks. Still, you might think it's a chance worth taking. Personally, I'd take the hundred thousand."

"And if I did?"

"You have carte blanche. With just one exception. Timing. It has to be Thursday night. We'll talk about a hand-over point, but whatever it is, it can't be later than 0230 Friday morning."

"You're joking!"

"I never joke. Those are the limitations."

"Don't be a fool. You'll jeopardize your own people. A job like this can't be set up in less than a week. You're giving me less than seventy-two hours."

"Time waits for no man, friend. The choice, unfortunately, is not ours. You'll have to move quickly. Have you any idea who you'll give the contract to?"

"That's my business."

"Or course. Of course. Just interested. All we require is the man. Cash on delivery."

"Half down. The rest on delivery."

"Agreed."

Guilfoyle stirred, stretched and climbed to his feet.

"Well, that's all really rather satisfactory." He held out a hand to Driscoll, who ignored it. Guilfoyle practiced another smile but his heart wasn't in it.

"I'll have the first half of the payment in your hands tonight. Deliver it myself."

He opened the door and turned, a finger to his lips. He mouthed "Good night," and slipped out into the hall. Driscoll watched the street door close on him. Seconds later, he heard a car cough into life and moan away in first gear into the night.

He slipped back into the study, picked up the telephone and dialed a nine-digit number. He waited impatiently as the automatic exchange clicked and buzzed. The dialing tone began; after six rings the cut-in operated and there were more clickings and crackling sounds before yet another tone began to ring.

Finally, a voice answered, heavy with sleep.

"Mowbray. Who's that?"

Driscoll said: "Mr. Mowbray, this is Dove. I'm sorry to trouble you, but the car you ordered for the morning will be late."

He waited five seconds for the scrambler to function. Then he said:

"Flag? Driscoll. Tomorrow morning. About eleven. No later. Usual place. You'd better make sure you're alone."

He hung up and turned to the door.

Julia was at the foot of the stairs. She looked very wide awake.

Through the parted venetian blind on the long window overlooking Exhibition Road, Driscoll watched the bland blue Mini pull into the curb. He turned and walked slowly toward the back of the museum, his heels drawing clacking echoes on the polished planking.

On the street below, Flag disgorged himself from the front passenger seat with the ease of a camel passing through the eye of a needle. He bent to talk to Duquesne, the driver, then stumped across the pavement through a disorderly crocodile of schoolchildren into the Science Museum.

Driscoll wandered casually through the Computer Room. It was deserted. Beyond it, the texture of the air changed perceptibly; the smell of clean oil on old metal. He stopped in front of one of his favorite displays: old ship's compasses enshrined in tall brass binnacles.

The Science Museum had been their trysting place from the beginning. Driscoll had chosen it himself; not for any obvious security it lent their meetings but simply because he'd never been there previously in his life. Bizarre reasoning perhaps, but as good as any. This would be their fourteenth or fifteenth meeting in three years. Maybe it was time for a change.

He walked to the head of the third-floor stairwell and listened. No sound, yet, of Flag's lurching step on the stone staircase. The old man took his time, these days. Paused every ten seconds to catch his breath, take the pressure off his heart. When Flag first approached him, a year after Herrick's had drop-kicked him into oblivion, they had arranged to meet on the ground floor among the steam locomotives and the giant water pumps, their conversation initially taking second place to a boyish fascination for the gaily painted old Glasgow Corporation tram and a group of antique fire engines.

Driscoll had said no that day. No—because the offer Flag had made bristled with suspicion; because he knew he could never trust a civil servant spy again; because a whole new legitimate business opportunity was opening at his feet and he couldn't afford to compromise it.

It took him a month of hard experience to realize that the
35

Flag initiative was unavoidable. In that month, he lost time, money and the top dressing off his reputation. What his operation lacked, he came to realize, was the very ingredient that had made it so profitable when it was still only a secondary occupation: Herrick's. Without that continuous intravenous drip of classified information, he was just another door-to-door salesman.

Driscoll called the second meeting. They met beside the old tram but the floor was packed with visiting school parties and they were forced up to the second floor. They shook hands like archetypal English gentlemen on the deal: Driscoll would accept occasional missions as Flag's dead runner for fees negotiable before each project. Operating outside the formal intelligence network, and often against its declared interests, Driscoll served as bag carrier, spy, disinformer, catalyst, shepherd, convener, messenger and activist. The benefits Flag drew were positive. Driscoll was not only a crystal mirror of Arab opinion and political motive, he was a two-way mirror offering insights into the curious system of Middle East checks and balances. For Driscoll, the rewards were high; Herrick's was a safe-deposit of high-level government intelligence and, even more importantly, a computer designed to anticipate national appetites, shifting loyalties and alignments and commercial expansion in the Arab world.

The bond he and Flag had forged had nothing to do with mutual trust and integrity—but mutual benefit was a satisfying substitute. You could bank it.

They had come to know the Science Museum well. Six months earlier they had quit the newspaper-machinery section on the second floor and moved up to sailing ships and small boats on the third. Each meeting, they moved on to another display. Today it was the model of Nelson's *Victory* at the far end of the sailing-ship arcade. Driscoll stationed himself in front of the glass and watched Flag lumber into sight.

He turned. The old man's face wore a ripe mottling of heliotrope. Staircases were getting steeper by the day.

Driscoll turned back to the case and said to his reflection: "I said on the phone it would be better to come alone."

Flag unwound the black wool scarf from his neck and stuffed it into the pocket of his aging black raglan.

"Duquesne is as good as being alone, you know that."

"I hope *he* knows that."

"Oh, come, David. I've explained Duquesne. Anyway, I have far more to lose than you."

Driscoll swung on him viciously.

"You lose your job. I lose my neck."

Flag pressed his lips into a thin unyielding line.

"It's a little late in the day to start doubting my veracity, isn't it? We'd better get on with it. He'll be back in fifteen minutes. I have a busy day ahead of me. What's the problem?"

Driscoll chuckled drily.

"The *problem* is Mr. Laurence Dean Guilfoyle."

Flag managed to raise an eyebrow without registering surprise.

"I don't understand."

"He dropped in on me last night—early this morning. I called you just after he left. He's a double."

He searched Flag's face for a flicker of emotion. The cupboard was bare.

"He wants me to spring that Arab, Assad, from the Scrubs. The deadline is Thursday night, just in case MI5 switch him to a safe house somewhere."

"And?"

"And if I don't, the Israelis beat seven shades of shit out of me and my operation, or Cindy and the boy, or Julia."

Flag murmured: "Julia?"

"Spare me the innocence, for God's sake. She lives with me. I've told you about her. You must have a file a foot thick on her by now."

Flag's face remained impassive.

"Did he say that?"

"He spelled it out, step by step. He's already thrown the switch on a deal that should have gone through yesterday."

"No. I mean did he mention the Israelis?"

"He didn't have to. He admitted he wasn't touting for the Arabs. It's the Israelis, all right."

"I see." Flag unearthed a massive blue-polka-dot handkerchief and blew his nose vigorously. "And how much is he prepared to pay?"

"What the hell does that matter? They're quoting a hundred thousand. Half as down payment tonight. Guilfoyle's delivering it himself."

"So." Flag backtracked along the arcade and came to rest before a perfectly detailed model of an eighteenth-century British man-of-war. Driscoll followed him reluctantly. "So you've agreed to take his money. You've presumably accepted the contract, then?"

Driscoll bridled.

"What else was I expected to do? He left me no way out. At three-thirty in the morning you take the line of least resistance. So I let him think it was on."

"And what do you intend to do now?"

"Do? I intend to drop everything in your lap, that's what I intend to do. As of now, I'm out. And I want protection. For me, Cindy, Richard—and Julia, too."

Flag edged away to another display case. The schoolchildren he had encountered on the pavement outside chattered and jostled up the stairs and spilled onto the floor at the entrance to the shipping arcade. A harassed young man in a tweed jacket and jeans marshaled them impatiently and marched them off to the computer section.

When they had gone, Flag said: "I'm afraid I can't take this off your hands, David."

Driscoll was beside him in two strides. He hissed angrily: "You take it or we're finished."

Flag turned to face him. His eyes were distant.

"You're being naïve. No protection I could afford would keep a determined group under control for long; you know that as well as I. Your ex-wife and your son would be difficult enough to keep under surveillance. But how long would we have to keep it up? A lifetime? And this young woman Julia. They could take her at any time. Rather more to the point, your business interests lay outside my jurisdiction *and* my power."

"That's balls. You just have to switch Assad to a safe house now and pull in Guilfoyle. Finish."

"Now you're being astonishingly stupid. Guilfoyle, I imagine, is just a pawn. Valuable, insofar as he's a link with Herrick's, but that's at an end now. If the intention to take Assad is there, Guilfoyle's removal won't change anything. They would switch their assault to another level. It would merely suspend activities for a few days and force them to take an initiative we couldn't hope to anticipate. No—if you're to have any future, David, we have to be in a position to arrest them all—Guilfoyle, his controller, the network, everyone. Leave one fish unhooked and you might just as well not bother at all."

Driscoll stared unseeing into the display case.

"You're setting me up."

"Intentionally, no. But I can see no other choice."

"I have another choice. I could drop the word with SIS Central. You, director of Middle East CAPE, conspiring to release a political assassin. Your feet wouldn't touch."

Flag said equably: "I'd deny it, of course. Embarrassing, but you'd achieve nothing yourself. You'd be in precisely the situation you are at this moment *and* you'd be forced to reveal to Central the extent of your relationship with me. We'd both be out of business. A very shortsighted concept, David. Rather like a bankrupt saying he's invested his capital in debts."

"You bastard!"

"I take that to mean you agree we have no alternative?"

"To what?"

"To do what Guilfoyle demands. What exactly does he want?"

"He wants Assad sprung, but with outside labor. Preferably organized criminal labor. He thinks I've got the right contacts."

"Which you have."

"Maybe."

Flag bent his face into a shallow smile.

"A hundred thousand pounds, eh? They must have considerable funds. I can imagine how they're getting their hands on them. That's a gap we can close fairly quickly. But you can see their point of view of course. A public trial in Israel on the lines of the Eichmann production. Show the Arabs—certainly the Palestinians—they can't get away with murder. It has its virtues."

"Not from where I stand."

"I don't expect you to like it. But look at the advantages. We know their intentions. We know their timing and we can nominate the hand-over point. They're making us—well, you—responsible for the entire operation from start to finish. I take it they don't want an observer in on this?"

"He didn't say."

"Good. Resist it. We have at least forty-eight hours to plan a covering mission. With careful organization, Assad will be out for no more than four hours. We can get him back inside, round up Guilfoyle's operation and keep your identity intact. I'd say we're in the perfect position."

Driscoll turned from him and walked back to the model of the *Victory*. Flag gave him a moment's contemplation, then joined him.

Driscoll said bitterly: "It's bloody impossible. You realize that? It leaves me forty-eight hours to make a plan, find an outfit to accept the contract, establish some kind of a link on the inside, organize the hardware and make it work first time. No rehearsals. No reconnaissance."

Flag checked his watch pointedly. He dragged his scarf from his pocket and wound the black wool round his neck. He stuffed the ends under his coat. He looked like a pregnant crow.

"Not hopeless. Hazardous, dangerous, yes. But that's what you're in business for, isn't it? You knew the pitfalls when you agreed to work with me. If you didn't you're a fool. One day, one of them was bound to threaten your existence—and everyone and everything associated with you. Your problem, David, if I may say so, is purely psychological. You refuse to inhabit your own mind. You're happy enough to take what you can get as long as it can be justified in cold, calculated material terms. Success justifies everything, eh? Even putting your life at stake. Well, now you're going to have to think about putting other people's lives at stake, David. And that isn't easy to justify, is it? Not Cindy's. Not Richard's. Not the girl's."

Driscoll breathed: "Believe me, I could justify yours."

"Now that I don't doubt for a second. But I think I can rely on your sense of perspective."

He half turned to go.

"The curious thing about you, David, is that you can be concerned in a perfectly *cold-blooded* way about the few really decent people in your life. They arrest your sense of purpose. Not your conscience. Because, I know, as surely as if I had an X ray into your brain, that you're also thinking what you claim is out of the question: Who will do the job and how it can be done. And do you know something else? You've already decided who'll do the job. I'll tell you his name if you like."

Driscoll spat back: "Just tell me if he'll pull it off."

Flag shook his head and walked away. He stopped and turned.

"I wish I could do that, David. I really wish I knew. But I think you know." He tapped his forehead with one finger. "Up here, if you care to look. You're the author of your own salvation. You'll be the author of your own destruction."

Albert Duffy lived in a gray-stone terrace house in Elm Place, a barefaced gray shoebox designed in more graceful days for artisans. The Fulham Road neighborhood had bettered itself socially since then—Duffy's fellow taxpayers were now expatriate American actors, pop guitarists and brass-hung City whiz kids.

Along the pavements Rolls-Royce Silver Ghosts squatted with Aston Martins, Ferguson Formula Interceptors vied with bloated American Corvette Stingrays. It was a street to be seen in if you were parking a metallic silver Ferrari Dino. Driscoll was.

The last trailing growths of summer had long blown and died and in the pocket-handkerchief paved gardens, bushes and shrubs drooped disconsolately in progressive stages of decay, but Duffy's eight-feet-by-ten estate was a perfection of military neatness and husbandry. No plant had become tinged with brown: every one had been amputated swiftly and cleanly. Driscoll could see the evidence of the knife and the pruning shears in every corner and bed. There was nothing crazy about Duffy's paving, either. A regimental sergeant major would have loved the layout. That was Duffy: an RSM's dream.

The door opened before Driscoll could reach out a hand to the brass lion-head knocker. That grinning metalwork had a peephole in it somewhere. Duffy was grinning too.

He was an enormous man made gargantuan by cultivated muscularity. The stubby quarter-inch-long brown hair and the tiny buttonback ears were almost invisible from the front. The head was vast. Eyes, nose and mouth were squeezed into a central enclosure so tightly packed that an observer could be forgiven for thinking that the Creator had embarked on a dwarf and lost his way. Duffy wore a dark blue Chester Barrie with a fine chalk stripe but he might as well have worn leotards for all it did to conceal the development of his body.

His hand was like a baseball catcher's glove. He wrapped it around Driscoll's and squeezed gently. "You wanna come up the shop, guv?" It was not a question.

They walked toward Fulham Road, Duffy a full head and

shoulders over Driscoll's six foot two.

"You ain't seen the shop," said Duffy amiably, as though they were continuing a conversation adjourned from the night before. "Took over the electrical place next door last year and a coupla months back I got the picture framers' the other side. Remember the picture framers? They done all the nobs' work—landed gentry, you know. Stuck me for fifteen grand for the goodwill— and they was doing theirselves down at that price, too. Making up very nice. Give us a sorta comprehensive service, see? Antiques, artifacts, furniture, pictures— and hey! course, you ain't heard, have you?—guess who we got on the old gold and silver side, eh?"

He grabbed Driscoll's arm and shepherded him across Fulham Road.

They turned the corner by the Queen's Elm and pushed on down Old Church Street.

"So I'm down the Elephant one night, meeting some joker —you remember the Urbino job, don't you? February '75. A Raphael and a couple of Piero della Francescas nicked from the ducal palace. Well, we talk a deal, see, and we have a couple and I'm on the way home doing a quick in-and-out round the back-doubles, when I come round this corner, and, wallop. Turk."

Driscoll looked up at Duffy with sudden interest. "I thought he got fifteen for that Piccadilly job."

Duffy snapped his fingers; it sounded like a leg fracturing in an empty tomb.

"Eight to ten; he did seven. Thought he was on to the lot, then they give him the old laying on of hands. Six months later, bingo—out he come. Naturally, I take him on, don't I?"

"Isn't he a bit rare for respectable antique dealers?"

"Oh—we don't let him loose. I gotta couple of real clued-up poofters for the front work. Good-quality background and the right accent and they know every dealer in the book. Old Turk is for the back-room stuff. When he's settled down— coupla years, say—maybe I'll give him a little bit of exercise, just to keep his hand in. Early days, though, yet."

The shop was impressive; a long sleek run of plate-glass-work webbed with anti-burglar wire, nestling in a cul-de-sac off Dovehouse Street. Hanging baskets of flowers and trailing fern swung from the black-and-gold-painted wood framework; five-foot-high bay trees stood sentry in black-and-gold half tubs along the pavement frontage. Inside, the atmosphere was ripe with the musk of controlled decay. Duffy, or one of his pin-

42

striped minions, had arranged the huge floor space in a series of room displays: sixteenth-century Dutch, seventeenth-century Italian, eighteenth-century French—boudoir, music room, ladies' drawing room. Duffy led him to an office (TV set designers' gentleman's club) and nodded Driscoll to a ruby Chesterfield.

"Okay, guv. What's the job?"

The words, and his manner, came as no surprise. From the moment they met, Driscoll had known the big man was bursting to ask; only his own peculiar brand of protocol had insisted that he prattle first.

"Usual strings?"

"Sure. What else? We don't have nothing to haggle, you and me. Unless . . ." He let the implication hang.

Driscoll took out his cigarette case, offered Duffy a Gitane and lit one himself.

"You could say there was a catch or two this time."

Duffy overflowed a studded leather swivel chair.

"There's always catches, guv. Depends what they cost. Let the dog see the rabbit."

Driscoll sat quietly for twenty seconds, watching the blue smoke.

"I want a joker lifted out of the Scrubs."

Duffy smiled. His tiny rosebud of a mouth stretched about a yard across his face, exposing a portcullis of giant white teeth. Any wider, thought Driscoll, and the muscles would be unable to bear the weight of the chin.

"Is that all?"

"That's just the prologue. There's a time limit. Thirty-six hours."

"From when?"

"About half an hour ago."

"Thanks a million."

"I didn't say it was easy."

Duffy sucked on the cigarette. "You didn't say you was in the market for miracles, neither. I mean, springing some bugger from the Scrubs—okay. Not easy. Not imposs. But thirty-six bleedin' hours? You can't pull a spring like that without help on the inside, right? Where's the time?"

"That's the situation. Can do?"

Duffy clamped a hand around his jaw and peered through his peephole eyes into the long distance. The Sheraton desk in front of him glowed with depths of age and polish, the gold tooling on its surface leatherwork perfectly imperfect. A

James Bucknell of Crediton long-case clock chugged away in one corner. From a long oak cupboard, a brass student lamp burned electricity under its green cowl; above it, five wall-length shelves bore the leather-bound weight of the kind of books interior designers bought by the yard. An Aubusson carpet covered the area of floor in front of the desk. A superb Second Empire glass-fronted case behind the door rioted with gold and silver plate.

"We'll need an inside man, no getting away from it."

Driscoll shook his head. "We'll need at least two."

"We?"

"I'll be going in with you."

"With who?"

"You, Duff. You know what they say: accept no substitutes." Duffy's smile wrinkled again and died quickly.

"You want to tell me some more about this, guv? We're talking about another kind of ball game, aren't we? If it's you and me, you're either paying off a favor or some bastard's got enough shit on you to put you under. Right? And if you need me—me personally—that's 'cause you can't trust a livin' bloody soul. You don't have to tell me a thing, you know that, but . . ."

Driscoll reached out to the desk top and nudged cigarette ash into a glass ashtray shaped like a swan.

"I'll tell you this, Duff. Two men on the inside, one night behind a wheel, ten minutes inside the wall—the hospital, not the cell blocks—and you're fifty thou richer. That give us a basis for discussion?"

The great white teeth said all that was necessary. Driscoll inclined his head in a gesture of courtly gratitude.

"Your big problem is to find a friend who can put someone in the sick bay."

Duffy spread his hands wide.

"The fifty thou. Where would you . . . ?"

"Zurich, Geneva, Lugano, Liechtenstein, the Caymans . . . you name it. It'll be there. No problems."

"Y'know—I gotta hand it to you, guv. You don't miss a trick. Everything neat and tidy."

"What about the inside men?"

Duffy raised a thumb thick as a brussels-sprout stalk and equally lovely. "Can do."

"I don't want any melodrama, Duff."

"I said I'd do it. Okay? There'll be expenses."

"It's a big purse."

Driscoll got to his feet and stubbed out his cigarette in the glass swan. When he had finished, Duffy deposited the debris in a black-lacquered wastebasket.

"You want to tell me about the MO?" asked Duffy.

"Plenty of time. Five o'clock tonight; you, me and Turk. Room 520, Savoy Hotel."

"What's Turk doing in this?"

"Just sweeping up, Duff. Get his hand in."

"I don't know about that, guv. Bit dicey. He's only been out a year. One step out of line and he's knackered. For life."

Driscoll reached up and patted him on the shoulder.

"If I read the situation right, Duff, Turk could be a knackered any hour of any day, without moving a foot outside this place. Anytime you or your pooflers drop a clanger, Turk's in it up to his hairline before they even take your name and address."

"Well. Just so's you know."

Driscoll winked. "I know, Duff. I know."

WEDNESDAY   1400

Cindy had been washing up. She came to the door with her hair in an untidy chignon, her hands elbow deep in pink rubber gloves, her figure blanketed in a dark blue plastic apron. She said: "Oh, it's you," and turned on her heel, leaving the door open. He followed her down the black-and-white-tiled hall to the kitchen and leaned in the doorframe.

She had been a bold, provocative creature when they first met; big bones under ripe curves; a sexual chemistry set designed for chain reactions and deep heat. They came together in 1956, two months before Suez. He had been spirited away for ten months during the Emergency and they had never recovered from the separation. At least, she never recovered. Richard was born eight months and twenty-two days after the night of Driscoll's return from Beirut in May 1957. They both knew it was a mistake. A month later they separated.

Driscoll had heard nothing about her breakdown, the over-dose (too many for a good night's sleep, too few to kill), until her mother wrote to him. It closed the door, that letter, on any contact between Driscoll and Cindy and Richard for five years. They had met again in the rain, outside the Law Courts in the Strand, on the day she had won the decree nisi. Typical of him, she'd said; it took a divorce to bring them together.

Scott's in Piccadilly for lunch. She got high on a '59 Bollinger and he injected himself against emotional contamination with foie gras, Black Velvet and California strawberries. He took her back to Eaton Square and they drank some more and fought like tigers and wept like junkies. Then he leaped at her like an animal. They had both known he would.

In the postcoital stupor, they had heard the Scottish nanny come in with Richard and Cindy turned off like a tap. They never made love again. They never shared anything again. Except, maybe, regrets. He could never understand why he kept coming back.

Her body could still perform the old trick of clouding his concentration. He lit a Gitane to give himself time to take her in.

"How's everything?"

She turned to look at him, or through him, then bent back over the cloud of detergent suds. "Since when have you been interested?"

"Please yourself."

She processed a half dozen small tea plates. Sullen silence was not her style. "I had a letter from Richard last week. He wants to leave school."

"What do you mean—leave?"

"He won't go to Oxford. Wants to get a job, he says."

"He'll do as he's told."

"He'll do as he *pleases*." The cutting edge on her voice drew a razor across his throat. "That's the kind of boy he is—not that you can be expected to know."

"Okay. Okay. Have you talked about it?"

She picked up a dish towel and draped it over his arm. "You don't know anything about your son, do you? Richard doesn't talk about anything that's important. The psychotherapist calls it aggression. Not too difficult to understand, is it? When you can't trust people, you keep your frustrations and your problems to yourself. That way you don't get hurt. You of all people should appreciate that."

He stirred himself and began to dry the crockery with slow, circular precision.

"You don't have to do this," he said, nodding at the cluttered sink. "Or has the Morrison girl quit again?"

She flashed him a hard, brittle smile; all show.

"The Morrison girl is having a day off. It may surprise you

to know that I'd do it anyway. God knows, there's not much else."

He picked up a pile of saucers and shuffled and dried them like a pack of cards, miniaturized in his prizefighter's hands. "You could get a job if you wanted. You could teach. Stuart Henderson would grab you in a second if you gave the word."

"When I decide to work I'll do it my own way."

They worked on in silence. Driscoll wondered vaguely how he could put it without provoking her. There could be no loose ends. Particularly this loose end. They finished the crockery and he waited while she mopped and polished the stainless-steel draining boards and folded and stacked the dish towels.

She walked through to the sitting room, abandoning him, but he followed, uninvited. He poured a tall Glen Morangie (at least she was still carrying his brand) and dumped himself into a suede Chesterfield. It was a *Homes and Gardens* room, opulent and expensive and graceful, primed with Cindy's designer's instinct. Gold and brown and royal blue; suede and leather and walnut and wool; silken Bokhara and deep blushing Hepplewhite. She made the most of his money.

"Why don't you get yourself and Richard away for a bit? Venice. You like the Lido."

"In December?"

She eyed him suspiciously through a curl of blue cigarette smoke.

"Why not?"

She blew smoke defiantly in his direction. "You could never lie to me, could you?" Her voice shook with the weight of her anger. "Why bother now? It doesn't matter any more."

"I never lied to you . . ."

"You just economized with the facts."

He shifted uncomfortably in the corner of the Chesterfield. "I did what I could to protect you."

"Oh, my God, he tried to protect me!"

She threw back her head and the action catapulted flakes of ash to the carpet. He waited for the tension to drain. She stubbed out her cigarette and lit another. She saw his eyes on her. Her face stiffened.

"Yes, sad, isn't it? A forty-a-day girl—that's what comes of trying to protect me. But that's all over and done with, isn't it? The need for protection? You told me so yourself—when? —three years ago? Four? You got out of it, you said. They let you go."

She put a hand to her face and for a moment he thought she was going to cry. She raised her head again and pulled hard on the cigarette.

"Do you know what, David? You tried to keep too many lies in your head. You never knew where fact ended and fantasy began—you lived your life as if it were a cheap novelette. You could never cover your tracks. They came to me, after they kicked you out. You didn't know that, I suppose.

He gulped a slug of the malt whisky.

"They weren't giving anything away. Not to me. But I knew. God, I knew you better than you know yourself. They were thinking of charging you under the Official Secrets Act. Oh, it was only implied, of course. Meant to frighten me, I suppose. It couldn't come to anything because at the time they didn't know the whole story. But they took one look around this room and you could see the questions queueing up in their minds. Like: How does five thousand pounds a year stretch to *this*? Like: How does he pay for it? Like: What, besides his soul, does he sell?"

She closed her eyes and leaned her head back on the upholstered chair. "I probably knew more than they could even guess."

He said quickly: "What did you tell them?"

She laughed. It was a hard, heartless sound. "Rest easy, David. I don't hate you that much."

He said doggedly: "All right. You win. I want you out of London for a few days. It's important."

She sighed. "There's that word again. Everything was so *important*. Everything, except me and Richard. We could always wait, couldn't we? Remember his last day at prep school? I've kept that letter he wrote you.

" 'Please try and come, Dad, even if you can only be there for prize-giving.' Something important kept you away from that, too, didn't it?"

"You know that . . ."

"I only knew what you chose to tell me—and by then we weren't your problem any more, were we? Just another tax-deductible item buried somewhere in a corporate balance sheet. "To miscellaneous items outstanding: ten thousand pounds per annum.' I suppose we come under 'petty cash' now."

He tried desperately to control his temper.

"Will you go?"

"Where would you like us to go, David? You know we're always anxious to please."

"What about Venice, then?"

"Yes. Why not Venice? Or New Guinea? Or Van Diemen's Land? Or the moon? Who cares, as long as we're out from under your feet?"

"The break will do you good."

"It won't do Richard's headmaster any good. There's almost a week yet before term ends."

"Tell him it's a family problem."

"Oh, certainly. An *important* family problem."

"Richard won't mind."

She sat upright and blinked at him through a flurry of tears.

"Oh—don't worry about Richard. He'll do what's best for me, David. He'll do whatever I ask. He'd break an arm or a leg or his neck to make up for the years when he was too young to do anything. He told me that. Straight out, like a man. 'I'll never let you down,' he said. Here in this room, standing over there by the fireplace. He didn't add: 'Like my father let you down,' but then he didn't have to, did he?"

Driscoll got to his feet, emptied the glass and replaced it on the silver tray. He was already late.

"I'll arrange everything. Phone Richard's headmaster now. He can get a train home tonight. I'll handle everything."

He turned at the door. She was still looking at the empty Chesterfield, the smoke curling unnoticed into her face.

WEDNESDAY   1450

Guilfoyle's back was braced hard against the curved wall. He could not bring himself to look into the void beyond the stone balcony, but the thought alone was a magnet tugging him forward and outward and down, down to oblivion among the tourists a hundred feet below.

For a man who had suffered vertigo all his life, the Whispering Gallery of St. Paul's Cathedral is the mental equivalent of a Torquemadan thumbscrew. Guilfoyle fixed his eyes on a crocodile of giggling tourists on the far side of the gallery.

Why in God's name had he agreed to come *here*, of all places? When the meeting had been arranged he should have realized, but the venue had been tossed out in that characteris-

49

tically offhand manner. Anyway, how could he have refused?

"Shit!"

The word hissed at him from the wall. On the far side of the gallery, a red-haired boy grinned at him and put his mouth to the wall again.

With superhuman effort Guilfoyle dragged himself from the sanctuary of the wall and leaned heavily on the balcony rails, meeting disaster head on. He allowed only his mind's eye to focus.

Four minutes. If the bastard did not arrive in another four minutes he would leave. A man can only take so much.

Ten minutes later there was a movement at his elbow and the voice shattered his self-hypnosis.

"Not sleeping on the job, are we, Guilfoyle?"

He didn't need to look up. That voice would follow him to the grave. Guilfoyle straightened and faced the newcomer.

"It's heights, sir. Vertigo."

"My dear fellow, why didn't you say? I mean . . . I had no idea. Are you all right?"

"I'm all right, sir."

The gray eyes narrowed slightly.

"Good man. Now. Tell me."

Guilfoyle wiped a trickle of sweat from his temple. His hair was wet with it.

"You were right, sir. It's Duffy. He went straight to Duffy's. Stayed just over an hour and left in the Ferrari. Went to the house in Chester Row, had lunch there and left with the girl at two. She took the Spitfire; didn't travel with him. Last report she was in the John Bates Room at Harrod's. Met a guy there. They're having tea in the Georgian Room. We're still waiting a report back on Driscoll."

The newcomer shook his head slowly. Guilfoyle watched him uneasily.

"You know, Guilfoyle; lack of attention to detail has already compromised you once. I would be very scrupulous about a repetition."

He took a paper-wrapped mint from his coat pocket, sucked on it reflectively, looked down at the ant-like milling below.

"Faces . . . faces . . . 'It is the common wonder of all men how, among so many millions of faces, there should be none alike.'"

"Sir?"

"Browne, Guilfoyle. Sir Thomas Browne. A contemporary

50

of our mutual friend, Mr. Herrick." He turned his head sharply. "How do you know Driscoll was with the girl? How do you know he had lunch with her?" It was an accusation.

"The surveillance men across the street. They can see into the dining room on the second floor."

"And they saw a man?"

"Yes, sir."

"They saw a man eating and then they saw two cars drive away?"

"Yes."

Guilfoyle saw the way the questioning was going and tried to head it off.

"It was him all right."

It wasn't good enough and he knew it. If only they were at ground level. He felt disoriented, lost. The man with the steady eyes allowed them to flicker over Guilfoyle from face to hands and back again.

"As I recall, Driscoll drives a car with a blacked-out screen and windows. Am I right? And the garage is in the mews in Elizabeth Street. So what do we have? One: A Ferrari drives in. Two: A man is seen eating. A man. Three: The Ferrari drives away. Assumption: Driscoll drove in, Driscoll had a meal, Driscoll left. Right, Guilfoyle?"

"Right, sir."

"Wrong, sir! I could name five men on Driscoll's payroll who match him for height and weight and a couple who could fool his mother at fifty yards. Faces, Guilfoyle, faces!"

Guilfoyle brushed away another rivulet of sweat from his temple.

"But the surveillance men across the street . . ."

"Were expecting Driscoll. So they saw what they expected to see. I put it to you that they didn't see David Driscoll at all. Who's been watching the girl?"

"Cohen."

"And Duffy?"

"Weitz."

"I will hold you personally responsible if Duffy is lost, you understand? Duffy will be recruiting—now—and he has a habit of branching out on his own."

Guilfoyle shook his head. "He won't get lost. Not with Weitz on him. I guarantee it."

The man leaned on the rail and said conversationally: "Let me tell you a little story.

"Some years ago, a man left a shop behind the old Opera

House in Alexandria and walked due east. He was shadowed by five Mossad agents, the best in the business, working both singly and in harness. They knew their Alexandria better than a muezzin knows his Koran. Really—they were very, very good. It was three in the morning and the man they were following carried arms-supply contracts for three of the fringe PLO groups. Mossad had been waiting for this moment for six months. The messenger would lead them to people they wanted very badly. So . . . the man turned south after a while, and set himself on the Cairo Road.

"Out of Alex it's as straight as a die. The shadows had him permanently in their sights, all of them. But after an hour the man disappeared. He didn't climb a tree. He just evaporated. The contracts he was carrying were worth half a million sterling. It was a very expensive mistake. Think about that, Guilfoyle, because your Mr. Weitz is now tailing that man."

He tugged at the collar of his coat and skewered Guilfoyle on a long stare. "We have less than thirty-six hours to make sure Mr. Driscoll is very dead indeed. Good day to you."

Guilfoyle leaned back against a pillar and stared at the wall. Things would have to be tightened up. He reached automatically into his pocket for a flattened Turkish cigarette. His hand trembled. It had nothing to do with vertigo.

WEDNESDAY   1900

From the sitting rom of the suite, the curved corner window looked down over the Thames. The gray-white span of Waterloo Bridge was encrusted with fleeing commuters and, on its eastern side, jammed with columns of cars and trucks, buses and taxicabs. Driscoll concentrated on the flickering patterns as they changed shape and volume in the dull, orderly, law-abiding world below.

There should be more time; much more time. On the surface Duffy seemed to have it gift-wrapped. He was a great salesman of an idea, Duffy. The fact that he was involved, that his own neck was on the block, made no dent in his enthusiasm. That was dangerous, too. Duffy was a support man, a manipulator of nuts and bolts; but he had no creative imagination and Driscoll knew he would have to rely totally on his organization at the prison end.

He turned from the window. Duffy had ordered, and consumed, coffee and sandwiches for four. He was now two thirds of the way through his second order.

Driscoll balanced on the escritoire by the window.

"Tell me again."

Duffy's face was bulging with one whole lettuce-cheese-and-tomato sandwich. He swallowed it instantly.

"Well." He chewed away on the remaining debris. "They're good boys. Don't fret yourself about that, guv. Both of 'em done their porridge clean, no misdemeanors. Terry's got a minimum of one left; Donnie's on to a five stretch with two done, so they ain't got a bundle to lose. Both of 'em got wives and kids, so the money's welcome."

Duffy took another salad sandwich and posted it into his mouth.

Driscoll said: "They could cop another five-to-ten if they're rumbled. I hope they realize that?"

Duffy looked wounded. "Look, guv—my lads trust me. I wouldn't let 'em walk into the shit without spelling it out. They know they gotta stand the racket. Personally, I think it's a goer."

"All right," said Driscoll. "Carry on."

"Tomorrow morning they get a visit. Terry's solicitor. Which is to say, my solicitor."

"Which is to say a two-faced crook every screw in the business knows. He couldn't put a toe through the gates of hell without arousing suspicion. Jesus, Duff!"

One of Duffy's hands opened like the business end of a mechanical grab.

"Fair enough. I gotta give you that. But you know what I said this morning. I laid it on you square, right? You said thirty-six hours and I said that ain't time enough. Okay—so I've got the word through and I got them on the payroll and it's only been"—— he consulted his watch—"it's only been five, maybe six, hours. I'd've thought, myself, that wasn't bad, considering."

"But *have* you got them on the payroll?" Driscoll insisted. "You say they're your people. I want to be sure."

Duffy shook his head, bewildered.

"If I didn't know you better, guv, I'd swear you were pulling my pisser."

Driscoll's mouth hardened.

"When I say 'it's on,' guv, It's On. Remember—I got more'n *your* interests to protect. I got a business to run, same as you. I got a payroll. I got people drawing pensions, even; bet you didn't know that. I got families on Duffy's National Assistance, you know that? You don't think Terry and Donnie's wives and kids is left helpless, do you? Twenty a week each, both of 'em. On the nail, every Friday, rain or shine. Expensive, but good business. Them guys is professionals. They won't take their skills to anyone but me, see. Now you understand?"

Driscoll grinned. The audacity of it took his breath away. He nodded.

"What about this solicitor of yours?"

Duffy raised his hands as though acknowledging applause.

"Perfect. Terry's boy, Shane, he's signing on for this apprenticeship. Toolmaker. Smart boy. Fact is, he gotta have his dad's signature on the forms. That's the law, see."

"So your solicitor takes the forms . . ." began Driscoll.

"And gets his autograph, all nice and legal"—Duffy beamed, enjoying it—"and slips him the pills. Tomorrow."

"They could be seen."

"No chance. You don't know the Scrubs, do you? They don't pay that much attention to every fiddle-farting solicitor that comes along." He winked. "Even my solicitor."

"How much will they need to know?"

"What we decide to tell 'em. I told you, they trust me."

Driscoll pushed himself off the escritoire and turned again to the window. The surging patterns of people and machines were less dense. Across the river, the vaulted roofs of Waterloo Station would be thundering to the passage and press of humanity scenting hearth and home and television set at the end of another lackluster day.

He turned back into the room.

"Right. I think we've left Turk alone long enough. Get him in here."

Duffy stretched and got to his feet, brushing crumbs from his jacket.

"You definitely want him in on this?"

Driscoll nodded.

"You're the guv'nor." Duffy paused in the center of the room. "You said something about your own contact on the inside. You want me and Turk to know about that?"

Driscoll opened his arms wide. "What's mine is yours. It won't do him any harm to know. And it won't do him any good. My contact doesn't know he's a contact yet."

Duffy and Driscoll took a taxi back to Chester Row. A filigree of snow was settling over the city and both of them wondered independently if it would materially affect the schedule. Twenty-four hours to go. They would need the devil's own luck as it was.

Julia was in bed. They went to the study.

"Drink?"

Duffy shook his head. "You know me, guv. Dry the day before, pissed the day after."

"I don't like this snow." Driscoll downed a neat scotch, enjoying the rawness of it on his tongue.

"No sweat. Less people about. We'll just have to watch the roads." Duffy raised one eyebrow quizzically. "You got something on your mind I don't know about?"

"Everything you ought to know, you know."

"You're sweating this one, though. I know you too well."

"I love you, too. If this goes wrong . . ." He shrugged. "But it won't."

Duffy pulled on a pair of skintight driving gloves.

"Are you sure there ain't nothing else?"

"Else? No! Christ, what's the matter with me? Do I look that bad?" Driscoll peered theatrically into the mirror over the Adam fireplace. "I see what you mean." He emptied the glass. "I need a good night's sleep."

The dusting of snow had become a blanket. Driscoll and Duffy stood on the steps at the street door. The air had the tang of aftershave, stinging their cheeks. Duffy clapped a paw on Driscoll's shoulder and trudged off in search of a cab. Driscoll watched him go. He felt isolated; exhilarated by the scent and feel of snow, but isolated. In Avoriaz now, there would be a couple of meters of it on the pistes. Powdered snow; the passage of skis, hissing and crackling like frying bacon. Mastery of movement and momentum. He scooped a stray flake of snow from inside the collar of his shirt. When this was over he'd go there. He and Julia. The thought made him feel better.

The two yellow eyes glowed off, on—off, on from the curb in Elizabeth Street. For the first time he noticed the white

Jaguar 3.4. He turned up the collar of his jacket and walked across to it. The window wound down.

Guilfoyle said: "You'll forgive me if I don't come in."

Driscoll had a sudden urge to wrench open the door and shake him like a rat.

He said: "Have you got the down payment?"

Guilfoyle reached over to the back seat and handed out a green plastic Harrod's shopping bag. It bulged attractively.

"Count it if you like," he suggested helpfully. He opened the passenger door. Driscoll ignored the invitation.

"I nominate the hand-over point," he said. "Take it or leave it."

Guilfoyle held his peace for five long seconds.

"Fair enough. Where?"

"Culpin's warehouse. It's off Wapping High Street. Derelict, so you'll have no problems with snoopers. Turn off the High Street into Green Bank and right into Cinnamon Street. Double gate. It'll be open. We hand over on the top floor."

"I'll find it."

"You'll be there at 0230. Not before; not after. Two-thirty dead. Clear?"

"Crystal."

Driscoll turned to go, but stopped in mid-stride.

"Don't do anything stupid. It isn't worth it. I've taken out insurance, just in case."

Guilfoyle nodded.

"Bear that in mind yourself, friend. We've got cover, too. Thirty-six hours and you can afford to go play for a few days. Take the girl friend somewhere nice. Venice, maybe, huh?"

He wound up the window abruptly and engaged gear. The car surged away in the direction of King's Road.

"Shalom," breathed Driscoll.

As he slammed the door of the house, the bedroom curtain above twitched and fell back into place.

Julia stole quietly to the bed, slipped between the sheets and settled herself in the fetal position of sleep. Silently rehearsing her opening lines . . .

"I've got to talk to you!"

Driscoll's reply was to reach for her breast. He gave one twentieth of his mind to the task of massaging the nipple with slow, sure fingers. The reaction was swift. The nerve endings swelled at his touch, pressing his hand; hard and tactile as molded glass.

"Did you hear what I said?"

He sighed and bent over her, trying to find her mouth with his. She pushed him away.

"For God's sake When somebody tells me he wants to talk I don't just grab his balls!"

The hysteria was close. She dropped her voice.

"David—are you all right?"

"Far as I know. Pulse normal, blood pressure fine, dandruff under control. Of course I'm all right! Let me off the hook, will you?" If you don't, he thought moodily, nobody else will.

She banged her head into the pillow. A moment later she sat up abruptly, reaching for a cigarette that wasn't there. "You haven't spoken to me all day. Do you know that? You put me through hell, then—nothing. No explanation. Why won't you talk to me?"

"Do we have to talk about whether we've talked!"

Duffy would have to work fast. Would he be so keen if he knew what lay behind it all?

"Well. I want to."

"What?"

"Talk. We've got to talk. *I've* got to."

"We'll talk tomorrow."

"Now."

"No!"

She flung her legs over the side of the bed. "There's something you've got to know."

What if they accidentally knocked off Assad? If the dose was too strong? Badly administered? What happens if Special Branch move him from the Scrubs? No, Flag would avoid that, somehow. What if . . .

"Christ!" Julia slammed her hands palm down on the bed. "You don't care a damn."

Driscoll rolled over to her.

"I care."

"No!"

"All right. What do I have to say? It's half past God-knows-when and you give me the runaround like some sex-starved hausfrau—so tell me. What have I got to know?"

She was breathing heavily. Sulking. Or . . . He sat up concerned. His tone was gentler this time.

"What is it, lover? What's wrong?"

"Tell me who I am, Driscoll. Go on, tell me. Do *you* know? Because I'm damned if I do any more."

The tension snapped and she slumped forward, her head cradled on her knees. He slipped an arm around her waist but she knocked it away. He knew there was only one kind of remedial therapy left. He muscled her back on the bed. She struggled angrily.

"No! Leave me alone."

He thrust his full weight on her. His mouth found hers, his tongue forcing a brutal passage. She brought her teeth together and the pain shocked him, but he could not withdraw. Slowly, slowly, she relaxed the grip on his tongue. His knee pushed between her legs and, as if in spasm, her back arched, thrusting her body greedily at his.

Fifteen minutes later she lay quiet beside him and he could still taste the blood on his tongue. Sleep was impossible. He got out of bed and found the cigarettes and lit one. He sat in the window seat and watched the snow; big flakes, now, floating like parachutes in the still air.

Something made him check the digital watch. Twelve midnight exactly. It was going to be a long, hard day.

He went to the bed and rolled back on the pillow, his eyes focusing the pictures in his head.

For God's sake, why hadn't he realized? Flag had given tongue to it at their meeting this morning: "Guilfoyle is clearly just a pawn." So who was the king? And was the king another Herrick's man?

A sharp sliver of light from a streetlamp sliced upward through the badly drawn curtains and outlined a crescent on the wall beyond the bed. Driscoll fixed it hypnotically.

Now think.

If Guilfoyle's controller was at Herrick's—and it would be a damned fine arrangement if he were—he would need to be on the Executive. Well, it was a pretty fair bet. He would need to be a deep-cover double, probably with a whole career of perfectly loyal service behind him. He would be triggered for only the biggest deal, because after it he would be blown forever.

He would be shrewd, resourceful, confident and secure. He would kill to preserve that status. Herrick's was an anthill of such men. It manufactured them. Still, not all of them had the stomach for it—or the originality.

Process of elimination.

There was Basey, Flag's chief of staff; a conventional Brigade of Guards throwback, shoehorned into a sinecure at the Defense Ministry when it was still the old War House. Drafted to a desk in Admin at Defense Intelligence in Holborn, he had, by a process of osmosis, become a senior SIS desk man. His brother-in-law was on C's personal staff at Century House.

There was no way it could be Basey. An Olivier couldn't maintain that façade of tweedy idiocy for twenty-five years without cerebral hemorrhage.

Then there was Hugh—Hugh Davidson. He was Herrick's executive field controller, their procurer-in-chief. If he had vices, in the professional sense, they sprang from a habit of ignoring his "executive" role in favor of building missions around himself. He felt neutered by walls and paper work. He was a bundle of frustrations when he was forced to sit at a desk during an operation. He handled recruiting in the field and coordinated the disinformation process. In the art of coercion, persuasion, bribery, corruption and subversion Davidson was pure Picasso. An original. He had a French wife, three cherubic little girls who knew Driscoll as Diksol, and an eighteenth-century thatched farmhouse near Saffron Walden, where he played English squire at weekends. He was the only member of Herrick's Driscoll still occasionally met on social ground.

Without Davidson, Herrick's had no cogs. But if he were the sleeper, the very specialized nature of his job would have blown him immediately. Out.

Three others fell into the same slot: Anderson of Political Intelligence; an academic sadist with no outside interests. King, of Project Analysis, Weatherby's ball boy; at home with juggling possibilities, but no experience of the field. Durrance, Communications; limited access.

That left the Big Three. As a group they were ill-assorted,

individualistic, antisocial; uninterested in each other as people, suspicious of each other as professionals.

If they shared anything it was a mutual repugnance, yet no matter how tenuous the bond, together they made one of the most clinically efficient teams British Intelligence had ever assembled.

Wernher, Grant and Weatherby.

Martin Wernher had actively worked against Britain's interests before transferring his allegiance. He had doubled for East Germany's AVO and the French SDECE, then bartered his way into M16 in the mid-fifties. No one could have anticipated that he would rise to the higher echelon. Although he had never been able to prove it, Driscoll was convinced that Herrick's had an unbreakable armlock on Wernher. And he was a man who could let old resentments run strong and deep. As Controller of Logistics, his could be a potent resentment.

Grant, Controller of Support and Supply, was a different kettle of fish. A freak from the English thirties, he dated back to the later years of Sir Vernon Kell, the original "K" of M15. In one job or another he had lived alongside most of the intelligence "greats." There was six foot five of him weighing eleven stone. He had a marked effeminacy of manner and a habit of wringing his hands in neurotic spasm when drawn into conversation. His hatred of verbal communication amounted almost to lalophobia. His wartime work with the Norwegian underground, with the marquis in Marseilles and with Tito's guerrillas in Yugoslavia was legendary.

He had broken his own mandatory silence in one very positive way. As early as 1951, he had warned of the activities of one of the most successful intelligence operatives in the service: Kim Philby. He had said nothing when his warnings were ignored. He had said nothing when they bore fruit.

Far from receiving praise he had earned almost universal resentment. Somewhat ungraciously, a nickname stuck: the Fourth Man.

Driscoll could see no circumstances in which Grant would "turn." Except one. In the past year he had been drinking heavily. In itself this was hardly surprising. Intelligence was a career in which alcoholism claimed men as a matter of course, but in Grant, the weakness was at least out of character.

Julia murmured in her sleep. Still sleeping, she turned

toward him. Driscoll's hand drifted softly, absently, to cup her breast.

And finally there was Weatherby.

Alexander Mansfield Weatherby. Flag's right-hand man; the operational linchpin of Herrick's. Weatherby was Strategy Analysis. Sally Ann. All brain, no heart. He had been plucked from the Tree of Knowledge when he was twenty-five, a visiting professor at Yale and indisputably in line for a chair at Oxford. "They" had brushed him down, knocked off a few corners and fed him into the system. It had been a masterstroke. A slight mid-course correction took him from M16 to Herrick's, and they had created a man every intelligence service in the world dreams of.

But it made no sense for Weatherby to go over to anyone. He had put too much into Herrick's. He was marked down as Flag's natural successor. An overwhelming point against his being a double; like most academics, he was obsessively ambitious. It wasn't in Weatherby's character to turn from the Holy Grail when it was within reach at last.

The room blanched with light and faded into darkness again as the headlights of a passing car raked it.

As Flag had said . . .

Flag.

The slow rise and fall of Julia's breathing began to communicate itself to him. He slid toward sleep. In the dying moments, a thought jabbed insistently at his brain.

One cog missing. One man.

Flag. What about Flag.

Beside him, Julia stared emptily into the dark, feigning sleep, warring with the things that hadn't been said, couldn't be said now.

Thinking of Flag. Hating him.

THURSDAY   0930

Dr. Raymond Barney turned the spade in the damp soil and watched two pink-gray slugs wriggle tormentedly. He threw a pellet of slug bait into the hole and allowed the earth to fall back on killers and victims.

He loathed gardening. Twice a year he was compelled to turn over the unsightly sprawl of grass and weed and ground-running creeper to pacify his wife Shirley and conform with the lease. It was an exercise in despair. He did little more than upend the earth on itself. The landlord was a Cypriot and initially had been markedly impressed to have a doctor as his tenant. The house had never been more than a staging post for a long line of impecunious Pakistanis or Irish laborers. It was not a carriage-trade house; Blickenden Road was not carriage-trade country.

When Raymond Barney came out of nowhere with his quiet ways and his doctorate and his legal wife, the landlord had cherished a fleeting vision of Blickenden Road flowering sweetly as another fashionable slum. The vision died of terminal disillusionment. Barney had turned out to be one of those doctors who earned virtually nothing. He had a captive audience. He was an assistant MO at Wormwood Scrubs Prison.

A half hour of slothful spadework was enough. He walked around the semi-detached house and stood in the front garden. There was a choice, he decided: either he made passes at the rank flower beds; or he took the shears to the privet hedge. He chose the latter as measurably less soul-destroying, deposited the spade in the garden shed and returned with the shears. He glanced at his watch. Shirley had taken Iain to the local doctor's surgery. His asthma again. Tonight Barney would have to leave the house at five-thirty to get to the prison by six-fifteen. At least it gave them a whole day together. He attacked the distended privet shoots.

Driscoll wound down the passenger window and focused the telescopic lens. It was not difficult to cover Barney from all angles, full face and profile, because every car that passed, every jingling cyclist, magnetized the young man's attention. Driscoll wound on the thirty-sixth frame and dropped the Hasselblad on the back seat.

Barney was tall and thin and angular and sad. His income topped seventeen hundred pounds a year but only just. He was twenty-eight and his track record suggested he had little to look forward to professionally but stopgap jobs, holiday relief posts or a fate as a traveling locum. He had no car; no bank balance and no overdraft; no extramarital connections, no hang-ups with queers. He was not a sniffer, he didn't smoke grass, he drank only beer and that very rarely. By the accepted standards of the seventies, he was honest. And weak.

No—you didn't trust people like Barney to take a bribe,

not if you wanted him to hang loose. A bribe would frighten him, panic him. And moral confusion begat guilt and guilt begat a telephone call to the governor.

What else about him? Edinburgh degree, decent hard-working student who nearly didn't make it; no paternity suits in the murky past. No murky past.

The grocer on the corner (to whom Driscoll had introduced himself as "a credit-evaluation agent") said the Barneys were a decent, respectable pair, a bit hard up except when it came to young Iain, their eight-year-old. Do anything for him, said the corner-shop man. He had a sneaking feeling, he had, that Dr. Barney felt he hadn't done right by the little 'un. You know; rushed into marriage, scored a direct hit on the wedding night and suffered for it since.

Driscoll was about to start the engine when he saw Barney straighten suddenly, then run into the house, hair flying. Driscoll picked up the camera and focused the 300-milimeter lens on the ground-floor windows. He picked up the shadowy outline of Barney through the lace curtains. He was leaning on a cupboard . . . a sideboard . . . a piano . . . something. He was talking into a telephone.

Telephone. Driscoll turned the telescopic lens to the roof line, found the black line of the outside feeder cable and followed it down to the front door. He lowered the camera absently. The telephone.

At nine-forty, there was a shriek of childish joy from behind Driscoll's car. Barney came alive as though he had been injected with a bicycle-pumpful of adrenalin. His head came up, a smile wiped the boredom and the care from his face, his mouth opened. He sprinted across the street and swept a chubby little boy into his arms. A young woman, pallid and mousy, embraced them both and pecked at Barney's cheek.

Driscoll turned the ignition key as they disappeared into the house. He pulled the car into the road and drove back toward the city.

Telephone.

Flag squeezed out of the car on the corner of Birdcage Walk and Horse Guards. The wind had lost its early-morning razor edge and the sky was piled high with gray marshmallow cumulus. There would be snow again tonight. Tonight . . .

He dawdled across Horseguards Parade, stopping twice to relight his Peterson. He passed through the arch, reached the back garden gate of No. 10 and flashed his MinDef accreditation wallet at the police constable on duty.

There were still bloated patches of snow on the winter lawns and the rose and dahlia beds were white islands, but the path had been scraped and shoveled clear.

Entry by the back door of No. 10 was a privilege granted to only a handful of trusted men, but there was a second uniformed policeman by the house to emphasize that even that trust was conditional.

The Prime Minister was in the private flat on the second floor, a modest suite which he personally declined to use as a residence. He had converted the sitting room into a spartan reception room where he could temporarily escape the machine of state below.

Flag was escorted up by an aide. The PM offered his hand. He still had a lot of sleep to catch up on; last night had obviously given him small measure.

Flag removed his coat and was gestured to a moquette armchair on one side of an empty grate.

"You'll have to forgive me, Flag. We haven't much time, so let's get down to it. I've called an emergency Cabinet meeting for two-thirty. All I want from you is a few straight answers. God knows, they're hard to come by. What are the odds on a retaliation by Assad's people, whoever they are?"

Flag sucked on his dead pipe, contemplated lighting it again to rehearse, dismissed the idea.

"I should say the odds are pretty short, Prime Minister. That's a personal opinion, of course. I've nothing to substantiate it. Central, as you know, are playing this very close to their doublet."

"Yes, yes." The PM's scowl indicated that he was in no

mood to referee a domestic Intelligence squabble.

"You wouldn't have been consulted at all if I hadn't insisted. So now I'm asking you man to man. Do we expect a second assault or don't we?"

Flag nodded, slowly at first and then decisively.

"We do, sir. Ordinarily, I'd vote against it; it's not the Palestinian way of doing things. In—crunch—out; that's their form. But this is obviously a prestige strike, carefully planned. Meticulous. I don't think they'd consider launching it without a support operation. They would want their conquering hero safely home to claim his laurels."

The Prime Minister fidgeted on his chair.

"C considers it's a one-off suicide mission. A glory hog working on his own. The PLO have disowned him; you know that, I suppose? They issued a statement this morning in Beirut. They dissociate themselves entirely from Assad, his action, his intentions—everything."

Flag poked his pipe bowl with a match.

"Diplomatically, I don't suppose they could have done anything else, sir. If you strike a legitimate political posture, you don't sabotage your new respectability by embracing an assassin."

"You think they might support him privately?"

"Not exactly. They might be tempted if the conditions were right, but this is too public, even for them. No—they're probably telling the truth. This is a fringe group operating alone. It's nothing new. The hardliners have actively encouraged it since Yasir Arafat got his ticket to the UN. The fringe think they've been sold out. Arafat and the PLO are in the same boat as the Provisional IRA Council. They created the perfect climate for militant offshoot gangs and when the time came for diplomacy they couldn't conrol 'em."

"So what are we to expect?"

"With respect, I think the real question is *when* are we to expect it? Bombings, a shoot-out, kidnapping, a take-over of one of the embassies. We can prepare against all those eventualities, to some extent at least. It's the time factor that worries me. But I'm just not equipped at present to offer you facts, sir. My hands have been tied by Central. I'm under orders not to make contact with our operatives abroad. I can't mount an investigation in the field. I can't even brief my section heads."

The Prime Minister got up and strolled restlessly across the room. He put up an elbow on a glass-fronted bookcase and rested his chin on his hand.

"How long would it take to get this—er—field investigation under way?"

"Hours. Half a day, no more. But it could take thirty-six hours to get a playback. Twenty-four if we're very lucky."

"And what if Assad's group strikes before then?"

Flag shrugged. "In that case we've already wasted too much time, sir. At best, we could take some kind of political initiative, perhaps, to avoid the necessity for a strike."

The Prime Minister pushed himself upright and walked to the window. There was no movement in the street below. The police had thrown a fence of portable steel frames across the entrance to Downing Street, minutes after the shooting on Monday morning.

"I've made that clear, Flag. We're not going to hand this man back to his people. Give in once and we give every tuppennyha'penny crook with a grudge carte blanche to hold this nation to ransom."

This time Flag lit his pipe and took his time doing it.

He said quietly: "I would agree with you there, sir."

The Prime Minister walked back to the hearth and sat down opposite Flag.

"Very well. You have my permission to go ahead with your investigation. And I want you to make it clear to everyone concerned that it has priority over everything else. Everything. But thirty-six hours is too long. Twenty-four is barely acceptable. Impress that on your people. I want accurate information and I want it fast."

He stood up. Flag took the hint. He got to his feet and pulled on his coat.

The Prime Minister held open the door. As Flag moved to pass him, he reached out a hand and rested it lightly on Flag's shoulder.

"I'm counting on you. This is between you and me. It's your operation. Don't fail me."

Flag looked squarely into the tired face.

"Just give me twenty-four hours, sir. This time tomorrow afternoon."

"I'll expect you here. Two o'clock."

Flag smiled. "You'll have your package, sir. Signed, sealed and delivered."

He had gone too far.

Thirty minutes of cool reassessment, a twist of self-justification, and it still came out the same way. He had fashioned a scenario for disaster.

Flag stared emptily at the carpet by the window where pale sunshine spilled in cold geometric pools. He got to his feet, strolled restlessly to the fireplace and turned to study his desk and chair as though the vacated space held the answer to his actions. The green-shaded desk lamp breathed its aura over scattered papers, encapsulating the isolation of the chair and the man who occupied it.

The bandwagon was moving, accelerating. All passengers accounted for. Nothing could stop it now. Only his own sense of duty; his conscience. Childish conceits.

The mistake was Driscoll. Everything else could be retrieved but the Driscoll factor was irredeemable. Never deliver yourself wholly into the hands of a dead runner. It was a fundamental of the trade.

A dead runner, by definition and by nature, was an outsider; a freelance pulled into the net to perform functions too dangerous, too compromising or too visible to risk a staff operative. A dead runner was expendable, unprotectable. More often than not the only successful outcome of a dead-run operation was the runner's grave.

No one read the implications of that definition better than Driscoll. He couldn't be trusted to obey instructions at all costs.

That's where the real danger lay. Driscoll would be on his own. What he chose to do would make the difference between success and total disaster.

Flag fretted all the way to his desk. His whole strategy was based on a calculated prediction of what Driscoll would do in a crisis. Yesterday, it had all seemed so clear, so obvious, because he had convinced himself that he knew this man. Today . . . ?

He stabbed the Dictograph.

"Get me a couple of paracetymol, will you, Mrs. Lamb? I've got a bit of a headache."

His crombie buttoned to the neck, a copy of *The Times* folded under one arm, the man threaded purposefully through streets crowded with last-minute shoppers.

At the corner of Sloane Square he paused in front of a garish window display. A guitar-playing Santa Claus in flared trousers, surrounded by chipped and yellowing children, spelled out the Christmas message: Buy Denim for All the Family.

He went inside.

Moving leisurely between the counters he made his way across the store, occasionally stopping to turn over some object on display, wincing gently at the price, and replacing it with the precision of a chess player.

At the far end of the store he joined a crocodile that was being fed into a lift and found himself on the third floor. Men's Outfitting. Millinery. Linen. The crowds were feverish, milling like refugees around sacks of grain. He shouldered his way amiably through them and walked down the stairs. Halfway down he paused and unlaced a shoe, retying it with exaggerated deliberation. He was alone. He waited a full minute, then walked back up the stairs and took the lift to the fourth floor. Gardening Equipment. Hardware. Accounts. He took the stairs to the ground floor and exited by a door marked "Emergency Only."

Tonight the crowds suited his purpose perfectly.

In all his years with the Company he had never quite come to terms with the cloak and the dagger. The world of ciphers, invisible inks, handguns and dark glasses filled him with acute embarrassment. He saw intelligence as being precisely that; a flexing of the intellect, an exercise in offensive wit and ingenuity. But he had long ago recognized it for what it really was; a ragbag of expediency and ruthlessness, planned in the mind maybe, but played on the street corner.

He allowed himself a wry half smile. Sometimes, he had to admit, the techniques that made up the ragbag came in useful.

Down Sloane Street and into Knightsbridge.

He turned up his coat collar as the wind funneled its way

across Hyde Park, dry and fresh as ice.

Just three months before, it had been a very different scene.

At the height of the rush hour, a bomb had exploded without warning at the entrance to Knightsbridge tube station. The very spot now seething with shoppers clutching tinsel and trees. What was left of the car carrying it had scythed its way through the crowds like high-velocity grape-shot, slicing indiscriminately into bodies and metal and stone. He had helped pull a young woman from under a shroud of shattered plate glass, screaming in delirium for her hand-bag, unaware that both the bag and the arm that clutched it were lying ten feet away in a blood-running gutter.

It had been the fifty-third bomb the IRA had planted in the city and it claimed three lives and forty-six wrecked futures. He shuddered at the recollection. His fear of blood was a phobia he knew he would never conquer.

A child crashed into his knees, wailing as its mother dragged it irritably to its feet. Disentangling himself, he nodded away her apologies, ruffling the wretched child's dark hair.

Non est vivere, sed valere vita est.

Life is not living, but living in health.

The pub off Old Park Lane had been open ten minutes by the time he arrived and business was brisk.

He waited patiently as the regulars went through their ritual greetings and shuffled away like opium addicts to their time-honored pews.

"Gin and Drambuie, love?" The barmaid's pinched lac-quered face leered at him above a cleavage of spotted goose-flesh.

"A rum. By itself," he said. He never drank. He picked up his glass and moved down the bar.

The man was here, somewhere. Watching. Waiting. He could feel his presence. Taking *The Times* from under his arm, he placed it on the counter and stood his glass beside it.

Nobody had given him a second glance, but he still felt awkward, out of place, a gate-crasher. The less time he spent here, the better. He walked across to a cigarette machine by the door and fumbled for some coins. A stamping gaggle of office workers gave him the opportunity he needed. Behind the smoke screen of their exuberance he slipped through the door and into the street.

"Same again, love." The stranger at the bar nudged his

empty glass across the counter and glanced down at the folded newspaper. He flicked through it idly and turned to the back page. The crossword had been partially completed and he studied the penciled answers with interest. He found what he was looking for.

Three words, bearing no relevance to the clues provided, had been heavily scored in.

They read:
JULIA
PARTY
TONIGHT

THURSDAY   2100

The house was full of shadows. The fridge was bare of instant food.

Driscoll toyed with the idea of building himself a club sandwich. He made a halfhearted forage for ham, cheese, salad and eggs, then abandoned the search. Sending Julia to stay overnight with Janie Davidson at Saffron Walden had seemed a good idea at the time. Maybe it still was—if he could ignore an empty stomach.

He poured himself a Glen Morangie in a fat Rosenthal glass, but put it down without taking a sip. Later, later.

One hour and fifteen minutes.

He went back to the kitchen and rifled the fridge again. He found a packet of chocolate Olivers and a bottle of milk and returned with them to the sitting room. The biscuits were good. He drank the milk straight from the bottle. If Duffy could see him now . . .

One hour and eleven minutes.

That meeting the Arab Emirates had canceled on Tuesday morning. That was another notch he intended to cut on Assad. Up to the moment of Asher Landis' assassination there had been no question but that the contract would go through—except, perhaps, for a few minor amendments to pacify Defense Sales and the national conscience. With spares and servicing, instruction and maintenance teams, and the bulk purchase of ammunition, everyone would have drunk deep of the gravy. Particularly the Exchequer. His own rake-off on base-line supply of forty units would have been a

70

conservative 750,000 pounds, paid through Neufeld AG in Geneva, in nice stable Swiss francs. Somebody was going to pay for that.

Like Flag.

He reached out to the radio and pressed the medium-wave selector. A velvet female was crooning a bad imitation of Barbra Streisand. "When on foreign shores I am, Truly, truly, yours I am . . ." He terminated her passion with an abrupt flick of a finger and tried again.

It was a man's voice this time, City-suburban and intense: ". . . but the market remained unsettled and falls in some long-term stocks extended to one and one eighth pounds sterling. Short-dated loans also met with increased selling pressure and there were falls of between five eighths and three quarters of a pound in Transport Four Percent, 1972-77, at eighty-eight and three quarters pounds . . ." Driscoll cut the cackle and switched off.

One hour and eight minutes.

Cindy and Richard would probably be safely asleep by now. Their two-bedroom suite at the Danieli overlooked the Grand Canal. The last of the ferries would be pumping their human cargoes onto the quayside of the Piazza San Marco; the last water buses snarling through the darkling canyons. In spite of herself, Cindy would love it; the graciousness and the instant service and the marble and gilt and the musky stench of water-logged history. It brought out her creative instinct. To be in Venice without paints and canvas was a uniquely sophisticated form of torture for her.

He upended the bottle and glugged milk into his throat to quench the guilt. In the beginning Cindy had never tried to conceal the joy she found in living with him. It colored their days and swaddled their nights. Perhaps it should be *made* to work again. Richard was tripping over his feet into manhood. He needed a father now to set him straight.

Driscoll pressed the button on the digital Omega.

One hour five minutes.

He was getting old. Senile. Only old men sat in judgment on their lost opportunity. Only old men doodled with their past, reliving it the right way. And where would that leave Julia? Was there a right way of erasing Julia from the past year?

He lit a Gitane and swallowed the smoke until it hurt. Julia was changing, strictly according to pattern. The first time they had made love in a bed, she had handed him her

71

Declaration of Independence. Her phrase. My life is my own. My body is my own. My mind is my own. Take it or leave it. Something like that. A lot of crap about no strings attached; butterfly flitting from flower to flower. About trying every dish at the banquet because woman couldn't live on bread alone.

His father had forecast all of it, right down to the time scale. There were two things you had to know about women, he'd said: When sex was the only way out, and when it was the only way back. He had a theory, too, that an affair was over when the taste of a woman's mouth reflected the last thing she had eaten or drunk or smoked. Lust or love were great sweeteners. They lent the serpent's tongue a taste of honey.

When would Julia begin tasting of garlic bread? Soon, maybe.

According to another of his father's theories, there came a point in an extramarital affair when the demands of the lover were so maddening that the wife became the "other woman." Julia was pushing that point. A year ago she had declared her total disinterest in his private and public life. Now a day didn't go by without her talking him into a corner. But what the hell were you supposed to to? She was part of the built-in furniture of his life. She saw, she heard. Too much.

Trouble was, she understood, too. There was very little landing space for flies on Julia.

Now it was all getting far too emotional. Like last night. "There's something I've got to tell you."

Jesus Christ! The cry that echoed over the primeval swamp. Once upon a time it was: I'm going to have a baby. Now it was: I've got to have an abortion. Or in Julia's case, since she seemed to be working up to some cataclysmic personal decision: I want to marry you.

Fifty-five minutes.

He got up and took the milk bottle and the remains of the biscuits to the kitchen. He held the bottle under a tap and flushed and cleaned it.

After this is all over . . .

Tackle first things first. Why not? Get Julia away for a spell. Avoriaz or Jamaica, or Alec Peel's villa on Lesbos. It could be the end of the beginning or the beginning of the end. Either way, it would hustle a decision for both of them.

On impulse, he picked up the wall phone and dialed Hugh Davidson's home. Janie answered.

"Janie, darling. It's David. Glad I caught you before you all turned in. Can I have a quick word with Julia?"

"Julia? She's not here, David. I got her room ready and she called me at—oh, it must have been seven-thirty—to say she was on her way. I assumed she'd decided not to come after all. I was just going to bed."

"But—" Driscoll stopped. He eased the panic out of his voice. "Sorry, sweetheart. You know Julia. Probably found herself a party and a Brazilian millionaire somewhere. Not to worry. If she turns up, tell her I called her. See you soon. Love to the kids." He replaced the receiver.

He perched on a high stool at the breakfast bar and lit a cigarette. Goddamn the woman. Did she have to pick tonight of all nights to exercise her bloody unpredictability?

He'd told her exactly what she had to do, when and how. Leave the car. Take a cab to Liverpool Street and get a train. Plenty of taxis at the other end. He'd emphasized the importance of traveling in the rush hour. The more people around her, the better.

She'd argued and refused and backtracked and finally surrendered, but he knew this wouldn't be the last he heard of it. The look on her face when he refused to explain the sudden overnight stay at Janie's should have been warning enough that she might sabotage the whole thing.

Driscoll caught himself.

Sabotage? That was a curious choice of word. Is that what he was really thinking? Julia a saboteur?

She had said nothing when he found her at the foot of the stairs, literally seconds after Guilfoyle left the other night. God knows, that was out of character. She'd accepted his excuse that he couldn't sleep, that he had gone to the study to read.

Had she seen Guilfoyle? Overheard the phone call to Flag?

There was a simple answer to that: she'd have grilled him endlessly. Unless . . .

Unless she knew Guilfoyle was coming. Unless he'd planted her right under Driscoll's nose. Unless . . .

He stubbed out the cigarette viciously.

After Cindy, he had vowed never again to allow a woman to get under his skin. A man gave of himself until he had nothing left but he still finished the day emotionally in debt. The more he gave, the more he owed. And when he could give no more, he drowned in his own guilt. Cindy had drained him because she wouldn't trust him. Julia would drain him because now he couldn't trust her.

He walked back to the sitting room, grabbed the tumbler of scotch and knocked it back.

Forty minutes to go.

THURSDAY   2130

The departure lounge at Schiphol Airport, Amsterdam, was packed. Four ski charter flights bound for Zurich had announced delays because of thick fog, and in the seventy-degree central heating, the Christmas vacationers were beginning to lose their sense of festive humor.

"British Airways announce the departure of their flight BE 146 to London Heathrow. Will all passengers proceed to Gate 6. Please have your passports and boarding cards ready."

Most of them were businessmen, hotfoot for home, their briefcases bulging with duty-free cigarettes and liquor and cheap Delft bought in last-minute desperation for wives who would never know the difference. A small posse of Pakistanis, chirruping hysterically around three fat old matrons in saris, galloped away to be first at the exit gate.

"All right then, you old cows. On your feet."

The photographer wore his equipment like badges; around his neck, strung from his arms, bulging from the pockets of his black leather windbreaker. The four incredibly cool, unbelievably thin model girls in his charge grumbled to their feet and strutted behind him, their furs and silks decanting a cloud of perfume.

There was confusion at the gate. A petite girl in KLM ground staff uniform was attempting to apologize for yet another short delay. Brays of protest and despair greeted the announcement. The Pakistanis surrounded her, twitching pathetically at her sleeve. The ground hostess was clearly at the end of a long and eminently forgettable day. She couldn't bear to stand still for a moment. Every thirty seconds, she walked to the glass wall of the exit area, peered hopefully into the darkness, then returned to the queue, her gloved hands writhing one in the other. After five minutes she was joined by two young men. A seasoned traveler would have been surprised to note that they wore the uniforms of a

KLM pilot and flight engineer, but the seasoned travelers had lost interest in everything but the passage of the minute hand across the face of the electric clock.

The exit door opened abruptly from outside and the wind hurled wreathing fog into the tightly jammed embarkation area. The little ground hostess shot a look of relief at the man who stood framed in the door and called out to the herd: "Your boarding cards, please. Have your boarding cards ready."

It occurred to no one to wonder why there was no security inspection, no examination of clothes and luggage. But the cold was beginning to bite into heat-coddled bodies. There was no room in minds clogged with impatience for bureaucratic reasoning.

The passengers were processed with indecent haste. The man at the door, obviously the driver of the airport bus, devoted more fixed interest than his uniformed colleagues to the passengers and their hand luggage, but even he urged them to move along quickly to avoid further delay. He was an uncommonly swarthy man among the white faces of England and the hearty ruddiness of the Dutch.

The bus was a small one and most of the passengers found themselves wedged upright. Three minutes, five minutes, eight minutes elapsed, and then three young Yorkshire salesmen broke into the chorus "Why are we waiting?" sung to the tune of "Oh, come all ye faithful."

The bus moved off suddenly, throwing the human weight displacement backwards and forwards. The hymn singing rose in volume.

The lights in the interior of the bus made it impossible to see beyond the windows and, after five minutes' driving, the passionate songsters' voices trailed away. The chatter stilled; faces set hard, eyes glazed.

The bus braked and the wheels locked and skidded on the new snow. The doors swung back on automated glides and the driver, the ground hostess and the two flight-deck officers appeared from the darkness.

"This way, if you please, ladies and gentlemen. This way." They surged like cattle down the steps into the snow. The island of light around the central airport complex sparkled more than a mile away.

Ahead loomed the mass of a hangar. Some of them made out the legend stripped across its doors: Fokker Friendship. Then, they were inside, anxious in the dark, falling over each other's feet, complaining bitterly. The Yorkshiremen were whooping like choirboys on an outing, "Ey—watchit!" Then one of them raised a mellow tenor in a reprise of the old hymn, this time to the words: "Oh, why can't we see you?" His friends took it up and other voices began, half-heartedly, to join in.

The steel door of the hangar slammed shut with a thunderous reverberation that echoed and re-echoed from every wall and girder. The singing stopped abruptly.

For the space of ten heartbeats, the silence of the grave settled around the blinded passengers.

Then a woman began to scream.

PART TWO

EXODUS

Blickenden Road slept under its mantle of snow and greasy poverty, the few streetlamps left intact spilling muddy yellow pools on the sludge-filled gutters. The Austin A50 van squeezed into a gap between two down-at-heel family saloon cars and switched off its lights. In its interior a lighter flared and snapped out and two red pinpoints grew and blossomed and faded. The two men sat without speaking, their eyes on Raymond Barney's sad little semi. Occasionally, one of them checked the luminous green ring of a diver's watch.

Duffy had said the timing was critical. Never mind if the lights are off, he'd said. If there's a phone by the bed, the woman might take it into her head to call someone—and it would be a right stumor, wouldn't it, to cut the poor cow off in mid-sentence. Get all worked up, wouldn't she? So worked up she might go out and use a public call box to phone her hubby. And that wasn't part of the deal.

The last possible moment, Duffy had said. It was all programmed down to seconds and every move depended on the one before it. One minute to midnight and not a second earlier.

The driver sucked his cigarette down to within an inch of the cork tip and crushed out the lighted end between finger and thumb. He raised the watch to his face, waited for a full minute, then dug his companion in the ribs.

The door creaked indelicately as the passenger got out into the street. He checked the road ahead and behind, then walked confidently through the garden gate and down the short path to the front door. The pictures had shown the telephone cable quite clearly: an ancient installation, running from the eaves to a point at the base of the doorframe where it entered the house.

The man slipped a pair of cutters from his pocket and opened the mat-black jaws. He forced one jaw under the cable and snapped the cutters cleanly. The severed cable ends bent outward.

It was exactly one minute to midnight. It didn't do to play silly-buggers with Duffy.

THURSDAY   2400

The hospital block at HM Prison Wormwood Scrubs is tucked away in one corner of a worn gray complex. On the second floor of the block, Dr. Raymond Barney sat at his night desk and doodled on the back of a prisoner's sick return.

He doodled squares; some with diagonals cutting across their edge, some with arrows penetrating the sides. Always squares. The hospital psychiatrist had told him, jokingly, of course, that doodled squares implied an innate desire to escape the womb. The hospital psychiatrist doodled squares, too. When a man is forced to spend up to twelve cheerless hours a day in prison of his own volition, escape is at the core of all his mental processes.

Barney looked up from his handiwork and stared emptily along the rows of beds. The ghostly orange glow of the night lights cast indefinite shadows across the figures beneath their blankets. At least, they weren't here of their own choice. For them it was time out from intrigue, violence, danger, chance. Barney envied them. None of them had a sentence as long as his.

Murderers, thieves, con men, embezzlers, poisoners, blackmailers, even the occasional sex maniac. Hogarth's people. And now an assassin. His gaze dwelt on the far corner bed. The young man had been brought to him under heavy guard from an isolation cell in the high-security wing at six forty-five. On admission, his stomach had been one solid knot of muscle, as if a clenched fist had bunched inside him. He had been like that, in his cell, for two hours before the screws began to think it might be genuine. Another hour and he might have died of exhaustion.

The name on the treatment card was Assad. Three days before, in the heart of London, he had shot the Israeli Defense Minister dead at point-blank range.

One thing was certain: whatever fate lay ahead of him, the Arab had had a ghastly introduction to retribution.

Into one end of him had gone a continuous ingestion of starch, barley and water. Into the other, gastric lavages. Morphine shots had kept down the pain. Then the stomach pump. Assad had lain there for three hours, his throat on fire, his stomach burning, blood streaking his vomit. His skin was clammy to the touch, his feeble pulse was racing, and his eyes had constantly pleaded for water and more water. They had stabilized him after six excruciating hours. Now, weak as a kitten, he lay drained and empty.

Barney pushed the doodles to one side and reached for the night report sheets. It hadn't been difficult to pinpoint the cause of Assad's melodramatic condition. It would be infinitely harder, though, to discover who had caused it and why.

Someone, somehow, had slipped him three quarters of a gram of iodine. Just a fraction under the lethal dose. Maybe it had been a warning. The Arab had obviously resisted, though. Someone had used a pointed stabbing weapon, presumably to quell him long enough to administer the oral iodine. The wound was high on the right of the chest in the clavicular head. He had lost a lot of blood.

Halfway through "Initial Diagnosis" the flickering light of the telephone broke his concentration. Barney looked at his watch. It was two minutes past midnight. "Dr. Barney?" The switchboard operator's voice was impersonal.

"Yes?"

"A call for you. Outside."

Barney blinked away the fog in his head. There was obviously some mistake. He had told Shirley never to phone him at work, except in an emergency. Iain! The line crackled.

"Your call, Doctor." There was a click and silence.

"Hello? Shirley?"

"Dr. Barney? Dr. Raymond Barney?" It was a man's voice. He did not recognize it.

"Dr. Barney speaking. Yes?"

"Dr. Barney, listen carefully to what I have to say. There will be no time to repeat it. You live at number 34 Blickenden Road, Ealing. Your wife is named Shirley. You have a son, Iain. He is eight years old. You will finish your shift at six this morning . . . I could go on but we have very little time, Doctor."

"Who are you? What is this?" Barney felt a tightening in his chest.

"Just listen carefully, Doctor, and don't be alarmed. My colleagues and I are at your home and I am speaking on your telephone. Your wife and child are with us. They're quite safe. In eleven minutes' time—and it's now exactly four minutes past midnight, please check your watch—in eleven minutes' time, I want you to pick up your telephone and inform the governor or his deputy that one of your patients is dying."

"At my home! I don't understand. What? . . . Dying?" The voice cut in.

"Pull yourself together, Doctor. Do exactly as I say. You will inform the authorities that your patient has had a relapse and needs urgent attention. You will advise that he be sent to Hammersmith Hospital. He will need specialist treatment if he is to survive. You will insist that his condition is critical and deteriorating. You will say that you wish to phone immediately for an ambulance from the hospital. That is all, Doctor."

"Let me speak to my wife. What are you going to . . . ?"

"Calm yourself, Doctor, or you'll regret it for the rest of your life. A dead wife and child hang heavy on a man's conscience."

"You swine! What have you done?"

"Do you follow my instructions, Doctor?"

Barney's hands were shaking violently. It was unreal. "I understand."

"Good. Very good. Now take complete control, Doctor. Complete. People are depending on you. Particularly your son. Don't let him down." Barney stared, unblinking.

"The name of your dying patient, Doctor, is Assad. Now make your phone call."

The line clicked dead. Barney checked the time. Seven minutes past midnight. His finger trembled as he dialed the switchboard operator.

"I want my home. Quickly, please."

It had to be a joke. It had to be! He waited.

"Sorry, Doctor, I think the line's out of order. Shall I keep it in?"

"No! No, it doesn't matter. Thank you."

They were there. With his child. With Shirley.

He began to feel sick. His head ached abominably. He stared fixedly at his watch as the minute hand crawled its course. At fifteen minutes past midnight he snatched at the telephone.

"Hello? Get me the deputy governor. Yes, I know it's late. Just get him! It's an emergency!"

From the ward windows of Hammersmith Hospital's West

Wing there is an uninterrupted view into Wormwood Scrubs Prison and the barred windows of one of the larger cell blocks. The return view was once said to be a source of pleasure—albeit frustrating for the inmates. The hospital's West Wing housed Women's Medical.

The hospital is separated from the prison by a narrow unnamed lane leading to Wormwood Scrubs, a wide, sloping stretch of open land, curving down to the Grand Union Canal, that serves as a recreation ground. Along one side of the lane runs a fourteen-foot wall, equipped with closed-circuit television cameras.

It was at this point, directly opposite the hospital, in October 1966 that George Blake removed the sawn-through bars from a landing window and sprinted twenty feet to the wall. A ladder made of wooden knitting needles and rope had been thrown over the wall from the lane where a van lay in wait. The escape had been one of the most mortifying blows the British prison service had sustained. Blake had been sentenced to forty years. He served five.

Concrete bollards are now spaced at intervals of ten feet along the base of the wall in the lane to prevent a repetition of the Blake caper.

One stable door had been closed.

Another was about to be opened.

FRIDAY   0005

The line appeared in cool green computer type on the Flight Information Display. Beeline 146 was estimated on schedule to arrive at 0035. The duty superintendent spared the information no more than a perfunctory glance. He had already seen the teleprinter tear sheet on 146, filed on takeoff from Schiphol by Air Traffic Control in Amsterdam. Beyond the anti-dazzle windows, a heavy scum of black cloud settled at a ceiling of 3000 feet and snow was sweeping the field with curtains of silver. Beeline 146 had thirty minutes to touchdown.

The superintendent ran a hand over his eyes. He had a strength-five headache. There would be time enough to worry about 146.

At London Air Traffic Control Center, West Drayton, the

senior controller also threw an eye over Schiphol's rundown on 146. There was a direct telephone link between the two centers and flight-plan confirmation was dispatched automatically. Beeline 146 was routed on Red One, steering 257 at 300 knots, climbing through 10,000 feet and accelerating. The flight plan included its routing, height, number of passengers (there were 106) and alternative dropdowns in case of diversion. Red One was the invisible path running from Amsterdam to a point halfway across the North Sea where, at 23,000 feet, 146 would pass from the hands of Amsterdam radar to London Control.

The cloud ceiling at Heathrow slumped to 2800 feet. The superintendent wrenched his tie loose and unbuttoned the neck of his shirt. He learned silently for a shower, a long cool pint, a cigarette, or the freedom to remove his dark blue pullover. He sensibly blotted the discomfort from his mind.

He lived among men keyed to a set of conditioned reflexes. Every action, every word, was predicated and planned to an infinite point of recurring-decimal accuracy.

They were hypersensitive men who reacted coolly to crisis and impending mega-death; but that built-in calm was founded on system and sequence and predictability.

He walked slowly through the diffused strip lighting, his feet sinking into deep, sound-swallowing pile carpeting, his mind ranging the bandwidth of stored knowledge and new information as he passed from controller to controller.

He stopped behind a balding head, its headset band cradled in protective cotton wool.

"Roger, Beeline 146. Maintain Flight 2230 squawk 1154 route Longsands–Ongar. Red FIR south. Over."

The superintendent paused and waited for the pilot's confirmation. The response was cackling with static but the voice was colder than a corpse in a charity ward.

Beeline 146 was now officially beyond the hand-over point and in FIR, London's Flight Information Region. It now had yet another classification tag: Squawk 11 (inbound Heathrow) 54 (its personal landing number). The plane would make a course correction any minute now to bring it over Longsands and Clacton-on-Sea to Ongar and the stack over Heathrow.

"Beeline 146. Clear to 160. Over."

"One-four-six. Clearing to 160. 21,500 feet, speed 600 knots."

The superintendent gazed out at the snow muffling the floodlit apron below the tower.

He was not one for globe-trotting himself; not that the job didn't make it easy—and cheap. He had never seen the sense in it. Four years in North Africa and a painful crusade through Sicily, Italy and Germany in the wake of an evaporating war had given him little appetite for foreigners or their cultures.

"Super? Emergency call from Schiphol."

The girl, cool and unruffled, handed him a teleprinter tear sheet.

"106 passengers your Beeline 146 Amsterdam–Heathrow located abandoned Schiphol stop. Please confirm with pilot Captain John Sharland. Ends."

The superintendent read it again. One hundred and six passengers abandoned? He flashed the sheet at the girl.

"Get them to repeat that, please."

Beeline 146 was about twenty minutes from touchdown. Over Burnham-on-Crouch, maybe, now. The ramp allocator had already given it space at Charlie 16 on Pier Three, near the terminal building. The notification had been passed to the tower.

All systems were working perfectly.

The superintendent picked up a green telephone and jabbed a button labeled LATC.

"Air Traffic Control, West Drayton. Senior controller here."

"Duty superintendent, AOR Heathrow. You have Beeline 146 Amsterdam–Heathrow?"

"Just a second, please."

The sound faded as a hand cupped the phone at the other end. The voice snapped back.

"I'm told there's some emergency signal about stranded passengers."

"Right."

"I'll check it out. We're handing over shortly. Keep this line open, okay?"

"Okay."

The superintendent waved to a girl checking a list at a desk beside his. He handed her the phone.

"West Drayton," he said shortly. "Keep the line open and report any message to me at once."

The teleprinter girl returned from her bank of stuttering

machines. The tear sheet confirmed the original message from Schiphol.

The superintendent folded it.

"Get me Schiphol on the phone, please. Air traffic control superintendent."

He strode to the control console handling the run-in of 146.

"I may want to relay questions to 146." The controller nodded and returned to his display.

"Beeline 146. Contact London Control 127 decimal 95."

The West Drayton operator's voice was comforting.

Sharland's voice—it seemed somehow more human with a name tabbed to it—came back steel cold.

"London Control, Beeline 146. Good morning. We'll be at Longsands in one minute. Leaving 230 now for 160."

The controller responded.

"Roger, Beeline 146. You're clear to flight cover 140."

He looked up questioningly, one eyebrow raised, as the pilot's voice crackled over the loudspeaker.

The superintendent shook his head. He wanted a word with Schiphol first.

FRIDAY   0018

Had it not been for the blood-red stripe with the brilliant blue vein at its center, the white Bedford Automatic would have been invisible as it stood in the snow in the forecourt of White City Stadium. Its engine purred softly.

Driscoll tapped Duffy on the shoulder. Duffy released the hand brake. Half turning, Driscoll knocked on the small communication window and Turk slid it open and gave him the thumbs-up sign from inside. The girl in the nurse's uniform was reading a paperback with a penlight.

The ambulance pulled out of the forecourt and picked up speed along Scrubs Lane.

"Left here," Driscoll muttered unnecessarily. Duffy turned the vehicle into Ducane Road. "Take it easy now."

Driscoll was worried about the "nurse." She was too attractive. Bordering on the tarty, but memorable. Still, any distraction would help once they were inside. As long as she kept her mouth shut.

In the distance, he could see the black-and-gold railings that guarded the warders' houses in front of the prison. Careful now. If the headlights came on too soon it might capture the attention of a hospital gatekeeper. If they came on too late, a watchful prison gate guard could become suspicious.

Luck was on their side.

The main-gate area of the hospital was deserted.

"Right," said Duffy. "Here we go."

He flicked a switch and the fog beams came up full. Another flick and the pulsating red lights set like eyes on either side of the radiator grille began to flash. They were committed. Driscoll felt the sweat trickling under the arms of his thick gray uniform.

Duffy swung the ambulance into the tree-lined avenue and the lights flared on the huge studded doors of the prison. He slammed on the brakes, theatrically. Driscoll felt a dull thud behind him. He glanced into the back through the observation window and saw the figure of the girl spread-eagled on the floor. Stupid cow!

The yellow-and-white-banded pole in front of them swung up immediately. From the small sentry box on their left, the pinched face of a prison officer appeared and nodded them forward. He walked alongside the driver's door, stamping his feet, for the twenty yards to the tower-flanked gate. Duffy slid open the door and jumped down.

"Jesus Christ, it's a shocker, mate," he whoofed, slapping his sides.

The officer exhaled a stream of frosted breath. "Brass monkeys, all right."

The small inset personnel door cut into the gate opened and another officer poked his head into the headlight glare.

"Leave it here, chief? Or do you want us inside?" asked Duffy.

"Hang on a minute."

The officer disappeared back behind the door. A full minute passed. Duffy trudged over to the ambulance and Driscoll wound down the window.

"What's keeping them, Duff?" He kept his voice low.

"I don't know. Just keep acting natural. We're on the telly, don't forget."

Duffy nodded imperceptibly at the twin cameras mounted above the gates. He pressed his hands to the hood of the ambulance, feeling for its warmth.

"What about the girl?"

"I don't know. She banged herself when we hit the anchors, I think."

"Daft bitch! She could screw up . . ."

The personnel door opened again and yet another head appeared around it. The officer jerked a finger at Duffy.

"You! Come here!"

Duffy ambled forward.

The officer maneuvered his clipboard light, a pencil poised over it.

"Name?"

"Stansted, Eric Stansted." Duffy had done his homework.

The pencil moved efficiently down the list and ticked off the name. The officer jerked his head at the ambulance.

"The others?"

"Charley Cummings up front. Wilf Toland and Nursing Sister McBride in the back."

Again the pencil squeaked. The names corresponded with the list of authorized ambulance personnel on call from Hammersmith Hospital.

"Okay. Identification." The officer held out his hand.

Duffy half turned in a show of weariness.

"Do me a favor, mate. Bloody freezing out here. We got other jobs coming up, you know." Still grumbling, he dug into his tunic pocket for the forged ID pass. The officer's pencil tapped on his clipboard as he studied it.

Duffy stamped and blew into his hands, hoping the sweat on his temples wasn't noticeable.

"Right." The officer handed him back the card.

"You don't want the others do you?" pleaded Duffy. "Me hooter's going blue."

A faint flicker of what might have passed for humor crossed the officer's face.

"In you go," he said, and jerked a finger at one of the warders by the gate. "Open up."

Duffy dashed across to the ambulance and slid into the driver's seat, his heart pounding. They eased toward the gates.

A small lead ingot that had been turning in Duffy's stomach was slowly disappearing.

What even Driscoll didn't know, nor ever would know, was the appalling chance they had just taken. Had had to take.

For neither Turk, nor the girl, nor Driscoll had an identity card.

Even at the speed Mendelson worked it had been impossible for him to turn out more than one in the time allotted.

"Do you vant one that gets you through, or four vot gets you caught?" he had shrugged.

Duffy had settled for one and an advance on his luck. He knew if Driscoll had found out that each one of them needed cards he would have called it off. But too much had been invested to throw it all away. Now they were in and nobody was any the wiser.

Duffy made a mental note not to bet on the horses for the next six months. He'd just used up all the winners.

The gates swung wide and they inched inside, halting under the arch of the main lodge. To the right of them behind the duty officer's desk, the bank of tiny television screens flickered their surveillance. Behind them the main gates swung shut.

One officer appeared alongside the driver's window.

"I'll walk you through. Keep it slow and quiet, eh?"

"Won't wake the sleepin' beauties," said Duffy, sliding the ambulance into gear.

Two warders dragged back the inner doors just wide enough for them to squeeze through and they were led into the main yard at a steady two miles an hour.

The officer turned them sharp left beyond the lodge, through a maze of workshops, cell blocks and huts scattered haphazardly facing the outer wall.

Driscoll breathed deeply. "Halfway there," he said softly, swinging a foot up to brace against the dashboard.

To their left the walls glowed with a live, throbbing fluorescence.

"They did that after Blake hopped it," said Duffy. "Stand in front of it and you're as sharp as the fingers on your watch. Pretty color though, ain't it?"

They drove for two hundred painstaking yards. At the far wall Duffy was ordered right, and right again. On their left towered K Wing, the pre-medical section. In front of it the oval exercise yard was flooded with light from the lamps high up on the wall.

Driscoll reran the maps and aerial photographs through his mind.

The four turreted cell blocks ranked equidistant across the

compound; the factory with its smoke-blackened chimney in line with the front lodge, marking the exact center of the prison; the squat library with its modern extension; the dominating incongruity of the chapel with its Norman windows and triangular flower bed.

But even Driscoll knew that the most such information could do was humor his need to set into complete context every aspect of a job he undertook. To know the unnecessary details, the trivia, had more than once paid off the hours of research and surveillance.

Not here.

He could know it like a rabbit knows its warren, but one thing was certain: if something went wrong, there was no place to run.

A group of warders waited at the entrance to the hospital wing. Driscoll picked out the face of Raymond Barney. Ashen.

The ambulance stopped and they got out.

"Right, then, where's the poorly boy?" said Duffy, clapping his hands together noisily. The rear doors were already open and Turk and the girl were looking efficient. Duffy joined them to wheel in the stretcher as Driscoll waited by the ambulance.

Barney's eyes had never left him. Driscoll met his stare. Don't be silly, Doctor. Just don't do anything silly. Easy, easy. Remember your wife. Your kid. Especially your kid.

Barney read the message in his eyes and turned away. Drawing a shaking hand across his forehead, he walked into the hospital.

The body on the stretcher was muffled to the eyes. Gently Assad was eased into the back of the ambulance, an appreciative audience of warders thawing visibly at the long, long expanse of nylon as the girl stepped up to join Turk. The doors were closed.

Duffy had kept the engine running and was hauling his bulk up into the driver's seat. Driscoll was only inches from joining him when a hand pressed his shoulder.

The man in plain clothes smiled pleasantly as he shook open his black leather-covered identification card.

"Name is Hayes," he said. "Special Branch. I'd like a word with you."

Driscoll could see nothing through the communication window. Just the reflection of the streetlights ahead.

It was up to Turk now. The Special Branch man who had insisted on traveling with them would be shooting the second he realized they had passed the hospital gates. He was standing in the aisle of the ambulance between the stretchers, one hand on the overhead equipment rack, his eyes riveted on Assad. His back was turned to Turk and the girl.

They had traveled a fast hundred yards when Duffy threw out a restraining arm and stamped savagely on the brakes.

Staggering wildly, the Special Branch man swung in a half circle. Then Turk hit him, a single blow delivered with incredible force at a point directly over the carotid artery. The man's legs folded under him and his body collapsed vertically, like a punctured concertina.

For the space of a second he assumed an attitude of prayer, his eyes wide. Then he pitched forward. His nose struck a raised ledge and the bone broke with a thin snapping sound.

He lay still, bubbling softly in his own blood.

Turk banged the rear of the driver's cab and Duffy pulled the ambulance to a halt two hundred yards beyond the furthest hospital gate and well out of visible range. He slicked the sweat from his brow with the side of his hand.

"Christ, just what we needed! You never told us he'd be coming!"

"Because nobody told me," said Driscoll, his face set in anger. They got out and walked to the rear of the ambulance. Turk peered at them from the open door.

"Everything under control. He's dead though. Sorry."

"Dead!" Driscoll scrambled into the back and prized open Assad's eyelid.

"Not him, chief!" Duffy angled a thumb at the Special Branch man. "Old Bill. Gone to Jesus."

"I couldn't take any chances," Turk said coolly. "You only get one chance." He stared at the body on the floor.

"It happens sometimes. Couldn't be helped."

Driscoll eyed the broken figure at his feet. It was too late for recriminations, too late for sadness, pity, disgust. He could feel nothing for the luckless victim. Nothing at all. What was important now was the time they had left in which to cover their tracks and the man's death. It made sense that he would have been ordered to stay with Assad all night. He wouldn't be missed until morning.

Duffy would have to arrange a scenario for the corpse and, when the hand-over deal was complete, Flag could exert the necessary pressure in the right areas to avoid any awkward questions.

"We'd have had to get rid of him anyway," said Driscoll to Turk, his voice toneless. He looked across at the girl sitting on a jump seat in the corner. Her hand shook as she dragged on a cigarette.

"I don't want no part of this," she said. "No part, do you understand?"

"Shut your face," said Duffy offhandedly. Then, remembering something, he stumped across to her.

"And, while I'm at it . . ." He grasped the hem of her uniform and with one sweep lifted it to the top of her thigh. "Bloody nurses don't wear bloody fully fashioned nylons at five quid a time. They wear black ones with bloody great seams. Okay?"

He let the hem drop and turned to Driscoll.

"Detail. They never learn."

Recoiling from his glare, the girl shrank back, whimpering excuses as Duffy and Driscoll returned to the cab. The ambulance plunged toward the Westway Flyover.

In the back Turk blinked away with difficulty the vision of white thigh and tightly stretched panties and busied himself with the man on the floor.

There was, he reflected ruefully, a time and a place for everything.

FRIDAY   0025

The girl hanging on to the West Drayton line signaled quickly and the superintendent took the receiver.

"Yes?"

"Amsterdam confirms. They have a hundred and six passengers and five crew. One-four-six is empty except for the pilot, I imagine. Otherwise, all standard procedures observed."

The superintendent looked at the mouthpiece quizzically. All standard procedures observed *otherwise!*

"Thank you."

He settled the phone back onto its rest. Amsterdam was on the line. Mijksenaar at Schipohl made it fast and lucid. The passengers had been taken to one of Fokker's repair hangars way out on the perimeter and simply locked in. They had broken out after an hour and made contact on the bus transmitter.

"Nobody hurt. Nobody too worried." Mijksenaar might have been talking about a schoolyard prank.

"Right. Thanks, Pieter."

"You're welcome. What're you going to do? We register no transponder."

"Nor do we. I'll keep you informed."

The initial approach phase was on and Sharland would soon be going onto auto-land, his eyes glued to the situations display screen in his cabin. The Trident would pick up the localizer, the radio beam that lined up the aircraft with the runway. When it was settled on the center line the plane would intercept a second radio beam, the glide path, about eight miles from touchdown point. The computer master-minding the exercise would force the aircraft's nose down at thirty feet per second. At an altitude of seventy feet the throttles would close automatically and the auto-pilot would reduce speed from thirty feet a second to two feet.

"Beeline 146. London Control. Flight level 130 . . ."

The superintendent closed his eyes and opened them again. He could see heads beginning to turn, eyes widen in silent curiosity. Everyone was listening to the loudspeaker. This was wrong.

He said quietly to the girl at his elbow, "Inform Heathrow police. I want fire tenders and an ambulance on standby. Make sure there's a doctor, too. No panic, understand. It's all speculation, tell them. Just covering eventualities."

The 146 controller at West Drayton was saying, ". . . on that heading."

Sharland's reply was innocent of panic or frustration.

"Beeline 146. One-three-zero. What forward speed would you like?"

"Keep up your speed for the moment," returned the controller quietly.

"One-four-six," crackled Sharland.

The Trident was now approaching Ongar and the thirty-mile-wide coil of the holding stack. At Heathrow Approach, the No. 1 radar director would identify the aircraft as it left the holding pattern to join the landing sequence. Then the No. 2 director would take over.

The flight strip illuminated 146. Its call sign, its type and estimated landing time were all displayed. They listened as the disembodied voice of the West Drayton controller signed off.

"Contact Heathrow Approach 119 decimal 2. Good morning to you."

Sharland ran through his procedures. Heathrow Approach director cut in as 146 drifted over Westminster. "Roger 146. Twenty-two miles to touchdown. Contact director 127 decimal 4."

It was too late to cross-examine Sharland now. It had been too late from the moment they picked him off Red One.

But why hadn't he hit the transponder code button? Why?

The explanations would have to wait. The superintendent felt the perspiration on his palms prickling through his fingers. Up there, 146 would be hanging over black mountains of cloud, the Thames to its left, Hyde Park over to the right.

Heathrow Approach ordered: "Beeline 146. Turn right, heading 260. Planned ILS approach, runway 28 left. Range is fourteen miles. 1018 millibars."

There was a break, then Sharland was on again for an establishment check.

"One-four-six. Range eleven miles down on runway 28 left. Call Heathrow Tower, please, on 118 decimal 2."

The superintendent walked quickly to the controller who would talk down 146. Sharland changed frequency and came on again.

"Heathrow Tower. This is Beeline 146. Establish 28 left."

As Sharland and Beeline 146 swept over the radio beacon ten miles from the end of the runway, fixing the final, precise position of approach, the superintendent called Jeff Parrish at Heathrow CID.

Julia opened her eyes.

Above her, on a stainless-steel rod, hung a line of spotlights. Each one shivered and multiplied as the tears mounted from the ducts and washed the burning surface of her pupils. Her head had the texture of an inflated balloon, stretched to the point of explosion.

Slowly, the rest of her body registered a return to life. Her arms and legs had the density of lead. Low down on her back, just above the hip, a pinpoint of sensation raged in its own private, piercing torment.

She closed her eyes and allowed her mind to range gently over the areas of pain, feeling from the inside for broken bones, torn ligaments, cuts.

Nothing there. But how . . . ?

The sharp shrieking pain in her back. Now she remembered. She had felt that first. She had been walking—that was it. She had waited for a taxi on the corner of Elizabeth Street and Chester Row and when none came she had walked down toward Ebury Street.

Yes. And by the pharmacists' some people were getting out of a car. She hadn't looked at them; they meant nothing to her. Besides, she was already late.

And then they seemed to be all around her. And then she felt the sharp deep pain in her back.

Realization flooded her and for a moment she struggled to move in the first throes of panic. Her body would not respond.

A hypodermic. Sodium pentothal, probably. She tried to think rationally. Who? Why? The spotlights beamed down cruelly into her closed eyes, boring through the thin pink walls of her eyelids.

Oh, David—I'm sorry.

It was all she could think. It had to be because of David, because they needed a hold on David.

Why, oh why, hadn't she told him last night? He would have understood. And this would never have happened.

From her right, a voice snapped: "Three kings! What're you using for luck, Tony? A marked deck?"

94

The victor raked in a pot of coins and paper money.

"You play with your wits, Leo. Try your brain next hand," he returned good-naturedly. "You want to raise the ante next time or . . ."

He stopped. Julia heard the chairs scraping as they got to their feet. They were over her, overhanging her, like vultures around a carcass. Four of them.

"Well, well, well—the dreamer awakes," said the bad loser.

"Get her up, Leo," said the winner. "Give the lady a chair."

Strong hands gripped Julia and she shrank from their touch but it was useless. They picked her up as though she were no more than the clothes she wore and set her down on a wooden dining chair. One of them stood behind her to hold her upright. His hands held her arms pinioned.

"Okay, Leo. Let's get it over with."

The winner bent at the knees so that his face was level with Julia's. There was something near to regret in his eyes.

He said to her: "Keep still and stay quiet. It'll be over in a couple of minutes."

Julia felt the blood drain from her face. She tried to turn away but the giant hands on her arms tightened like a vise.

The leader said: "More pentothal."

The man called Leo turned to a small table by the wall. There was a flat black case. He opened it. A glint of steel.

Julia couldn't take her eyes from Leo's back. Then the hypodermic needle was plunged into her arm. She ignored the pain. The anesthetic of terror had already engulfed her.

Leo turned towards her tight-lipped.

In his hand was a surgeon's saw.

FRIDAY   0038

The superintendent wore the headset himself.

"This is Heathrow Tower, Beeline 146. I repeat. Complete your taxiing procedure. Your ramp allocation is Charlie 16 on Pier Three. Confirm, 146. Over."

He repeated the message. Then again. There was no reply. He handed the headset back to the console operator and walked to the tinted plate-glass windows and stared out.

For thirty seconds he hesitated. Then he swung on his heel.

"Emergency procedures, 146."

He turned back to the window and began to count the seconds. On twenty-five the first fire tender skidded into the penumbra of light and flashed away across the field, hurling a jet stream of snow behind it. Three more followed in quick succession.

Seven vehicles were on their way before he had counted to thirty-six, their full headlights dancing and threshing in the darkness.

The superintendent returned to his desk, snatched up the internal telephone and depressed a red key.

"Dennis? Jack. We've initiated emergency procedure on Beeline 146. No communication with the captain since landing. Taxiing procedure ignored. He's parked his aircraft at the arrowhead junction of Number Two and Number Six runways. We tried to raise him. Got nowhere."

He listened intently. "No, there's more to it than that. West Drayton have four in the stack and holding. We have five minutes to make a decision to divert them. Maybe longer. It's a sticky one. Schiphol advise 146 is carrying no passengers. They were dumped in a repair hangar. No— I don't know why."

He slumped into his chair, one eye on the 146 controller across the room.

"We've had BA check Sharland's file. Right as rain: High stress threshold. No history of depression. No flight-fatigue problems. Good domestic background. Unmarried. First-class officer. So what have we got?"

He listened again. "No, Dennis, it doesn't add up. We've got a 9052 on our hands."

Every operator in the room heard it: 9052—the International Code for aircraft hijacking.

The 146 controller waved agitatedly. Sharland's voice hammered out of the loudspeaker unit.

"This is Beeline 146 to Heathrow Tower. This is an emergency. Come in, Heathrow Tower."

Behind Sharland's voice rose a hysterical chatter. The pilot came on again.

"One-four-six. You will order the immediate withdrawal of all rescue units. All fire and rescue tenders must keep away."

The controller turned his head interrogatively. The superintendent touched him twice on the shoulder.

"Heathrow Tower to 146. We read and confirm."

"Get those bloody tenders back here," the super yelled over his shoulder. "Now!"

He reached down and angled the operator's headset mouthpiece and said into it: "Heathrow Tower. Tenders returning. Confirm your intention to complete taxiing procedure, please. Over."

The loudspeaker snapped off.

"Keep trying," he said to the operator and, striding back to his desk, picked up the phone.

"Dennis? It's a 9052 all right. There's someone on board. On the flight deck. Yes, I'm pretty sure. I'm keeping all tenders on standby. No—no idea. Just a babble of voices behind Sharland's. One thing's certain; they aren't day-trippers."

The duty officer in the Cabinet Office received the call at twelve-forty. He was most particular about the time and duly entered it in the Duty Book in bold, unmistakable figures.

But first he called the Prime Minister. He was reading Rousseau in bed and seemed to welcome the interruption.

He ordered that his car should be available in five minutes and gave the duty officer a string of calls to make. Ministry of Defense, Scotland Yard, Home Secretary, Curzon Street, Century House.

The last call was to the commanding officer of the 22nd Special Air Service Regiment at Hereford.

FRIDAY   0055

They were two hundred yards onto the Westway Flyover when Duffy saw the police motorcyclist. His hands instinctively strangled the wheel and Driscoll shot a look into the nearside mirror. The headlight of the Triumph was less than thirty yards behind.

Duffy fastened the top button of his shirt, one-handed, and slipped his tie into place. "He was waiting at the junction. Down that side road. You don't think . . ."

"Keep moving," ordered Driscoll. "Don't slow down whatever you do."

It couldn't have gone wrong. Not yet. Unless Barney . . . Driscoll obliterated the fear.

The motorcycle swept in front of them in a graceful controlled arc. The white-helmeted figure raised his arm. Duffy's foot automatically eased off the accelerator.

"Don't slow!" Driscoll fisted Duffy's knee downward.

"He's telling me to stop! For Christ's sake, guv. I'll run the bleeder down."

As if in answer, the motorcycle accelerated away. The rider's left arm motioned them on with a sweeping circle of forward movement and his emergency light flashed on.

"Christ! Follow-my-leader," breathed Duffy. "He's taking us through!"

"We're an ambulance, aren't we?"

They cut through four sets of linked traffic lights, all showing red. At King's Cross Station the policeman threw them a final wave, accelerated to a safe distance and pulled in to the curb.

Duffy roared up the hill to the Angel crossroads and turned left toward Islington. At the Ball's Pond Road he swung viciously right, then hurled the Bedford into a warren of dimly lit back streets. Driscoll lost the thread after the seventh turn.

They skidded to a stop finally in a small courtyard, a mews lined with the flaking double doors of workshops and small factories. The nurse, red-eyed and only semi-conscious, was led to a waiting car and dumped unceremoniously in the back seat. Duffy and Turk returned to the ambulance and dragged the body of the Special Branch officer from the stretcher.

They humped it toward the car and the girl sat bolt upright.

"Oh no, Duffy! Please!"

"Shut up!" growled Turk.

They propped the corpse against her and Duffy wiped its cold white face with a Kleenex.

"Won't have any trouble from him, love," he said comfortingly. "He's pissed as a newt, ain't he?"

The girl froze.

"Shove up," ordered Turk.

He caught the girl's rigid arm and draped it over the dead man's shoulder.

She gagged.

Turk arranged himself behind the wheel and glanced into the rear-view mirror.

"You throw up on my upholstery, kid, and I'll put you where he is."

The engine turned, caught and roared into life. Duffy and Driscoll watched Turk back it down to a turning and drive away.

A battered Volkswagen crouched in the shadows in one corner of the mews. Duffy roused it, backed it out and put the ambulance in its place. It would stand there for less than five minutes after they had gone.

Duffy began to whistle softly to himself as they cruised through an avenue of sodium lights on the main road. Driscoll slipped off his uniform jacket and tie. Almost casually, he lay back in the seat, letting the tension flood out of him. In a few hours the game would be over. In a few hours . . .

Then he remembered Julia.

FRIDAY   0105

The superintendent shook his head at the proffered cup of coffee.

"No, thanks."

From his swivel chair he could see the traffic building up on the display board. He picked up the internal telephone and pressed a key on the panel.

"Dennis? Jack. Look—we're in real trouble."

He listened intently.

"Of course. We're trying every thirty seconds. Nothing. Not a peep."

He listened again.

"I don't give a damn about 146, Dennis. All I want is some kind of directive. We've got to divert. Gatwick for the Continent; Manchester Ringway or Prestwick for Transatlantic. Both are clear."

There was a long silence and he rubbed his eyes with his hand.

"You there, Dennis?"

He pushed himself back in his chair impatiently and swung it left and right. The line came alive again.

"Well, for God's sake why not? Look, Dennis: I'm not accepting responsibility with that bloody thing sitting out there." He rolled his eyes helplessly.

"Well *somebody's* got to make the decision. I don't care what Security say."

The voice at the other end spoke for a full minute. The superintendent clutched a sheaf of hair with his free hand.

"Then let Downing Street *make* the decision. But let them make it now. If they can't see that . . ."

The operator at the console immediately to the superintendent's left raised a hand dramatically over his head. He waved it, beckoning.

The superintendent cupped his hand to the mouthpiece.

He heard the operator say: "BE 146 on 118 decimal 2."

The superintendent dropped the phone and ran to the console. He reached over the operator's shoulder and threw a switch on the display panel.

The voice boomed out from the loudspeaker; ". . . on this wavelength."

The operator said urgently: "Heathrow Tower, 146. You are transmitting on London approach wavelength. I say again, 146, you are on operational wavelength. Did you ident on transponder 3100? Over."

The special 3100 code is designed to alert ground control stations to a mid-air hijack: Sharland should automatically have hit the button which would have transmitted continuously, allowing ground stations to identify and track the aircraft. The moment the 3100 code was activated, there would be complete radio silence between all ground stations and pilots.

Sharland replied. "BE 146 to Tower. I read you. No ident on 3100. We have flight-deck problems. Over."

"This is Heathrow Tower. Change to 140 decimal 6. Do you read and confirm, 146? Over."

"One-four-six. I read. Changing to 140 decimal 6. Changing to . . ."

The voice cut off abruptly.

"Try him again, man. Call him again," urged the superintendent. "This is Heathrow Tower. Do you read, 146? Do you read?"

A door at the end of the room opened and shushed shut, but no head turned. A minute passed. Another. After four minutes the supervisor pushed himself upright and massaged the small of his back. His eyes were fixed on the loudspeaker grille; it breathed a muffled static.

Then it clicked and the carrier wave hissed from it.

"BE 146 to Heathrow Tower. BE 146 to Heathrow Tower."

"Heathrow Tower. We read you . . ."

"Heathrow Tower. I am changing now to 140 decimal 6."

There was a sibilant buzz and then a click. The console operator adjusted his dial. Back came the voice of 146.

"This is Captain Sharland. Heathrow Tower. Do you read?"

"Strength five, Captain. We read strength five. Over."

"Heathrow Tower, I am relaying a message on behalf of"—the hesitation was fractional—"on behalf of my passengers. I shall read it once. I am not empowered to repeat, Heathrow Tower. Do you read?"

"Record. Record!" snapped the superintendent. The operator pressed a key.

"I shall now read the message, Heathrow Tower."

"We read and register, 146. Over."

"Message begins. Quote. No further attempt must be made to approach this aircraft. All fire and rescue units will be withdrawn from the area of the tower. There will be no further landing or taking off of aircraft. This is an order. This aircraft is carrying an explosive device. It will be detonated if anyone approaches this aircraft."

A jabber of voices rose in heated argument behind Sharland's. Sharland spoke again.

"Heathrow Tower. Do you read and confirm?"

"We read and . . ."

The operator looked up at the superintendent, who nodded quickly. "We read and confirm, 146."

"Message continues: When this message ends, you will report the following to the appropriate authorities."

Again there was an argumentative babbling.

Sharland said: "I am instructed that you will report personally to the Prime Minister. Here is the message: Mahmoud Assad, who is in your custody, will be brought at once to this aircraft. This aircraft will then be given immediate clearance for takeoff. You have one hour in which to comply. Do you confirm, Heathrow Tower?"

"We read you, 146."

The babble began again. An edge of discomfort crept into Sharland's cool, professional drawl.

"And confirm, Heathrow Tower. And *confirm!*"

Once again, the operator looked to the superintendent for

guidance. The silence was deafening.

"Please confirm, Heathrow Tower." Sharland's voice was breaking slightly.

"We confirm, 146."

The superintendent spoke the words himself into the headset microphone.

"Over and out."

FRIDAY   0200

The Special Branch commander wagged a finger of salute at the staff colonel and the Home Office man. Behind them he recognized the Heathrow internal-security superintendent, the head of the Bomb Squad, the deputy assistant commissioner, one of the SIS stooges from Central Clearing House and the Home Secretary's terrorist activities adviser. There were at least a dozen others packed into the room.

The commissioner was on his way by car. So was the Home Secretary and the Chief of the General Staff. Exactly what an admiral was expected to do to advance a situation involving a paramilitary terrorist group aboard an airplane was debatable; but this was a night no self-respecting brass hat would dare miss.

"My men are in position," the commander reported.

The colonel nodded vaguely. His Guardsmen at the perimeter points had reported precisely that five minutes ago. Police cooperation was a requirement of law in this situation, but he had no confidence in uniformed civilians. He was uneasy at the convoluted chain of command.

The Home Office man said primly: "I hope they understand there's to be no shooting except by direct order."

"They understand, sir."

"This is a political matter, and I hope you chaps realize it. The Home Secretary will take control as soon as he arrives. We can't have itchy fingers triggering off international incidents."

"The Yard says the PM is taking charge, sir," the commander said mischievously. "Perhaps he's on his way, too."

"He's not."

Their heads turned as the Intelligence Clearing House executive loomed over them.

102

"Cabinet Office. The Home Secretary will merely be making an on-the-spot assessment."

He looked down, hawk-nosed, at the diminutive Home Office man.

"I think we're in danger of having more chiefs than warriors here."

"The warriors will do their job, don't worry about that," retorted the colonel stiffly. "Just leave it to the Army."

"We left Ulster to the Army, Colonel," said the man from Clearing House silkily. "But not to worry. I hear the SAS are on the way from Hereford."

The door jerked wide behind them and the commissioner plowed into the room with three harassed aides in his wake.

He looked briefly at the Home Office official and the Special Branch commander.

"Paul. Harry. Who's in charge here?"

The man from Central Clearing House covered his face with his hand. The others looked uncomfortable.

"The Home Secretary's on his way, sir," said the commander. "He'll be reporting direct to Downing Street, I believe."

"Right. Come with me, gentlemen, if you will."

The commissioner pressed through the crowd to a long table at the far end. He took an ashtray in his hands and tapped it firmly on the table, three times. The talk ceased. Heads turned.

"Let's sort ourselves out, shall we?" said the commissioner briskly. "The Army first. What's your ground status, Colonel?"

The door opened again and the colonel swung around resentfully. A naval lieutenant commander poked his head into the room.

"The CGS is here," he snapped. "He wants all officers and civilian personnel to stand by for briefing. He'll be directing operations himself."

FRIDAY   0212

"Minutes now."

Duffy's forehead wrinkled with anxiety. When things went this well, there was reason to worry.

"Keep it steady. Not too early, not too late."

Driscoll ran over the scenario in his head for the tenth time. Arrive 0215. Duffy leaves 0220. At 0230 the hand-over, neat and tidy. Gentleman's agreement. At 0231 Herrick's assault team moves in.

It had to be a nice, straightforward, right, tight pickup. Classic Flag: simplicity concealing detail so complex that if one man moved one yard at the wrong moment the exercise collapsed. Flag's men didn't move at the wrong time.

The car traveled in a wide arc to approach the ominous outline of the Tower of London from Limehouse. Driscoll could make out the bulk of the World Trade Centre, its flags hanging in icy paralysis. The half-ruined Mint Tea warehouses and the barred and bolted arches of Tower Bridge like dungeons where they dipped to the river. Duffy changed down into second, turned sharp left and nosed the car through the arches and pillars of a hotel.

"Look after sonny boy, guv," said Duffy. "It's a bit important we don't wake up the wrong people."

They slowed to a crawl and wound through the hotel parking lots.

Driscoll tapped Assad on the knee. "If you move or speak I shall hit you. I shall hit you very hard in the stomach. Now, let's all settle down and enjoy the ride."

A narrow bridge crossed an inlet from the river to the bowl of St. Catherine's Dock guarded by a red-and-white drop barrier. Duffy got out. He walked to the swing arm, picked up a metal key from the ground, turned it and swung the pole skyward.

He placed the key on top of the bollard and took from his pocket a fat brown envelope. Balancing it gingerly alongside the key, he returned to the car.

They moved forward again, past the skeletal shapes of yachts in the marina basin. The smooth metal of a bridge gave way to cobbles as they veered slowly right. Through the rear window, Driscoll saw a figure emerge from the hotel, pick up the gate key and stuff the envelope into a pocket.

Through two white gates.

Driscoll read the notices: "HIJACK: Drivers, secure your vehicles at all times," and filed away the implication automatically, just as he had filed away the names of the yachts in the basin: *Emilia, French Connection, Capricorn, Waterjoy.* One day there might be profit in recalling such details.

Through the darkness, Driscoll could make out the smashed

façade of gutted flats; Matilda House, its windows sheets of corrugated iron, looked out blind-eyed at the gray walls of the British and Foreign Wharf. One-legged cranes stood sentinel by the river, guarding a wasteland of demolition. Signs: W. Badger, Ship Repairers. No Parking. Strictly Private. Wapping High Street.

Driscoll's nostrils flared as the stench reached into the car.

"Pongs a bit," grinned Duffy. "Old rag merchants. One of the biggest around here. Enough old knickers down there to knock out a regiment."

Assad retched and slapped a hand to his mouth.

"DOGS: Beware guard dogs."

As the car headlights raked the frontage of a long, high fence, two Alsatians, bristling and edgy, raced to the wire netting.

Wapping Old Stairs.

They swung left off the main road and drew up beside the ruins of a warehouse. Duffy eased the car through rotting gates into a small courtyard.

"This way. Watch the antique woodwork."

At the top of the fourth flight of stairs, Duffy snapped on a light. He stood back and ushered them across a catwalk spanning a narrow alleyway. Driscoll pushed open the facing door.

The room was wide and low and cork-lined throughout. A half dozen black leather chairs crouched at random on the pile carpeting and a functional bar filled the far wall, dispensers at shoulder height. Behind the bar was a door.

Duffy poured Driscoll a Glen Morangie and himself a cold Guinness.

He nodded to Assad.

"What is it, old flower? Sake? Firewater?" He waved an arm expansively at the array of bottles.

Assad's eyes moved around the room. He shook his head.

Driscoll sipped the scotch. It dropped into his stomach like bubbles of mercury.

"Cheers," said Duffy.

"Cheers. Okay, Duff, drink up and go."

Duffy peered at him over a mustache of foam.

"Come again."

"Sorry, Duff. This is as far as you go. I want you out. Like now."

Driscoll checked his watch. Ten minutes to pickup.

"You've done your bit. Now it's my game."

Duffy shrugged. "Whatever you say. But . . ."

"Duff!"

"Okay, I'm gone."

He slung down the last of the Guinness and made for the door. Assad sprang forward and gripped his arm.

"No!"

There was panic in the Palestinian's face. "He will kill me! You cannot go!"

"You must be joking!" Duffy tore his hand free.

. Assad swung around to face Driscoll.

"You are paid to kill. I will pay much more. My friends have money. A lot of money. Take me to them and . . ."

"Belt up!" Duffy winked at Driscoll. "You going to be all right left alone with him?"

"Leave him, Duff. He'll be all right."

Driscoll knew the signs. The monologue of the man who believes that as long as he talks, he lives; as if death wouldn't interrupt a sentence. I talk, therefore I am. Assad would do nothing. He had too much sense.

"You think I am a killer, too?"

The words spluttered out of the Palestinian. "But not like you, my friend. The cause in which I killed . . . I do not murder for money . . ."

The sentences splintered and died. He wiped a fleck of spittle from the corner of his mouth.

Driscoll slowly placed his glass on the bar.

"Listen to me. I don't want to repeat myself. Anything you've got to say I've heard before. Before you were born. Freedom fighters like you have been blowing hell out of the human race since Cain and Abel and they'll go on doing it long after you've copped yours. All they ever left behind were widows and cripples. All they ever created was a reason for someone else to carry on killing. I don't like your style, sonny. You turn my gut. So be a good boy. Shut up."

Assad's eyes glittered and his mouth twisted with venom. He spat on the carpet at Driscoll's feet.

It took Duffy three strides to reach him. His knee slammed into the back of Assad's legs and the young man crumpled stiffly to the floor.

With one foot, Duffy rolled his face in his own spittle.

"One thing I do like, Abdul. I like guests to observe the house rules. Rule one: don't spit on the carpet."

Driscoll waved an arm.

"All right, Duff. You've made your point. Push off."

Duffy dragged Assad to a chair and threw him into it. "Gone."

He walked to the door. "See you, guv. Good luck." He pulled the door shut quietly behind him.

Driscoll shoved his whisky glass hard against the dispenser and splashed out four fingers. From the fridge he took an ice bucket shaped like a golf ball and hammered free two lumps with a miniature putter. The fridge shook into life as the door closed and Driscoll's nerves jumped.

Guilfoyle was due in eight minutes.

His overdeveloped sixth sense was trying to say something. He crossed to the door and put his ear to it. The low moan of a ship's siren boomed across the river. Even cork walls couldn't drown a sound like that. Nor the sound of a car's starter. Duffy should have driven off by now.

"Right, you. Up!" he rapped at Assad.

The Arab stretched out his hands to use the arms of the chair as leverage. The barely perceptible glint of metal caught Driscoll's eye. He leaped forward and caught Assad's left wrist in his hand.

The Arab was wearing a watch, a black-faced, intricate chronometer as thick as a bun. Driscoll stared at it. Then his spine took a cold shower.

He thrust the watch into Assad's face.

"Where did you get this?"

The Arab looked at it blankly.

"It is not mine. I did not know . . ."

Driscoll unbuckled it and took it to the bar. He unscrewed the backplate. Inside, on a slim platform built over the clockwork, was a wafer-thin black tablet of mat plastic. He lifted it gingerly. Two wires, thin as gossamer, led to the button operating the stopwatch. The button was not solid. It was a fine gold filament. Like the mouthpiece of a microphone.

The watch was a miniature transmitter. With the right kind of equipment, anyone at the receiving end could follow the wearer, probably at a distance of a couple of miles.

Driscoll scooped up the pieces, strode to a curtained window and raised the lower half. He hurled the pieces into the night and swung around on Assad.

"You knew, didn't you?"

"I know nothing. I had no watch when they took me to the prison hospital."

No, thought Driscoll, because they waited until you were unconscious before they strapped it on your wrist.

Before *Flag* had had it strapped on his wrist. Flag had said that Herrick's team would be with them from the moment Driscoll and Assad reached the warehouse. So why this stupid Dick Tracy gadget? It was unnecessary. If Flag had his men poised to move in the moment Guilfoyle and Assad reached ground level, electronic tracking gear was irrelevant.

Driscoll's spine slid into its sub-arctic state again. How could he have been so dumb? Accepting Flag's word at face value was akin to playing catch-as-catch-can with a killer shark. Mutual benefit was the name of their game—but only as long as each of them looked out for himself.

So why did he need a bug? Obvious. He wasn't going to pick up Guilfoyle's group and Assad at the warehouse. He was going to let them run. Run until they allowed him to snatch Guilfoyle's controller and the pipeline operators nominated to get Assad out of Britain.

His heart began to bounce warningly on his ribs.

It also meant Flag expected the worst. Guilfoyle couldn't allow anyone in on the prison break to live.

Driscoll rounded on Assad.

"Over by that door. Move!" Driscoll waved him to the cork-lined door behind the bar. "When I say 'Open,' you open it fast. Understand?"

Assad nodded.

Driscoll moved swiftly to the landing door. There was no real break in the silence outside. Just a muted scratching. A shuffling. He could be imagining it, he thought.

"Duff?"

He opened the door an eighth of an inch. Now he heard it. A harsh, snuffling, rasping pant. A dog! One of the bloody guard dogs! He could hear it clearly now. He snatched the door wide.

A figure was crouched on all fours in the blackness of the landing, black streams bubbling from its mouth. It half rose, arms outstretched, begging. Then the last breath scraped through its throat on a tide of blood.

Duffy fell against Driscoll's shins and slid to the floor.

There was no time for etiquette. Driscoll hooked his foot under Duffy's shoulder and hurled the body backwards. He slammed the door, the Walther already in his hand.

"Open! Open!" he shouted.

Assad heaved at the bar door as Driscoll raced across the room.

"Open the bastard! Open it!"

Assad tugged at the handle frantically.

"It's locked."

"You stupid bastard!" Driscoll turned the handle and pushed. The door swung open.

They were on another catwalk, longer this time and stretching over the cobbled street along which they had driven. Driscoll saw a car tucked into the foot of the building.

"Get across!"

Pushing Assad in front of him, he covered the car, but there was no movement, no sound. A half-hung door ahead of them offered no resistance and they were in a windowless room. Assad tripped and crashed to the concrete floor, dragging Driscoll to his knees.

"Get up!" Driscoll hissed. "Bloody get up, or so help me . . ."

He pressed the Walther deep into Assad's cheek.

Assad almost sobbed. "My chest. It's bleeding."

They groped their way across the room. It stank of cats.

"A door. Here!" hissed Driscoll. "Out!"

Faint light filtered up from the greasy reflections of the street. The fire escape wrapped itself like a frail steel muffler across the front of the building. It was pitted and rusted and buckled by generations of misuse.

Driscoll moved down, no longer caring whether Assad followed him or not. His foot slipped and a sliver of metal tore his hand as he grabbed at what was left of the rail. Within feet of the ground he turned to find Assad crouched above him. He pointed the Walther into the Arab's face.

"Move!"

"My legs." Assad shook his head. Tears of pain were coursing down his cheeks, and then he just let go. Slipping and bouncing, he fell down the remaining steps to the ground. Driscoll hauled him to his feet and hooked an arm under him.

He froze, his breath caught deep in his chest. Someone was running along the catwalk above. A silencer coughed faintly and three inches from his face the wall grew a ragged tear and thunked, and brick dust showered over them.

Driscoll began to run, the deadweight of Assad pulling him crazily into the wall. A shout echoed wildly from the catwalk and from somewhere in his rear a car door slammed and an engine burst into life.

Driscoll's lungs fought for air. On either side of him loomed the wharf buildings. No openings, no doors, no windows. He half turned as twin shafts of light blazed into his eyes and bounced wildly from pavement to sky. The car surged forward.

He slammed Assad into the wall. One, two, three, four, five . . . Driscoll dived bodily into the road, the Walther clenched two-fisted. He fired three times in rapid succession at the blackness of the windshield above the lights.

The car squealed, veered crazily and rammed its nose into a wall. A man leaped from it and Driscoll saw the outstretched arm. With agonizing deliberation, the figure took aim as Driscoll frantically rolled out of the arc of light.

The first shot richocheted off a steel grille six inches above Driscoll's head. The second hummed angrily into the night.

The anesthetic of shock died. Driscoll fired, arms extended.

The bullet took the gunman in the neck and erupted with a monstrous force that poleaxed its host to the ground.

"Assad!"

Driscoll stared wildly around him. The Palestinian was slithering along the wall, like a wounded rat. From behind the car came the rattle of men's voices.

"One more try! Come on!"

Driscoll grabbed Assad around the waist, but it was no use. Neither of them had the strength to save themselves. They sagged like drunks against the wall. But this time it was not brick. A fence. Driscoll felt it yield under their weight. Interspersed between stretches of six-foot planking, the plastic sheeting had been nailed to fill gaping holes in the woodwork.

Driscoll flung himself at it.

They collapsed headlong into the gut-turning stench of the rag yard.

FRIDAY   0300

It smelled like a field hospital at Balaclava.

Driscoll crawled forward on hands and knees, Assad groveling and puking in his wake, through foul clothing stacked like gray tripe. Around them dangled arms, legs, tattered buttocks; the obscene jetsam of shirts and vests and underwear. If the body died in a place like this, the soul was already halfway to hell.

Driscoll raised his head briefly to judge direction and distance.

Over his right shoulder a dog yelped suspiciously.

BEWARE GUARD DOGS.

Driscoll reached back with one hand and tugged at Assad's shoulder. He led the way forward into a mountain of putrid cottons, burrowed unheeding into its stench and distributed the foul rags over Assad's body and his own.

He heard voices from the direction of the fence he and the Arab had broken through. Immediately, the dogs gave tongue, baying like wolves as they raced and jumped across the yard. There was the unmistakable phutt of a silencer and a sudden whine that ended in a gurgle. One of the Alsatians had leaped into a bullet. Another barked savagely and the gun spoke again. The barking grew louder.

Driscoll felt Assad's body shaking. He whispered confidently: "Take it easy. They won't find us here." He wondered if Assad believed him.

In the lane beyond the fence, tires squealed. One car. Two. Three. Doors slammed and voices burbled, too low to hear. The remaining Alsatian had found its dead partner. It began to howl a requiem.

The voices beyond the fence were suddenly stilled. One man was speaking, fast and urgently. Driscoll strained his ears. Was it Guilfoyle?

The talking stopped. Feet pattered in the lane and car doors clunked shut. Engines started; tires whirled in the snow and slush, found a hold and swished away.

Assad made a move to raise himself from the cotton mountain but Driscoll pushed him flat. There was still the dog and maybe a sniper sitting up on the old iron staircase of the warehouse, a telescopic night sight on his rifle.

Driscoll resettled his body, scooping the rags into place under his pelvis to cushion the effect of the broken stone and concrete of the yard floor.

It was almost funny.

Flag, the one constant in his life, had led him by the nose to his own funeral. And he hadn't suspected a thing. The deal had been struck as all past deals had been struck— on a basis of mutual profit and mutual deceit. Driscoll had never agreed to a dead-run operation unless he was satisfied that the profit motive was uncontestable and Flag's Machia-

111

vellian reasoning at least within his power to control. He had never gone into a tight corner without first preparing an escape route. Until now.

Assad tried to whisper something. Driscoll cracked an elbow into his ribs.

The trouble with supping with the devil was that you used a spoon twice as long as you needed. In the end, it was so long you couldn't see the pot. Flag was no longer a man to him, he was a label. None of his actions, none of his motives, were meaningful in a human context, so they became labels, too. Herrick's was a world of fairy castles and ogres and princes who changed into frogs and cardboard kings who wore clothes no one else could see. To live out that fairy tale for each other's benefit, they wore their labels and expected recognition of them. It was the only way the Flags and the C's and the Davidsons could protect themselves when they switched off the office lights at night and went home to wives and children and mortgages and the dull suburban moralities of love and happiness and freedom of choice.

Driscoll closed his eyes and lay his head on crossed arms. He had made the mistake of viewing Flag as a predictable constant. Dead runners paid for that mistake with their lives.

Unless . . . unless Flag also saw *him* that way. What exactly would Flag expect him to do now?

Obvious answer: Run. He had bugged Assad with that wristwatch precisely because he knew Driscoll would run. That devious bloody mind! He'd also predicted that Driscoll would shake off Guilfoyle and hold on to Assad. Wherever Driscoll ran, the Israelis would have to run. And, sometime, there would be a point where Driscoll could run no further and the Israelis would step in and take Assad.

Driscoll raised his head, shocked at the direction his own logic had taken him.

But that was nonsense. Another unless. Unless Flag's objective was to go that final step over the line and actually give Assad to Israel.

In which case, Guilfoyle's visit to Chester Row that night was no chance free-lance shot in the dark. He had come hotfoot from Flag.

And that made Flag . . .

They lay interred like maggots in offal for more than three quarters of an hour. Incomprehensibly, Assad managed to fall asleep. By the time he decided to move, Driscoll had programmed the next six hours.

There was no disputing the fact; he *would* have to run. But not necessarily in any direction Flag had anticipated. It had to be the cottage near Littleport. Not even Julia knew about it. Cindy hadn't, either. It was the place he had used to escape the Cindys and the Julias, the place where the tug of a roach at the end of a line was the quintessence of existence. It stood on the banks of the Old Bedford River, deep in Fenland. In December, it was the end of the world.

Next question: How did they get there?

FRIDAY   0315

"Hey, Taff. Take over for a sec, will ya? Freezing me bloody cobs off down here."

The soldier rolled over on the groundsheet and stretched to his feet, shivering. His companion handed over his carbine and settled down behind the Bren.

There were four of them: a lance corporal and two para-troopers, and the sergeant in command, who had positioned himself twenty yards ahead, closer to the aircraft and just off the perimeter runway.

A piercing northeasterly whined across the airfield, biting deep into their flimsy camouflage jackets and battle-dress trousers. The regiment had been alerted, wakened and heli-coptered out of Hereford in twenty-five minutes. But they had been unprepared for snow.

The colonel had sent a wagon to Central Ordnance for as many arctic white combat suits as they could find, but no one was holding his breath. At one in the morning, COD would be warm in their pits and dead to the world.

The Bren gunner swung his arms stiffly to revive his circulation, grunting with the effort. They were all the same, these airport alarms. Hours, maybe days, of standing to, waiting for someone or something undisclosed, while the cold screwed into your bones and the damp turned your clothes to pulp. They never told you why you were there. And when you stood down and returned to barracks no one was any the wiser.

The grapevine said it was the wogs again—maybe the

113

bunch who turned over the Israelis at the Munich Olympics.

"Hey, Corp. Have a snout, can I?"

"Snout, my arse. Get a grip, you manky bastard. Where d'you think you are? And keep your mouth shut."

"Just asking."

"Just asking!" The corporal wound his arm into the bandolier of his carbine and rested the butt on his hip.

Just asking. No information. Just a whispered conversation between the company commander and the sergeant and "Right, you four—follow me."

For all anyone knew, it was just another exercise. Trust the Army to pick Christmas. The sergeant had led them off into the snow and dumped them and taken his walkie-talkie up ahead. He had a pair of night glasses too, but he was keeping those to himself.

The corporal heard the crunch of steps too late and whirled, carbine leveled. The policeman reached out gently and tapped the barrel to one side.

"Easy, mate. Police—Special Patrol Group. I'm on your side," he said.

The corporal whistled nervously in his teeth. "Bleeding hellfire; I nearly *had* you."

The policeman threw back one side of his cape. He held a Lee Enfield 7.62-mm. sniper rifle with telescopic sight in his armpit like a crutch.

"That would've made two of us." He grinned.

"Long way off your beat, aren't you, mate?"

"Long way," agreed the policeman equably. "I've been detached. You in command here?"

"The sarge is up there, somewhere. What are you supposed to do?"

"Just obey orders like you, son. Better tell your sergeant I'm here. He'll want to check back."

"You tell him," the corporal said with relish. "He said, 'Stay here and wait,' and that's what I'm doing."

The policeman slid his cape from his shoulders and spread it on the snow. He wore navy blue overalls over plain clothes. He dropped down on his stomach and brought the rifle to his shoulder.

"Jesus! Hang about a bit," the corporal hissed.

The policeman squinted into the viewfinder. He said casually: "It's a night sight. I like to know what I'm shooting at."

He focused the Passive night sight and the blackness

114

turned bright green inside the object intensifier. If needed, it could brighten an object 100,000 times.

The tail plane soared disproportionately high over the foreshortened slug shape of the Trident's fuselage.

He inched the sight steadily to the right and stopped. The forward passenger door was open. He held the position rigidly. Was that movement? He took his eye from the rubber sighting cup. A pair of burnished toe caps were staring him in the face.

He raised his eyes. He couldn't see the face.

"What's this then, Corporal?"

The sergeant was an old hand. He had the kind of barrack-square voice that did not adjust easily to a whisper. The corporal instinctively straightened.

"Police, Sarge. On detachment, he says."

The sergeant turned his back and whispered into the walkie-talkie swinging on a web strap at his neck. A series of squeaks issued from the transceiver. The sergeant turned back to them.

"You take your orders from me, Sergeant," he said to the policeman. "You don't make a move 'less I tell you. Okay?"

The policeman grunted to his feet, the rifle threaded over his shoulder. "You're in command, Sergeant."

He pulled open the collar of his coat and revealed the neat walkie-talkie strapped to his chest. "But I open fire only when this says so."

The sergeant nodded and turned to the corporal.

"All quiet. Nothing moving up there. I want these men kept on their toes or I'll have your guts for garters. Right?"

"Right, Sarge."

The sergeant flicked his head and they moved a few paces away from the group.

"Now I'm putting you in the picture, lad, in case of accidents, see? We're in the rear of the plane. Forward HQ is in a Nissen hut two hundred yards over there, back toward the main airport building. There's groups of our lads up ahead, about a hundred yards in front of the plane and either side of the emergency pad. And there's another lot across the runway, square with us. You got that?"

"Sarge!"

"We got 'em boxed in, in other words. Just in case they decided to take a little walk, see. This 'ere"—he tapped his walkie-talkie—"is a direct link with regimental HQ in the control tower. That's your nerve center. You don't do nothing 'less they give a direct order. You don't listen to nobody else. Right?"

"Right, Sarge."

"Any questions?"

The corporal cleared his throat.

"Who's in the plane, Sarge?"

"Don't concern you who's in the plane, lad. Wouldn't concern you and me who's in the plane if it was your fucking mother and all the little kiddie-winks, would it, Corporal? You just keep your men awake and ready for action and I'll do the same for you. Right?"

"Right, Sarge," mumbled the corporal.

FRIDAY   0415

The Prime Minister signaled for quiet and switched the telephone to his other ear. His face gave away nothing.

"Wait a minute," he said.

He flicked the control arm on the telephone and said to the switchboard operator, "Put this through to my office."

The faces at the table waited expectantly.

"This won't take a minute, gentlemen."

"Right, then," he said when he had settled behind his desk. "Let me have that again."

Flag had had time to rehearse.

"Three men and a woman turned up at the prison in an ambulance. The duty officer there can't be sure whether they had appropriate identification or not. God knows why they fell for it but they did. The deputy governor's in a spin. He says the night doctor called him and informed him Assad was in a critical condition. He gave permission for immediate transfer to Hammersmith Hospital next door, as long as the Special Branch man went along.

The Prime Minister closed his eyes and knuckled his jaw.

"What about this doctor?"

"Barney, Raymond Barney. We'll have Special Branch check him out, of course, but I don't think it will take us anywhere. He said he received a call telling him exactly what to do. The called claimed he had Barney's wife and child. He was calling from Barney's home."

116

"Were they? Holding his wife hostage, I mean?"

"No. But the telephone cable at the house has been cut. Barney rang back immediately after he got the call and the phone was out of order. He put two and two together . . ."

"And made a fool of himself," finished the PM disgustedly.

"He's no hero, sir. He was scared stiff. Still is."

"And what's happened to the Special Branch man?"

"We don't know. I've had a check run on Hammersmith Hospital, of course, but they have no record of an emergency call."

"And the prison people just let them drive in, pick up a top-security prisoner and whisk him off into the night?"

"The doctor was the clincher, sir. His word, backed by the deputy governor, was all they required. And apparently the Special Branch officer never left Assad at any time."

"I find the whole damned episode incredible. Have you any idea at all what this means?"

"I received word of the Heathrow situation a couple of hours ago. That's why I checked with the prison."

"You mean, nobody else checked?"

"Not as far as I know, sir."

The Prime Minister laid his head in his hand.

"Very well," he breathed heavily. "I take it you've alerted the usual agencies?"

"Yes, sir. Before I called you. I hope we're not too late."

"I'll call C. I'm putting you in personal charge of the search, Flag. I want that fellow back in jail. Use whatever facilities you need. But I want no word of this to leak out to anyone. *Anyone.* Is that clear?"

"Of course, sir."

"If this got out to the press . . ."

"Yes, sir."

"Well, at least we know where we are. We shan't be needing your field operation now."

"No, sir."

"Very well. Get on with it. And Flag . . ."

"Yes, sir?"

"Well done. At least you've won us a little time."

The Prime Minister took off his glasses and tossed them wearily onto the massed paper work in front of him.

There were twenty men at the table. They all registered varying degrees of tension and acute depression. A half dozen were noticeably furious. Their outward signs of frustration peaked in restless eyes and hands, aggressive gestures, barely controlled vocabulary.

The coffee was a welcome diversion. It had been a stormy half hour. Army and police were colliding on fundamental points of principle and members of the Cabinet had divided their favors strictly according to ministerial responsibility. The Prime Minister had lost his temper, openly and with malice aforethought, on three separate occasions. The gambit had borne no fruit.

From Heathrow, the Home Secretary reported similar clashes of temperament. The battle had been a long and bitter one and he was no nearer a judgment of Solomon.

The Prime Minister swilled coffee into his throat and got to his feet. He singled out the Secretary of State and telegraphed an unspoken summons. As the assembly rose from the Cabinet table and crowded around the dumbwaiter, the two men stood in brief isolation.

"Well? You see any chance of getting a compromise out of this lot?"

The PM jerked his head ungraciously at the crowd.

"No, I don't. Have you got any ideas?"

"Aye. One idea. It won't solve anything long-term, but it might give us breathing space in the morning."

"Breathing space for what?"

"For measuring priorities. For thinking. And for keeping the media out of it for a few hours. Are you sure none of this has filtered out?"

The Secretary of State shrugged.

"As far as anyone can be sure. We have Special Branch men on every telephone switchboard. No one is being allowed to leave the airport. No one's getting in. But you know as well as I do, newspapers have their tip-off men everywhere. Airports. Scotland Yard. You only need someone to pass
118

the word to the British Airline Pilots' Association, for instance, and . . ."

He turned down the thumb of his left hand, graphically.

"Yes—the longer we wait, the less chance we have of containing the situation."

The Prime Minister swallowed more coffee, swirled the cup speculatively, then gulped the remains.

"Look—I'm going to take a chance. And, one way or another, the fewer who know it the better."

His friend fingered the stubble of beard on his jowl. "If it affects the life of the pilot or the people living round the airport . . ." he began uncertainly.

"Doesn't affect anyone. Not in the way you mean. Let's face the facts. We've got to take attention off that plane and we don't want the media sniffing round the airport. At least, not yet, we don't. I can think of one way of distracting 'em."

He put down his mug and took out his pipe and tobacco pouch. "It'll cause a bloody pantomime if it ever gets out, but it'll buy us time and it'll explain why the airport's closed to traffic."

"Are you saying you intend to take action yourself? Without reference to Cabinet?"

The PM glanced down the room at the scrum of drinkers.

"Yes, I am. Look at 'em. You think I'd get agreement to anything out of *them*? Particularly what I've got in mind."

The other man perceptibly withdrew. "Perhaps you'd prefer I didn't know either, Prime Minister."

The formality was unmistakable.

"Dear God. You walking out on me, too? Growing too hot for you, is it? Well, you make your own moral choice. Stand and be counted or get down there with the rest of 'em."

"You know me better than that." The tone was apologetic.

"Do I? You can't keep every situation impersonal, you know. Comes a time you have to start thinking in terms of the people who've got to get hurt. Well, I'm going to have to decide who gets hurt first. Can't avoid that decision, whatever which way I turn. I've also got to keep that airport clear. I've got to hold off a national panic. I've got to give myself time to deal with whoever's on that plane. And I've got to avoid endangering the lives of ordinary people."

He sighed. "In my book, that gives me the right to fool some of the people, some of the time."

"What do you want me to do?" asked the Secretary of State bluntly.

"I want you to watch and listen and keep your fingers crossed. One day, it'll make a chapter for your memoirs—if you can get it past the Attorney General. I'm about to change my spots."

"How do you mean?"

"I'm about to become an enemy of the working class. In a manner of speaking. Just for a few hours. God help us if it doesn't work."

FRIDAY 0500

The twelve Flying Squad cars were unmarked. They flowed in a stream of light and a wailing of klaxons through the airport tunnel and peeled off in groups to the three main terminal buildings.

The raid was swift and perfectly executed. In ten minutes, the policemen had arrested thirty airport baggage handlers on suspicion of theft and receiving stolen property. There were a few scuffles as the traditionally independent baggage gangs rallied in defiance, but they were overcome with a minimum of actual bodily harm.

Within fifteen minutes, the senior union shop steward was demanding the right to call his branch secretary at home. The detective chief inspector in charge dialed the secretary's home number himself and handed over the phone.

Within a half hour, all members of the Union of Airport Employees working on the night shift had been called out on strike. The union general secretary, roused from his bed across London, called his brother leaders of the Transport and General Workers' Union, the Transport Salaried Staffs' Association and the British Airline Pilots' Association. Electricians and engineers offered immediate sympathy.

The circle was complete. By six o'clock Heathrow was closed to all air traffic.

Flights were diverted to Ringway, Manchester, to Gatwick and Prestwick. Picket lines mushroomed at the main road approaches, augmented by local police squads. Both had explicit orders: no one was to enter or leave the airport until further notice.

The thirty men helping the police with their inquiries included eight union committee men. They were denied access to a telephone and the advice of solicitors until the preliminary police examination was complete.

The airport would lose revenue and incur costs amounting to two million pounds for each day of closure.

It was cheap at the price.

FRIDAY   0600

Driscoll kept the Transit in the mews lockup off Lancaster Gate. Its side panels advertised Sheridan's Butter ("Spreading around the World") but its real activities had been rather less innocent. It was ideal for moving small, valuable shipments without attracting attention. Guns traveled safe as butter.

The traffic was dense, the Doomsday chaos visualized by every urban planner since Colin Buchanan concluded that the inner city was no place for the motorcar.

Driscoll sheered off his proposed route to the A1(M), forked right beyond the Angel into the jammed tube of Green Lanes and crawled through the controlled crossings of Harringey toward the North Circular.

In these conditions, his choice of the van was little short of inspired. The snow had first trickled out of the sky at five, and within half an hour became a thrashing blizzard.

Ten minutes on the road in a conventional saloon car—like the Toledo Sport he had considered using at one stage—and the windshield would have become a muddied blur, showered incessantly by spitting wheels. Up here, foursquare behind the Transit's flattened wheel, visibility was near perfect.

Driscoll jinked the wheel right and squeezed suicidally across the bows of a slow-witted Marina. The startled driver braked instantly and stalled. A cacophony of horns opened up a barrage of protest in his wake. Ten minutes later he was playing ducks-and-drakes past the Thorn Electrical factory with a youth in a reconditioned Triumph TR2 and a gasoline tanker. He won, and ploughed on through the storm.

At Wadesmill, an oil tanker had broken down on the upper shoulder of the hill and the crocodile of cars behind it was too dense to permit any one of them to pull out and release the pressure.

A police motorcyclist roared down the hill. At the sight of the black waterproofs, the glinting gaiters and the virgin white orb of the helmet, Driscoll's memory did a backward flip to the incident on the Westway Flyover. He dug a hand into the slip pocket of his pea jacket and clicked a flame to the cigarette in his lips.

The policeman was leaning out from his machine flailing an arm as he passed each vehicle. Driscoll interpreted the soundless formation on his lips: "Back. Back." He slipped into reverse, squinted quickly through the two rear-view mirrors, waited for movement from the car behind, then inched backwards.

The policeman did not spare him even a fleeting glance. If he had actually picked up an APB he couldn't possibly be expected to know that the getaway had been made in this commercial van, bright and innocent in its spring colors of white and gold and green.

The queue shook itself free of the obstruction at last, but the swishing passage of oncoming traffic was continuous, leaving Driscoll no chance of leapfrogging up the mile-long procession in front of him. He would have to grit it out; there was no other choice.

At 0725, the Transit crossed the invisible line into Cambridgeshire, mounted the last upland barrier and coasted down into Royston.

FRIDAY   0700

The controller's tone was dispassionate.

"He came on less than a minute ago, sir," he told the Home Secretary over the telephone. "We recorded every word. One second, sir. I'll plug the tape in."

The Home Secretary raised a hand as the CGS made to speak. Captain John Sharland's recorded voice emerged tinnily from the receiver.

"Sharland to Heathrow Tower. Do you read?"

"Tower to Sharland. We read. Over."

"This is an important message. I cannot repeat. Do you understand?"

"We read and copy. Over."

"The message reads . . ."

Sharland coughed to clear his throat.

"The ultimatum delivered at 0105 hours this morning has not been acted upon. You have had six hours in which to bring Mahmoud Assad to this airport. *You* have failed to comply or your Prime Minister has failed to comply. It is now imperative that you convey to the Prime Minister the following instructions:

"Mahmoud Assad must be brought, unharmed and alone, to this aircraft and permitted to walk unaccompanied to this aircraft. If this is done, no one here will come to harm. If Assad is not here in three hours' time, the entire population of this great city will be put at the gravest risk.

"There is aboard this aircraft an atomic device. I repeat. An *atomic* device. It will be detonated in three and a half hours' time, at 1030 hours, if you fail to produce Mahmoud Assad. Message ends. Out."

The Home Secretary had unconsciously placed the tip of his tongue between his lips. As the message ended and the recording clicked off, he blew a hiss of disbelief. Every eye in the room was on him. The CGS was in an agony of suspense.

The Home Secretary scrambled his thoughts together and said into the phone, "Hand me back to your supervisor, please." He waited.

"Hullo. Thank you. Yes. I heard all of it. Let me know the minute he comes on again. For whatever reason. Thank you."

He replaced the receiver.

He turned to his aide. "You'll find the Bomb Squad chaps in the next room. Ask the commander if he'd be good enough to step in here for a moment." The aide scurried away.

"They're claiming the explosive device is an atomic bomb."

The Home Secretary watched the admiral's face. It registered instant disbelief.

"Rubbish!" boomed the CGS.

He leaped to his feet and pointed an accusing arm toward the window.

"If at first you don't succeed . . . I doubt if even *they* expect us to believe that. They're piling on the pressure. You know the sequence. It's happened often enough. Jordan, Munich, Copenhagen, Amsterdam, Entebbe. Delay, delay, delay. Threaten, pressurize, terrorize. We can expect any deadline they give us to be postponed two or three times at least in the first forty-eight hours. Probably indefinitely, if we apply pressure in return.

"*Atomic bomb.* Rubbish!"

The Home Secretary watched the performance with ill-concealed distaste. He said quietly: "Are you prepared to gamble innocent lives on that?"

"It's not a gamble, don't you see?"

The CGS walked to the window and gazed out.

"Where do you suppose a rabble of amateur gunmen would get an atomic device *from?* Oh—I've read the NORAD reports on uranium stock thefts. And I don't believe a damn word. CIA scare-mongering, take my word for it. And d'you suppose these people would have gone through the panto-mime of killing just one Israeli politician if they thought they could have blasted London to a pile of rubble instead? Of course not."

The Bomb Squad commander entered the room and stood silently. The Home Secretary nodded to him.

"We have a disturbing report from the pilot of the plane, Commander. He claims—*they* claim—that the explosive device on board is atomic. Do you have a nuclear specialist on your team?"

The commander shook his head, his eyes round with interest.

"No, sir. But I could have an expert here in"—he looked at his watch—"in an hour, perhaps."

"As quick as you can."

The commander left the room.

FRIDAY 0700

The patrol car rounded the corner of Brompton Road into Egerton Terrace and crept watchful through the cars parked on both sides of the road. The driver began to open the throttle but his partner whispered urgently: "Hey—hold on a minute."

His head twisted around over his right shoulder.

The driver pulled in to his left and double-parked the Morris 1100.

"Whatcha got, Dave?" He turned to follow the other's gaze.

124

"Old bugger over there. In the doorway. See? Just the other side of that Volvo. He's turning some poor bastard over. Come on. Let's have a look-see."

The policemen swung out of the car and sprinted down the middle of the street.

The down-and-out was gray-bearded, bent with age and arthritis; a filthy bundle of rags. He was bending over a second man, who lay sleeping on a pile of newspapers in the recessed side door of a carpet shop.

The graybeard started wildly at the sight of the two policemen and made a pathetic attempt to pretend that he was not stripping the sleeping man of his clothes at all.

"Out 'e is. Freezin'."

His voice had the tonal quality of sandstone on slate. "Puttin' some clo'es on 'im, I was. See?"

He demonstrated one half of the coat he held in his hands.

The driver stood arms akimbo, looking at the pair of them, his head shaking. "Gentlemen of the fucking road. Would you credit it?"

His partner approached the tramp, who bent quickly and tucked the coat back around the sleeping form.

The policemen leaned over the figure and sniffed.

"Jesus!"

He pushed the graybeard to one side.

"Smells like a Pakistani stoker's jockstrap," he said. He got to his feet. "You want to take a look at him, Joe?"

"Hey, you." He prodded the graybeard in the ribs. "Over by that car. That's right. Now turn your pockets out. Yes. All of 'em."

The driver dropped to his haunches beside the sleeping man and swung a gloved hand lightly left and right across the alabaster cheeks.

"Come on, then, Sleeping Beauty. On your feet. Wakey, wakey."

The head sagged drunkenly.

"Hey, Dave," he called over his shoulder. "Come here."

He pulled off a glove and felt for the pulse in the throat. "Strewth!"

His partner dropped down beside him. "What?"

"This one's dead."

He picked up a corner of the coat. "Look at that. That's good schmutter, mate."

He pulled open the coat and bent back the label above the inside pocket. "Jaeger. Well, he didn't find *this* in a dustbin. Look at the suit. And the tie. See his face? Clean. Well shaven. Just a minute."

He dug into the corpse's inside pocket and withdrew a small leatherbound folder.

He flipped it open. His partner whistled slow and low, then got to his feet. He walked menacingly toward the tramp, who backed away until he was almost prostrate over the hood of the Volvo.

"All right, dad," said the policeman. "What you been up to then, eh? Knocked him off for his coat, did you?"

"Never did," rasped the old man hysterically. "Honest, mister. Never did. Never touched no one. Not me. I comed here, see? And there he was, all sleeping in the papers and them paper bags they put out. And I said: 'How's about me squeezing in?' I said. And he don't say nothing, see? So I fink: 'Ad too much! Meths, see. So I squeeze in. Tha's all. Swear to God. Swear to God."

The driver got to his feet.

"No blood. No wounds. I think the poor bastard got his neck broken."

He eyed the graybeard witheringly. "Hold on to him. I'll call in."

He raised his voice at the old man. "They'll have your fucking toenails out for this, mate. One by one. You know what you done, do you? You've laid one on the Special Branch, you have."

FRIDAY   0805

Assad whispered out of the gloom behind him so suddenly, so sepulchral in pitch, that Driscoll's hands reacted like plucked nerves and the Transit slewed wildly across the narrow road.

"Where are we going?"

There was no fear in his tone. The venomous hysteria of the night before had gone. It was as though he were another man entirely. Driscoll was irritated by his coolness.

"You'll see."

Assad chuckled gently, wasting no energy on words.

"I must be of some importance to you," he tried again. He waited in vain for a reply, then went on: "Every man has a price for dying. Your price must be very high. I assume you are being well paid for this."

The van was caught in a cross fire of headlights as it rounded the traffic island on the Cambridge road and roared off toward St. Ives. The left-right-left flick of the wheel rolled Assad like a log as he lay, arms pinioned, in the belted sleeping bag.

"Silence is golden," said Assad patiently. "Is that not your English saying: Silence is golden? Now that is very English, I would say. To say nothing is to admit nothing is to embrace innocence."

"Shut up," growled Driscoll.

They were approaching the one-way stone river bridge in the town center of St. Ives. "Stay still and stay quiet."

He need not have bothered. The town was empty. He struck off through the stock market and snaked through the S-bend into Needingworth Road. Assad said: "May I talk now? I do not wish to irritate you, but talk is a medicament."

Daylight was blushing the sky; cold gold and amber streaks weighted down by purple storm clouds.

"All right."

Driscoll sighted along the main road and urged the Transit in the direction of Needingworth.

"In my country, we associate a man's price for dying with his reason for living. We suffer, you see, from the worst kind of naïveté. You would call it patriotism, I suppose. Or—what is the fashionable usage? Nationalism. Yes?"

"You're doing the talking," Driscoll returned coldly.

Assad chuckled again in the darkness. "Of course. Silence is golden."

He practiced it for a full five minutes.

Then: "You are a civilized man. A creature of the controlled environment. An anthropologist would find us an interesting study in contrasts. Primitive man and the product of advanced social organization. Would you agree?"

Driscoll refused to take the bait. Assad sighed.

"Have you read of the Kurelu? An interesting example of the human equation at the primitive level. They live on the island of New Guinea. Until 1954, no white man had set foot in the valley in which they live. In which they survive, because they could truly be described, I think, as Stone Age men. Unique. Untouched."

Driscoll dropped down to third gear and crossed the

river bridge by Hermitage Sluice, yanked the van hard left and settled down to a steady forty-five along the twenty-foot wall of the dike retaining bank. To his right, across the dimly lit tableland, the twinkling of streetlamps and household lights pricked the phosphorescent snow with diamonds. Three miles or so ahead was the flickering tinsel of Haddenham, the longest village in England.

"The Kurelu," intoned Assad, like a lecturer assaulting the citadel of indifference of a tutor group, "are bred to pursue warfare as you and your society are bred to embrace the ideal of peaceful coexistence. War is a ritual, in fact, just as the acquisition of wealth and social power is the ritual of your society.

"Consider it. Ritual war. Aggression as art. As religion. To draw blood, to wound, is sufficient to bring battle to an end for the day. And, of course, a man acquires great merit in proportion to his skill in violent combat."

He fell silent again.

"You are familiar with Professor Washburn? *Conflict in Primate Society*? No? He tells us that man's history reveals that society has always depended on its young adult males to hunt, fight and maintain the social order with violence. So I am very much the primate. We Palestinians are primitive men. Our own social order—and it enjoyed great refinement—our order was summarily, arbitrarily, indefensibly destroyed for reasons that could not be explained logically or historically. Restitution, you see, cannot therefore be achieved logically."

He made a dismissive hissing sound through his teeth.

"We are little more than the Kurelu—except that we fight to recover and they to protect."

Driscoll pegged two fingers in his pea jacket and drew the cigarette pack up to his face. He lit the cigarette without taking his eyes from the road.

Assad's voice mocked him from the rear.

"You find comfort in tobacco? A fine subject for psychological research. Could it be that your infliction of tobacco on yourself is an act of violence? Violence directed against oneself. That is truly formidable behavior modification. Don't hit out. Hit in."

The laughter tumbled out of him. "How can I expect such a man to understand?"

Driscoll ignored him. He was poised on the triangular confluence of the Haddenham exit and the dog-leg sweep of the main road to Ely. A group of young people marched across the nose of the van, wrapped and cosseted in coats and waterproofs and talking heatedly.

They turned to stare through the windshield.

Ely was a tomb. He fretted at the traffic lights by the hotel and had time to study the cathedral, mantled for the benedictions of Christmas.

Flying buttresses sliced dramatically on the smooth heightened gray of the lower walls, harboring shadows.

Driscoll bent forward and allowed his eye to travel to the summit where a vague orange luminance threw the lantern tower against the black sky like a Byzantine golden crown.

An organ was booming and the voice of a choir, sharp and fragile as crystal, interwove the swelling Gothic chords. The spell held him motionless, unthinking, for all of fifteen seconds before he realized the lights had changed.

FRIDAY   0815

The Home Secretary pushed open the door into the control room and went immediately to the superintendent's desk. He indicated a disheveled young man at his heels.

"Supervisor, this is Professor Lockhart. I've had him flown in from Harwell. He should be able to tell us precisely what that device is aboard 146."

"Well, sir, that's . . ." began the superintendent.

"I want to you to contact the pilot now," the Home Secretary went on quickly. "I will talk to him personally. Just make contact, then hand over to me."

The superintendent looked at him curiously. "Very well, sir." They walked to the console and the superintendent took the spare headset.

"Heathrow Tower to Sharland. Come in, please."

There was a long pause. "Sharland to Tower. Over."

The Home Secretary took the headset and strapped it on clumsily.

"Captain Sharland, this is the Home Secretary. Will you tell your—ah—passengers that I have a message for them."

"Go ahead, sir. They're listening."

"Tell your passengers we cannot accept their claim that there is an atomic device aboard the aircraft."

Sharland's shock was tactile. Before he could reply, there was an uproar of shouting behind him. Then contact was switched off abruptly.

"Do you—ah—hear what I say?" intoned the Home Secretary.

The carrier wave buzzed emptily in his ears. He looked appealingly at the superintendent, who averted his face.

The pilot's voice crackled back.

"My instructions are that there is an atomic device aboard this aircraft, sir, and your proof will be its detonation in less than two hours from now. Over."

"Captain Sharland. Explain to your passengers that we cannot accept their word in these circumstances. My government will not yield to threats. To unsupported threats. There can be no question of our handing over Assad unless we have the opportunity to satisfy ourselves that there is such a device aboard."

The Palestinians jabbered passionately in the background.

The Home Secretary made a mental note that there were at least four of them.

"Sharland to Tower. Your proposal is not acceptable, sir. They refuse to let anyone aboard."

"Then tell them this: Unless they permit an expert aboard to examine the device, there will be no further communication between us."

This time, the pandemonium was virulent. The Home Secretary heard Sharland arguing heatedly.

"Tell them the bomb expert will come to the plane alone. He will be unarmed and he will return immediately his examination is completed. Tell them that."

Sharland came on again. "They say, sir, that they will permit an inspection of five minutes. No longer. The man must approach the plane on foot and he must be naked. He will be allowed to look at the device but he can't touch it. Over."

The Home Secretary sighed.

"Very well. That's agreed."

He took off his headset and turned to the young scientist.

"I'm afraid we'll have to do as they say, Lockhart. D'you think you're up to it?"

"I'll freeze to death out there with no clothes on, sir," said Lockhart. "I need something. I can raise an anti-infection suit, if you give me time. It's made of transparent plastic. At least it's a covering. I don't think I want to go naked

130

into the chamber if they really *are* sitting on an atomic unit out there."

"I think they'll accept that."

The Home Secretary turned back to the supervisor.

"Raise Sharland again, please. Tell him the professor will wear a transparent suit. He will come aboard in exactly half an hour's time."

FRIDAY   0849

" 'Ey, Sarge. Cop a look at this."

The corporal pointed back in the direction of the terminal building. A figure emerged from the night, a hundred yards away. It was encased from head to foot in rippling plastic, its movement stiff and bizarre as the man inside fought to stay upright in the snow.

The sergeant turned his night glasses on the zombie, and watched its ponderous progress up to the open main hatch of the Trident. "Observe, but don't touch," the command post had radioed.

A steel ladder swung to the ground from inside and arms reached out to assist the struggling Lockhart.

The soldiers watched him disappear.

FRIDAY   1000

Two tubes of cardboard, one half-inserted in the other, were balanced precariously on the table. The end of one tube had been sealed. At the end of the other was taped a small square of cardboard, slightly larger than the tube's diameter.

The Home Secretary pressed his knuckles hard into the tabletop and, arms braced, stared down at the object before him.

"It's a bit Heath Robinson, sir," said the CGS apologetically from across the table. "The best we could do under the circumstances."

The Home Secretary nodded impatiently, then turned to the scientist beside him.

"Tell me about it," he said.

Lockhart cleared his throat self-consciously and picked up one of the cardboard tubes.

"The principle itself is relatively simple, sir. I'll run over it as briefly as I can. The whole thing is about three and a half feet long. It has seven main components. Projectile, target, initiator, reflector, propellant, container and firing system. Weight: roughly five hundred pounds.

"We have a cylinder made from, in this case, a sliced-up naval gun barrel. It contains molded uranium. Another cylinder"—he picked up the other tube of cardboard—"fits inside it, like so. A plug. That too contains molded uranium. Around the whole assembly is a reflector; I'll explain that in a moment. These two particles of uranium are, you understand, totally harmless in isolation. Now, at the rear of the plug there's a steel plate—that's this piece of cardboard here. The object is to bring these two subcritical masses of uranium together . . . with force.

"The projectile at this end weighs about thirty-five pounds and will need to travel five hundred feet per second down the gun barrel."

He looked across at the CGS.

"Less than two ounces of gunpowder are sufficient to achieve that, as you know, sir. The powder itself needs to be in a container; anything will do, plastic bag, whatever. Detonation is the simplest thing of all. A flashlight battery wired to the bag."

The Home Secretary flattened his hands on the table. "Carry on."

"Well, sir, as I said, the aim is to bring the two particles together *violently*. The charge blasts the projectile down the barrel and penetrates the companion uranium at high speed. At the same time, this"—he tapped the small square of cardboard taped to one end of the tube—"this seals off the whole device."

The CGS looked at him quizzically.

"It's essential that happens, sir, otherwise . . . phuttt! When the uranium conjoins, it becomes supercritical and this shield allows no neutrons to escape. The reflector that also helps stop this happening is made from a solid block of three-inch steel. It's sufficient. How much steel the reflector needs is obtained from calculations I won't go into

132

here. Suffice to say they are readily available to anyone who has the time and energy to look for them. . . . Where was I? Ah, yes. Now the neutrons, reflected back on each other into the core, initiate a chain reaction and . . . and . . ."

The young man's voice trailed away.

"And?" said the CGS.

"It explodes, sir. It explodes."

"I see," said the Home Secretary. "At least I think I do. Is there anything else?"

"A few technical things, sir, but I think you have the essentials. I mentioned an initiator. As it stands, this particular device could be undependable. Relies on chance, so it might not work. As I said, neutrons must be emitted; that's vital. To ensure they are, you need an initiator. Again, this depends on two substances being brought together. In this case, lithium and polonium 210. The lithium is glued to the projectile, the polonium to the target, the end which is to be struck. A collision of the two will ensure that the neutrons burst into the uranium."

The young man paused.

"It seems they thought of everything, sir."

The Home Secretary moved for the first time, flexing his shoulders. He walked across the room, paused and stared abstractedly at his toe caps.

"And that is it?"

"Yes, sir. The whole thing's encased in a bin. Metal. Like a dustbin, sir. It's all that's needed. The essentials are there."

"And will it work, this bomb?"

"No one can say for sure. There are always imponderables. It might crack, neutrons might escape, anything. But, in theory, yes. It could work."

"And do? What will your bomb do?"

"The blast would be in the region of one kiloton, I think. It could raze the airport to the ground and surrounding buildings would collapse under the shock wave. For example, one tenth of a kiloton would be sufficient to reduce the Post Office Tower to rubble. This"—he shrugged—"it would be very bad. And, of course, there's the radiation hazard."

"Of course," said the Home Secretary drily.

"In this case, sir, without doubt it would be very dirty. This bomb would send a lethal dose of radiation through free air for up to at least half a mile. Gamma rays would strike first. Next the light, then the neutrons, then the air shock, then the missiles."

"Missiles?" queried the CGS.

"Bits of concrete, telegraph poles, fragments of cars, anything could be propelled by the blast for over a mile. Tons of it. Like grapeshot. Of course, we must bear in mind that the blast itself would be erratic, very difficult to program because of the bomb's amateur nature."

"Amateur?" The Home Secretary pinched the bridge of his nose and looked across at the CGS.

"Tell me something. Why go to all this trouble? Why didn't they just steal one? They have the means, obviously. Manpower. And money. It's not impossible, surely?"

The CGS shook his head.

"Near enough. For years people have been speculating on how it could be done. Hijack, straightforward purchase, it's kept a whole battalion of novelists in business. But that's what it is. Pure fiction. Nuclear security has been made practically watertight since the end of the sixties. What these people have done—built their own—has totally bypassed it all.

"No, sir, to answer your question, to steal a bomb would take an army. There's no loophole for amateurs."

The Home Secretary leaned over the tubes of cardboard and slid one, experimentally, into the other.

"Amateurs," he repeated tonelessly.

Slowly he crushed the contraption in his hands.

FRIDAY   1000

The road took a sharp turn and on the elbow of the bend lay the gate, its foot buried deep in frozen mud. Driscoll dragged the gate wide, drove through and shoved it back in place.

The Old Bedford ran straight as a die. A bank of blackberry taller than the van paralleled it right up to the walls of the house.

For no immediate reason, the memory of Duffy's death flashed into Driscoll's head. Duffy's body lying still and disfigured in a spreading pool of blood at his feet. The flapping mess where the knife had entered Duffy's black pullover and turned and sliced his flesh. The leaden weight of the corpse as he lifted it with his foot and kicked it back onto the landing.

Sorry, Duff; there was nothing else I could do.

Driscoll brought the van to a halt under the fluted plastic of a carport and slid open the van door. The carport roof wore a six-inch crust of snow. Twenty yards away, the Old Bedford whispered in its winter reeds. Nothing else stirred.

Driscoll flattened himself against the wall of the bungalow, edged to the French windows and darted a glance inside. Satisfied, he pushed himself upright and circled the house, then moved a few yards to the rear, to a point where he could see everything from the jetty to the house to the blackberry hedge and the gate four hundred yards back along the path.

He stood still for two minutes, imprisoned by his thoughts, letting the bite of the wind and the obsessive fingering of the snow drain every last ounce of torpor from him.

There was no sound from inside the Transit. Assad would be communing with his new surroundings, too; breathing in the scent of freedom.

Driscoll pulled his hands down his face, wiping away the exhaustion. It did not come off. He wandered back to the clapboard porch, dug a key from his zipped top pocket and fitted it into the lock. It was unnecessary.

The door creaked open. He waited for the muted *phutt* of a silenced bullet. Nothing. He released the Walther from the sprung holster under his arm and touched the door gently. It swung wide on protesting hinges. He dived, forward and down; his shoulder struck one of the chairs by the table, deflecting his dive and flipping him onto his back.

The silence settled on him like a mist.

He got to his feet sheepishly and flicked on the light. The room was undisturbed . . .

Except for a neatly wrapped oblong parcel placed in the center of the mantelpiece. Propped against it was a long white envelope.

He touched the parcel gingerly, put his ear to it and traversed every millimeter of the brown wrapping paper. He took a knife from his pocket, sprang the blade and surgically incised the upper surface, cutting well clear of the natural folds.

The paper came away in one piece. Inside was a cardboard box, perhaps ten inches long. Driscoll traced a tentative fingertip along the projecting shelf of the lid, then made four incisions, an inch in from the edges. He lifted the central portion.

His stomach heaved. He turned his head as the vomit rose into his throat. Tears flooded his eyes.

He swung away from it into the room.

The box was cushioned inside with cotton wool. The padding, once white, was stained crimson.

On it lay a severed hand, the butchered bone of its forearm glinting through a torment of tendon and artery and flesh.

On one slim finger was a ring fashioned in the shape of a coiled python with diamond eyes. The python was Julia's soul brother. Her guardian spirit.

She was mesmerized by that line of Kipling's: "We are of one blood, you and I."

Driscoll bowed his weight on the mantel and spat adrenaline into the fireplace.

Julia. Julia.

Why?

It was several minutes before he remembered the envelope. He swept the tears from his eyes and took out the single sheet of notepaper.

It said simply:

THOU SHALT NOT STEAL.

FRIDAY   1015

A gust of wind whined off the Old Bedford, thrashing the copse of stunted bushes, rattling the dead leaves that carpeted the sunken dell in which the four men crouched.

They had been waiting for five hours, taking turns to shelter in the warmth of the car parked a quarter of a mile away in a plowed field. When the Transit pulled through the gate, the leader had sent Leo to fetch the others.

"He's been in the house a damn long time," growled one of them. "You think he's taken off through the back door?"

The leader shook his head, his eyes glued to the Transit van, two hundred yards away.

"There isn't one. Anyway, what else do you expect? He's found the box."

"Don't tell me that's turned him over," growled Leo. "The

Man said it wouldn't force his hand." He grinned at his own unintentional symbolism.

"The Man said she was just a girl friend," snapped the leader. "Maybe Driscoll has other ideas."

Leo curled his lip.

"The Man doesn't get it wrong. He said he knew which way Driscoll'd jump and, by God, he's been on the button every step of the way. You start thinking you know better and we could be in trouble."

The leader ignored him. Leo was right, of course. The Man was never wrong. That was the essence of his achievement, the rock on which the legend had been built. For years, every staff officer of Mossad, Israel's intelligence service, had known about the Man in London. Only two men in the service knew his name; only the director himself had ever met him. Among the commandos of the Wrath of God assault unit, the strike arm of Mossad, the Man was a totem, the unattainable archetype of their profession. To be working directly under his command, even by remote control, was an honor that would now set them apart from their fellows.

There was no denying he knew Driscoll. He'd worked with him, controlled him in the field, ordered his career and observed the shadowy corners of his private life. His right to total obedience was unquestionable.

One of the men shifted his position painfully, scrubbing his legs with gloved hands to encourage the circulation.

"He's got to move soon."

"He'll move," said the leader absently.

The Man had plotted Driscoll's reactions to a T. It had all happened exactly as he'd said. Right down to the house on the Old Bedford. How he knew was beyond understanding. It was just part of the magic that made him the ultimate spy.

The Man had been explicit. His message had left nothing to their imagination. Getting Assad into their hands was all-important; getting him to Israel was the objective that outweighed all others. Driscoll, said the Man with unchallengeable prophecy, would realize at the warehouse that he was on his own; that Herrick's was not giving him the cover he had been led to expect. Therefore, he would run and his destination would be the Fens. From there, he would have to get out of Britain fast and he would take the obvious route: by sea.

That was to their advantage. Let Driscoll get Assad out of the country. Let him run on the Continent. There were a half dozen points he was likely to make for, in France, Switzerland and Italy. Those points would be covered by Mossad search groups. When the time was right, when the Man was satisfied, they would simply pick up Assad and freight him to Tel Aviv by the most accessible route.

For the moment they would have to wait. It was essential, said the Man, that Driscoll should know they were on his tail. But he must not see them.

The leader checked his watch.

The twin-turbine motor launch was ready and fueled at King's Lynn. It would take them no more than half an hour to reach it by car.

The wind howled again, flinging snow across the leaden sky.

FRIDAY   1030

The Home Secretary adjusted the headset and nodded curtly to the superintendent.

"Heathrow Tower to Sharland. Come in, please."

"Sharland to Tower. Over."

"Are your passengers listening, Captain?"

"They are, sir. Over."

"Do they speak English?"

"Yes, sir. But they will not use the radio. Over."

"I want them to understand this. Please explain if they have any difficulty. Mahmoud Assad has been injured. He is in hospital and his doctors inform me that to move him could jeopardize his recovery. Do they understand all this?"

"Affirmative, sir."

"We cannot move Assad until he is well enough to travel."

The jabbering rose to a crescendo in the background and became muffled as Sharland cupped a hand over his headset mouthpiece. He came on again.

"Sharland. That is not acceptable. Assad must be allowed to come to the airport and walk unaccompanied to the aircraft."

"Assad is incapable of walking, Captain. Can you make them understand that? He is not able to move from his bed."

138

A hand blanketed the mouthpiece again. This time, the silence lasted for two minutes.

Finally, Sharland said: "They won't have that, sir. It's Assad or nothing."

He paused, listening to a voice over his shoulder. "Yes. Right. They say you have thirty minutes to get Assad here."

"That's impossible. Assad is in hospital on the other side of the city. Even if we could get him up, there's no hope of crossing the city in thirty minutes."

There was a scuffling sound and a long pause. A new voice spoke; younger, more brittle.

"You are very wrong to be dishonest. You will be responsible for many deaths. You must bring our brother Assad to us here. Now. We will delay exploding the bomb until . . . until midnight tonight."

He was very young. It was an educated voice, well modulated, with a faint American broad-vowel inflection.

The Home Secretary felt a momentary flush of triumph.

"Who am I speaking to?"

"That is of no matter."

"Then I must ask you to believe me when I say that I am not being dishonest. Assad is very sick. He has a severe wound and has lost much blood. He is weak and he cannot move. Would you have the death of your brother on your conscience?"

"You are trying to confuse us. We will not delay beyond midnight tonight."

"Your brother Assad will not recover by midnight tonight. You must believe that."

He had a sudden breathtaking thought.

"If you will undertake not to explode the bomb, I will permit one of your group to leave the plane, unharmed, and go to the hospital to see your brother."

He waited until the heated whispering died.

"I will permit any one of you to see him if you decide now."

"It is a trick. You will arrest anyone who leaves this plane."

"You have my word."

"We do not accept your word. You lie."

"I do not lie. It is too important to us and to you. If you see Assad, you will know that I am not lying. You will see that he is sick and cannot move. Is that being dishonest?"

The line snapped off. The Home Secretary leaned back in

his seat and lit a cigarette. His hands were trembling with concentration. The young man switched on again.

"You have in London a brother of the Palestine Liberation Organization."

"Yes. We have."

"You will find him and bring him to the airport. We will talk to him."

"He will be able to tell you nothing."

"We will speak further only to him."

The line closed abruptly.

The call to the Prime Minister took five minutes.

There was a further delay of half an hour as Special Branch officers drove to the headquarters of the Arab League in Hay Hill, off Berkeley Square, where the PLO leased office space. It took another fifteen minutes to establish the representative's whereabouts.

The Home Secretary opened the line to the plane again. Sharland responded, then handed over to the young Arab.

"The representative of the PLO is in Beirut," explained the Home Secretary. "He left London four days ago and is not due to return until January the fourth."

"This is another lie."

"It's the truth. We have made contact with the office of the PLO in Beirut, and the London representative is believed to be with his family in Tripoli. It will take some hours before they can contact him."

"If you are lying to us . . ."

"We are doing everything we can do to bring him to you. He will be on board the first available flight from Beirut."

"How many hours will this take?"

"That depends on how long it takes the PLO in Beirut to find him. He may be with his family or he may be traveling."

"You think to make us wait so we will not explode the bomb."

"I think only of the safety of all of us—you and us. We do not want the bomb to explode. We will do all we can to bring this man to you as quickly as we can."

"We will wait. But not too long."

Driscoll scuffed through the snow to the bank of the Old Bedford and raised his face to the air. It had the demon sting of true Fenland winter in it.

The whipping curtain of snow made it impossible to strain eye or imagination into the distance. He should get Assad into the bungalow. Out of sight. Fast.

Why? What was the point? They knew, whoever they were. They could see. They were out there, somewhere, waiting, measuring his indecision and misery as surely as a tiger drools over a tethered goat.

He turned back to the van. He released the straps around Assad's sleeping bag. He watched the Arab will circulation back into his dead muscles and prize himself out into the air.

Assad flashed a bleached-white grin as the effort wrenched at the stitches in his chest and pushed himself upright. He was still unsteady. Driscoll threw an arm around his waist and half carried him into the bungalow. He kicked the door shut and eased the Arab into one corner of a battered settee camouflaged in a flower-printed stretch cover.

Without a word, he picked up the letter and the box and thrust them under Assad's nose.

He had hoped for shock, for an emotional collapse, a shudder of revulsion. He was disappointed.

Assad looked first at the box and the hand, then turned to the paper and read it with a perceptible movement of his lips. When he finished he looked coolly into Driscoll's face.

Driscoll stared savagely into the deep eyes. He said: "I just wanted you to know how far they're prepared to go."

Assad shook his head, mildly surprised.

"I have no doubt of my value. Many people, many interests, are involved. They will pay in gold or in blood. It makes no difference."

"It makes a difference to me."

"Ah, but of course. You are an outsider and a good businessman. Yes? A good businessman. By the code of your society that permits you any course of action that shows profit. In this case, your safe conduct in exchange for me.

141

I suppose our friends are"—he made a swirling motion of his hand toward the window—"outside?"

Driscoll placed the box on the table, and went to the window. He drew the curtains, screeching, along the rusted rail, and stood for a moment, staring through the material into the timid morning light.

"Why do you suppose we're still alive?" he asked flatly.

Assad shook his head.

Driscoll lit a cigarette and threw the battered pack to Assad.

"No one knew about this place. No one."

Assad let smoke curl lazily from his mouth.

"That is illogical. How many places could you have taken me? A dozen? Two dozen? More? Yet you chose this house. And they knew you would come."

Driscoll interrupted, impatiently. "So either they covered every place I *might* have turned to, or they read my mind . . ."

"Or the unfortunate owner of that hand was in a position to tell them."

Julia? How much had he told her? *What* had he told her? The hairs pricked along the base of his skull.

Memories. Sealed boxes echoing with lies. Truth lies bleeding.

In his head the words had always been savage with passion: "Fight me, you little cow, fight me and make me rape you," but his mouth had formed the same bland lie over and over again: "I love you, I love you, I love you."

Assad was studying him intently, the cigarette tight in the center of his mouth, nostrils flaring with released smoke.

"She didn't know a thing."

Assad nodded, as though in agreement.

Driscoll found himself qualifying the assertion.

"She was never involved in anything. She never asked. She was a . . ." He stopped himself, angrily.

"A friend?"

Assad's expression was free of cynicism.

Driscoll ignored him. "They're waiting for me to make the next move. They're holding back. They don't want you—yet. Maybe they don't want you at all. Maybe they want . . ."

What? Both of them? They *had* both of them. And Julia. And Duffy. Poor bleeding Duffy. What else?

They could put an end to him as a dealer in arms, of course, but they could have done that with a bullet. A waste of time, anyway. He would be replaced easily enough by an American Driscoll or a French Driscoll or a Swiss or a German. No one was irreplaceable.

He got to his feet, so quickly that even Assad's rock-like imperturbability was momentarily shaken.

The cigarette in the Arab's fingers was within a quarter inch of total immolation but he sucked deeply on it once more before grinding it under his heel. It was a nervous gesture. Driscoll liked that. It was the first sign that Assad shared his apprehension.

Driscoll prodded open the door into the cell of a kitchen at the rear. It smelled of old plastic and coagulated cooking oil and damp.

He said to Assad: "I'm going out there. Five, maybe ten minutes. I'll go through the kitchen window."

Assad nodded and smiled nervously. "And if I am not here when you return?"

"You'll be here."

"Our friends may decide otherwise."

Driscoll buttoned the front of his pea jacket.

"I'll take that chance. Here." He tossed the lighter into Assad's lap. "Turn on the radio. If we can make them think we've settled down for the day, so much the better."

He stepped into the kitchen, pulled the door shut behind him and swung open the tiny window above the sink. He paused to judge the distance through the snowfall, then swung quietly over the sill.

FRIDAY   1115

The Prime Minister turned savagely and slammed both hands hard on the desk.

"I *know* what it means, man. I'm asking you what you can do to stop it."

Flag examined his hands.

"In any preventive sense, we've done all we can for the moment, sir. Special Branch have detached a hundred men and we're augmenting with every officer we can lay hands on. MI5 are covering every point of exit, every airport, every private flying club. We shall be combing every ship's manifest, every aircraft freight list. The regional crime squads are on a full alert in all the embarkation areas for Ireland and the Continent. The Royal Navy will cooperate and so will the coastal stations."

"I told you we had to keep this quiet. You seem to have confided in every blasted man, woman and child in the country."

"As far as they're aware, sir, we're looking for two men wanted in connection with the murders last night at Wapping. Nothing more."

"Then I hope they're as stupid as you seem to think."

Flag got to his feet.

"If you'll excuse me, sir . . ."

He hooked out his half hunter and studied it pointedly.

"Oh, yes, of course. Whatever you want. But don't let that man out of the country. I don't care what it takes. Just get him."

Flag stopped at the door.

"With the best will in the world, sir, I can't guarantee that."

"Then be prepared to preside over your own destruction. I will not tolerate failure in this. By you or anybody else."

For five minutes after Flag had left, the Prime Minister sat at his desk, his fingers drumming a tattoo. At length, he got to his feet and opened the communicating door into his secretary's office. Sir Lionel Harvey, the Cabinet's chief scientific adviser, had commandeered the room the night before. His appearance gave every indication that he had not slept.

Sir Lionel was bent low over a sheet of yellow paper, his old Conway Stewart scratching noisily in long flowing strokes. His half glasses, thick as doughnuts, threw reflected sickles of light on the paper. Through the wispy white baby hair, his scalp glowed pinkly.

He looked up, unhurriedly, his eyes blinking as they adjusted to the extended focal length.

"Ah! I thought you might have been called away."

The Prime Minister shook his head.

"Any of this make sense to you, Lionel?"

The half glasses performed a flashing genuflection.

"Well, now—there's a question. If you're interested in facts the answer is yes. If you're looking for comfort and reassurance the answer's no. Lockhart says the bomb could work and on my assessment of what he found, I have to agree."

144

The Prime Minister groaned into a chair.

He said helplessly: "But how, in God's name? Are you telling me the Palestinians are capable of designing an atomic bomb?"

The old head sank into frail shoulders. Old eyes stared across the desk, surprisingly wide, uncompromisingly sharp.

"I may find it oppressively difficult to avoid telling you 'I told you so.' However." He removed his glasses and polished them with a square of chamois leather.

"If you're asking me: *Have* they produced a bomb? I must admit in all honesty I don't know. *Could* they? Another kettle of fish entirely."

He arranged the glasses low on his snub nose.

"Let's stick to known facts. They're not too technical.

"First, this is a uranium bomb, pretty obviously. At its heart is a nugget of uranium 235. They used sixty kilograms of it at Hiroshima. Now, you'll have to take it from me that the powder from which 235 is made, uranium oxide, is far from being as rare as you think. Tons of it moves almost continuously around America, usually by road transport, and it's an irrefutable fact that hundreds of tons of it have been misplaced, lost, call it what you will, since the early fifties.

"Now—if you can lay your hands on some of that uranium oxide, if you can afford a £75 laboratory furnace, a £2 graphite crucible, £4 for a quart of hydrofluoric acid, £12 for a pound of magnesium oxide and £30 or £40 worth of ancillary equipment, you're in business.

"Next you find yourself a bright university lad, a bright schoolboy even, who can apply his physics.

"Then, you buy yourself a copy of *The Los Alamos Primer*. It reveals all the mathematical fundamentals of fission bombs and it's openly available from the American Atomic Energy Commission for two or three dollars a copy. It was declassified in 1964.

"For another four or five dollars, you can buy a book called *Manhattan District History: Project Y, the Los Alamos Project*. Again readily available, postage and packaging included, from the Office of Technical Services, U.S. Department of Commerce. It carries all the details of the problems that arose in the building of the first atomic bomb. It was declassified in 1961.

"You won't believe this, but I assure you it's true. On its inside front cover it has a little note to the effect—I can't

145

remember the exact wording—that the United States and the Atomic Energy Commission accept no responsibility for the use of, or damages resulting from the use of, anything disclosed in the book."

He rubbed his hand through his white fluffy hair.

"Hope springs eternal in the mind of bureaucrats. Put all of those factors together and you have a bomb like this one. That's one method.

"Personally, if I were an amateur I'd use plutonium as a base. The mass you need for a sustained chain reaction is a third that of uranium. And, of course, a bad bomb made with plutonium would produce a bigger yield than a fair one made with uranium.

"And with reactors spawning plutonium all over the world nowadays, it would be supremely easy for a determined group to lay their hands on it. It's shipped and stored as plutonium nitrate in four-foot flasks, rather like thermos bottles. Three or four flasks would be enough for a good big bang. You'd need a fairly substantial induction furnace. It has to have a magnetic field and be capable of bringing to high temperatures anything resistant to electricity. Like plutonium.

"It might cost something on the order of a thousand pounds.

"Both uranium 235 and plutonium could be held for months without any harmful effects. Long enough for the people concerned to design and construct a firing mechanism for their bomb."

The Prime Minister closed his eyes and nipped the bridge of his nose between finger and thumb.

"You make it sound child's play."

The half glasses flashed excitedly.

"Yes—isn't it?"

FRIDAY   1130

The shape of the cottage emerged slowly. It was half hidden by a belt of young willows. Over to the right was a five-barred gate and presumably a track. Driscoll reached it in a series of zigzagging runs and nestled into the under-branches of the outlying trees.

146

No light, no sound, no movement. Wood slat walls, characteristic hooded porch, one room—two at most. He walked boldly to the front door and knocked.

He circled the house once, then a second time.

The door gave quietly; he felt the tongue of the old lock riding over the restraining socket.

Very cozy: split level with the upper part looking out through a picture window onto the Old Bedford. Big fat armchairs and a settee, dining table for six, heavy blue wallpaper and dark blue carpet. Somebody cared.

There was a bookcase and under it a triple row of drawers, unlocked. Bills, a Perkins marine diesel handbook, Stanford's Chart No. 21: "Navigation on the Broads," Hoseason's inland cruising map of England for larger craft, two or three old copies of *Yachting World* and *Practical Boat Owner*.

Driscoll switched off the lights and crossed to the window. The ground rose to a slight eminence twenty yards to the right, upriver. Another irrigation ditch, probably. Or . . .

He ran from the cottage, turned the corner by the picture window and blundered to the top of the rise.

Even under her winter canvas, she was every inch a thoroughbred. He recognized the design at once.

A little over twenty-five feet overall, twenty-one feet six inches on the waterline and seven feet plus abeam.

Made of fine teak, she had that look about her—half maiden, half Amazon—that turned seasick landsmen into daredevil circumnavigators. He slipped down the bank onto a frail woodplank jetty, released the canvas and swept it back over her stern.

He forced the door into the saloon, switched on the flashlight and ran it over the interior. Galley immediate left at the foot of the companion steps, chart table right, a full berth amidships behind a folding table. He pushed through forward; hanging lockers, lavatory and, beyond, two vee berths.

He climbed back up into the cockpit and opened the lockers. The sails were stowed in neatly marked bags: jib 1, jib 2, jib 3, spinnaker, genoa.

He fished around, produced a flat plastic dipstick and plumbed the tank: seven gallons, maybe a shade less. Lucky if there was any water in the tank, but that was easily remedied.

He pulled himself up short.

So, she was an outstanding blue-water cruiser. But this

147

was December and, if he had fully grasped what was churning in his mind, the idea would lead him out into the Wash and beyond to the North Sea. In midwinter.

He unbattened the canvas, rolled and flattened it and hefted it onto the jetty. Back in the house he tore through cupboards and drawers until he found a coil of green plastic garden hose. Back to the boat and a long stumbling hunt-the-slipper game with his fingers crossed and his tongue sandwiched between his teeth.

Thank Christ; the standpipe, topped by a bright brass tap, had been sited in one corner of the cut, abaft the jetty. He coupled on the hose, stabbed the business end into the watertank pipe and turned on. The little boat's stomach gurgled happily and finally fizzed and spat when it had had enough.

The house was empty of food and drink—fresh, frozen or dried. The place had obviously been closed at least a month earlier and the house-proud woman who had so jealously lavished her attention on the appointments and furnishings had been careful to remove all possible sources of putrefaction and decay from the larder and the fridge.

Nothing to be done in that direction, short of trekking alone cross-country to the nearest village or isolated farm and stealing what he could. But that would waste valuable time. Run now, starve later.

He squinted up into the snow. The wind had died. Light airs now scarcely moved the floating flakes, but it could be a different story in an hour's time. A full twenty-four hours from now he could be on his beam ends in a squall anywhere between Vinegar Middle and Bob Hall's Sand, waiting for the wind and the sea to crush him and this frail little shell to a pulp.

He slipped into the cockpit and flashed the Flarepath into the lockers again.

Eight distress flares, four of them the rocket-parachute type, towrope, lifeline, engine tool kit, fenders, four life jackets, four neatly wound warps, two stout canvas dodgers. He unshipped the dodgers and shook them out.

The name was painted boldly in letters twelve inches high: *Blind Virtue*.

Driscoll grinned in spite of himself.

Touché.

Below, the chart locker was stuffed with Stanford colored charts. He was interested in only two: No. 20, "East Coast of England, Haisborough Sand to Tees Bay," and No. 19, "Southern North Sea." He breathed with relief when he found both.

The owner was a gadget man. Along the ridge of the hatch he had mounted a Midas instrument console that would have done justice to an Admiral's Cup racer; gauges to measure boat speed, distance traveled, wind speed, efficiency, wind direction and performance close-hauled.

There was an expensive Seascribe echo sounder and a Seavoice VHF radiotelephone that must have set him back at least 250 pounds. In the hanging lockers in the saloon, he found a first-aid box comprehensive enough for heart-transplant surgery, and, on one of the vee berths in the fore-cabin, a masthead radar reflector.

Now that was something he could do without.

He reached the house, having traveled sixty percent of the distance on hands, knees and stomach.

He was half over the windowsill when the voice cut through from the living room. For a full minute, Driscoll hung motionless, taking his body weight on trembling arms, as his ears tried to overlay form and meaning on the stream of sound.

He squeezed into the kitchen and closed the window without noise.

Assad's nerves were at fine pitch. His face momentarily flinched as Driscoll threw back the door and burst into the room, gun in hand.

The Arab's recovery was instinctive. With a gesture of his hand he indicated the radio.

A voice was saying: ". . . history of unfortunate labor relations. The bare facts are these: Early this morning, a force of Flying Squad officers swooped down on the baggage-handling areas at Heathrow. No warning was given and the airport police themselves were not, apparently, notified. The usual explanation has been issued, that 'a number of airport employees are helping police in their inquiries,' but so far Scotland Yard is refusing to go into detail.

"What strikes the union leaders here today as remarkable is that the police struck at a time of the morning when only a trickle of baggage and cargo passes through the airport. That, and the fact that the police action was almost a text-book exercise in industrial confrontation. As the handlers' senior shop steward, Gus Williamson, put it this afternoon: 'If they wanted to bring the airport to a total standstill, they couldn't have chosen a better way."

Driscoll crossed to the radio and switched it off. Assad watched him with a half smile on his lips, a mark of expectancy.

Walking quickly to the window, Driscoll touched the curtain aside and observed the van. Then he moved to the door and slipped outside to the Transit.

He took a plastic bag from the dashboard shelf, weighed it thoughtfully in his palm and made a face. There were a few bars of chocolate in it, some apples, an orange or two and a half dozen packets of Gitanes.

Hardly provision for a sea passage.

Back in the cottage, the Arab raised his head inquisitively. Driscoll stood over him, silent for a moment, then said: "On your feet. We're taking a little trip."

He pulled Assad to his feet; then, to the Arab's astonishment, ripped the flimsy stretch cover from the settee and tossed it on the floor. He tore open a couple of cushions and scattered the contents on the stretch cover.

In the kitchen cupboard, he found a can of paraffin. He slopped the liquid on the mound of fabric and feathers and hurled the rest over chairs, settee, tables, curtains and walls.

Assad watched, fascinated.

Driscoll flicked his lighter and carefully set the flame to the material. The paraffin whoofed and flames ran, licking, across the room.

Assad looked at him blankly.

Driscoll said: "For our friends outside, whoever they are. Give them something to think about. It might keep them busy long enough to give us a head start."

He turned at the kitchen door, a thought electrifying his eyes. He crossed quickly to the mantel and took down the cardboard box and forced himself to look at the dismembered hand.

The flames had caught the hanging folds of the tablecloth and a circle of fire writhed over the table. Gently, he placed the box at their center, ignoring the pain. He stood for a moment, then turned abruptly, aggressively.

"Okay," he said. "Let's go."

Someone with a wry sense of humor or none at all had named it Newgate. The Newgate Hotel: a crumbling neo-Gothic façade festooned with a tatty bunting of wet nylons and shirts. Half-empty milk bottles cooled on windowsills in the winter Frigidaire.

The visitor stepped over a sleeping dog in the hall that passed for a foyer and waited by the reception desk. A half-eaten abandoned sandwich lay on the register and two inches of dead ash hung impossibly from a cigarette perched on an ashtray emblazoned: "Colwyn Bay 1953."

Somewhere in the bowels of the building, a woman was singing. Dreaming of a White Christmas. But there was no one in sight.

He walked slowly up the stairs, pausing by each door. On the second floor a man burst from one of the rooms cursing, his breath foul with stale beer. A torrent of abuse followed him into the corridor. At the door, a hollow-eyed bony girl clutching a greasy negligee around her yelled: "Dirty bastard! Pig"

The pig stumbled down the stairs and half turned at the bottom.

"Frigid bitch!"

The visitor ignored the girl's swiftly accommodating smile and moved up the next flight. The hotel narrowed as it got higher, the rooms crowding in on each other like Russian boxes.

On the fourth landing, he stopped and closed his eyes. There were only two rooms on the floor. He stood equidistant between them and sniffed.

Abdullah Turkish.

He moved to the door on his right and turned the handle. It was locked. He knocked. The voice behind the door was giving away nothing.

"Who is it?"

"Me. Open it."

A bolt slid back and the door croaked open on protesting hinges. The visitor walked to the middle of the room as Guilfoyle hastily relocked and bolted the door. He was un-

151

shaven and his hand shook as he dragged on the cigarette like a man recovering from a long bout of malaria.

"You took your time getting here. I said eight-thirty. I can't afford to be here long."

The speaker glanced around the room with a frown of utter distaste.

"No, there isn't much time."

Guilfoyle's eyes became slits. His tongue flicked momentarily over his top lip.

"Do we have a postmortem, or does that come later?" He met a withering gaze and slumped into a frayed and leaking chair.

He tried again. "I told you it was in the cards. I told you the risk."

"Oh, no. No time for postmortems, I think. Waste of time. Spilt milk." The visitor intoned the words preciously. He ran his finger through the dust coating on the mantelpiece.

Guilfoyle said: "Driscoll must have known something. He was one step ahead all the way. Work that out!" There was a hint of menace in his voice.

A raised hand cut him short. "No need. All is clear. There was a Quisling in our midst." He paused for effect. "And now we have him."

"No!" Guilfoyle came out of his chair. "That's not true! You know it!"

"I know only this: I know I spent years building up an organization second to none. None! In the course of one night you have put that organization in jeopardy. You, Guilfoyle! I feel very sad it should be you." His nose wrinkled as the pungent gray cigarette smoke drifted into his face. He turned to the window, pushed both frames open wide and breathed in the cold air.

Guilfoyle ran his fingers through his hair and lit another cigarette from the dying butt.

"I've worked for the organization, too. Almost as long as you. Do you think I'm stupid enough to throw all that away? For what? That Beirut scum? Herrick's? Come on, you know better than that!"

The visitor allowed his eyes to fall to the cracked overgrown paving stones that formed the dingy yard of the hotel. He moved fractionally to one side, his back still to Guilfoyle.

"Are you expecting visitors?" he murmured softly.

152

"What?"

"There's somebody down there. Somebody watching the hotel."

Guilfoyle stubbed out the cigarette on the way to the window. He peered over the man's shoulder.

"Impossible! No one followed me! No one!"

"But they did, my friend. And they're waiting outside. Stand back from the window . . . until we know who they are."

"Can't be!" Guilfoyle's voice began to crack. He pushed the visitor roughly aside.

"There."

A guiding hand settled between Guilfoyle's shoulder blades. The push was slight, almost gentle, but it was enough to impel him through the open casement.

Guilfoyle hit the yard below, headfirst, before he could even scream.

FRIDAY   1530

The snow began to fall heavily again, driving into Driscoll's face in stinging sheets on a light wind now veering northeast. The sputtering of the little engine was muted by the rush of wind in his ears and Driscoll began to fashion its beat, as sailing men do, to the doggerel of the sea.

Dah, de-de-dah-dah, de-dah, de-de-dah. Way-hay, blow the man down . . .

The land flowed like white silk on either side, flat as a bed sheet and empty as the moon. At every bend of the river, the wind whipped the scurrying snow into whirling eddies before settling once more into an angle that maximized the assault into his eyes and ears.

Even so, he experienced a strange contentment, as though the air and the water and the land and the snow had plucked him from life and set him down in some timeless, painless no-man's land. The wind stripped ghostly perfumes from the land and mingled them with its sea tang and Driscoll felt his landsman's indifference ebbing away as body and mind reawakened to the old stimuli.

He left West Lynn to port at five-fifteen and minutes later passed the entrance to King's Lynn docks. He deliberately averted his head as he came abeam of the harbormaster's office upriver at Common Staith; it was the official point of no return.

He searched the gathering dusk for the slightest hint of official activity ashore, but the town and the harbor had already locked out the bitter day. The engine thundered in his ears as they sliced through the town; there was a deliberate anarchy in the way it snatched echoes from jetties and walls and quays and volleyed them across the water, massively magnified.

Driscoll's body was tensed throughout the passage and when the last warehouse and street fell astern, the flood of relief that surged through him left a wracking trail of muscle fatigue and cramp.

All he had to pray for now, he told himself, was that the fuel held out long enough for the engine to get him through March Cut and out beyond Daseley's Sled. He did not want to think about navigating a way through those sandbanks under sail on a falling tide.

There was a sharp plopping sound from below. Driscoll ducked in time to watch Assad push himself to his hands and knees on the cabin sole.

Their eyes locked and Assad attempted one of his all-concealing grins but his heart wasn't in it.

Driscoll turned back to the gently swinging bows just in time to avoid a sixty-point collision with a moored dredger on his starboard bow.

He shouted to Assad: "You'd better get yourself up here. Find a blanket first."

The two fixed lights south of Training Walls reached out of the gloom on the starboard bow and Driscoll shook himself in his snow-soaked pea jacket. They were doing well.

For a full half hour *Blind Virtue* thrashed her way through the flickering beacons along the course of the main channel. Then the gale hit them. Out of nowhere, as though a giant fan had been switched on by some maniac hand, the snow curtain switched direction and angle and howled through the little boat's rigging. It was almost horizontal, whipping and stinging Driscoll's right profile. Force Four or Five at least and beam on. If the engine died now, he would have to beat up into the wind to weather Blackguard Sand.

"Get below," he bellowed at Assad.

His companion cocked one eyebrow, lifted a hand to his

154

forehead in comic salute and gingerly squeezed through the hatch.

Around six-thirty *Blind Virtue*'s sizzling bow wave began to gather luminescence.

They had clipped the heel of Pandora Sand and Driscoll brought up with the triple flash of the beacon on Seal Sand.

To starboard, beyond Blackguard, there was an orange tinting to the tar-black horizon, the faintest possible inkling of civilization.

And at that moment, *Blind Virtue* herself shuddered with the recognition of unsettling new influences in her life. Her bows lifted horribly and smacked down on wave tops already rising to meet her again across her line. The shallows were gone; she now had three fathoms under her keel. She began to yaw as the seaway built up on her windward side.

Driscoll rifled the cockpit locker, found a coil of nylon and lashed the tiller. He dug out the storm jib from its bag and staggered forward into the plunging bows.

It took an endless time to bend on the jib and raise it clattering into the wind. But the effect was electric.

The boat gathered way instantly. Her head came around and she dragged herself upward and onward as though trying to shake the sea from her heels.

Driscoll clung to the grab rails all the way back to the cockpit and killed the engine. It was like switching off a blast furnace at the peak of its run. Even the wind seemed to lose weight and power in the blanketing silence.

How in hell's name they had failed to waken the whole of Norfolk and the Isle of Ely in the past two hours he would never know.

SATURDAY 1130

The Prime Minister hooked the telephone receiver into the booster unit and took a pull from his tenth cup of coffee of the morning.

"And what does the CGS propose?"

"An assault on the plane," said the Home Secretary. "Under the cover of darkness, of course. A swoop by the SAS. They would surround the plane, then attack the front, rear and mid-section of the aircraft from both sides."

The Prime Minister clattered his cup into the saucer.

"Does he have any suggestions about what we do if some-one—our men or theirs—puts a bullet into the device?"

"Lockhart's view is that a bullet merely striking the mechanism is unlikely to set it off, sir."

"Unlikely?"

"A direct hit on either section of the canister in which the uranium is located wouldn't create an atomic reaction. For total effect, the uranium core at the—ah—firing end must be propelled into the parent core at the other. Rather like firing one bullet head on into another."

The Prime Minister turned in his chair and raised an inquisitorial eyebrow at the elderly, round-shouldered man at his elbow. He received a hesitant nod.

"Has there been any further contact with the pilot?"

"No, sir. Nothing since the ultimatum."

The Prime Minister sighed. He took up his pipe and stroked it along one side of his jowl.

"Of course, this is all entirely academic, sir, if you intend to do as they wish. This man Assad . . ."

The Home Secretary gave the sentence air.

The Prime Minister flared.

"Don't ask me to repeat myself. Get it firmly into your head. I don't want Assad to enter your consideration in any form. As far as you're concerned Assad doesn't exist."

"Then I have to say . . ." The Home Secretary stalled for time. "I have to say that the assault plan is the best plan we have."

"Yes. At the moment, I think you're right. Very well."

The PM got to his feet and scratched a match to his pipe. "You will plan the assault for . . ." He consulted his watch. "For 0200 hours on Monday. That's provisional, you realize. I will give the order and you will accept it from me verbally."

"Of course, sir."

"Then we have a great deal to do in a very short time. I want the whole of the airport area—and you'd better take that to read the western Greater London area—completely evacuated."

The silence at the other end became interminable.

"Did you hear that?"

"Yes, Prime Minister."

Silence, long and full-bellied.

"Is the commissioner with you?"

"Yes. He's here."

"You've discussed the probability of evacuation, obviously?"

"Yes, we have, sir."

"And?"

"There is no contingency plan for an evacuation on this scale, Prime Minister."

The Prime Minister snatched the phone from the amplifier unit.

"That's bloody ridiculous. Of course there's a plan."

"No, sir."

The Prime Minister closed his eyes tightly. His jaws closed around the pipe stem as if to snap it. He brought himself under control.

"I see. Then you will call a meeting. At the airport. Now. All necessary powers in the Greater London area. All emergency services. You'll need to contact provincial agencies as well. All the help you can find. I want a plan, I don't care how makeshift it is, within two hours. I want organization, lines of communication and control, areas of responsibility, a monitoring system, safe areas and destinations. You can make an immediate start by alerting local hospitals, old people's homes and so on. They'll need priority."

"Two hours, sir . . ."

"That's all you've got. It's all the time we have. Get to it."

He slammed the telephone back on its cradle.

He turned to the old man.

"Lionel, I want the Atomic Energy Commission to give me a computer model on the probable destructive capability of this device. Talk to your man Lockhart at Heathrow. I want exact zones of blast effect and fallout. I want your plans for anticipating the aftermath of an explosion. Use one of the Cabinet offices."

SATURDAY   1540

In his dream, Julia was tracing a finger across his arm, as she always did in the mornings because abrupt awakenings had him jumping in a conditioned reflex for the Walther. She avoided erratic or unsignaled movement; she had seen its effect on him and it frightened her.

He could smell the coffee, Mocca Mysore, harbinger of

renewed life, bringer of the day. The cup was in her other hand.

Hand . . .

He opened his eyes wide and wild. Assad's black eyes were dulled and their depths reeled away into an eternity of repressed suffering. There was a whiteness around the eyes and mouth as though pools of bleach had lain there.

He was thinner and older and emptier and his chest was concave under the intolerable weight of his head.

Driscoll came up from his stupor like a diver with the bends. Assad tried to restrain the first animal spasm but an arm swept the Arab onto the cockpit sole like cotton flicked from a sleeve.

Driscoll stared around him like a madman, seeking escape. The sun was in the southwest, prodding inquisitive fingers down through the gray-black cloud, spraying gold on the sea. The sails flapped idly in ghostly breaths of faint air.

Blind Virtue's protest. She had come up into the wind and rooted herself like a sodden sack on the heaving gray silk. How long had he been asleep? Where in God's name were they?

His watch face was coated with salt. He rubbed the glass free. Three-forty. Where . . . ?

Assad climbed out onto the locker seat. He pointed wearily astern over Driscoll's shoulder.

Driscoll's head came around with a speed that stitched a pattern of excruciating pain along his neck and shoulder. He opened his mouth to cry out but the sight of the wedge outline of the motor launch cut off the sound at the source.

It was at least a thirty-footer and the creaming wave at its bow suggested she was making at least twenty knots. She was a mile and a half away and her course was laid across *Blind Virtue*'s stern.

In the southeast, the cloud was piled high on the horizon like black-currant fool; probably raining heavily. It was too dark to make out whether the base of that cloud layer was a smudge of land. It should be.

"How long since you first saw it?" Driscoll wheeled on Assad, accusingly.

"Three minutes. I cannot be sure. I was very weak. I have difficulty to move. I heard . . . something. A change in the sounds. I got up and I saw it."

Driscoll whirled his arms to hustle the circulation. He sucked in the wet air.

He said curtly to Assad: "Get below. Get the smog out of your head and tidy up down there. You'll find the bilge pump alongside the head. Get it working."

Assad's face was blank.

Driscoll said impatiently: "Handle. Beside the lavatory pan. Work it up and down. It pumps out the water in the cabin."

Assad nodded. He turned painfully and crept through the hatch onto the companion steps. Driscoll shouted after him.

"When they come alongside—if they do—you stay up forward in the forecabin. Where you've been sleeping. Okay?"

He watched the launch again. He wrenched the helm over and stared expectantly at the sagging sails. Nothing happened. He pushed it to starboard. *Blind Virtue* sat rock still.

He cursed his stupidity. She was aground. Judging by the whisper of movement in her bow, she was stern on to a bank.

But where? As far as he could judge he had slept for seven hours or more. Before he had dozed off *Blind Virtue* had been on the port tack and his course was zero-eight-zero.

Seven hours . . . but possibly no more than an hour or two hours of that had been spent under way at, say, three and a half knots before *Virtue* gave up the game and came up into the wind.

The motorboat's profile changed. She had triangulated on a point about a mile on his port beam and was punching her way toward him.

The thought hit him like a kick in the stomach: the watchers at the Old Bedford!

He glanced into the saloon. There was the clanking shush of the pump from the heads. At least, Assad was functioning.

Driscoll felt under his yellow waterproof jacket for the Walther. It lay warm and substantial under his armpit. At worst, if they only wanted Assad . . .

If they only wanted *Assad!* After the rip-off at St. Catherine's Dock, they'd want everything. Everyone.

In a mopping-up operation you don't leave loose ends floating in the sink.

He shouted down to Assad: "Okay. Knock it off and get yourself up front."

The Arab appeared in the hatchway. "You think they are unfriendly?"

"Everybody's unfriendly—and out here you can bet no

one's dropping in for a social chat. You'll find a wrench in the toolbox under the bottom step of the companion. There! Under your nose. Take it with you."

Assad turned and made his way forward.

Driscoll stopped him with a curt "Hey!" Assad bent his head to look back.

"If you're thinking of using that on me, forget it. I'll blow your brains into the sea before you get within a yard."

Assad nodded, grimly at first; then the old detached smile blossomed across his lips, savoring a joke too abstruse to explain.

The launch eased off about thirty yards short of the boat, and burbled around to show her starboard sheer line. She wore a pram dinghy at her stern.

Driscoll could make out at least five men. He felt for the Walther again as three of them climbed over the stern into the dinghy and whirred the outboard motor into bubbling life.

The pram buzzed across the water and the thin-lipped, sallow man at the controls brought her up ten yards away. The youth in the bow was corpulent under his yellow oil-skins; his round bovine face free of artifice.

"You're aground," he shouted helpfully.

His voice was unusually high-pitched and the flat-voweled Norfolk drawl lent it a comic dimension. Driscoll didn't smile.

The fat one tried again.

"We seed you 'asmornin'. Funny time bein' out for a tiddler like that 'un, we say—din' we, Alf?"

He turned for confirmation to a fair-haired man in the waist.

"A's roight," his companion grunted. The helmsman sat silent, watching Driscoll's face.

"Then, arter dinner, we been up to Burnham Ridge and we'm comin' back and I say to Alf 'ere, I say, 'There's that tiddler again. Oi reckon she's up, y'know.' Wull . . . we give the *Witch* another hour sea time—'a's her triles she's on, y'see, winter refit—an' we seed you agin. Same place.

" 'E *is* up!' oi say to Alf. 'Bet 'e'll want to git orf there in a 'urry.' "

The young man fell silent. He was a stranger to one-way conversations and the stoicism required to support the other party's silence was beyond his range.

Driscoll looked at all three in turn. He raised his glance

to the launch, the *Witch*. There were two men visible, one of them lounging dangerously in the heaving pulpit over the bows, the other half in, half out of the wheelhouse.

"I could use a hand to get off this bank," he said.

The fat lad's face bloomed with happiness.

"A's the ticket," he shouted. "You'm up on the Woolpack. Didja know that? Oi say to Alf 'ere, 'Bet they's foreigners, not knowing that old Woolpack, sorta like.' Not the first, you int. Nor the last. Come on then, Alf, git this thing over so's oi can git 'im a line across."

Alf stared resolutely at Driscoll but did not move. "Wha's it worth, you 'int ast 'im."

The fat man spluttered embarrassedly.

"Oh, yeah—oi forgit that. You c'd be done for salvage, mister, up 'ere. Lucky oi warn't no lifeboat, that you are. Take you in for nothin' they tell you, but once you git ashore—bugger my weasel, they don't 'alf gollop up your seervin's. Oi reckon 'a's worth a penny a two to you. Whaddyou say?"

Driscoll sat silent, stretching the fat man's embarrassment to the full.

"I'd say it was worth a tenner to me, friend," he said at last.

"Oh ah."

The fat one glanced hopefully at the older man at the helm. The fair-haired Alf leaned across and whispered.

"Wull . . . oi'd say twen'y m'self," shouted the fat one. "Oi meanta say, she's makin' up for a blow and with a big sea you'm arse over tit in a split minute out 'ere on Woolpack, y'know. See what oi mean? Twen'y int too much when you come to think."

"Okay. Twenty."

The fair-haired man whispered again. There was a brief but feverish argument. The helmsman ignored them. Finally, the spokesman turned shame-facedly to Driscoll.

"Oi'd say another tenner for the diesel—for comin' orf course and jillin' around and pickin' you orf. Whaddyou say?"

"And a tenner for diesel. Now—let's have that line aboard."

The pram nosed in and Alf slipped the line under and over *Virtue*'s bow fairlead. Before Driscoll could raise an objection, the fat youth leaped aboard. The pram chugged slowly back to the launch and the double end of line was made fast astern. The pram returned and stood off.

The maneuver was over in seconds.

There was a grating, plopping sound as *Virtue*'s rudder and propeller came free of the fine sand and suddenly she was alive again and swinging to the call of the wind.

The fat young man sideslipped nimbly along the deck and dropped lightly into the cockpit. He had called for one end of the line to be released by the launch and threaded it free of the standing rigging as he came aft.

He began to coil the wet line self-consciously around him—over the right shoulder, under the left arm—as he shaped up for the final bite.

"Now, that warn't no trouble, see. Noice little boat, this 'un. Woulda made a nice mess of 'er all noight up on Woolpack, ye see. Reckon oi'd be glad a someone comin' along to pull us orf, oi was in your shoes."

Driscoll called out to the man in the pram. They came alongside.

"Well, now. Thirty quid, you said."

Driscoll slid a hand into the jacket of his oilskin. The fat young man sat on the thwarts, one leg in the pram, the other on *Virtue*'s cockpit locker.

"Well, there's a turn-up."

Driscoll withdrew his hand. The Walther stared the fat lad full in the face, black and stubby and evil. The sallow face of the helmsman tensed. "I seem to have left my wallet at home. You'd better leave your name and address and I'll post you a check."

The fat youth paled. Alf leaned back on his seat, in quivering disbelief. The helmsman's fist tightened like a spring on one knee.

"Yeah. Wull . . . oi s'pose tha'll be orroight. Whaddyou say, Alf?"

The fat youth slid inelegantly into the dinghy, his left leg and boot angled incongruously in the air on *Virtue*'s side in his anxiety to leave without a display of movement.

Blind Virtue began to pick up way. The tiller slapped Driscoll's thigh and he leaned into it. The scowling helmsman urged the dinghy forward to keep pace with the little boat to avoid tearing his shipmate apart.

There was a sudden commotion in the wheelhouse of the *Witch*. Water boiled at her stern as the twin screws roared and she turned her bows onto an interception course.

With elaborate care, Driscoll raised the Walther, gripped

162

the wrist of his gun hand with the fingers of his left, took aim at the floodlight mounted on the launch's wheelhouse and squeezed the trigger.

The floodlight exploded with a shower of glass and chipped steel. The launch healed to port instantly; her engines opened to full throttle and her bows lifted magnificently.

There was a scream from the pram. Driscoll flashed a look down but he was too late.

The fat youth was already in the sea, the line from the *Witch* still wound tight across his shoulders. He was on his back, head and shoulders rearing above the break of the sea, moving in reverse at a speed not far short of twenty-five knots.

From his mouth came what would have been a bellow but for the tourniquet of coiled warp.

The dinghy burst away from *Virtue*'s side in pursuit, the fair-haired young man spilling invective over his shoulder.

When Driscoll looked over *Blind Virtue*'s stern ten minutes later, the launch was an indistinct blob on the horizon, hove to and presumably disentangling the unfortunate salvagers.

Another incident he would probably have cause to regret. But not now.

Every man had the right to win, sometimes.

SATURDAY   1600

"You have had many hours and you say you have not found him?"

"Not *us*. The Palestine Liberation officials in Beirut cannot find him. There is fighting in Beirut. Heavy fighting. It is difficult for people to move from place to place."

"We shall not wait much longer. You have the lives of many people in your hands. You must bring him to us."

"We shall. I have promised that. But no aircraft can land or take off from Beirut Airport today, and until the fighting stops, we dare not risk the life of the man you want. The government in Lebanon have brought both sides together for peace talks and . . ."

"You think our brothers will talk peace with the Maronite jackals? We would rather die in the street."

"We shall all die if your brothers cannot send us the man you wish to speak with."

"You waste your time with Yasir Arafat and his gang. You must speak direct to George Habash. You must speak only to Habash."

The Home Secretary caught his upper lip with his teeth and gnawed at it absently. Habash was the leader of the Popular Front for the Liberation of Palestine, an academic who had coordinated and directed the most violent of all the groups in Middle East terrorist politics. He now lived in semi-retirement in Beirut, a father figure of some potency.

"We will try to do as you ask."

"You must do as we ask. We will wait another twenty-four hours."

SATURDAY   1700

High over Brook Street, Rear Admiral Sir Charles Wharton-Stone brooded on the mechanics of human nature.

The universal, ritual version of it was being played out below him as the last of the weekend shoppers clogged the road with their homegoing cars and the first of the evening drinkers struggled against the wind to the warmth of Claridges' bar.

Ellie had been on the telephone fifteen minutes ago with some nonsense about the Richardsons' party and how she couldn't face going alone after promising faithfully they would both be there. It was important to her, he knew that, as any evening out was important. There were precious few of them in her life. He'd told her it was impossible. She'd put the phone down on him. No arguing, no recriminations. Just that abrupt breaking of contact between them.

What did Ellie think? *Did* she ever think?

She'd lived with it long enough, but surface acceptance of the unexplainable never guaranteed anything. All his life, or the greater part of it, had been spent working toward Herrick's. From the moment he got the Naval Operations job at NATO in the mid-fifties. Quietly, zealously, he had developed and extended his Middle East identity until, in the end, they *had* to give him Middle East CAPE.

Ellie had never asked questions. She had brought up her

children single-handed and made home wherever he decreed it should be and walked her dogs and taken the kids away on holidays alone and knitted and sewn and cooked and waited. She was, he supposed, an outsider, in every sense. He had no place in her world, nor she in his.

His lip curled with self-recrimination. She was as much part of him, as separate from him, as David Driscoll. Both of them were a constant source of irritation to him; both of them took and devoured his thoughts, his time; both of them had claims on him and both of them knew that he gave to them no more than was absolutely necessary. And both of them were more important to him at this moment than they would dare to believe.

Ellie because she was sanity. Driscoll because he was salvation.

There was a hesitant knock at the door and Mrs. Lamb pushed her face around it, her spectacles dangling on black cord.

"If there's nothing else, sir," she hinted.

"Sorry, Mrs. L.," he said. "Yes, of course you can go. I'm afraid I've made a mess of your weekend." It was a lie, but he knew she would appreciate it. Mrs. Lamb was a wife in all but fact. Her husband had run off with a bus conductress from Chigwell nearly twenty years ago. Mrs. Lamb knew that Flag knew, but it was never mentioned. She had her pride.

"Will you want me in tomorrow?"

"No. Well . . ." Flag paused. "Yes, I think it would be as well, if you can manage it, Mrs. L. A nuisance, but there it is."

He had a sudden thought and called out to her as the door began to close.

"I shall be staying here tonight. Do me a favor in the morning, will you, Mrs. L.? Call my wife and ask her to pack me an overnight bag. She can have it sent round to my club. Make sure she gets it there by midday."

A Laurence Bagley painting of a twelve-meter running close-hauled in a ripping Solent sou'wester arrested him on his way back to the window.

He stared at it.

Running free.

A heavy swell rammed *Blind Virtue* amidships and the northeaster spat freezing rain into her canvas. Driscoll gave up any hope of sighting the Blakeney Overfalls buoy. Its five-second flash should have blinked out at him a good hour ago.

The mental and physical exhilaration of the *Witch* incident had worn off with chilling speed. Night had doused the sun with a hydraulic suddenness that took him completely by surprise and with the loss of vision came the panic erosion of common sense and sound practice.

He allowed his eyes the hypnotic comfort of the compass as though, in itself, it held the power of total salvation. There had to be a compass error but he had no way of judging it.

He had also chosen to ignore the leeway she must have lost in the fourteen-mile run from the Woolpack and, as the horizon closed in, he found himself straining his ears for the telltale boom of sea on coastal rock or sand. Given some sort of luck, Blakeney Point ought to be out there on the starboard quarter and hopefully four or five miles off. Sheringham Shoal should be fine on his port bow.

But he hadn't weathered the Overfalls buoy. . . .

With sudden decision, he heaved up the helm and *Blind Virtue* reared with displeasure. He sheeted in, his frozen fingers fumbling and clumsy. He tried to hold the straining craft on to 121 degrees but with the wind now moaning over her port quarter and roaring in Driscoll's left ear, the boat would have none of it. Her head took the wind and the compass writhed in agony like a virgin at an orgy.

One-two-eight degrees. One-three-four. One-three-zero.

He swore at her, smashed his foot into the cockpit sole and leaned into the tiller. It was no good.

He released one hand and let her have her way. She came around. One-three-zero degrees. Let the devil have his own.

The wind freshened, as if aware of this new opportunity for destructive advantage, and the sea lengthened its stride, lifting the stern precipitously into every trough and showering her cockpit with blown spume. If there was to be any chance at all of making good, he knew he had to hold this course.

The French coast was a long way away and there were the restricted traffic lanes of the Channel in between. Eyeless in Gaza.

The boat was racing, canvas tight as drumskins. Still one-three-zero and he was sitting there, the sitting duck again, just waiting to be pooped.

He eased himself off the cockpit locker and raised it. There had to be a drogue aboard somewhere. He found it, buried and forgotten, attached to a warp that must have been thirty fathoms long. A sea anchor wouldn't prevent a drift to leeward altogether but it might reduce it.

He checked the thimble at the conical foot of the canvas bag, tugged the four-legged bridle sewn into its sides and tested the galvanized iron ring in its mouth. It would do.

He made fast and heaved the anchor and twenty fathoms of warp over the stern. *Blind Virtue* snapped up the slack like a bull terrier. Driscoll reefed in the main and raised the tiny storm jib. The effect was comforting.

He felt his muscles relaxing as though he had been lowered slowly into a bath of warm olive oil.

Driscoll checked his watch. It showed 12:46.

This was turning out to be expensive time. The Gulf tank deal was in suspension. The Armalites sitting in a Boston warehouse were no nearer Beirut and he had only eight days left before the penalty clause took effect.

In a Lausanne warehouse, the seven hundred Sturmgewehr Model 510's were boxed and sealed awaiting delivery to Damascus. This was the first consignment of many. The machine guns were silent, expensive and very, very deadly. They represented a fortune. Diverted via South Africa and Greece in a clandestine shipment back to their country of origin, they were too hot to hold much longer.

In the arms game, time was a bomb. A day lost could blow a contract sky high.

So many clients were waiting in the wings: the American Brewer, who dealt exclusively with Indonesia through Driscoll; Manzetti, who had sewn up the East Africa trade; Heinemann, who was having a field day in Angola. How many days before the delicate mechanism of the Driscoll organization fragmented?

A light sprang on in the saloon below. The intensity of it

blinded Driscoll instantly, filling his eyes and head with dancing pain.

He screamed at the top of his voice: "Get it off! Get it off!"

The saloon plunged into darkness.

Assad appeared in the hatchway. Driscoll heard rather than saw him; his head seemed to be an echo chamber of ricocheting light.

"I am sorry. I was looking for food and water."

Driscoll shouted at him through the mental firework display: "I'll tell you when you can eat and drink. And I'm telling you this for the last time. Raise one more light on this boat and I'll put a bullet through that pin brain."

Assad protested: "I could not stay down there, doing nothing. You must be very tired. You must have food."

Driscoll rolled his eyes up to windblown heaven. He was right. He was making a habit of being right. Either that or Driscoll was beginning to like him.

"There's a bag. Wedged in the sink unit. In the galley. Get me an apple and some water. No. Wait a minute."

Assad stood spread-eagled in the hatch to keep his balance.

Driscoll shouted: "Get a bowl, a breakfast bowl or something. Slice an apple and an orange. Small. Mix 'em. Half for you—half for me. And water."

He lashed the helm again when Assad was ready and went below.

The few steps from the cockpit to the settee berth behind the table in the saloon told him that his body had taken as much as it was prepared to take without some positive promise of relief.

He dropped his head into his hands and allowed his brain to sink onto a soft cushion of semi-consciousness. He became aware of Assad's hand on his forearm, feather light, nagging. He raised his head. The bowl was invisible in the darkness but he could hear it sliding to the set of *Blind Virtue*'s bucketing roll.

He stuck his fingers into the cold, sticky preparation and began to shovel the fruit into his mouth. Citrus and apple and water. It was the worst possible diet. But the choice was simple: be seasick or starve. He felt Assad squeeze alongside him on the berth.

They ate in silence in the heaving darkness. Driscoll was aware of a strange disembodied sense of freedom, as though

168

he had withdrawn entirely from physical participation in this madness. He stopped eating.

Assad read the silence.

"If it is possible, I could take charge of the boat. I am much stronger. I have lost my sickness. I have slept while you worked."

It was so tentative it was nearly funny.

Driscoll said wearily: "Forget it."

He waited for Assad to renew the offer and when it didn't come he said: "You ever handled one of these before?"

Assad's voice grew in confidence.

"There are many things I have never done before. If you will tell me what must be done, I can follow instructions. And I shall feel much better where there is air."

Driscoll elbowed him in the ribs. "Okay. Get out of here and I'll talk you in."

He found another set of oilskins in the locker behind the companion steps and waited as Assad climbed into them. The Arab had still not found his sea legs. Driscoll wedged him into one corner of the cockpit and unlashed the helm. The first brutal kick of it took Assad unawares, but he had prepared himself for unscheduled shocks and quickly muscled the boat into submission.

Driscoll was pleasantly surprised. His body was already allowing its energy responses to become sluggish in the sweet anticipation of sleep, but he forced himself to repeat the vital statistics of watchkeeping until Assad insisted that he understood.

"If the wind shifts out of this quarter, call me. Okay? Wake me up right away. No messing."

"How will I know?"

"Oh, Jesus," Driscoll groaned.

He tried again. "If the wind stops blowing from behind your left ear, call me. If it pushes the boat over at an angle, call me. If there's a flashing light on any point—anywhere round the boat—wake me up. If you hear a foghorn or an engine or a bell, I want to know. Don't try to work it out for yourself. Got that?"

Assad raised his voice powerfully over the wind.

"I understand. Please get some sleep."

Driscoll stripped off his oilskins and got up to the fore-cabin. *Blind Virtue* rolled accommodatingly and upended him on the port vee berth. He was asleep before he touched the mattress.

The commissioner took the helicopter to Hammersmith and the waiting squad car sped him to the Belvedere Road entrance of County Hall.

He was half asleep and dizzy with pain. The duodenal ulcer he had lived with for eighteen months had woken from its pampered hibernation and was radiating hairline fractures across his abdomen and down into his loins.

He slipped a white-and-yellow tablet of Equigesac onto his tongue.

In two frantic hours, the Prime Minister's Civil Contingencies Committee had cobbled together the makings of an evacuation team. Its assembly point, the nerve center, was the council chamber at County Hall.

The Committee has a continuing, although inactive identity. Composed of thirty-five permanent high-ranking civil servants, all administrative experts of one kind or another, its function is to quantify, analyze and organize national effort in the event of a civil emergency. But the commissioner was far from comforted.

The emergency the government visualized when it breathed life into the Committee was the ultimate one: a nuclear attack. The principle of evacuation had never been a consideration. The Committee's role was based on establishing a code for survival—not arming itself against a holocaust. God alone knew what they thought they could do in this situation.

The Commander, Civil Affairs, met him at the door of the council chamber and they went inside. The huge tiered, paneled room was echoing with noise. Some thirty or forty men and women had collected in a group on the sunken floor of the chamber beneath the raised desks of the chairman and officers of the council.

A dozen Post Office engineers were burrowing into cable channels in the floor to install more telephones, and a teleprinter bank had been set up on hastily erected steel trestles. On the far right of the chamber, a police telecommunications team had already completed a temporary RT transceiver unit.

The commissioner strode over to it.

"Can you get me through to the Heathrow command room on this?" he snapped.

A plainclothes officer keyed in and presented a headset. The commissioner sank gratefully into a chair and called the Special Patrol Group at the airport. He waited for them to find the deputy assistant commissioner.

"Gerald? I'm at County Hall. Any reports yet from your evacuation units?"

"Yes, sir. None of it good. We were able to put two hundred men on the streets immediately in Stanwell and East Bedfont, nearest the plane. They've covered most of the houses in that corner, but it hasn't helped not being able to use loudspeaker cars. They've met a lot of resistance, I'm afraid."

"What d'you mean—resistance?"

"People won't leave their homes, sir. We've literally had to winkle them out and drive them to the reception areas. It's taking a damned sight longer than we can afford. I'm getting reports from some of the mobiles that officers are having to go back three and four times to the same house to persuade people to leave."

"We knew that was likely."

"Yes, sir. But we didn't anticipate the worst. I'm told that two dozen or more families have barricaded themselves in. If we're going to have to break into every damn house, it'll take the whole day to clear this area alone."

"You know the answer to that," retorted the commissioner. "I want this line kept open. Keep me posted. And get that area cleared."

It was unfair of him, he knew, but if civilian resistance snowballed across the board in the semi-suburbia of Stanwell, any attempt at a mass evacuation of West London was doomed to total failure.

As it was, the temporary reception areas nominated by the Contingencies Committee could not hope to function for more than twenty-four hours without being overwhelmed. For the twentieth time in the past three hours, the commissioner tortured himself with a mental picture of the chaos.

One hundred thousand men, women and children, their cats and dogs, out on the snowbound streets, milling and protesting in massive disorder. Fleets of closed police vans and trucks; commandeered army and civilian trucks, buses and coaches; private cars, motorcycles and scooters—thousands of vehicles strung across miles of the A3 and the feeder-road network of West London.

Somehow, all of them would have to be channeled along specially selected routes to the immediate reception areas; the civil airports at Kidlington, Oxford, Luton in Bedfordshire, and Elstree in Hertfordshire.

And that was just the beginning.

As the day wore on and pressure mounted on the facilities at these points, traffic would be diverted to the old Battle of Britain airfield at Biggin Hill.

It was just not good enough and everybody knew it.

The Home Secretary had spent an hour on a conference line linking him with Downing Street and the Contingencies Committee already established in the High Holborn deep shelter. Their hastily hatched provisional emergency plan was subject to refinement and redevelopment as the situation progressed—or regressed, thought the commissioner moodily.

Stage Two of the plan was a proposal to funnel evacuees from the airports to the near-derelict camps last used in 1974 to house the Asian immigrants banished from Uganda by Idi Amin. There were sixteen such centers available for immediate, if comfortless, occupation and they could handle around twenty thousand evacuees; but the support operation necessary to house and feed the people was still merely a scribbled note in one corner of the grand design.

When the camps were full . . .

Not for the first time since his appointment, the commissioner cursed the amateurism of the whole counter-terrorist machine. Too little, too late, too cheaply.

The miners' strike of 1972, ludicrously, had set the ball rolling. Even then the government was thinking only in terms of protecting itself against domestic squabbles. Terrorism was a bunch of micks raising hell in Ulster.

The real aim had been to coordinate national defenses in the event of violent picketing, the kind that led to the closure of the Saltley coke depot near Birmingham that year. Six thousand miners had massed at the gates of the depot to stop trucks loaded with supplies of fuel from leaving for power stations starved of direct supplies from the mines. The chief constable of Birmingham had withdrawn his seven hundred men when it became obvious they could not match the muscle power and determination of the strikers.

The Prime Minister of the day had been appalled at this blatant collapse of law and order and astonished that there
172

were no contingency plans for military assistance to the police.

But the Committee of Inquiry he appointed under Lord Jellicoe had barely set its feet under the table when the Palestinian terrorist assault on Israeli athletes at the Munich Olympics shattered all conventional thinking on state security.

Jellicoe's brief was promptly widened.

The police had jealously protected their pre-eminence as defenders of the civil realm. While acknowledging their need of army support, particularly against the new breed of sophisticated and ruthless international terrorists, they had been quick to point out that they could still act more swiftly, more effectively in emergency situations.

Unlike the Army, they didn't need ministerial sanction to pull the trigger.

They had their priorities straight now.

The Army and the SAS regiment at Hereford, in particular, had proven its unassailable superiority in a tight corner. They were good. How good, the next few hours would put to a punishing test.

But that wasn't the commissioner's problem. Not now.

The Civil Contingencies Committee was another brontosaurus born of civil disobedience. Its members, in discussion with the Cabinet, could authorize three critical lines of defense.

MACP, or Military Aid to the Civil Power, was the device that had brought the SAS from Hereford to Heathrow. A number of specialized military units were on call under an MACP operation but only in cases of armed terrorism.

MACC, Military Aid to the Civil Community, released the Army's medical, engineering, ordnance and telecommunications services for disaster relief.

MACM, Military Aid to the Civil Ministries, permitted troops, transport and equipment to be drafted in to maintain essential services during a strike.

In some form, all those categories had to be brought into play in the next forty-eight hours. If there *was* that much time.

As of 0400 that morning, the National Emergency Contingency Plan had been in operation. So high was its security classification that fewer than fifty people in the country knew its specifications.

At 0625 on the Day of Judgment, that was a terrifying fact to swallow.

SUNDAY   1100

The Home Secretary called the Trident from the tower control room. The young terrorist leader answered immediately. A good sign.

The deadline was four o'clock but the speed of his reaction suggested that with five hours to go he was already strapped into the headset.

"We have spoken with an intermediary—a contact—of George Habash. Great efforts are now being made to send a group of your brothers from Beirut to find the representative of the PLO in London."

"You lie! There is no need to bring this man to us if you have talked to George Habash. Habash will send one of our brothers to us now. Tell him to send Abou-Khaled or Abou-Ahmad."

"I must write these names down."

"I repeat them. Abou-Khaled or Abou-Ahmad."

"They are friends of yours, these men?"

"You cannot trap me. The names will mean nothing to you. They will have meaning only for George Habash."

"They are code names for your brothers?"

"I will not talk more. You must act quickly."

SUNDAY   1200

At the evacuation center in County Hall, the Incident File was already three times thicker than the Street Clearance Roll.

In the first five hours of carefully logged police activity, forty-seven children had been reported lost; eighteen men and three women had been arrested on charges varying from assault and battery to obstruction; twenty-seven homes had been forcibly entered to remove reluctant families; thirty-five vehicle breakdowns and nine road accidents had halted
174

main traffic flow for a total of fifty-five minutes; three household fires had broken out, one as a result of burning fat
from a deserted breakfast frying pan; one baby had been
born prematurely in the back seat of a Ford Escort saloon
car; and the Hounslow police had detained eight looters
posing as local-authority safety officers.

Main roads from the area were so jammed that county
police forces within a twenty-mile radius had been ordered
to empty the London-bound lanes of all motorways and
trunk roads; evacuation traffic was now given priority on
all carriageway lanes.

Word of the exodus had grown like pandemic cholera.
Mainline railway stations were inundated with travelers willing to buy tickets anywhere, but frenzied attempts to marshal
operating staff, drivers and rolling stock were still in the
early stages.

The skeleton Sunday shifts had been overwhelmed by
nine o'clock.

The temperature had dropped to three degrees Centigrade, light snow was falling, the wind was in the northeast
and lunch dominated the waking thoughts of a million snug
homes.

The Sunday papers were as predictable as ever and, at
two minutes past midday, Jean Challis introduced "Family
Favourites" on Radio Two.

For some it was still just another Sunday.

SUNDAY   1700

The beginning of the end was bizarre.

On the M4, just two miles west of the main-gate approach
to Heathrow, a man recently expelled from his home in
Spinney Drive, East Bedfont, stalled his Ford Taunus in
the middle lane of the westbound highway. He got out and
raised the hood to locate the fault.

He failed.

A police motorcyclist using the sidewalk and shoulders
as an emergency road, stopped to give assistance. His patience
gave out and this led to argument.

The driver's wife intervened and, according to the subsequent Incident Report, claimed that the policeman pushed her.

Her husband grasped the policeman around the waist and flung him to the ground. The officer bounded to his feet and arrested the driver.

More blows were exchanged and the two men fell to the ground, shouting and wrestling.

All traffic stopped.

In a matter of minutes, other drivers left their cars and formed a ring around the combatants.

From the van tumbled five children, all of them under ten, all of them cold and hungry, all of them frightened. Their screams of fright and their wailing harmonized with the squeals of their mother.

The crowd grew, and its tension hardened into animosity. The events of early morning, the enforced awakenings, the dragooning by overworked officialdom, the growing resentment against uniformed authority, exploded in one mighty outburst.

It was impossible, later, to piece together the sequence of events. All that was clear to the evacuation center at precisely 1726 was that the entire westward flow of vehicles stopped.

By 1735, mobile patrols reported that thousands of men, women and children were pouring back to their homes along roads, over fields and recreation grounds bordering the M4.

They left their cars where they stood.

Initial appeals to them to return were ignored.

Many of them were singing "Show Me the Way to Go Home."

SUNDAY   1730

The briefing had been called for five o'clock and the waiting men railed at the Press Secretary's tacit refusal to explain why they had been ordered to No. 10 at such short notice—or why they were being kept waiting.

National newspaper editors are unaccustomed to the role of acolyte and obedient silence sits uneasily on them. For the men in the room, time wasted at such an advanced stage of the day was priceless.

Latest copy time for first-edition front pages was nine-twenty and this urgent summons clearly had front-page implications. A thick cloud of cigar and cigarette smoke rose to the level of the chandeliers and sat there like mist in a Highland glen.

The Prime Minister arrived at last, spilling apologies and first-name greetings. The agitation diminished measurably, a striking example of the palliative effect he exercised among newspapermen.

He had, over the years, both in government and opposition, achieved a finely balanced relationship with the editors of Fleet Street which defied rational analysis. In public speeches, he affected to despise them; he had given the word "media" a despotic definition that served him well as an instrument of justification.

In private, however, he distributed his patronage meagerly, but with unerring accuracy. He cultivated his friendships beyond the coarse milieu of working politics and maintained a broadly detailed file on journalists' domestic backgrounds, anniversaries, birthdays and children.

He seated himself at the table facing them and dug immediately into a pocket for his pipe and tobacco. It was an integral part of his I-am-but-one-of-you persona projection. It was a stability factor.

"I must ask you all to forgive me, gentlemen. I apologize for the delay, but as I'm sure you know, I'm dealing with a situation here that is quite unprecedented."

He realized he was slipping into characteristic platform doggerel and silently reprimanded himself. Keep it friendly. Keep it intimate.

"Now, I know you've all had a busy day."

He waited for their smiles to break and went on, encouraged.

"I can see you want answers and I'm sorry we've had to cold-shoulder your reporters and your lobby men all day. I've called this meeting to invite . . . to *appeal* for your help. In the national interest."

He studied them intently. The first inevitable frowns settled over the two rows of faces.

"But first—an explanation."

That was better. Curiosity is an ally.

"Briefly: The death of General Landis on Monday was, as some of you were quick to point out, a natural springboard for retaliation. I think four of you carried stories last

Tuesday morning suggesting that Israel would undoubtedly make air strikes or commando raids on the usual Palestinian targets in the Lebanon. I think it's to the great credit of the Israelis that they haven't done so.

"My own concern was closer to home. The man who shot General Landis is in custody and still seriously ill—which may answer some of the questions you've all aired this past week. He's not yet fit enough to be formally charged in court. However . . ."

He allowed the word to float, studying the anticipation it precipitated in his audience.

"My concern, as I've said, was the possibility of another kind of retaliation. A retaliation to secure the release of this man by his own kind."

He paused dramatically. "That retaliation has come."

If he had expected a stirring of excitement, he was disappointed. A dozen pairs of eyes examined him shrewdly. No one spoke.

"I had hoped, initially, that we could contain this—er—retaliation. In view of today's events—and I'm sure you all plan extensive coverage of the chaos of the past twelve hours—I can see no likelihood of containment. What I cannot permit, under any circumstances, is an outbreak of national hysteria. Equally, I must leave my hands free to deal with a desperate situation in whatever form is expedient."

A graying, hunched man in his late forties broke in gently.

"Perhaps it would help, Prime Minister, if you were to tell us exactly what the situation is."

"Of course. Shortly after midnight on Thursday a British Airways jet landed at Heathrow. It was on a scheduled flight from Amsterdam. I'm afraid I can't go into detail—I'm sure you understand. That plane is carrying a group of Palestinian terrorists. They claim to have a nuclear explosive device on board."

He had them this time. Sprawling figures pushed upright in their chairs. Heads inclined instinctively to watches.

"Let me say quickly, gentlemen, that we are not dealing in supposition. We have been able to send an expert aboard the plane and he was permitted to examine the device. There is no doubt that it is some form of atomic device and we must accept, in theory at least, that it can be detonated."

"May I ask why this was not revealed earlier, sir?" asked

a donnish editor. His frameless spectacles glittered pugnaciously.

"Containment, as I said, was our primary objective. I considered it essential to delay any formal announcement until the last possible moment."

"And that moment has been passed?"

"It has. I hoped we could resolve the problem with the least amount of civil disturbance. Unfortunately, the one prerequisite of a defensive strategy was that we should be in a position to evacuate an area of ten miles around Heathrow. We have to concede, now, that that isn't possible."

"With respect, sir," began a crumpled, overweight man in heavy horn-rims, "we might have been in a position to help if we'd been informed. The evacuation at East Bedfont today—I assume that's what it was—was a disaster. I can't speak for the others, but my own paper's interpretation of the chaos out there today is pretty close to the facts. If anything, our assumptions were far worse than the facts."

"I accept that possibility," said the Prime Minister coolly. "But I still believe I was right to attempt a solution without publicity. And that brings me to my reason for asking you all here this evening. I said I was appealing for help. I am. That's why I've been completely honest with you. I recognize you can't ignore the situation and I won't insult you by suggesting you either suppress or distort it.

"What I do ask of you is that you don't reveal in your stories the fact that the device on board that aircraft is an atomic bomb."

There was a stir of movement along the rows of chairs.

"How long would the embargo last, sir?"

"You don't expect me to answer that, surely. I can only judge on the public's reaction to your stories tomorrow."

The horn-rimmed man in the front row said petulantly: "Can we expect some *official* quotes from you, then, on the situation at Heathrow? Something attributable."

The Prime Minister frowned.

"No—I can't do that. Not yet. I want to be sure that bomb is under control before I talk on the record."

The donnish editor said politely: "Can we at least get nearer the aircraft than the main road, sir? Even if it's on a rota basis."

The Prime Minister bunched the lower half of his face angrily.

"Out of the question. You must know that. What do you
179

expect me to do in a situation like this? Let you stand out there in full sight of the plane taking pictures?"

SUNDAY 2100

So far, so good.

It had taken two minutes of bluff and bluster at the police checkpoint before they let him through, but it had been worth every second.

Get me your commanding officer, get me the CGS, the Commissioner, Airport Control. He had challenged them and gambled they would contact no one.

And if the letter of approval he had waved was not exactly what it at first glance seemed, as always he had got what he wanted.

He made his way across the airport lounge, a short stocky figure made broader by the kapok-filled parka; small, bright eyes glittering above a full, badly trimmed beard. A scrum forward ill at ease in marble halls. He set his face with a look of surly authority.

A flak-jacketed soldier nursing an Armalite eyed the new-comer uncertainly, guessed wrongly and half saluted. He nodded and strode out onto the apron.

The plane lay in the distance like a stranded whale, bathed in a cocoon of unwavering white light from beacons placed at four points near the emergency pad.

Beautiful. Just beautiful.

He tore at the lining of the thickly padded shoulders of the parka and slid the object carefully into the palm of his hand.

He breathed deeply, letting the cold night air stabilize his nerves. Leaning against a wall, he checked the heel of his shoe. The three-inch wedge slid to one side, revealing a small, crudely hollowed compartment.

It would do.

A voice called from the darkness away to his right and was answered by a muffled grunt. The patois of soldiers. He moved along the wall.

The long hours in the pub, the endless rounds of drinks, the patient sifting of disconnected small talk to make meaningful fact. It had all paid off. They were there, exactly as the chatterers said they would be; a line of army jeeps on standby, waiting for the swoop.

It took only seconds to stroll over to one and climb behind the wheel.

If it goes wrong, it goes wrong now.

He waited for the shout, the click of a drawn bolt, but none came.

The key was in the ignition. He turned it.

Nothing. Keep calm.

He tried again. If they were poised for a quick assault it made no sense to immobilize the vehicles. And why leave the keys?

Then it hit him; the jeep was trembling, its muffled engine pulsing faster than his own heart. He slid it into gear and released the clutch. He began to move, heading for the pool of light.

"Jesus Christ!"

The sergeant trained his night glasses through the slit window of the corrugated maintenance hut commandeered as a forward observation post.

"There's something moving out there. Here!"

He flung the glasses to a corporal and grabbed the portable radio transmitter.

"Heathrow One? This is Darrow on Green Four. What the hell's going on? There's a jeep out there. Shouldn't somebody have told us something?"

He bent his knees to peer through the slit window into the darkness. Covering the mouthpiece of the transmitter, he grated at the corporal: "Bloody marvelous, if we'd shot the bastard colonel!"

The speaker crackled.

"Darrow, Green Four. This is Heathrow One. Vehicle is monitored. Stand by. Move only on orders. Out!"

"Bloody marvelous!" muttered Darrow.

Less than three hundred yards now. Easy, easy. Smooth and easy.

The jeep approached the Trident from the rear, its engine shuddering defiantly as the speedometer danced on seventy. It would take a platoon to catch him at this speed, even in the blinding light playing over the plane.

Slow down, now.

He took one hand from the wheel and raised the tiny Olympus camera to his eye.

He touched the shutter button; the motor drive whirred into play . . . one, two, three, four, five, six. Every one a winner. The whole length of the plane in six frames.

The ice crackled and hissed under the wheels as he pulled the jeep right onto the perimeter runway, and pressed his foot hard on the accelerator.

Starting price for this one was twenty grand.

No question. Fleet Street first. Then *Time, Paris-Match* and television.

Move over, Zapruder; farewell, Robert Capa!

One-handed, he took the exposed film from the camera and slotted it into the hollowed heel of his shoe. The jeep swerved wildly as he fed a fresh reel into the Olympus. This one the Army could keep.

He never knew what hit him.

Streaking along its remote-control beam, the Blowpipe guided missile took the jeep side on, lifting it bodily into the air. Man and machine became a whirling fireball, spewing fragments of hot metal and oil and blood into the snow.

Momentarily, a blazing human shape cartwheeled into space, arms and legs splayed grotesquely, a thin plume of smoke trailing from its heels. It plopped into the snow at the end of its pirouette, still clutching the camera.

Behind the sandbagged embrasure on the perimeter fence a hundred yards away, an officer spoke swiftly into a transmitter.

Alongside him, a sergeant eased his thumb from the guidance button and lowered the smoking launch canister. He propped the weapon in its carrying frame and stared across the snow at the guttering beacon of flame.

A hand reached out and grasped his arm firmly.

"Nice shooting, Sergeant," said the officer.

"Bang on."

In the control tower, the Home Secretary slammed down the phone that linked him with the forward command post. The nervous twitch that habitually pulled his mouth into a diagonal slit jumped uncontrollably. He was a man who regarded display of emotion as intellectual weakness. At the age of fifty-seven, he was no longer able to reduce anger and frustration to mere electrical flexing of the brain. He was ashamed of himself.

He took the CGS to one side.

"I want the name of the man responsible for that act of"—the overwhelming anger bubbled up in him and nearly overflowed—"idiot *barbarism*, Philip. I want his officer's name and I'll make it my personal business to . . . to . . ."

His hand strayed up to his mouth and he quelled the twitch with savage fingers.

The CGS hesitated, embarrassed momentarily by the passion of this quiet man and the animated working of his face.

"Yes, I know," he said gently. "But they weren't to know. Until we can identify the body, we can't be sure who the devil he is. He could've been one of theirs. Or some crank with a rifle. He could've sent the whole lot of us to kingdom come."

The Home Secretary had clasped his hands in an attempt to repress their shaking. His voice hovered between rationality and frenzy.

"He was a photographer. We know that. They've found the camera. Some suicidal fool out for a con*founded* scoop, I suppose. But don't you see—it doesn't matter *what* he is. He's dead and there can't be a soul for miles who didn't see or hear that rocket hit him. It's only a matter of hours now before the whole world will know what's happening here."

He walked a few yards, wringing his hands vexedly, then returned. He was unaware that he had even moved.

"I'm telling you, Philip, your *damned* people have ruined everything."

The CGS was uncertain.

"Well, I wouldn't say it's as bad as that. We can still . . ."

The Home Secretary waved wildly.

"*Everything.* You can't kill a man in cold blood in the middle of a civil airport and expect to keep it quiet. It's finished, Philip. Finished. We're out in the open now."

SUNDAY   2400

There was no theme to the dream, just the rise and fall of some shapeless menace and whipping shrieks of discordant sound and the icy touch of Death on his flesh.

Driscoll came awake falling, falling.

His body and head and arms and legs struck solid, unyielding reality and struck again. It took a whole minute to
recover from the shock and adjust his eyes and his ears to
the surroundings.

The forecabin was like the antechamber to hell. Blood
spurted from his right hand where the cutting edge of the
radar reflector had stabbed him in his fall from the berth.
The cabin sole was awash; maybe three or four inches deep.
The stench of diluted vomit was everywhere.

He pulled himself to his feet.

The neat orange berth palliasses from the saloon were
swinging fore and aft along the cabin sole on an agonized
tide of bilge water. Careening with them were pieces of
smashed crockery, pulped apples and oranges, paper bags,
books and—dear God!—the charts.

He bent to grab the corner of one sodden sheet and the
boat reared on her heel and the paper parted in his hand.
He fell into the swirling scum and swept the debris from
the sheet and wrestled it from the water.

It was Stanford's "General Chart of the Southern North
Sea," and it was beyond salvage. He stuck it to the heaving
chart table and stared down at it helplessly.

The shivering brought him back to life. His body was a
mass of vibrating nerve; the thick gray sweater he wore and
the corduroy jeans were saturated and freezing. Salt had
rubbed blisters into every aching contact point with his skin.

He looked around for the suit of weatherproofs he had
shrugged off. They lay under the companion steps, drowning.
He pulled them on.

The hatch was shut. He pushed at it. It held fast. He
turned his shoulder and smashed at the swollen woodwork.
He tried again and again. It gave, without warning, in one
groaning, ripping collapse and he fell forward onto the
cockpit draining boards.

He thought the Arab was dead.

He looked up into Assad's face and it stared back owlishly,
unseeing, into his. The face that had been the color of worn
leather was caked white with salt. From out of it, the nose
glowed like a beacon and the brown eyes stared, red-rimmed,
as though they had been transfixed by the ultimate vision.
The body slumped forward at an angle of forty-five degrees,
the tiller enclosed in the left armpit, an arm and a hand
clamped to it as if carved in stone.

184

Driscoll threw himself onto the port seat and braced his right arm over Assad's.

He was alive.

He checked the compass. Course 126 magnetic. He reached out and rubbed caked salt from the face of the anemometer on the cockpit coaming.

The reading shocked him: forty knots of wind. Force Nine.

The sea was a yellowish-grayish green, streaked with foam and rioting with white horses. The waves were breaking badly, mountainous and threatening, twelve to fifteen feet high.

He turned to check the stern warp that held the sea anchor. It was gone.

Driscoll leaned into the tiller; Assad, rock still as a graven image, resisted every millimeter of movement. He was functioning now on pure instinct, on a primitive reflex to survive. Driscoll shouted into his ear, but it had no effect.

Slowly, Driscoll forced the deadweight of Assad's hand and arm back along the tiller until he had leverage. *Blind Virtue* came around to 124 degrees.

The sky was black with spitting cloud and freezing rain thrashed the water in the cockpit as though it harbored a school of feeding piranha.

Visibility was down to less than a couple of yards. He thought: If there's land out there, I won't know about it till we hit.

He bent his mind to the wave pattern.

A half dozen near-vertical monsters, pursued by three or four quieter, smoother hillocks, then a half dozen short ones that beat a staccato rat-a-tat-tat on *Blind Virtue*'s bottom to prepare her for the next round of raging combers.

He settled himself and the boat into the pattern and felt some of the old confidence returning. She would hold out, the bouncy little cow. She'd hold out. He gripped the tiller in the vise of armpit and hand and turned to Assad.

He never made it. He heard the sound building up over his left shoulder like the run of a fast-burning fuse.

His eye caught the spuming crest as it slid off the top of the rogue wave, but there was no time to move. The roar engulfed heart, mind, body and boat.

Blind Virtue reared like a mustang, turned side on and rolled down the wave. The mass of water that filled the cockpit erupted back into the sea and the drains gurgled angrily.

Driscoll grabbed Assad by the shoulders and felt for the harness he had buckled on. It held firm. He leaned back into the wind and prepared to raise himself and the lid of the port locker to withdraw his own harness.

The sea was not done with him.

A galloping roar grew on the port beam.

The boat rose sickeningly, as if trying in one final act of desperation to escape the clutching sea altogether; then with a helpless drunken roll she crashed down on her beam in a torrent of exploding water.

Driscoll flung himself upward and grabbed the guardrail above him in an attempt to reach Assad, but he was gone.

The following wave roared gleefully in for the kill and plunged down on them from behind. Driscoll's head smashed into the swinging tiller and his world erupted with light.

Assad was head down in the water, his harness taut and strumming behind him.

Again the sea attacked from astern. Again the hissing became a hollow pause, then exploded like an atomic warhead on an oil refinery.

All thought of Assad evaporated. Every single roaring, cascading second stretched into infinity. Driscoll could feel his fingers slipping on the guardrail. The sea was sucking him down.

The noise stopped.

The coldness slid from his hands and his body and penetrated his mind. He thought quite casually: Assad may still be alive.

He touched a coiled line thrashing in the water under the submerged hatch door and grabbed it and strung it through his leather belt and bent it onto the guardrail.

Another wave blitzed *Blind Virtue* but Driscoll neither heard it nor felt it.

He lay into the line and it held; took a firm grip of Assad's straining harness with both hands and heaved. There should have been no strength in him but Assad came up, bleeding water.

Driscoll clutched him to his chest. He fought the tiller into a hugging position across Assad's chest and made it fast to the guardrail with the end of his own safety line.

No sound. No feeling. No movement.

The sea had gone away and taken the pain and the fury

with it. Assad would be all right. They would both be all right now. He couldn't move but he didn't want to move. They would be all right now.

Then he lost consciousness.

MONDAY   0530

The noise came back but it was no longer cold. Driscoll's body was warm and dry and cocooned in indescribable softness.

He could not see because there was something over his eyes; over the place where the pain was, where the tiller had struck his head. It didn't matter. He didn't want to see; just feel.

The noise was not the voice of the sea any more. That was curious. It was a pump-pump-pump-pumping sound, regular as breathing; solid and sure and man-made. Engines. Powerful engines.

He flexed his fingers and gauged the texture of the cocoon around him. Sheets. Blankets. He tried to raise his head but the pain was horrendous and, as he strained upward, the nausea surged from his stomach into his throat and he fell back.

A door snapped open and slammed hard shut. He felt a hand on his, a finger on his pulse. It put his hand down on the soft sheet and took his head and moved it left and right.

The voice made words, but Driscoll couldn't frame them. He shook his head. This voice must be made to understand.

The words changed. "Français—heh?"

Driscoll shook his head again.

"Anglitsch?"

Driscoll nodded.

"To dying very close you come, mister. Der boad ist kaput, heh?"

Driscoll gritted his teeth.

"Assad. Is he . . . ?"

"Der udder? He lif. He lif just."

Driscoll closed his eyes and the warm soft sheets seduced him back into unconsciousness.

The Dutchman stared down at him, lifted his battered peaked cap and scratched his head.

Why was this man smiling?
Mad Anglitsch.

MONDAY   1300

"This is 'The World at One.' "

The racketing signature tune gave the man at the microphone ten seconds for a final check with the producer in the control room.

He coughed his throat clear and settled himself.

The producer's raised hand cued him in.

"We are extending the program today by fifteen minutes to broadcast an important statement by the Prime Minister on the Heathrow Airport emergency declared this morning. We go over right away to No. 10 Downing Street. The Prime Minister . . ."

MONDAY   1330

Duquesne waited anxiously until Flag stumped away to lunch. From the window on the third-floor landing, he watched him cross Brook Street, stop at a tobacconist to buy his daily ounce of shag, then amble comfortably to Claridges. When he disappeared, Duquesne turned resolutely and climbed the stairs to Hugh Davidson's office on the fourth floor.

He was already regretting this. Integrity had always seemed to him a simple credo: it was that which you gave unto Caesar. Integrity was loyalty and you owed loyalty to only one master. Flag was master. Now it wasn't so easy any more.

But Hugh Davidson would understand.

Garth Duquesne was twenty-six, and a former Princeton forward, big as a house and bright as a pin. He had majored in economics and political philosophy and made Phi Beta Kappa. The CIA had kept an eye on him in his last year and snapped him up before science or law or Wall Street could get off the mark.

He was old-style All-American: crisp, clean, godly.

Flag had won Duquesne in an adroit game of nip-and-tuck with Walter Stoll, his opposite number in Washington. It came some months after Watergate had bloomed on every front page in the world; eighteen months before the CIA itself was put under an electron microscope by a Senate investigating committee.

Stoll was Navy, too. He and Flag had an understanding: they "got on." A year ago, Stoll had requested a face-to-face and he and Flag played three rounds at Troon over a long weekend.

Walter's outfit had sprung a leak. Not a bad one and not too high up the classification ladder, but it threw a lot of unsavory smells all over his middle-management structure and he was nervous.

Two things he didn't need: an interservice court of inquiry and/or the threat of a congressional witch hunt. He wanted peace and quiet and the assistance of friends.

His suggestion was a bold one: a student exchange scheme. One of ours for one of yours. A three-year contract, all on the up and up.

But what London sent Walker would be a walking, breathing memory bank, a files man, a ferret who could be dropped into the Records Building and left to hunt the rabbit.

In return, London would get a first-rate field operative, a little rough around the edges, but a man with style and ingenuity who could do the same job for Flag as the ferret would do for Walter.

It was a deal.

Duquesne had been flung by the scruff of his shaven neck into Willoughby's records department and the dust hadn't settled yet.

His baptism of fire had been a bottom-to-top re-evaluation of every filed personnel sheet in the cave that ran under Herrick's. Reputations had been won and lost; sacred cows had been put to the sword: Lotharios had proved to be mere men with penises of clay.

All this, yet Duquesne had never once broken faith with Flag because that would have meant breaking faith with himself.

So far, he had weeded out a couple of dubious clerks, married queers who had duly been hunted down and caught holding hands in a pub near Charing Cross; and a payroll clerk who had been moonlighting in a Soho amusement arcade.

Hugh Davidson was the first, and only, purely social contact he had made at Herrick's. They occasionally dined together; Davidson had proposed him at the Traveller's Club in Pall Mall and Hurlingham; they had a twice-weekly squash game and they never burdened one another with shoptalk.

Davidson beamed at him as Duquesne knocked and entered.

"Garth?"

"I need to talk, Hugh. Something's come up. I don't think I can handle it."

"Sit down, old chap." Davidson waved hospitably. "What's the problem?"

The young American's blue eyes clouded.

"I guess maybe it's nothing. I'm getting twitchy in my old age. Fact is, I should be telling this to Flag."

Davidson raked him with his opal eyes.

"And why aren't you, Garth?"

Duquesne ruffled his short yellow hair agitatedly. "Because . . ." He stopped, suddenly formal. "Well, sir, in the last few weeks, Flag asked me to chauffeur him around quite a bit. He's been meeting a guy. Outside the organization. Maybe six or seven times, but more important, last Tuesday, after the Landis shooting. They met off limits; this last time it was the Science Museum."

"So?" Davidson murmured.

"The guy's on the RPL. I checked it. Recognized his picture."

"Who is it?"

"I'd rather not say, sir."

"But if he's on the Restricted Persons List . . ."

"I'd have to face Flag with it first."

"So why are you talking to me?"

Duquesne breathed heavily through his teeth.

"I need advice. Something else I've turned up. Flag put me on to a close scrutiny of the personnel master files a year ago."

He said it in a rush. Davidson grinned steadily, but only with his lips.

"Only Flag was in on it and I did a provisional run-through. Coupla months back, Flag asked me to concentrate

190

a second time on Executive members and section chiefs only."

He shrugged uncomfortably.

"Everything's fine—except for one file."

He slid a buff folder from under his arm and opened it on the corner of the desk in front of him.

"And why can't you show this to Flag?"

"It's not a case of can't. It's—well, maybe you should judge for yourself."

Davidson leaned deep into his chair.

"Tell me about this . . . file."

"Well, sir. I got a complete breakdown on the guy. Running through schools and university and periodic surveillance assessments and so forth. But I get to look closely at the family and there's no birth certificate. I check back with Central Records and they have no copy either, but they got everything else—medical health records as a child, that kinda thing."

Davidson chuckled.

Duquesne looked puzzled.

"This is *basic*, sir.

"Anyway, I put the usual request in to Somerset House. Zilch! Fact One: there *is* no birth certificate. I go to the local authority—that's Coventry, sir—and I get the whole thing. No birth certificate because the subject was adopted. No information available on the adoption because the city's records were destroyed in the bombing during the war. I checked out all the adoption agencies in the country; all of 'em. No record of the subject being offered for adoption."

Davidson sat forward in his chair.

"Then I get a slab of luck dropped in my lap. The subject's adoptive father was a registered special constable during the war. The local police dig up his file and backtrack. The guy was an alien. Austrian. Came to Britain 1929. Name of Stroessner, Kurt Stroessner, which he changed in 1938 by deed poll when he gets his naturalization. I get the police to follow up on the family background—friends, neighbors. We were lucky.

"They find a Mr. Harry Groom, age seventy-six; knew Stroessner; remembered him and his wife taking the kid.

"The subject was age four when he came to England in 1938. The genetic father, as far as Groom could remember, was a German businessman. Just that. A businessman. Period. Well, sir. I checked that through with the West Germans in Bonn and they give me a selection of ten thousand kids it might have been and a million parents who might have snuck their children to England."

Davidson watched the serious young face.

"What did you do then?"

"Well, sir—I was kinda surprised nobody'd done this degree of follow-up before. Jesus, sir—no birth certificate!

"Anyway, I contact a guy I know in NATO command structure records—he's an old class buddy of mine. All I ask him was this: How do I finger a prewar German family, a man and woman, who were separated from their son?"

Davidson was there before the boy spilled the words.

"Right that moment, I coulda kicked myself. It's so darned obvious, you don't see it. He said: Try the Jews. They got the biggest damn list of motherless sons you ever saw.

"First thing I did was check out Simon Weisenthal's people in Vienna. They put me on to some guys in Bonn and—Bingo!—home and dry.

"A coupla ladies"—he flicked more file sheets—"here—Ellalina and Gerda Stroessner—laid claim before the War Reparations Court in 1948, '52, '55 and again in '58. Nothing after that and they don't seem to have gotten anywhere. They entered a claim to their brother Franz Stroessner's home, possessions, land and cash residue amounting to, let's see, about two million pounds.

"Stroessner was a director of the Bank of Rhineland-Westphalia, a collector of old masters, a landowner, big philanthropist."

Davidson stopped looking at Duquesne. His focus lengthened into infinity.

He said slowly: "Are you going to tell me that the father survived the war?"

"No, sir, he did not," said Duquesne. "All the documents are here, mostly the unofficial ones the Jewish committees tried to keep in the death camps."

"Death camps?"

Davidson could hear the small brass clock beating away the seconds over by the bookcase.

"Oh, yes, sir. Franz Stroessner and his wife were both liquidated. September 1942. By gas. Auschwitz. They were Jews, sir."

Jews. The phrase crystallized in Davidson's mind: the Children of Israel. Son of Stroessner—Child of Israel.

Duquesne persisted: "The son of butchered Jews, sir. A

man like that—well, sir, if he had any loyalties, I guess they'd be with the Israelis. It's a possibility."

Davidson wasn't listening. He didn't have to look at the name on the file. But he still couldn't believe it.

MONDAY   1700

Sharland was clearly on the brink of collapse. His voice was muffled with waking sleep but he reacted automatically to the call from the tower.

"Sharland. I read you. I have . . ."

The young Palestinian broke in. His voice, too, was beginning to display signs of breakdown. The exhaustion must be engulfing them all.

"You have news of my brothers?"

The Home Secretary shook his head, as though the young man were sitting across the console from him.

"We are in hourly communication with Beirut. The airport there is still closed."

"This is a lie!"

The young man was assailed by a mix of panic and anger.

"Fighting in the city would not delay takeoff from the airport. You lie to me."

"I dare not lie to you. This is too important. You must believe that. I do not lie."

"George Habash. Have you spoken again with George Habash?"

"No—not George Habash. But we have a message from Captain Ali of the PFLP."

"Captain Ali?"

"You know his name? You know Captain Ali?"

"I will listen."

"Captain Ali is in personal charge of this project now. He has Abou-Khaled at his side. Do you understand?"

"I am listening."

"They will leave for the airport as soon as darkness falls. That is Captain Ali's message."

"And when will they fly?"

"He said nothing more. I know he will leave as soon as possible with Abou-Khaled."

193

"I will wait."
The radio clicked off.

MONDAY   1800

Like a spectator who inexplicably finds himself sandwiched between the opposing packs at a rugby match, the British Airways chief engineer looked unhappily out of place.

Small and ferret-like, his sparse hair brushed forward in a vain attempt to hide the obvious, he tugged nervously at the corners of a small military-style mustache as he stood surrounded by a scrum of burly, black boiler-suited SAS men, their faces hidden behind thick woolen stocking masks.

Twelve pairs of eyes glittered through slits as he unrolled a large sheet of drafting paper and, arms at full stretch, pinned it to a makeshift blackboard barely high enough for those at the rear of the group to see.

One of the men dragged a rickety wooden bench from a corner of the hangar and the engineer gingerly climbed on it. A huge commando boot casually stretched out and riveted it to the floor.

The engineer half turned and let his glance play over the drawing. The Trident 2E. Son of 1 and 1E. Elegant and well-mannered, with a certain unobtrusive chic that came only with the very best of breeding.

How different from the loudmouthed, boorish monsters that were bulldozing them out of the sky.

There was nothing he didn't know about this plane; every inch, as surely as a surgeon knows his patient. He had crawled through its innards, juggled with its skeleton, stripped it to its bones and its multicolored electrical arteries, healed its wounds and stitched it up with steel.

It had no secrets left.

A shuffling of feet shook him from his reverie. He tapped the board with a rule.

"Gentlemen, by now I'm sure you're all familiar with many aspects of Trident. I have been asked to run over some of the basic points once more.

"This, as you can see, is an exploded view of the plane."

Unaware of the irony of his remark, the engineer blinked

194

uncertainly as a rumble of muted laughter ran through the group. He coughed nervously and plunged on.

"Two passenger doors . . . inward-opening and plug-fitting . . . total height of plane from ground, 27 feet . . . toilets to port . . . at front . . . galleys starboard . . . emergency exits above, center section, port and starboard, height 3 feet 4 inches . . . flight-deck length, 67 feet 1½ inches . . . three-seat units . . . interior height 6 feet 7½ inches . . ."

The rule rapped a drumbeat through the vast hangar as the engineer intoned his litany of statistics.

". . . five fuel tanks. One in the center section, here, and four in the wings. In all, a total of 6400 gallons."

He looked down at the squat metal of the Ingram 9-mm. machine gun one of the men held dangling at his side.

"I will leave the significance of that to you."

This time nobody laughed.

Out on the runway the wind had begun to gust strongly, picking up the engineer's muffled words from inside the hangar and shredding them in sporadic bursts of sound.

In the lee of a black Range Rover, three SAS officers and a trio of policemen sipped coffee from plastic cups, heads unmoving, eyes fixed on the barely discernible shape of the aircraft, as if a wayward blink would somehow lose it.

For the past four hours they had calculated and revised, abandoned and redrawn, the details of attack.

Now, for better or for worse, was the moment of truth.

They had worked with only one precedent: Lod Airport, May 8, 1972.

One hundred hostages inside an El Al airliner had sat for days as a tense game of bluff was played between Arab hijackers and the Israeli government. A game that gave vital time to Moshe Dayan and a handpicked team of commandos to make their plans; to hone and polish the denouement that would forever underline the fact that Israel no longer made bargains, that Jews no longer shuffled like sheep in the shadow of gunmen.

The world had watched and waited. And when the end came, it came quickly.

In thirty-four seconds, from the forcing of the plane doors, dead terrorists littered the gangway and panic-stricken passengers wept away their shock.

The men sipping their coffee knew that if it went half

as well tonight, it would be enough.

Thick coffee grounds slopped steaming into the snow as the hangar doors slid back and, stamping away the cramp, the black-garbed SAS men filed out, their briefing over.

Feeling the needlepoint of cold through his woolen mask, the assault leader turned his head to the sky. The heavy blanket of cloud was still unbroken. As long as it stayed that way; one sliver of moonlight at the wrong moment and they would be rabbits in a field.

He jogged across to the Range Rover as the rest of his team hitched the special aluminum extension ladders under their arms and partially unzipped the jacket tops of their boiler suits where their weapons nestled.

"A twenty-five-second flare, no more," ordered the assault leader. "It's enough to attract them. But then for God's sake don't silhouette us with the searchlights."

The officer nodded. Adjusting his throat microphone, he spoke to the backup units.

"All ready. One flare, a minute from now. Twenty-five seconds floodlight. Then out. Counting."

The assault leader rejoined his team. They stood motionless in the dark. From the tiny receiver hooked into his pocket, the seconds were counted away.

Suddenly, the flare soared in a low arc, scudding erratic as a fireball across the runway as the wind thrashed it wildly from side to side. Pitching and twisting, it maintained its height until, ten yards from the plane, it emitted one final shower of green flame, plunged into the snow and was gone.

It was enough.

In the plane all eyes would have been focused on it. The assault team shielded their eyes as two blinding floodlights cut into the night, fixing the plane in their beams, impaling it like an insect.

The men moved forward.

At twenty-five seconds the lights were killed abruptly. For those who had stared into its brilliance, it would take at least twice that time to begin to adjust to the dark.

The paratroopers broke into a run, their cramponed boots smashing into the ice.

In the Range Rover, the operation leader studied his stopwatch with the intensity of an Olympic coach.

They were under the plane.

In one smooth movement, the ladders slid into place

alongside the fuselage and directly below the forward and aft doors.

The assault leader was halfway up when the ladder began to sway, skating on the hard-packed ice beneath the snow. With a muscle-tearing jerk, he threw it to one side in search of grip, his leg ripping against the steps.

Below him someone grabbed the two jointed sections and dragged them upright.

He was up. At the front of the plane two of his men were already in place, waiting.

The leader's hand sliced the air and a simultaneous blast tore into both doors as the machine pistols etched a circle of bullet holes around the locking mechanisms. Two feet slammed against metal and the doors swung inward.

With whoops and screams, the soldiers threw themselves into the plane, pistols stitching the air with a pattern no man could slip through. From the flight-deck end, the same insistent hammering reverberated down the echoing tube.

"Run! Run! Run! Mooove it!"

The assault leader hurled himself down the gangway, spraying the seats. Behind him the toilet door became a grille as one of his men poured shots through it.

He poked his machine pistol into the galley and fired blind until he was satisfied no one could have survived.

At the rear of the plane, the assault leader tore off his mask as the forward team raced down to join him and his group. He drew back his sleeve, and stabbed at the stop-watch key on his Bulova.

One minute forty-five seconds.

At Lod it had taken ninety seconds before the commandos had been able to open fire and God knows how many dry runs like this they had had.

It would do.

From his radio receiver came the voice of the operation leader.

"I make it one-fifty. Repeat. One-fifty. What kept you, Harry?"

The assault leader flicked a bead of sweat and his face cracked into a rare smile. He pressed the transmit button.

"I laddered my bloody nylons, didn't I?"

For the second time they walked the length of the plane. The assault leader led the way, occasionally stopping to point out a bullet mark or to drop on one knee and illustrate an angle of fire. The operation leader, two fellow SAS officers and a ballistics expert from Woolwich Arsenal followed.

Behind them came the chief engineer.

The plane was a wreck. The high-velocity bullets had struck with the devastation of an ax, gashing the fuselage and mincing seats to pulp.

They called it a dress rehearsal. The engineer ran his hand along a headrest and slid four fingers into a hole that marked a bullet's point of exit.

From further down the plane police chiefs and Home Office men joined the SAS group. The operation leader paused to study the bullet-torn door-locking mechanism.

"It could have jammed," he said.

"It could have," said the assault leader. "But it didn't."

One of the Home Office men reached out and, with a flash of onyx cuff links, gently swung the rear door on its hinges.

"What if it jams next time?" he asked primly.

The assault leader glanced at the officer.

"Then," he said, "we'll just have to knock."

MONDAY   2345

His muscles woke first.

The stored tension of two days and two nights breached the barricade of flesh and sinew and radiated a web of perfect agony. He opened his eyes.

The darkened shell of the room was lit from one end by a faint luminous green glow that threw frail, impossible shadows onto a bare pegboard ceiling.

The bedclothes had been tucked in tightly around him, forbidding movement. He began to pull at them tentatively but they resisted the meager effort.

He was helpless.

As his eyes grew accustomed to the gloom, he rationalized the setting. Hospital room. Six beds. Desk at one end—the source of the soothing green light.

He raised his head furtively. No one at the desk. There was bound to be a night nurse nearby.

His head flopped back onto the pillow.

No strength. Not an ounce. You bastard, Flag.

He felt his whole body shake, not with anger but with the intolerable passion of terror.

He had often wondered if it would ever be like this. He had feared it and hated the fear, but with the blind idiocy of a Saturday-night drunkard he had stifled the fear with a preposterous machismo. Schoolboy heroics. Never show caution when you can show courage. Never admit that yesterday's resourcefulness had withered into apprehension and a fine regard for the sanctity of one's neck.

It was insane, all of it. He'd outgrown the histrionics, the night games and the puerile deceits. He was forty-two years old and his gut ruled his head. Yet he had been conned like a fly-fed trout.

He wriggled with a massive effort and felt the sheets and blankets wrench free on one side of the bed. He lay gasping, shattered by the outflow of energy.

At the end of the room, the door pushed open and its rubber draft excluder whooshed caressingly over the tiled floor of the ward. From the corner of his eye Driscoll saw the nurse silhouetted against the green light. She began to move along the beds.

He closed his eyes and heard her shoes squeaking from bed to bed; heard her breathing as she paused at his feet. She returned down the room, stopped at the desk to rustle a pile of papers, then retreated again through the door.

Driscoll raised his head experimentally. Stronger. Much stronger. He pushed his shoulders off the pillow, pulled back the bedclothes and swung his feet to the floor.

As he sat upright, his head staged a blistering fireworks display and he grabbed wildly for the steel bedhead as the dizziness engulfed him again. His throat began to bob with nausea; his chest surged with a tide of vomit.

What do you think you're doing? Where are you going? It's all over, can't you get that through your thick head? You're finished. Accept it.

It could have been seconds. It could have been half an hour. He had no sense of time. But his system settled and he listened to his own breathing.

Regular. Stronger. Not too deep, for God's sake; can't afford to be sick.

The sound hit him several times before he arrested it. Not breathing. Too sibilant. A hiss. He turned his eyes to the bed opposite. Assad was up on one elbow, his face half hidden by the sheet.

Driscoll made it to the Arab's bed in a series of coordinated collapses. He dropped down beside him and rested his head in one hand, forcing the nausea back.

Assad whispered: "Are you all right?"

Driscoll grunt-whispered back: "Bloody marvelous."

"What is this place?"

"Hospital. I dunno. You got anything broken?"

"Many cuts and some bruising. I will be all right if I can rest."

Driscoll glanced automatically to the door.

"Forget it! There's a nurse in and out of here. She could be back. Can you get up?"

The Arab tensed himself uncertainly. "I am very weak."

"Me, too. But we'll be a damn sight weaker if we don't get out of here before morning."

"It is better, then, that you leave me here. I cannot travel far. If one of us escapes . . ."

Driscoll wrapped a huge fist around the lapels of Assad's pajama jacket. He brought his face up close.

"You must be joking. While I've got you, I'm fireproof. You come with me if I have to drag you all the way by the scruff of the neck."

He dug his hands under Assad's arms, sucked in a chestful of air and lifted the Arab bodily into a sitting position. He waited for the wave of dizziness to subside, then got to his feet.

"Out!" he whispered hoarsely. "Come on."

Assad scrambled to his feet with difficulty and they moved along the room toward the light, their hands clutching at bed ends for support.

Driscoll edged open the swing door. The corridor outside was lit with the same subglow of green. From a closed door, ten yards along to the right, came a muted stutter of conversation.

He ushered Assad forward and inspected the young man's face. Suffused in the emerald lighting, it was furrowed with pain and blotched with exhaustion. But the black eyes gleamed with monstrous determination. Driscoll thought fleetingly: I'll give out before he does.

They crept along the corridor to the door. Driscoll tuned his ear to the talk behind it, judging its tempo. They tiptoed on.

Ahead was a T-junction and a facing door. Driscoll made

for it, tried the handle and pushed. The closet was in darkness.

He motioned Assad in ahead of him, looked for a switch, closed the door and turned on the light.

It was clearly a janitor's hidey-hole. Brooms, squeegees, dusters, boxes of cleaning liquids and soaps, towels. On the door hung blue boiler suits.

Driscoll unhooked one and threw it at Assad.

"Get into that," he whispered.

Assad began to unbutton his pajamas. Driscoll smashed his hand away impatiently.

"*Over* the pajamas, stupid. It's freezing out there. Here." He took another of the denim suits from a hook.

"Get this one on, too. You'll need all the warmth you can get."

They looked, reflected Driscoll when they had finished, like inmates of a mental institution. The clothing was grotesque, bulking their bodies beyond human proportion. Their hair was wild. They were unshaven.

Driscoll located two pairs of aged green rubber boots.

He beckoned Assad to follow him.

"Okay, sunshine," he breathed unsteadily. "Let's take a little walk, shall we?"

TUESDAY   0540

The old truck hiccupped to a halt that sent Driscoll tumbling down a hillside of cabbage sacks into the tailgate.

He had been sleeping and again the horrific nature of his dreams had dried his mouth and stretched his nerves like guitar strings.

The tailgate chains rattled and the driver beckoned his passengers into the dagger-thin light.

Driscoll focused stupidly on the furrowed old walnut of a face, on the steady brown eyes and the white Franz-Josef mustache—framed ridiculously by a hand-knitted gray balaclava.

Life and cold reason flooded through him. He nodded his understanding and turned his head to look for Assad.

The Arab was perched high on a cabbage summit, one of Driscoll's Gitanes in his fingers, an expression of acute curiosity on his face. He had watched the manner of Driscoll's awakening, listened to his childlike whimpering and the stream of subconscious hysteria. In those fleeting, disjointed words, he had recognized the cry of the naked child, the fearful repentance of the tainted innocent.

Assad stared at his keeper with a new boldness. He knew with striking clarity that he had nothing now to fear from this man.

He tobogganed down to the tailgate and landed on his feet in the road. He reached out a hand to Driscoll.

"Come," he said. He couldn't keep the warmth from his voice.

The old man waited patiently and, when they stood before him, weighed them speculatively for the value of their gratitude. His analysis lasted no longer than the passage of one steamy breath cloud on the freezing air. He made a short decisive sound deep in his throat, shook his head disgustedly, then turned from them and bustled back to the driver's cab.

Driscoll stepped onto the pavement over a gutter piled high with frozen black slush and followed the uncertain progress of the truck until it turned the corner and disappeared from sight.

The street was full of light, a theatrical mix of blazing shop windows, twinkling Christmas decorations and the rose glow of the as yet unrisen sun.

He looked about him.

A street sign twenty yards away on a corner read "Hendrikstraat." Over the roofs, where the old truck had turned, loomed a willowy stalk of concrete with a flat mushroom cap on its head. Driscoll recognized it instantly. The revolving restaurant of the Euromast that soars over the harbor installations of Rotterdam.

When the old man had picked them up on the road out of Ijmuiden, Driscoll had permitted himself the luxury of assuming the journey would carry them inland, down toward the Belgian border.

But Rotterdam!

Hours of freezing discomfort and they had gained only inches.

Time lost. Energy lost.

The cold penetrated the double layer of boiler suit and he winced. He caught Assad's almost apologetic glance of sympathy and snapped himself upright.

"Okay. Let's go."

He strode away, forcing Assad into a jog trot to catch up.

"Where are we?"

The Arab was gasping for breath as the icy air plunged deep into his lungs.

"A long way from home," snapped Driscoll. "Rotterdam. The docks are over there on the right."

"Have you decided what we must do now?"

"Food first. And some clothes. That means laying our hands on some ready."

"Ready?"

"Money. Cash. Currency."

Easier said than done. There was no one in Rotterdam he knew well enough to trust. No one he would dare contact in his present state, anyway. There were a half dozen shipping men in the city who would willingly give him anything he wished—and feel privileged for the opportunity.

But then, they had dealt with quite another human being—*Mr.* David Driscoll, chairman of this and that, inhabitant of a gracious world, rider in executive aircraft, Rolls-Royces and choice foreign sports cars, habitué of exclusive clubs, diviner of good food and formidable wines. Man of power and influence.

An unshaven fugitive squeezed into two layers of blue boiler suit was no match for that reputation.

They reached an intersection. A few cars were beginning to break the frozen spell of dawn with their high-pitched whinings, their hoods and roofs clogged with snow, their chained tires spluttering and clumsy on the packed ice.

Driscoll paused on the pavement edge. This was too damned silly for words. There had to be something . . . someone.

Assad grabbed his elbow and nodded silently across the street. Under an awning heavy with snow blazed the windows of a café. It was deserted but for a chubby little fellow in a blue-and-white-striped apron who sat on a high stool behind the bar.

The opening of the door triggered a bell somewhere in the back of the café. The proprietor looked up from his paper and beamed a welcome.

"Morning," Driscoll said cheerily. "You speak English?"

"Yaw," said the landlord. "Yaw, Anglitsch I speak some gut."

"Right. Coffee for two."

Driscoll pointed at his chest, then Assad's.

"And—er . . ." He ranged his eyes hungrily over the brilliantly polished chrome of the hot plates, grills and coffee machine. "And ham and eggs. Two. You savvy?"

The happy burgher nodded enthusiastically.

"Sure. De ham en heg. Sure. Sunnyside hop?"

"Sure," said Driscoll, "sunnyside hop."

The food was placed in front of them, hot and crackling fresh, in minutes. They wolfed it. The coffee was served in percolating cups, black and thick as molasses. Driscoll ordered a large Bols to settle a final warm blanket on the feast.

At last, they got to their feet. Driscoll moved to the bar, where a gleaming IBM cash register stood proudly. He reached across to a shelf and selected a half dozen packs of Gitanes.

He dug a hand pointedly into the pocket of his outer boiler suit and the proprietor got the message and bounced briskly down the bar. He rattled an efficient tattoo on the cash register keyboard. In the cash sale window, "23 florins" crystallized in orange type and the cash tray slid open into the proprietor's chest.

Driscoll's hand streaked across the bar and seized the little man by the loose skin of his neck. He raised a stifled screech of surprise but offered no resistance. Driscoll pulled hard, dragging the perspiring head down onto the bar top.

"What are you waiting for?" Driscoll snarled at Assad. "Get it!"

Assad dodged swiftly behind the counter, stepped around the recumbent bulge of the proprietor and pulled paper money and coins from the till.

"Now get out here and pull down the blinds. And lock the street door. Come on!"

Driscoll tightened his grip on the folds of flesh in his right hand. The action drew a gasp of pain from the fat man. His wide brown eyes were round with terror and sweat slicked the few carefully grown hairs plastered across his bald pate.

"You got a car? Hey? A car?"

"Sure. Der car."

The words squeezed out on a wave of asthmatic wheezing. Driscoll tightened his grip again.

"Where?"

The man's bulging eyes moved fractionally in the direction of the back of the café.

204

Driscoll snapped: "Take a look out the back there. Check if he's got a car."

Assad pushed through a doorway hung with multicolored plastic strips and Driscoll heard him unsheath the bolts on the back door. Assad returned quickly.

"There is a car."

Driscoll bent his lips over the man's ear.

"Keys!"

A pudgy arm detached itself and gesticulated wildly at the cash register. Driscoll looked into the cash tray. A bunch of keys was lodged in one corner.

Assad touched Driscoll's arm and winced down at the perspiring head on the bar. Driscoll released the flesh folds and the fat man collapsed onto his stool. He was shaking violently, moaning to himself as he tested his neck and throat with fat feeble fingers.

Assad said: "We have no further need for him. We should leave now."

Driscoll unzipped a threatening smile.

"We go when I say so."

He walked around the bar, picked up the telephone and banged it down in front of the crooning fat man. Driscoll put a hand on his shoulder and the proprietor almost fainted with apprehension.

"Easy now. Easy. You know how to dial London?"

The proprietor shook his head doubtfully. Driscoll grabbed two telephone directories and dropped them into his lap.

"Find out! You dial the number for London."

The little man's shaking fingers tripped and jerked through a half dozen pages. Assad watched, unsure.

Finally, the man wheezed: "Sure. London ist here. Sure."

Driscoll took a pencil and a receipt book from the cash register and scribbled down a number. He pointed to the directory, then to the number.

The proprietor nodded, and dialed. Driscoll waited until he had finished, then tore the scribble to shreds.

The dialing tone rang endlessly.

Then: "Yes?"

Driscoll said: "Morning. This is the long arm of coincidence."

"David?"

"Give the man a coconut."

"Where in God's name are you?"

Driscoll clicked his tongue on his teeth.

"Dear oh dearie me. That's very indiscreet. You really must learn patience."

Weatherby said impatiently: "Have you got Assad?"

"Right here in my hip pocket."

"Not funny, David."

Weatherby's tone was taut but friendly.

"I don't know what you've heard, but there's all hell hanging out here. We've got a terrorist group at Heathrow with an atomic warhead. David, I must have Assad back here. If that bomb goes up, half of London goes with it. Flag . . ."

"To hell with Flag," said Driscoll.

"I'll second that. Look—it's imperative you talk only to me from now on. There are reasons I can't go into on the phone. You've got to let me help you. What do you say?"

"So *help* me. What do I have to do?"

Weatherby chuckled with pure relief.

"That's my boy. You don't have to do a thing. Just tell me where you are and give me your phone number. I'll get help there. Just sit tight."

Driscoll read back the phone number and as close as he could approximate to an address.

He heard Weatherby muttering the words and numbers as he wrote them down.

"Good, David. Excellent. Now—whatever you do, promise me one thing. You'll keep your hooks into Assad and you won't budge till you're both picked up. Is that a bargain?"

"That's no bargain. But okay—it's a deal. One condition. Flag is kept out of it."

Weatherby clicked his tongue impatiently. "Flag will be taken care of. But it'll take time. Be careful—he wants you badly. You know too much, David."

Weatherby dropped the receiver on its cradle and Driscoll heard the click. But there was something about the quality of the dead line that made him keep the receiver to his ear. The line still had a hollowness, a pulsing half-life in it.

Two seconds. Three. Click. The line died again.

Driscoll replaced the receiver thoughtfully. Weatherby's line—his own private outside line—was being tapped. There was only one man at Herrick's with enough muscle—sufficient reason—to run a tap on Weatherby. That was Flag. And there could be only one reason for tapping Weatherby: because Flag knew that he was Driscoll's last line of defense.

And he was right, wasn't he? He was always right. Congratulations again, Flag: you win the star prize . . . burial at sea with the rat of your choice.

He tossed the bunch of car keys into the air and caught them. He picked up the telephone and wrenched at it savagely. The cord burst out of its anchorage in the wall.

"Let's get out of here," he said.

Assad moved to the plastic-hung doorway but stopped halfway through.

"What about him?" he asked, nodding at the bewildered fat man.

"Forget him," said Driscoll. "He's not going to say a word." He shouted at the proprietor. "You stay here. Right? Stay here." He weighted his fist in his hand.

The fat man shuddered.

TUESDAY   1620

"Captain Ali is at the airport. We have spoken with him and we await his flight. We can do no more."

"You do nothing. *Nothing!*" The young Palestinian's voice was thick and slurred.

The Home Secretary looked up at the CGS, who was leaning over the console in front of him. The Chief shook his head.

Both of them knew they were entering the most dangerous phase. It was obvious that the young leader of the group had renounced sleep; at this moment he would be in the emotional no-man's-land between eruptive anger and resignation. One false move now and he might be pushed over the edge.

"We have nothing to lose. You have much to lose."

It was a game try but the men in the tower accepted the weary threat for what it was: a desperate attempt to shore up the young man's flagging resolution. There was something new, too; the young voice broke midway through the second sentence, like the wobbling falsetto of a boy soprano succumbing to manhood.

Hysteria? The prelude to actual physical collapse? No doubt about it—he was very shaky.

"We all have much to lose. Life is sweet."

"Death is sweet. We will die well."

"There is no need for anyone to die."

"It is a privilege to die. I will talk no more."

The click closed the circuit, then it opened again immediately.

"Are you there?"

"I hear you."

"You will not talk to the pilot again. You will talk now only to me. We will talk again only when Captain Ali and Abou-Khaled are here."

The Home Secretary got to his feet and stretched and yawned wide.

"How long do you think we can keep this up?" he asked of no one in particular.

No one in particular answered.

For the last two days, all such questions had been rhetorical.

PART THREE

REVELATIONS

The newspapers had gone as far as inspired conjecture could go.

The story of the spectacular death crash on the runway at Heathrow plastered every front page. Fleet Street's backbench makeup men must have had seizures at having no pictures to illustrate the story, but they had made do with action shots of union strikers trying to break the police barrier at the airport entrance.

No details were available to identify the body or how the stolen jeep had inexplicably exploded under him just as he was within striking distance of the imprisoned Trident; but the graphic artists had ingeniously forged scenarios of what he might have been up to.

Hugh Davidson stepped onto the platform at Liverpool Street and joined the swarming race for the ticket collector. The station was packed. According to the news on television, last night, every station was. Parents all over London were using every remote relative they could think of to get their children away to the country. The schools in the Inner London Education Area had closed officially and many of the county authorities had followed suit because absenteeism had rocketed, in some cases to as high as eighty percent.

Davidson spotted the waiting car and sprinted across to it. There were no taxicabs at the station, as far as he could see. He settled back in the seat.

A D Notice had been issued shortly after the fool photographer met his fiery end at Heathrow on Monday, so the papers had been forced to avoid putting two and two together. There was no mention of atomic bombs, but the *Daily Express* had found an acceptable way through the net by splashing an exclusive story on the arrival at a Wiltshire RAF station of West Germany's anti-terrorist chief and the American FBI's top adviser on siege psychology. Both of them, claimed the *Express*, had gone to Downing Street.

Hugh Davidson pushed the papers aside and looked out at London. The City was deserted. So was the Embankment. He noticed, as they drove by, that the gates to the Temple were locked. Trafalgar Square, on the other hand, had something of a carnival atmosphere about it. Even at this hour, the crowds were out, standing or strolling, as if they believed the crack of doom would be proclaimed from the plinth of Nelson's Column.

Regent Street and Oxford Street were deserted; and for some reason, Davidson decided, they seemed utterly naked. Then it struck him. There were no buses, no taxis.

He didn't cherish the prospect of a meeting with Flag but there was no avoiding it. He had to be told. It would be disastrous if the old man found out himself.

His wife Janie had telephoned him at Herrick's on Thursday but Davidson had been tied up. Same again on Friday. On Saturday evening, he'd called her to say he wouldn't be home for at least the next few days. Try, she'd said. It was urgent. She couldn't discuss it over the phone. When he got to Saffron Walden last night, she'd told him about Julia. How Driscoll had asked if she could come to stay on Thursday night; how he'd called to talk to Julia; how she'd never arrived.

For the twentieth time since he'd left home, Hugh Davidson tried to fit the pieces together. Flag's refusal to discuss the Assad affair or the Heathrow situation with the Executive. His curt dismissal of Weatherby, who had gone to him as spokesman. The suspension of all activities in the field. Driscoll's total disappearance. Julia's. The continuing refusal, direct from Downing Street, to permit any contact with the Arab in Wormwood Scrubs.

When the car rolled to the curb in front of the double doors of Herrick's, Davidson had made a decision.

For the moment, for reasons he couldn't yet understand himself, he would keep his peace.

WEDNESDAY   1000

Assad's head rolled onto Driscoll's shoulder again and this time he let it stay there. Better to let him sleep.

At least they were warm. When Driscoll had turned the café owner's Taunus into the hotel parking lot at Roosendaal, he had spotted the two sheepskin coats in the back of a sporty Mercedes. He had jimmied the window and lifted the coats. It had seemed the sensible thing to do.

211

At the station, he'd kept his heart in his mouth until the tickets were safe in his pocket and they had wedged themselves into a compartment already bulging with four young men, their luggage and their skis. Two of them wore ski boots; all of them were clad in the bizarre, puffed-up costumes common to the Alpine slopes. Alongside these, Driscoll's and Assad's sheepskins, boiler suits and boots seemed almost conservative.

The tickets had cost an equivalent of forty pounds for the two of them. There had been enough for the break in Paris when they reached the Gare de Lyon, a few francs' worth of coffee and sandwiches, and Driscoll had set aside fifty francs for the coach trip at the end and a taxi.

There had been no question that the train was the best way. Travel by road could have meant holdups for identity cards or passports; a casual process this close to Christmas, but one they couldn't afford.

So far, the trip had been uneventful. No police. No inquisitive, talkative passengers. Assad had been no trouble at all. Even before he had fallen asleep, Driscoll had realized that he had given the Arab an unspoken parole. He was relying on his cooperation, his help. He had, he thought, invested him with complete trust. It disturbed him. At some point in the game, they both knew their personal interests would diverge sharply and without warning. Probably at the other's expense.

The Palestinian network of brothers and sympathizers was impressively strong in France. Assad would have only marginal difficulty in going to ground there.

But if he had any ideas along that line, the Arab was doing a beautiful job of keeping them to himself. Food, hot drink, the warmth of the coat and the compartment, had lulled him into a sleep that left his face unfurrowed, as openly innocent as a baby's.

The journey from Roosendaal to Thonon-les-Bains would take close on twenty hours. A whole day lost. Or maybe gained. It was difficult to think of winning or losing now. At best they were going to get to Thonon and hop the coach to Morzine and grab a cab to the Avoriaz cable car and fall down in his chalet and sleep for a week. And after that, he'd think of something. Anything.

First off, before he slept, he would talk to Cindy. Richard, too. He'd call them at the Danieli.

Assad's head fell forward over the ledge of Driscoll's

shoulder. He put his hand on the side of the Arab's face and lifted the head gently back to safety. Now why did he do that?

Why was it so important to talk to Cindy?

Reaction, probably. I want my mummy figure. He grinned stupidly. The young man sitting across from him grinned, too.

Never ask why, he warned himself despondently. Never ask yourself for reasons. Ask yourself why and you get answers. Just take one at random. Why did you *really* leave Cindy? Need to think about that. Liar. You left because loving people gets in the way, doesn't it? Herrick's and Cindy didn't mix. Anyone who wanted to squeeze Driscoll had only to squeeze Cindy. If she got hurt because he was what he was, the guilt would kill him. So separate himself from Cindy. Now, if she gets hurt, he had nothing to blame himself for.

Was it *that* simple?

That—and Richard. Richard doubled the squeeze. He also doubled the guilt.

So Herrick's was more important? Questions. It was always like this. Questions just raise more questions.

Yes, damn you, Herrick's was more important. Herrick's was winning. Herrick's was the ultimate freedom; to play outside the rules, to be above reproach; free to act out the heroic fantasies of childhood, the ones every man had, and in the end to wipe the slate clean in one heart-stopping millisecond of sensation—kill or be killed.

He snatched a look at the faces around the compartment as though they were privy to the conversation in his head. They were lost in newspapers and magazines or sleeping, like Assad.

All right, then. You want to ask questions. Go ahead. What am I trying to do? What am I trying to be?

Rich. Powerful, whatever that means. Untouchable. That's getting nearer the truth. What else?

Sure—what else? When you've run the last dealer off the road and put the last war into the last lunatic's hands and you've stashed the last million in the last numbered account—what will you have? Well?

Forget it. Get some sleep and forget it.

No—keep thinking. Think—and for once in your life, goddamn you, believe what you hear in your head.

Believe in Cindy. And loving; believe a lot in loving. Believe in Richard and cross your fingers before God or fate or the zodiac that Richard will undo some of the damage. Not to save your devil-rotten soul. Not that. To save you, Driscoll, from happening all over again in him. The sins of the father. Remember? You've given him a great head start.

He slept all the way to Thonon.

WEDNESDAY 1215

Davidson's Dictograph buzzed insistently. Mrs. Lamb sounded terrified.

"It's the Prime Minister, Mr. Davidson. For Flag. I can't find him."

Davidson said: "Well, there's nothing odd about that, Mrs. Lamb. Tell the PM he'll call back as soon as you can contact him."

Mrs. Lamb was near to tears.

"I can't, sir. Flag's overnight case, the one he had me get his wife to pack; it's gone. I've checked round everywhere. Mr. Weatherby's gone, too. No one's seen either of them since last night."

"Right, Mrs. Lamb. Put the PM on to my line. The green phone." They might need the scrambler. He flicked off the Dictograph.

"This is Davidson, Prime Minister. I'm afraid we can't locate Flag or his deputy at present."

"Where is he?" The Prime Minister made it sound like a threat.

"No idea, sir."

"You should have. You say his deputy's with him?"

"I don't know, sir. He's not here."

The silence was a long one. Finally the Prime Minister said: "An RAF Andover took off from Calne in Wiltshire fifteen minutes ago. It had a full fuel load and no flight plan. No destination shown. What d'you know about it?"

Davidson felt the hair prickling on his neck.

"Nothing, sir. I'm sorry."

Silence.

"The plane was chartered on a Special Intelligence Requirement. Flag is aboard. Can you explain why?"

214

"No, sir. I can't."

The Prime Minister sighed heavily, distractedly.

"Very well. You'll consider yourself acting director at Herrick's for the time being, Davidson. I'll expect to hear from you the moment Flag contacts you."

THURSDAY 0900

The taxi driver curled his lip contemptuously at the one-franc tip but kept his peace. Driscoll was in no mood for haggling and his expression made that plain. He led Assad up the ice-rimmed steps into the teleferique station and took the owner's lift to the embarkation platform.

The cable cars were passing at the midway point, wreathed in early-morning cloud. On the platform, a ruddy-faced Alpine peasant was playing with crystalline snow with a broom, ignoring with calculated insolence the thirty or so skiers around him.

It was a cosmopolitan crowd: local French from Annecy and Thonon, curious Swiss from nearby Geneva, package holiday groups from Italy, America, Scandinavia and Japan.

Avoriaz was little more than nine years old, one of a string of ski villages that had mushroomed in the High Savoy during the boom tourist days of the sixties. Unlike the other stations, designed to capture a mass, low-income holiday market, Avoriaz had aimed its appeal at the perennial big spenders—the tax dodgers, the enthusiasts and the Beautiful People.

The best architects in Europe had created a thematic cluster of hotels and apartment blocks, sculpted to the line of the mountains and dressed with flakes of red cedar. The system of chair lifts and drags was arguably the best in Europe. When the tourist boom punctured in the early seventies, Avoriaz remained remotely, exclusively successful.

Driscoll was a founder-owner. His private chalet perched precipitously on the edge of the Avoriaz plateau, overlooking the valley and Morzine and the comings and goings of the cable car.

The chalet was clean but cold. The Italian central heating came good within the hour and both men fell into deep hot baths and marinated luxuriously in Badedas.

Assad's chest wound had been carefully cleaned and bandaged at the Ijmuiden hospital but Driscoll examined the sutured flesh and satisfied himself there was no infection.

The Arab's powers of recuperation were astonishing. The bath, the rest, the removal of pressure and stress, left him buoyant and assured. He politely refused the offer of a few hours' sleep but asked with some deference if they could find something to eat.

Driscoll's extensive wardrobe of French ski wear was several sizes too big for the diminutive Assad, but he fitted perfectly into the pants, sweaters and snow boots in Julia's wardrobe.

Driscoll set a match to the logs in the stone-flag fireplace in the sitting room and burned the blue boiler suits, the boots and the sheepskin jackets.

They took breakfast at the Hotel Dromonts and returned to the chalet at eleven in high good humor.

It was short-lived.

The men were waiting for them; two in the entrance hall, one on the stairs, two in the sun room overlooking the valley.

It didn't even occur to Driscoll to resist.

THURSDAY   1230

Through the corner window, Driscoll could see the children's classes planing down the narrow throat of the nursery slope to the reception area by the ski school.

Weaving dangerously around them came the adults who had spent the morning up on the plateau or on the powdery slopes of Lès Lindarets. The chairs and tables outside the café were already packed with sun worshippers.

The leader was a slim, controlled man in his mid-thirties. Every inch of him spelled athlete; every movement heightened the impression in Driscoll's mind of perfectly toned fluidity.

In an hour and a half, he had exchanged fewer than a dozen words with his captives. None of them had been threats.

Every quarter of an hour, he left the sitting room to talk quietly with the man on the stairs and the two guards positioned on either side of the main door. He was never out of the room for more than two minutes and he never once sat down.

At precisely 1235, he checked his watch and gestured to his companion, who crossed to the picture window overlooking the valley. He stared down at the teleferique station at the foot of the cliff, turned back into the room and nodded.

The leader pointed a finger silently at his companion's chest and strode from the room. They heard him whisper urgently to the man on the stairs.

Feet rattled down the pine staircase and the leader's voice addressed all three men in the entrance hall. The outer door scraped open and shut.

The staircase guard appeared in the doorway, nodded to his colleague at the window and dropped into a white leather chair, the Uzi tucked comfortably under his armpit, its sight aligned with Driscoll's head.

Driscoll shifted uneasily and the Uzi's snub nose moved fractionally in the guard's hand.

Why had three of them left?

As if in answer, the cable car swung into view in the wide window, slowing as it made the final three-hundred-yard approach to the Avoriaz station.

Of course! They'd gone out to meet the cable car. Someone important was on it.

The sudden clatter of the brass knocker on the front door shocked everyone in the room. The guard in the chair was on his feet and in the doorway before Driscoll's nerves had settled. The other moved into the center of the room.

They heard the door crunch open over the frozen snow. . . .

"Monsieur Drisque'l! Can I come in?"

Driscoll tensed. The gunman in the chair formed a soundless question.

"De Villiers. He's the director here. An old friend," Driscoll murmured. "He has nothing to do with . . ." The gunman waved him into silence. Without hesitating, he slipped the Uzi under his chair and whipped a mat-black Beretta from his jacket. He waved it without speaking, slid it back into his pocket and got to his feet. The second guard must have moved with equal speed, for when Driscoll turned to him, he, too, had performed a vanishing trick with his automatic.

De Villiers puffed into the room with two of his assistants at his heels. Driscoll rose to greet them.

"Alain! Michel! Monsieur de Villiers! Good to see you. I couldn't let you know I was coming . . ."

He never finished the sentence.

Assad had risen politely from the settee, arms hanging loosely at his sides.

Momentarily, the guard in the center of the room was surrounded and as he stepped uncertainly to one side Assad launched himself, arms outstretched, in a waist-high tackle.

Driscoll hurled himself between the visitors at the second guard. His shoulder caught him just below the breastbone and the concealed gun exploded inches from Driscoll's left ear. Across the room a Venetian molded glass nude erupted into a million flying fragments.

The guard staggered under the impact of Driscoll's charge, his spine met the solid pine of the stair rail and the impetus flipped him in a backward somersault. He thundered down onto the stone flags of the hallway.

Driscoll leaped to his feet and turned to help Assad. He met the Arab's black-eyed smile. His adversary lay brokenly at his feet.

The action had lasted no more than seconds and the three Avoriaz Location officials stood gaping.

De Villiers ran to the stairwell and looked down. He burst out: "*Il est mort!*"

Driscoll grabbed Assad and shoved him through the door. They bounced down the stairs and wrenched open the outer door.

"This way!"

Driscoll plowed through the snow to the ski *cave*, a concrete cell under the house where his equipment was stored.

He found a pair of snowshoes and buckled them on Assad's snow boots.

"Outside," he ordered.

He snatched a pair of 220 Head skis from their rest and thrust his feet into molded plastic boots. He kicked them into the ski bindings and strapped up.

Assad was on his back in the snow.

"Like this."

Driscoll performed a short-paced Indian shuffle in the snow.

"Don't try to walk or run. Shuffle. See?"

Assad followed suit, clumsily. Driscoll led him across the nursery slope.

They reached the flattened snow of the reception area and

jogged around the laughing, chattering lunchers.

The chair lift at Pas du Lac was still operating; for some people, lunch was an unwarranted intrusion into the sacred act of snow worship.

Driscoll relaxed and made a quick reconnaissance of the village receding below.

No sign of the two guards at the house, although he picked out three running figures who could have been the Avoriaz officials.

The newly arrived passengers from Morzine were spilling out onto the snow but it was impossible to distinguish the group leader and his two companions.

The chair bore them up and over the gully that dived away precipitously on the long, difficult run down to Morzine, and Assad gazed at the weaving figures of two skiers below as they raced in sweeping arcs, scything curtains of powdered snow in their wake.

The sun sat above the horned crest of Les Hauts Forts and dashed the eye-crinkling dazzle of a million diamonds from the towering piste of Tête au Boeuf.

Up there lay safety, but an acute form of physical punishment, too. He was out of condition and Assad was out of his depth. Driscoll's plan, if a vague hope could be called that, was to work around the eastern shoulder of Hauts Forts and move down to one of the drag lifts that would carry them up again to the Pas de Chavanette on the Swiss border.

No passports were needed for skiers making a day run over the border to Champéry and once there . . .

They made a long traverse across the face of the piste to the drag lift, Assad tumbling and sliding like an addict on his first mainliner.

Driscoll paused at the drag lift, ripped the heavy-duty nylon hoods from his own ski jacket and from Assad's, and bound them tightly over the snowshoes. This stage of the journey could easily be disastrous, but the nylon might overcome at least some of the friction.

He made Assad watch the next half dozen skiers as they slid into the approach guides to the lift, seized the flat circular "seat" of the drag and settled their backsides on it, legs stiffened, bodies lying slightly back to take the first ferocious pull of the spring.

Assad fell on his first seven attempts. The nylon hoods clung to the caked snow and his body was rigid in his fear.

On the eighth try he made it, clutching the steel haft in terror as his panic threw him from side to side like a dislocated puppet. Four minutes later they were at the top.

Several hundred feet above and to the left was the top of the Les Prodains chair lift, perched like an eagle's nest on a jutting shelf of rock. A narrow track ran across the face of the mountain from the chair-lift exit and the final approach to it was one hundred yards of backbreaking, sidestepping slog up a one-in-ten incline.

It took them an hour to reach that track. Assad's lungs were blowing like leathern bellows and his face was contorted with effort. Driscoll was bathed in sweat and his back and thighs and legs were numb.

They plugged along the track to the head of the chair lift and fell against a bank of snow.

The bulk of the mountain above them now blotted out the sun and the wind blew with a continuous contralto moan that slashed their clothing and cut to the bone.

Driscoll lit a Gitane and smoked it slowly. He allowed it to burn down to a half-inch butt, then flipped it outward into the void. He watched its progress until it was lost in the white blanket.

Then he saw them.

They were mere blobs of movement at that distance but he recognized the leader at once.

There were five of them, standing in a tight group at the head of the drag lift; one of them was pointing up at the chair-lift exit, although it was unlikely they could see Driscoll and Assad from there.

The Arab's heavy breathing stopped short.

"They are coming."

Driscoll spat a shred of black tobacco into the snow at his feet.

"What did you expect?"

"How could they have known we would come this way?"

"You tell me. They're bloody good, whoever they are."

"They can see us from there?"

"I don't intend to wait around to find out. We don't have much choice, do we? There's only one option."

He jerked his thumb upward over his shoulder. Assad gazed up at the monstrous slope above them. He rubbed the back of a gloved hand across the bridge of his nose.

"They will see us when we move," he ventured.

"But then they've got to catch us. Right?"

Driscoll pushed himself upright and pulled on his gloves. "It'll be cold up there if you stop, so keep moving," he said. "No more talking unless it's absolutely necessary. Save your breath for climbing. Keep side on to the mountain and always take your weight on the lower foot. Don't rush it. Take your pace from me. I'll be behind you, in case you fall—so don't fall! Okay, let's go."

The first hundred feet was a comparatively shallow slope with a thin crisp crust of frozen snow that made progress easier. Their breathing was more controlled now and Assad had begun to master the art of swinging his body weight rhythmically through a fifteen-degree arc as the bottom foot lifted to join the upper.

He was doing fine.

The gradient increased and a hundred feet higher Driscoll called a halt. He tunneled his hands before his eyes as a makeshift binocular and searched the slope below for the pursuers.

They were halfway up the snowfield to the chair-lift station, shuffling forward in line astern in the Norwegian cross-country style. They were obviously on walking skis; no one, no matter how expert, could make that kind of forward progress on that slope over soft snow without those cunning arrester teeth on the ski sole.

"Right. Time's up."

They crabbed on up the mountain. Driscoll measured the slope above them with his eye. When they climbed out of the shadow, they would be some four hundred feet from the ridge. That would mean a diagonal climb to the left on what looked like a one-in-four incline.

Maybe it really was hopeless.

Driscoll had maintained his rhythm throughout by running the words and music of "Good King Wenceslas" through his head. It was hypnotic and he clung to the imagery and let it blot out the fire in his muscles and the shrieking accompaniment of the wind.

He was into the line "Tread thou in them boldly" when Assad tilted helplessly into the mountain and the snow engulfed him. He sat up and shook himself free. The snow wave spurted on down the slope for fifty yards and finally expended itself in a sullen trickle.

Between Assad and Driscoll a wedge-shaped cave had developed.

"Pppphhhough!"

Driscoll pushed himself up and lifted his skis from their grave under the slide.

He should have realized. The faint tracery of old fall lines ran across the face of the mountain like tidemarks on a sandy shore. The dynamiters had been at work here, probably in the past day or two; creating mini-avalanches to avert the possibility of a bigger natural one.

Each day, before skiing began, teams of orange-suited experts moved up into the mountain to probe the snow for consistency and compactness. Any flaw judged to be a potential hazard was sown with explosive snowcaps and detonated.

The signs of that work were everywhere.

In the next hundred feet, three more slides burst from under them, one of them taking Driscoll twenty feet down the mountain on his back.

They broke above the shadow line at last and as the sun beat down on them Driscoll felt the first stirrings of hope. He called to Assad to take a breather and squinted back down the mountain.

The five men were strung out across the slope, less than four hundred feet below, and moving like pistons in a well-tuned engine. At no time in the last three hours had Driscoll looked back and found them at rest. Moving, always moving.

If they were thinking, suffering, doubting the wisdom of the chase, they hadn't allowed it to affect their inexorable, mechanical progress.

My God, they must need you badly, Driscoll thought, watching Assad's elephantine swinging action.

He struck off on the diagonal to the ridge. The snow was now like fine flour, its surface offering no resistance, no hold, no highway. In forty feet, Assad launched eight crumbling, suffocating snowfalls, each one bigger, progressively more dangerous than the last.

Driscoll finally stopped the Arab and overtook him. At this rate, they would still be on the mountain by nightfall— or buried deeper than love in a whorehouse.

The switch resolved nothing. Even Driscoll's skis, and the longer base of support they lent his weight, did nothing to avert the slides.

They fell and fell again.

Driscoll was picking himself out of the snow when the helicopter swept like an avenging angel over the summit of the mountain, its tweetering vanes whirling tall conical wraiths of transparent snow cloud from the crest.

It swung out over the slope, bouncing its roar off the semicircular vertical walls of the mountain, and circled around and down, combing every inch of ground.

For a moment, it hovered over the pursuing party of five in a flurry of talcum-fine snow, then lifted majestically and swung behind the summit.

The roar of the engine died immediately.

Driscoll checked the progress of the pursuers. They had closed the gap now to three hundred feet, perhaps less.

He measured the distance to the ridge. Three hundred feet and more. The group below had covered the same distance in less than two thirds the time Driscoll and Assad had taken and they were climbing as strongly as ever.

He said to Assad through great gasping breaths: "Faster. They're gaining. The ridge. Make the ridge. Come on."

Assad neither looked up nor checked his stride.

Another hundred feet on and Driscoll glanced behind and down again. The leader, ghostly in a gray ski suit, his head and face obscured by hood and goggles, was less than eighty feet below Assad and pumping his skis into the mountain with unbelievable speed.

His men were spaced out at intervals of fifteen yards, but their efforts were no less than his. They were automatons.

Driscoll willed energy into his legs and stumped on, but for every yard of mental effort expended, the physical reward was less than a foot.

His chest was bursting, the thin air tempting the blood but never satisfying it with the oxygen it needed. In the last few yards, his head had begun to swim and the ridge had grown a mirage of waving arms and elfin figures, beckoning, welcoming.

Assad groaned and sank down onto his snowshoes, half crouching, half conscious. His eyes as they turned up to Driscoll were glazed, the pupils pin specks of black, flinching in the brilliance of the sun.

They had no goggles, either of them.

Driscoll panted: "Up! Up, or I'll put this through your head."

He waved a steel-pointed ski pole menacingly. Assad attempted a smile and opened his mouth but no sound came. His throat had closed, tight and dry.

There is nothing left, he tried to say; but somehow he

pushed himself up and somehow he forced left foot up and right foot on.

Driscoll saw the leader of the pack behind stop and measure the distance left. He was forty feet short of total victory.

Driscoll knew that he would win now, this man who flowed like water. There was nothing to stop him.

He turned back to the slope. Twenty-five feet to the ridge. The tears in his eyes were playing distorting tricks again. Waving, beckoning, welcoming arms were rising from the crest behind the curtain of blown snow.

He dashed a glove across the tears and momentarily everything was clear.

He knew then it was finished.

The figure looking down from the ridge was short and black and menacing, made gigantic, monolithic, by the perspective. A huge enveloping black coat, smothered at the collar with a wide black woolen scarf wound many times. The head was grotesque in a fur hat with the earmuffs tied beneath the chin. But the face was unmistakable, unforgettable.

Driscoll hesitated, shriveling under the weight of his misery and his failure and the unwinking eye of death.

Suddenly the anger welled up in like like lava and he sucked deep on the air and slammed his skies into the snow.

A wedge opened at his feet and boiled down on Assad but he didn't stop to look. There was no time left for that now.

Oh, God, give me Flag and then do what you like with me. Just give me Flag. Let me take the bastard!

The shouts rang down at him and he raised his head.

Flag was wading down the impossible drop from the ridge, overbalancing at every step but still coming. The powdered snow surged away from under him in a vast bubbling tide but still he came on.

Driscoll raced to meet him, foot on foot, breath sucked and blown, the blood pounding in his head, his heart hammering, the life force crystallizing for one final volcanic burst of energy.

He saw Flag and he knew he couldn't reach him. The black bouncing boulder of a man was chopping, falling, smashing his way down through the snow, heedless of Driscoll and the monstrous danger below.

Driscoll stopped.

Flag was five yards to his left and staring fixedly beyond him, down the slope to Assad. The Arab lay where the snowfall had blanketed him.

The shouts from above increased. Driscoll saw figures dancing on the ridge; running, gesticulating.

The first shots roared down from the ridge like thunderbolts, picking out the hollows in the canyon walls and rebounding from them to magnify the sound a hundred thousand times. Driscoll threw himself, instinctively, into the mountain. But the shots were not aimed at him. The world was suddenly full of noise, but Flag heard nothing, saw nothing; only Assad, only the half-buried, burlesque scarecrow crouched in the snow. The man on whose shoulders his whole world rested. From below random bursts of shooting crackled in response.

Flag wrenched himself from a thigh-deep drift and plunged onward, but the snow fell massively away from him and, with a comic drunken wobble, Flag fell with it, head over heels, like an embryonic snowball.

Shots roared out again and again. And then the mountain woke.

Driscoll slewed around and saw three of the pursuers jump-turn acrobatically and launch themselves down the slope.

Their leader reached under his parka, but for the first time in his life, even he was too late.

The roar shook the earth, and the sky reverberated to it.

Half the mountain shuddered, a giant disturbed from a long sleep. And then it began to slide.

Slow at first, agonized and indecisive, but as it gathered bulk, breathing clouds of fine dust on its crest, the avalanche accelerated and threw drum rolls of thunder down on the village below.

Driscoll opened his mouth to shout. Assad lay paralyzed ten yards below on the brink of a ten-foot chasm where the canopy of snow had snapped.

They both watched the bumbling black-white rag doll figure of Flag. For a moment, it was suspended on the vast sinuous back of the avalanche, prostrate, face down, like a butterfly pinned to a board.

Then the surface parted and swallowed him whole.

Within seconds the leader of the group of five below was engulfed where he stood in frozen awe, and with him his nearest companion.

Beneath them, in turn, the slowest of the three fleeing skiers jackknifed forward as the wave struck him.

The others were barreling headlong downhill. They were buried alive at sixty-five miles an hour.

The boiling snow surged like a tide of detergent suds over the chair-lift station and dropped into the valley.

"For chrissakes, man! Driscoll!"

He looked up to the ridge. Somebody up there knew him.

THURSDAY   1700

The peaks of the High Savoy spread out below like a collation of magnificent soufflés dusted with sugar icing. The dying sun crouched on the horizon, raw as an angry pustule, inflaming the sky dead ahead and gilding their faces with bronze leaf.

The helicopter was a Sikorsky Commando, its capacious gut amply accommodating Driscoll, Assad, Duquesne and the three henchmen.

Avoriaz vanished, an isolated diadem of flickering lights. Geneva was a mere fifteen minutes away. Duquesne explained that they would be picking up an RAF Transport Command flight there. Flag's last instruction had been that they should lose no time in getting Assad back to London.

The young American shouted over the tweaking roar of the blades. "He said you wouldn't understand."

"Understand what?" bellowed Driscoll. "Understand why he played me for all he could get? That much I expected. But I had a right to *some* cover. He tossed me in a pool full of sharks. I was the bait on the hook and he cut the line."

Duquesne waved his hands angrily.

"For chrissakes, man, he just laid his life on the line."

"Sure. For him."

Driscoll hooked a thumb in Assad's direction.

"You think he'd whip up this bloody eggbeater if it was just my skin? Not on your mother's grave. Assad was his ticket home, you said as much yourself.

He brushed aside Duquesne's denial.

"Well, you implied it, anyway. If Assad had got lost along the way—and take it from me, he would have been if I hadn't broken my back to keep him alive—Jesus, what do

226

you think Flag would have done then? Chucked himself down a mountain to pick me out of the shit?"

"Yes! All the way. That guy gave you his word and he's been living with it for ten days."

Driscoll shrugged deep into his ski suit and glared defiantly into the sun.

The stupid, crazy old bastard. He didn't have to die. He didn't have to step off that ridge. He didn't have to do a thing.

He shuddered at the memory of those final thunderous seconds on the mountain. Flag tumbling and bouncing on the tide of shifting snow, dying blind. The paralysis of the leader of the pursuers; the paralysis of resignation. It would be in such a man, even at the moment of death, to await the grave calmly and without fear.

According to Duquesne, the group was a death squad of the Israeli Wrath of God organisation. Zealots, purists. Like Assad and his brothers. Blind dedication to an ideal: unquestioning, unreasoning worship of some goddamned samurai instinct for self-destruction.

So, where did that leave mercenaries like himself and Duffy and Flag?

Duquesne leaned over and shouted in his ear: "Your wife should be in London when we get there. She left Venice on the four-o'clock flight."

"How the hell do *you* know that?"

"Flag kept a tail on her. Round the clock. You don't think he'd take a chance on that? Damn good thing he did. The place was lousy with interested parties."

They hovered down to the Geneva airport in darkness and the three faceless helpers shepherded Assad away to a closed van with an oil company insignia on its panels.

Duquesne led Driscoll to a waiting car. Five minutes later, they were in the departure lounge, sipping good coffee at the refreshment bar.

Duquesne bought a morning edition of *France-Soir* and thrust it under Driscoll's nose. The splash was the Heathrow siege. "24 hours to Armageddon," roared the streamer.

There was a lot of speculative fiction in the story and more comic hysteria than a Feydeau farce, but Driscoll siphoned off the essentials quickly. He put the paper down.

"What're you doing with Assad?"

Duquesne shrugged.

"The Swiss are being helpful, all things considered, but

they want him out of here fast. We've taken him straight to the aircraft. Hang loose, man. He's not going anywhere you aren't."

"I want to talk to Weatherby."

"So do a lot of people," said Duquesne.

"I mean now. Is he here?"

"Search me."

Driscoll bunched his fist angrily.

"Look—I talked to him on the phone. From Rotterdam."

Duquesne leaned back in his chair and swung it back on two legs.

"We know that."

"You had his line tapped. Flag was listening in."

"What big ears you have. Sure. He was bugged."

"Okay—so you have your little secrets. I still want to talk to Weatherby."

"Like I said," said Duquesne gently, "so would a lot of people. Your friend took a powder last night. Pouff! All gone."

"You're telling me he was Guilfoyle's controller?"

"I'm telling you nothing. Nobody's trying to tie a can to his tail, because nobody can find him. All we know is he's gone. He took your call at Herrick's and he lit out around seven-thirty last night. He didn't leave a forwarding address."

Weatherby? A double? A sleeper? Take the greatest improbability, magnify it a hundred times and you have an anomaly.

The Gospel according to Flag.

In executive intelligence, he always said, you merely reverse the standard values. A man capable of exciting trust is a man capable of breaking it.

"And what did Flag do about Guilfoyle?"

"He identified the corpse."

"What!"

"Guilfoyle bought his around midafternoon Friday. Broke his neck falling out of a window. With a little help from his friends."

Driscoll felt the starch run out of him.

Flag's rules, his own rules, had never applied to Weatherby. At this distance—what, fifteen years after their first professional assignment together?—it seemed incomprehensible that the man was capable of running a double identity.

So he was a great actor. Doubles were always great actors. No—there was more to it than that. Professional doubles weren't born; they were made. The instrument of their making was compromise.

Weatherby was the last man on earth to submit to ideological compromise. He wasn't the type to make mid-course corrections; he had chosen his course in adolescence, or more likely fallen under the same kind of dialectic spell at Oxford that won over Kim Philby a generation earlier.

But why? For God's sake why? Communism was the classic philosophical war horse for embryo idealists. But Israeli nationalism . . . that was for—

"Have you checked out Weatherby's background? School, university?"

Duquesne dangled a tiny triangular sandwich in his fingers, examined it searchingly, then bit it in two.

"Maybe."

Driscoll's stomach knotted. So his own survival had been in the crucible for years. Middle East CAPE, every operator, every assignment had been an open secret in Tel Aviv, as open as a wall chart pasted up in the cool white Mossad office block.

His own organization, IMPACT, must have suffered at Weatherby's hands, too. Weatherby would have run a tight surveillance on every Arab deal IMPACT had ever made.

He would have watched everything—even Cindy and the boy.

Even Julia.

THURSDAY   1940

Richard dumped the expanding suitcase on the sitting-room carpet and collapsed like a poleaxed ox into a chair. Cindy followed with two airline bags and a deep plastic bag bulging with a holiday collection of Venetian glassware. She shed her coat and headscarf.

"Now don't get settled in, Richard," she nagged. "The car will be back in half an hour and you mustn't keep it hanging around. I want you on that train."

"Oh, God, Mum. Why?"

Cindy hefted the case from the middle of the room and put it to one side.

"We're not going through all that again. Gran expected

us today and she'll have everything ready. Now don't give me a pain. Please."

"I don't see the point of my going tonight and you dragging yourself up by car tomorrow. You know you hate traveling on Christmas Day. You've always said so."

"Richard! I'm not going to argue with you. Just do as you're told. I've promised Gran you'll be there tonight. She and Granpa will be at the station to meet you. Now leave it at that, will you?"

The boy hunched sulkily in the chair.

"I told you not to telephone them from the airport. You knew what she'd say."

He pinched in his lips in a creditable impersonation of his grandmother's contralto: "Let that young ruffian come up by train tonight. He'll only get under your feet."

Cindy's mother was a formidable woman who commanded and expected instant obedience. Christmas had traditionally been spent at her eighteenth-century mansion near Leatherhead and, in his day, even Driscoll himself had been unable to deny her.

"Don't be rude," snapped Cindy.

"Well. I thought I'd be more useful here tonight—helping you unpack and tidy up."

"I won't need any help, thank you very much," retorted Cindy. "I'm going to leave everything as it is. I'll make us a quick snack and when you've gone I'll get off to bed. I want to make an early start in the morning."

The telephone burped from the hall. Richard lugged himself out of the chair.

He called back: "It's for you, Mum. Some man."

Cindy didn't recognize the voice, but it had that odd mix of obsequiousness and command about it that she identified as upper-grade civil service.

"Rather important, Mrs. Driscoll. My apologies for calling you the moment you reach home."

"Yes?"

"David's on his way back to London. I'm afraid I can't go into detail but it's essential you meet him."

She felt a clutching hand in her womb.

"Is he all right?"

"Perfectly all right. I'm sorry—I had no intention of frightening you. He's well and whole but the matter's very important. He couldn't confide in me. He just said it was . . ."

"Very important!" Cindy's relief became anger. "Well,

what does he want me to do? Can't he telephone me?"

The man ignored the question.

"I suggest you take a taxi to arrive at the flat in Sloane Street—you know it, of course?—at about nine o'clock. I shall be there myself to meet you."

"Well . . ."

"Thank you, Mrs. Driscoll. I realize it's a bad time."

"Yes."

"Well, I'll leave you to get on with your unpacking. Till nine, then."

"Yes."

She was putting down the phone when the voice called out tinnily: "Mrs. Driscoll! Mrs. Driscoll!"

"Yes, I'm still here."

"I should have explained, of course, that I'm a colleague of David's. My name is Weatherby. Alexander Weatherby."

THURSDAY   2015

The RAF Andover put down at Luton airport and two cars pulled out onto the runway to meet it.

Duquesne, Assad and the three heavies squeezed into the Austin 1800. Driscoll was pointed toward the Park Ward Rolls.

The driver swung open the rear door for him and Hugh Davidson's opal smile glowed from the scented interior. For the first time in two weeks, Driscoll felt safe.

Davidson was full of questions. He was a good listener with a gift for weighing his silences with sympathetic understanding. Driscoll forgot his natural caution and spilled words in a torrent of graphic release. They were half an hour into their journey when Driscoll stopped suddenly.

"Where are we going?"

"Heathrow. No, please, David . . ." Davidson held up a magnificently gloved hand. "Please. This is critical. I have orders from the Home Secretary to take Assad there immediately. I must ask you to bear with me."

Driscoll leaned back into the velvety softness of the upholstery.

"Okay. It's your ball game."

"Not mine, David. The Prime Minister is handling this

himself. I'm just a body servant."

"Great casting," grunted Driscoll. "Why you?"

Davidson smiled apologetically.

"I suppose there was no one else to turn to."

"Like Weatherby?"

"Like Weatherby."

"Don't give me the yo-yo treatment, Hugh. I've earned *that* much. What *about* Weatherby?"

"We're not sure of anything yet. Not a hundred percent sure."

"Come on! So you've made a few guesses."

"A little more scientific than that," Davidson demurred.

"We've had problems, as you might imagine. Flag gone, Weatherby gone. It leaves holes in the net; unanswered questions. Most of them will never be answered. They each knew more than the rest of the Executive put together."

"Were they turned?"

"Flag? Never! He was a good officer. The best. He was very loyal to you, in his way."

Driscoll exploded.

"Loyal! He *lied* to me. He let me set up an operation knowing I was tying a bloody garotte round my own neck. He said Herrick's would step in at the warehouse and no one came. He *knew*—he *had* to know—that the idea was to put me out of business, once Guilfoyle had Assad. The bastard served me up on a plate. If that's your idea of loyalty . . ."

"There were extenuating circumstances, David."

"There always are, aren't there? My life or his sodding reputation."

Davidson clicked his tongue in his teeth.

"You're making noises for the sake of it, David. You know Herrick's well enough when you were on the strength to realize how they'd treat you in a dead-run situation. Flag accepted that. Good God, man—he *liked* you. But you agreed to play his game; and I have to say, David, that in your place I'd have told him to go to hell."

Driscoll shrank into the seat. Davidson was telling him nothing he did not already know about himself. When the spider throws out an invitation to come play in the web, the fly makes its own decision between life and death.

Davidson went on: "Flag was acting directly for the Prime Minister. No one, not even the Executive, was kept informed. All field operations were canceled. We sat in suspension for days. No explanations. Looking back on it, I can see why. I'd have done the same in his place."

"Don't kid yourself."

"Well—perhaps I wouldn't have had the courage to let you run with Assad as far as you did. Flag wanted the whole shebang—not just Guilfoyle and a couple of field men. He achieved that. We picked up a strike force of Mossad's Wrath of God unit at your cottage on the Bedford Level. Rather silly of you to burn the place. And that business with the launch off the Norfolk coast. That was trouble. It may've seemed odd to you at the time but the people in that launch were perfectly innocent boatmen. Flag had to work fast to cool the police over that."

Driscoll said: "Try it yourself sometime. I didn't have time to ask questions."

"Of course," soothed Davidson.

"And Weatherby? Where does he fit?"

Davidson coughed uncomfortably.

"He left nothing behind. He was a careful man. His files tell us nothing and his flat is a desert. I went there myself. A hermit has more to show for his life. No books. No letters. No pictures on the wall. No photographs. No record of relationships, no hint of a life of any kind outside Herrick's."

"What else did you expect?"

Davidson sighed audibly.

"I wasn't blessed at the time with your hindsight, David. It was possible he'd acted under instructions from Flag. How were we to know?"

"You've worked with him long enough."

"Without knowing him. As I protected *my* identity, he protected his. How many times do you think I looked across a table and wondered to myself: 'Can I trust that face?' Hmm? No doubt he did the same. The same goes for any of us. We're not there to practice friendship. You accept a man for what he can do. You accept him for what he tries to be, what he appears. But if he's good, you'll never be sure if he's a genuine, committed colleague or merely trying to appear to be. It depends what his loyalty *is*—to whom he owes it."

Davidson gazed out dreamily at the shredding light patterns of suburban London as the Rolls hummed through dirt-stained traffic, spurning contact.

"We are puppets, David. Interchangeable puppets. There.

but for the grace of God . . . Flag could be sitting here; Weatherby could be secure in Brook Street; Hugh Davidson running for his life. It's the nature of the craft. In every case, none of us are men. We're vessels churning with chemical reactions designed by somebody else. A spy is a good man embracing evil for the sake of good, or an evil man pretending good for reasons of his own."

He turned back to look at Driscoll.

"No, David, I don't know Weatherby. And even the idea of him I have at this moment may be wrong. Today, I suspect him of being a double, a traitor. Tomorrow?"

He shrugged and drew shapes in the silken carpet with the tip of his silver-topped ebony cane.

"Tomorrow, Weatherby may be a hero. Or a traitor who can be forgiven for the value of his information. Or a brilliant opportunist who duped a gullible enemy. Or he may be a martyr; or just another good man who bowed to intolerable pressure.

"One of our better novelists once said that the past is a foreign country; they do things differently there. Hartley, I think. True of people, perhaps, but not true of you and me and Flag. Tomorrow is the only foreign country. Everything's different there. My name may change; my face; the beliefs I'm ready to die for today. But the day after that . . ." He shrugged his shoulders.

Driscoll stirred.

"Weatherby's finished you. The Arabs have known for years that Israel had a man in London; someone built into the bricks and mortar."

"Tomorrow and tomorrow," murmured Davidson.

Driscoll changed tack.

"Have you seen Julia?"

Davidson's boyishly handsome face set hard.

"No."

"If I ever lay my hands on Weatherby . . ." Driscoll began.

"It's better you hear it from me, David." Davidson looked straight ahead of him as he spoke. "I knew nothing until Flag . . . until I assumed command at Herrick's. I swear to you. Julia is an agent. Flag recruited her from Special Branch."

Driscoll came upright, slowly.

"You're lying," he said. There was no blood in his face.

Davidson shook his head. "I'm sorry, David. Truly. It's a

234

terrible mess, all of it. Flag used you, so he had to protect you. He had to be at the center of your life and there was only one way to do that, be honest with yourself."

He paused unhappily.

"Her surveillance reports on you began a year ago. There was nothing . . . personal in them."

Driscoll lay back and waited for the flood of remorse. It didn't come. He forced his mind back to her, to the perfume of her and the touch of her body; to a hesitant soprano singing in the shower. Day by day a little more demanding, a little more like a wife. And under it all, Flag's ferret, combing the warren of his mind; what he thought, what he did, why he did it.

He said: "If anything's happened to Cindy and Richard . . ." It was almost as if he were talking to himself.

THURSDAY   2055

Driscoll bought the service flat in Sloane Street a few months after he went into the arms business full time.

He had discovered quickly that, in a world where the buyer held all the cards, the seller's hospitality quotient was an incalculable virtue. Too often, deals that had seemed to be in the bag evaporated like cheap perfume the moment the vultures learned there was money in town. The apartment was geared to keep clients featherbedded and isolated. Here, at the press of a button, were all the creature comforts a man could dream of; a blissful form of imprisonment that had seduced more than one foreign military attaché from his responsibility to shop around.

The setting was perfect, the security total, and the telephones worked only one way: out.

Cindy paid off the cab and mounted the short flight of marble steps to reception. It was more than three years since she had last been here. The girl at the desk was new. So was the impeccably dressed gorilla who hovered by the lift. The only bouncer in London with an Eton accent, according to David.

"Mrs. Dricoll?"

The girl had a smile an Avon lady would have given her wardrobe for. Cindy's agitation made it blossom wider.

"You're expected, Mrs. Driscoll, if you'd care to go up."

Some people, thought Cindy, can make invitations sound like commands. It came from a background of money and inextinguishable authority; subtle entities bequeathed at birth. She had the same feeling of overwhelming awe at those green-and-white signs in Harrod's. "Please try not to smoke." The implication was the same: obey or suffer social death.

She noticed a neat file card on the desk under the girl's hand. Clipped to it was Cindy's photograph. The girl ticked a visitor's book and nodded across to the gorilla, who had already summoned the lift.

"Please call if there's anything I can get you."

She was halfway to the third floor when she realized she hadn't spoken a word. They must have thought her stupid or ignorant or both. Or perhaps it was easier for them to recognize the shortcomings of someone who wasn't one of them.

It was irritating but she knew she would never be able to conquer her fear of efficiency in others. Secretaries, doctors, headwaiters, bank managers—they all had the power to reduce her to vocal paralysis, to numb her with a sense of her own inadequacy.

And so, in the quixotic way these things happen, she had been drawn like a phobic to the very heart of her fear. She had married David Driscoll.

She let herself in with the Chubb key and leaned back against the door, her eyes closed. The scented opulence of the room calmed her.

When she opened them, the room came in to smother her. Thick, specially tailored white Wilton rippled across the floor and broke like a wave on the elevated dining area. The upturned tulips of the Tiffany lamps; the Klee lithographs lining the walls; the gold brocade of chairs and settees—it could have walked off the pages of *House Beautiful*.

The man lounging by the windows fitted the setting perfectly. His smile was relaxed and warm.

"Nice of you to come, Mrs. Driscoll," said Alex Weatherby.

His body tensed and tuned to a whisker, the radio officer sat, eyes closed, like a medium willing the spirits to talk.

One hand delicately tuned the selector knob on the receiver, the other pressed one earphone tight to his head.

For the fifth time he ranged the wave band in search of a response. He had sat like this for three hours and his brain was full of junk.

A tap on the shoulder from the relief officer came as a reprieve. Thankfully he tugged off the earphones and scratched his itching head.

"Not a bloody thing. Either it's kaput or they're just not talking."

The relief officer scowled and prepared himself for his ordeal. His head was aching already. God knows what it would be like in a couple of hours.

Locked in a cocoon of meaningless whistles and hisses, he looked across at the group of bigwigs standing at the control-tower window. Like spare pricks at a wedding!

A moustache of perspiration prickled above his lip. He was sickening for a cold or, after those sausage rolls the Catering Corps had dished up, more likely food poisoning. Whatever it was, everybody in the room seemed to have picked it up.

The CGS turned from the window and beckoned over a leather-jacketed figure who had been slouched over the arm of a chair.

"I don't know what's happening out there, but the assault goes ahead. Are your men ready?"

The SAS officer nodded. They both knew the question was superfluous.

"Right then. We'll abandon the plan. No more waiting. We strike in the next hour."

"Cloud is good."

The SAS man looked at his watch.

"Say, one hour exactly, barring moonlight."

"One hour it is. Brief the backup team and everyone else who needs to know. I want no mistakes."

The officer paused as if to reply, but tact prevailed. With a grunt, he sauntered off.

The CGS blew his nose hard into a Kleenex. All day the signs of hay fever had been building up: now he felt it about to break over him. It was absurd. Midwinter, on an icy, desolate airfield, and he was getting hay fever? Maybe it was just a chill.

Still, in an hour it would be over. He could go home to bed and a hot rum toddy.

An hour.

He remembered the call.

Assad had been found and, like the good fairy, was homing in to solve all their problems. He doubted it.

By the time he arrived it would be too late. Anyway, this was a military affair. It could be solved without outside interference, he had no doubt of that.

A bout of sneezing shook him so hard that it was some time before he became aware of the man waiting patiently at his elbow. He wiped his eyes irritably and blinked away the tears.

"Yes?"

"Rigby."

The man spoke with the air of one who had no respect for uniforms. Small and lean with half-moon spectacles, he had a faint hunch to his shoulders that betrayed a life of books and workbenches.

Rigby was the Clearing House tape man. Monitoring and Surveillance Technical Officer, Grade One.

Rigby had been saving for fifteen years to buy a hi-fi and still hadn't made it, but for the past week he had driven them wild with his spaghetti of wires, tape machines and voice printouts. Nobody had bothered to look at them.

The CGS, still reeling from his attack, was not in the mood now.

"No, Rigby, please. I'll want this room cleared of all nonessential personnel in three minutes."

He motioned to one of his aides to deal with the persistent little man and strode over to the radio officer. Rigby trailed him doggedly.

"They're probably incapable," said Rigby. "The men on that plane." He spoke with a weary authority; expert to amateur.

"The sequence of voice patterns has changed completely. It's all here."

He held up a concertinaed sheaf of papers etched with pen lines. One of the Special Patrol Group who had been

238

keeping watch at the door took him by the arm.

Rigby shook him off.

"It's all on the printout. Their voice patterns have been deteriorating for the past two days. The last reading we have shows definite signs of sluggish . . ."

The CGS sneezed again. There was a taste in his mouth of bad port.

"Later, man, later."

This time there was no argument. The guard gripped Rigby's wrist and led him away.

The CGS leaned heavily on a battery of green metal boxes to steady himself. More infernal bloody machinery.

"Get this blasted rubbish out of here," he barked at an officer. He watched the needles dance on their dials. One of them, in a narrow rectangular display lit by a soft purple light, was banging frantically against the top end of the scale like a trapped bird against a window.

"What's that?" demanded the CGS, tapping the instrument.

His aide bent to look. "It's a Geiger counter, sir."

THURSDAY   2145

Davidson left them to go search for the Home Secretary.

The control tower looked like an officers' mess. Medal ribbons and braid and the smell of starch. Driscoll, hollow-eyed and unshaven, stood aimlessly with Assad as Duquesne tried to elicit a response from a group of brass hats hunched shoulder to shoulder over a table.

A civilian glanced briefly at Duquesne, then did a double take. He slipped away from the group, took the American by the elbow and drew him to one side.

His glance flickered over Driscol and Assad. He positioned his body so that they were excluded and dropped his voice to a conspiratorial whisper.

A leather-clad SAS officer strode into the room, his lips pursed for confrontation. He reached the group of high-ranking officers; voices were raised; arms waved.

Driscoll watched Duquesne and the civilian hissing like quarreling lovers into each other's ears, then shrugged and turned away. He had no idea what was happening and cared less.

He slumped into a hard wooden chair and looked up at the Arab. Assad seemed brighter, more alert, than he'd seen him in days. He radiated an excitement that formed almost a physical halo around him.

Driscoll said bitterly: "Relax. You're not home yet."

Assad smiled triumphantly.

"We must say our farewells. I shall go out to the plane and . . ." He waved his arm, graphically; a plane taking off.

Driscoll said: "Amen. A-bloody-men."

Duquesne appeared behind Driscoll's head. He touched a hand on Driscoll's shoulder. It was shaking.

Driscoll turned his head to study the young American's face.

"He's all yours," he said. "The Seventh Cavalry's arrived. Armageddon's averted. See next week's exciting episode."

Duquesne shook his head violently. A thin cleft of nerve fibers bunched between his eyes.

"Can I talk with you? Alone?"

Driscoll walked with him across the control room to the huge sloping windows.

"Well?"

"The Arab stays here."

"What d'you mean?"

Duquesne's bunched nerves twitched, creasing his forehead.

"He's no use to us now. We couldn't get him on that plane now if we wanted to. See for yourself."

Driscoll took the sheaf of stereotyped yellow sheets, but before he could read them, the wail of sirens came from below. A stream of ambulances, twenty strong, swung from behind the airport buildings and skidded into position below the tower. Drivers snatched open doors before waiting queues of technicians, soldiers and police.

Driscoll started. "What the hell's that all about?"

Duquesne tapped the papers.

"Read it. It's all there. On the first page."

The quarto sheet was headed: "Nuclear Research Council." It read:

Roentgen dose and fatality:
The exact mean lethal dose of radiation is unknown for man. Less than 300r is unlikely to kill. Between 400r and 700r will kill in sixty days in about half of all cases. A dose

of over 1000r will always be fatal.

There are four main phases:

1. A latent period.
2. Nausea and vomiting a few hours after irradiation, passing within twenty-four hours. Followed by malaise, anorexia, diarrhea, thirst, lassitude and somnolence for a few days.
3. Period of well-being. Low-grade fever.
4. Epilation. Increasing malaise and rise of temperature. Pain in throat and gums. Edema, ulceration. Infection of the gastrointestinal tract. Anemia develops as the red blood cells diminish. White blood cells follow suit.
5. Death.

Driscoll lifted his eyes from the paper and found the ambulances. One by one they began to pull away. Around him the room was emptying.

"Radiation," Duquesne said unnecessarily. "The plane's pumping it out. The bomb's deteriorated and it's leaking. The brass say even conventional nukes do it after a time. They need to be serviced, just like a car battery, I guess."

He moistened his lower lip.

"Let's get out of here. They're pulling everyone out."

Driscoll walked back into the room to Assad. He sat unconcernedly on a small formica-topped table. Duquesne followed. He turned to Driscoll, his voice low.

"You read the notes. We don't know exactly how long it's been pumping out radioactivity but I'd say long enough to kill everyone on the plane. If any one of them is alive, he knows he's dying."

He looked around the room. They were alone.

"Come on. No point in hanging around here."

At the foot of the tower, senior police and army officers and the mandarins from the ministries were testing out their divine right to be the last to leave. Driscoll, Assad and Duquesne shouldered a path through them.

Assad shouted: "Where are we going? What is happening?"

"Dunkirk," said Driscoll. "Without the Germans."

Duquesne was spotted by an officer and anchored to a knot of men by a truck. Driscoll pulled Assad on into the crush of bodies. They reached an exit door of the Number Two departure terminal and went inside. A few men were talking into telephones but the wide-open spaces were empty. Driscoll and Assad strolled quickly across the main lounge.

"I don't understand." Assad stopped impetuously, and faced Driscoll, his mouth working.

"Since when've we been supposed to understand? Just do what I do and keep your mouth shut."

A Tannoy burst into life above them, smashing down on them almost physically.

"Mr. David Driscoll. This is the emergency standby operator. An urgent call for Mr. Driscoll. Please pick up the nearest telephone and keep your conversation short. Leave the airport the moment you've finished."

Assad's face broadened with relief. He ran to a desk and lifted a telephone. He held the instrument out to Driscoll.

"Yes? This is Driscoll. You have a message for me."

"Yes, David." The voice was cold and crackling with tension. "I'll keep it short. Your wife is safe with me. You'll want her. I want Assad. We'll be at Sloane Street. And remember: Thou Shalt Not Steal."

The line went dead.

Driscoll was stunned. He felt Assad's hand plucking at his sleeve, heard his voice, but nothing registered. For no sane reason, he suddenly remembered Raymond Barney. The hysteria bubbled up from his stomach. Oh, Barney—you'd have loved *this!*

Assad finally got through to him. Driscoll dropped the phone on its cradle.

"That was a man called Weatherby. He wants to meet you."

THURSDAY   2215

They assembled in the hangar less than a mile from the Trident—twenty of them, in black suits and helmets with tinted Plexiglas visors.

The SAS officer checked his watch automatically. Only the lack of time concerned him.

The volunteer force satisfied him at last and he ordered them into the Range Rovers. One last check, one whispered conversation into the transceiver strapped high on his chest, and he signaled. They pulled out onto the field and drove across the snow, the engines unhappy at twenty miles an hour.

Outside the hangar doors, the radio operator gathered up his equipment. All contact now would be between the CO and the assault team. His ears ached and his head was full of fire. There had been nothing on the Trident's wavelength for a full day, but he had been tuned in for every empty second of it.

He cued in the dial and checked for the last time.

Nothing.

Over his shoulder, the Range Rovers whined into the distance. His head came round with a snap. There was a voice, half imagined, in the headset.

He touched the dial to a pristine exactness.

"This is London Control. Come in, Sharland."

He waited. Faint, very faint, But definite.

"Sharland to Heathrow Tower. Sharland . . . Tower . . . preparing . . ." It rose and died. He clamped the headpiece to his ear. A dull roar suffused his head, smothered the tinny tinkling of that weak human sound; booming like . . .

He turned his head from his equipment.

The Trident's engines had developed an insistent howl. The assault crew were less than a hundred yards from the plane, but the Trident was alive, moving.

The operator shouted across to an army officer.

"I think I'm making contact, sir. It's Sharland."

The officer raced across the snow and swept the headset from the crouching operator.

He shouted: "Sharland. This is Control. If you can hear me, stop that plane. Do you read? You are sick. The bomb is leaking radiation. You must . . ."

The boom of the Trident's engines grew in pitch and depth. Slowly, the plane pivoted on the emergency pad, a single searchlight holding it unsteadily. For a moment it held still as the engines built to a deafening roar, then it began to move along the runway.

The Range Rovers slithered to a halt and the team leaped down into the snow. All over the field, in the operations rooms and the tower, men stood suddenly still; entranced, impotent.

The plane gathered speed, seemingly incapable of lifting itself. The first searchlight was joined by three more, their thin fingers bobbing and weaving wildly as they fought to contain the silver shape.

Less than a quarter of a mile from the runway's end, the Trident's nose tilted upward.

Then, a falcon freed from the gauntlet, it lifted and plunged into the night.

THURSDAY — 2300

The road behind the control tower and the Number Two terminal was alive with vehicles and uniforms. The Army were doing their best to fashion an orderly withdrawal and a regimental sergeant major was courting acute laryngitis by screaming at three ranks of Guardsmen in dappled flak jackets.

Police and ambulance men were working feverishly to free their vehicles from a chaos that had grown through the night, and airport workers threaded through them, cursing, as they tried frantically to liberate essential equipment.

The snow had turned to brown slush and men and machines sloughed in its clutching filth.

Driscoll pulled Assad into the corner of an open door and surveyed the scene quickly. Over to their right, an airport policeman was shouting and waving at two army trucks as their wheels spun and threshed impotently. Behind him was a dark blue van with the police insignia on its door. They worked their way in front of the building, then traversed the outside of the mass of men. The policeman didn't even notice as Driscoll roused the engine of the van and pushed in the gear lever. Through the airport complex, they wedged into a line of retreating vehicles. At the far end of the tunnel, a dozen policemen and SAS commandos waved them through impatiently.

On the motorway, things were easier. Assad tried twice to interrogate Driscoll but never got beyond the first few words. Driscoll knew he couldn't afford to explain. He had read somewhere that lion tamers owe their survival to what they call the critical space factor. Not too close, not too far away. An animal's instincts, blurred between flight and attack, rooted it to the spot, permitting neither. By the time Assad knew which way to jump it would be all over.

Driscoll pulled the van to a halt, finally, in Belgrave Square, just up from the German Embassy. Another critical space factor. Not too near, not too far away from the Sloane Street flat. They walked the last half mile.

On the third floor, the familiar light burned through the venetian blinds.

"This way," he said shortly. Once again, the need to force Assad and his future out of his mind wracked Driscoll like malarial shivering. Giving him up. After all this, he was giving him up without a word. If it hadn't been for Cindy . . .

The reception desk was empty. So was the foyer. It took a lot of muscle to achieve that.

He made Assad knock at the door. It opened almost immediately. Cindy's face was a mask made of sugar ice; cold, bereft of feeling. Her eyes were red.

Assad stiffened, treading back into Driscoll's chest.

"This is my wife, Cindy."

The words were laughable, but they filled the necessary gap.

Cindy said: "David?" but there was no response. He couldn't bring himself to look at her.

Weatherby was on the raised end of the room, the gun in his hand as steady as a rock and pointed unwaveringly at Cindy's head.

"Sit down, both of you," he said. Gone was the beautifully balanced lilt, the coolness, the gentleness.

"Now, we haven't much time. I'm not interested in violence, David. Your wife for the Arab. I intend to leave now. I'm afraid it'll be necessary to lock you in. Now . . ."

Assad sat as if in a catatonic trance, stunned by the monstrous betrayal. Weatherby threw Cindy a roll of medical adhesive tape.

"Bind his wrists, Mrs. Driscoll. And tightly." He watched her shaking hands. Assad offered no resistance.

When she had finished, Weatherby rapped: "Right. Stand up." Assad levered himself forward on the chair and got to his feet.

Weatherby gestured the gun at Cindy.

"A coat, Mrs. Driscoll. There are plenty in the cupboard. There, by the door."

Cindy fetched a gray Burberry from the closet.

"Over his shoulders, please."

Cindy fumbled and the coat slipped to the ground. She bent to pick it up and Weatherby's mouth tightened in anger. It was the first slight crack in his icy precision, a fleeting wave of feeling that overspilled his control.

Driscoll bunched his last reserves and poured energy down

245

to the balls of his feet. He rocked slowly on the settee, checking his center of gravity.

Weatherby turned the gun on him before he moved, but by then it was too late to stop.

The gun barked and the blow spun Driscoll like a top.

"Jesus!" His cry was half a scream. He pressed his hand to his side and found the blood, just above the hip. Cindy had her mouth wide, screaming, but no sound came. Weatherby turned the gun on Assad, then on the woman.

"The coat, Mrs. Driscoll. Put the coat round him. Then you can see to your husband."

He stared down bleakly as Driscoll dragged himself into a chair.

"You're a damned fool, David. I could have killed you easily."

Driscoll felt the pain ebb and flow as the anesthetic of shock set in.

"You should have," he gritted. "You're mad. You can't get away with it. You'll have the world on your tail. They'll pick you up in hours." The words came out like broken glass.

Weatherby shook his head.

"We're not all dead runners, David. You may work alone but I don't. Assad will be out of the country before daybreak."

Cindy had been standing petrified, her hands cradling her face. Now she relaxed in one convulsive movement and ran to Driscoll. She fell to her knees beside him and tore away the jacket and shirt. Driscoll winced. His blood ran freely over her hands. She snapped open her handbag and ripped free a wedge of Kleenex tissues. Driscoll's face contorted as her trembling fingers plastered them over the blood.

Driscoll said: "You've got no fight with the people round that airport. That bomb . . ."

Weatherby cut in: "Is now a problem even Assad can't alter. Don't play chess with me, David. I know exactly what's going on at Heathrow."

"Then I hope to God you think it's worth it. Flag, Duffy and a few thousand others on your conscience." Driscoll levered himself upright. Cindy folded the torn shirt around the padding of paper.

"Conscience?" Weatherby nearly laughed. "How long have you had that word in your repertoire? You—a mercenary. A political gangster. A man who's never known a cause and never wanted one." His face reddened with emotion.

"You sicken me, David. You and all the rest. The Gestapo, the SS, the Palestinian murderers. They're your people."

Driscoll closed his eyes and lay his head back in the chair.

"And where would *you* be without *my* people? You name them, you need them. Because without them you have no fuel. Nothing to hate. No excuses for playing war games with real people. No justification for hiding behind your bloody sacred causes.

"Do you really think what you're doing would get a round of applause at Auschwitz?"

He opened his eyes and stared disinterestedly at the pointing gun.

"Well, go ahead and do it. What have you got to lose?"

Assad inched forward.

"We had better go. All this will solve nothing."

Weatherby's hand wavered. He lowered the gun.

"The boy's talking sense, David. You were never very good at that."

Driscoll tried to rise but the bullet wound gaped and forced him back into the chair. Cindy took his hand and they watched the two men leave.

Weatherby prodded Assad from the lift into the basement garage. There was no mistaking the sleek metallic shape of Driscoll's Ferrari Dino crouched against the far wall.

They walked across to it, Assad rocking robot-like under the restraining tape.

The engine rumbled into life immediately and Weatherby slid it smoothly toward the attendant's hut at the garage entrance. A flat-capped figure swathed in a vast greasy scarf sat pondering over the day's racing fixtures behind the smeared glass of his cubicle.

"One word from you and I shan't hesitate to use this," said Weatherby, patting his pocket. "On him, of course."

The attendant glanced up as the Ferrari growled to a halt. With a grunt of annoyance he swung himself down heavily from his high chair and shuffled across to remove the single chain across the garage entrance. For a moment he stood in front of the car, squinting at the passengers. Weatherby's foot hovered over the accelerator as the man wheezed his way to the driver's window.

"Merry Christmas, guv."

A hand was raised to an imaginary forelock and, slowly

opening, was dropped in what its owner considered a suitably subtle hint.

Weatherby eased his grip on the wheel and fumbled in his pocket. He wound down the window and held out two tenpenny pieces.

"Bless you, guv."

The fingers locked on Weatherby's neck in one movement. The bone snapped with the noise of a rifle shot.

Weatherby was dead before the coins hit the garage floor.

The tape tore at Assad's wrists as he reared in the seat, fighting to press down the door handle with one flapping hand. The lumbering figure grunted and began to move around the car.

Assad was out and running before it reached him, his feet skidding, his shoulders swinging awkwardly. Behind him the figure broke into a heavy jog but Assad had at least fifteen yards headway by the time he reached the steps that led up to the apartments.

The rough concrete of the stairwell tore the shirt and skin from his shoulders as Assad ricocheted from wall to wall. Below him, a voice barked something unintelligible and feet slammed heavily on the steps.

One flight. Two. Three.

The man was gaining ground as Assad stumbled into the corridor leading to Driscoll's apartment. He hurled himself at the door. It opened immediately and Cindy recoiled as Assad's scratched and bruised face struggled to mouth words.

Driscoll jerked to his feet through a sheet of pain.

His chest heaving, Assad nodded wildly at the corridor. Driscoll took two steps then folded like a jack knife. Cindy instinctively reached for him.

He grated: "No! The gun. In the chess table."

Cindy slid open the drawer and gingerly took the gun between finger and thumb. She held it out to him.

Driscoll was locked in agony, his hands plastered across the wound. He said: "I can't move. Stand in front of the door. Point the gun at it. When it opens—fire at the chest."

"I can't."

"Do it!"

"I can't!"

"DO IT!"

They heard the racking cough at the far end of the corridor. As a reflex, Cindy turned to the door, her arm outstretched and trembling under the weight of the automatic.
248

Driscoll snapped: "When I say 'Now'—fire."

The door burst open.

Cindy's eyes were rivetted on the gun. Her finger curled on the trigger.

"Don't!" screamed Assad.

Distracted, Cindy's head whirled round for Driscoll's confirmation. Before she could move, a bear-like paw plucked the Walther from her hand.

"Bloody hell, guv. Take it easy."

Albert Duffy looked at them reproachfully.

FRIDAY   0035

In their shock they waited for the mirage of Albert Duffy to dissolve and fade but his all too solid flesh had no intention of melting away. He found himself a six-pack of canned Guinness in the refrigerator and only then released Assad's taped wrists.

Cindy peeled the tissues from Driscoll's wound and washed and bandaged it as Duffy told his story.

How, halfway down the warehouse stairs, he'd heard cars arriving in the yard. How he'd frozen in the dark, gauging the opposition as their feet clattered on the stairs.

How he had guessed there were two of them. A fair match. How the first had died as cleanly as any man had a right to hope for, his heart stopping the instant Duffy's size-twelve boot smashed into his chest, collapsing the rib cage like a paper bag and propelling him wholesale down the stairwell.

A muffled curse had been enough to lead Duffy's bunched fist sweeping sideways, a bolt hammer slamming into the second man's temple.

How, then, the impossible happened. He had tried to shout a warning to Driscoll but it turned to a watery gurgle as the silent third man sliced a switchblade deep across his throat. He staggered to the door and collapsed. The last thing he heard before passing out were the footsteps of others racing up the stairs.

Driscoll stared at him, unblinking. "What can I say, Duff?"

Duffy's hand was raised, podgy and powerful, waving him into silence. "Forget it. You'd have lasted ten seconds if you'd left that door open. And where would we have been then, eh? Cheers. Here's to life."

He lifted his glass in salute.

Cindy poured Driscoll a scotch and sat down beside him. She felt herself a stranger in this room. She had never had any illusions about David Driscoll; about what he did and why he did it. But she had always kept it academic, remote. Now there was no running away from the reality of it. She had his blood on her hands to prove it.

Assad, too, seemed to feel a stranger. He pointed to the scarf around Duffy's neck and ventured: "You should not be here. You should see a doctor."

Duffy grinned and fingered the scarf.

"Who found you?" said Driscoll. "Was it Flag?"

"Dunno. Just remember waking up in hospital. Intensive care. The lot."

"And they let you out? In under a week?"

Duffy rearranged his huge rump awkwardly.

"Sort of. Well, not exactly. I decided to discharge myself. No way they could keep me."

Driscoll said: "And what about the Law?"

Duffy tapped the side of his nose. "Ask no questions, hear no lies."

"Why did you come here?" Assad said suspiciously. "No one knew we would come here."

"Dead wrong," said Duffy. "While you and the guv'nor were on the Grand Tour, me and the lads were doing a bit of checking. And one of your mates, guv, was acting very funny. Like he kept meeting people in strange places. And when he met Guilfoyle it stopped being funny. Because Mr. Guilfoyle suddenly finds himself slightly dead.

"So we check him out. Name of Weatherby. We been on his tail ever since. The rest, like they say, is history.

"When Weatherby came here, I thought I ought to meet him personally."

He threw the remains of the Guinness into his throat and heaved himself to his feet.

He said: "I don't want to break the party up, guv, but I think it's about time we weren't here." He tossed a glance at Assad.

Driscoll frowned. "What do you mean?"

Duffy dropped a huge hand on the Arab's shoulder and squeezed comfortingly.

"I've got plans for this one. He's going home the fast way.

Courtesy of Duffy Travel. All arranged, guv, don't worry yourself. There's a plane waiting at a little place I know and the couriers are the best in the business."

Driscoll tried to get up. It was wasted effort.

"You stay where you are," ordered Duffy gruffly. "This is my business. That's what I'm paid for."

He propelled Assad to the door. "Okay, Abdul, time to go. And don't think I'm doing *you* any favors."

Driscoll said: "Duff!" then swallowed an attempt at thanks. He added lamely: "Watch your back, okay?" His eyes flickered over Assad's face and then quickly away. "And his too," he growled.

Assad's face was expressionless. Duffy sensed the embarrassment and shoved the young Arab through the door into the corridor.

He flicked a comic salute. "You're on your own now, guv," he grinned. "Enjoy it while you can." The door closed on them.

It had all been too quick. Driscoll lay back, trying to connect. Assad was out of his life as quickly as he'd entered it and with even less formality. Things could have been said. Should have been said. Those seven days had been seven lifetimes. They had shared everything, resolved nothing.

Driscoll twisted around to look at Cindy. She was staring at her hands, but she felt his air of uncertainty.

"What happens now?" she asked. It was something to say.

"Nothing you need worry about." His voice was hard, rejecting her. She took a pack of cigarettes from her bag and lit one.

"Do you want me to go?"

He looked away uncomfortably.

"There's nothing to stay here for, is there?"

"That's up to you."

He ran one hand tenderly over the bandaging at his side. "Don't lean on me. Nothing's up to me. In a little while a guy called Davidson is going to walk through that door. I'm going to have to tell him Assad's gone and Weatherby's dead. If I were you I wouldn't hang around for another bloodletting."

She said: "One more won't make any difference."

He nodded. Match point.

"What are you going to tell him?"

"I'll tell him it was his fault. He was supposed to protect me. Weatherby moved too fast for him. Turned up at the airport, snatched Assad and me, brought us here . . ." His voice trailed away. There was silence for a moment. "What the hell does it matter?"

"Will he believe you?"

"Would you in his place? Of course he'll believe me. He has to. He's going to need a story, too, when the inquests start."

He looked at his watch.

"Christ! It's late."

"We'll have to get a doctor to look at that wound, David."

The sudden gentleness in her voice triggered his half-forgotten sense of guilt. The remorse burned.

"Do you realise something," he said. "This is the first thing we've shared for years." He bit on the irony of it. There was a long, long pause. "You were bloody good."

"Thanks."

"No. I mean it."

"So do I. Do you still want me to go?"

He looked at her long and hard. Then:

"Of course I bloody don't. But this time it's your decision."

Her blue eyes leveled unwaveringly on his.

"It was always my decision. I didn't marry you because you were perfect."

"No. But that's why you divorced me."

Game, set and match.

He pushed painfully to his feet.

"What are we trying to prove to ourselves?" he said.

She wanted to break the tension, too. "If you're going to have visitors I'd better find you a shirt," she said.

She went through to the bedroom and he heard her rummaging through drawers.

He shouted to her: "By the way. Merry Christmas. I haven't bought you a present. Anything you really want?"

There was silence and she appeared in the doorway. Her face was serious.

"No—not at the moment," she said. She measured him from head to toe with one look.

"But I'm working on it."

Captain John Sharland nudged the throttle fractionally and the airspeed indicator hovered back to 518 knots.

He collapsed back into his harness.

His eyes were streaming continuously, blurring the outline of the instrument console, blotting out the fevered twitching of meters and dials.

He tried again to raise his hand but this time his brain refused to cooperate. He sat with his eyes on the auto-pilot and felt the flesh slipping away from his bones like warm butter.

It wouldn't be long now.

He raised his head to stare through the window. The two Phantom jets sat above him and about a mile to starboard. From time to time one of them kicked and banked and dived away to come up behind him.

It was good to know they were there. He didn't want to be alone. Not now.

It was impossible to concentrate; impossible to remember. How long out from Heathrow? How long before . . . ?

No, don't think about that. Think arithmetic. Concentrate on arithmetic.

Economic cruising speed at 30,000 feet for the Trident 2E was 518 knots. Good. Good.

Range with maximum fuel and payload: 2,500 miles. Reserve for a 250-mile diversion at 15,000 feet would last 45 minutes.

So . . . she's made two trips, London-Amsterdam and return. Add pre-takeoff taxiing, circuit approaches, takeoffs, and that left . . .

It left him exhausted.

The pains attacked again and all but engulfed him. He began to cry softly, openly. It was strangely satisfying. It gave him the courage he needed.

He sucked in air, braced his back into the seat and poured the last of his energy into his right arm.

It moved. He pushed it forward. His fingers located and canceled the auto switch. Six inches more and he grasped the controls.

The plane reared and swung, then settled again. One of the Phantoms peeled away and came to stare.

Sharland's face bled sweat. His eyes made one last sortie over the instrument panel, hovering doubtfully from dial to dial, like fruit flies looking for a place to land. He sucked in one last morale-boosting gulp of air and pushed the controls forward.

The Trident plunged into the sea.

For several minutes, fragments of wreckage no bigger than footballs curled and bobbed among the waves and a thin scum of oil rose and fell like a silk net on the water.

High overhead, the Phantoms circled until the sea no longer boiled at the point of impact. When all was still, they banked against the breaking morning and turned for home.

JACK HIGGINS

High-voltage tales of adventure—suspense by
the bestselling author of THE EAGLE HAS
LANDED.